THE WORLD OF THE GATEWAY

The Gateway Trilogy (Series 1)
Spirit Legacy
Spirit Prophecy
Spirit Ascendancy
The Gateway Trackers (Series 2)
Whispers of the Walker
Plague of the Shattered
Awakening of the Seer
Portraits of the Forsaken
Heart of the Rebellion
Soul of the Sentinel
Gift of the Darkness
Tales from the Gateway

THE RIFTMAGIC SAGA
What the Lady's Maid Knew
The Rebel Beneath the Stairs

SPIRIT LEGACY

SPIRIT LEGACY

Book I of The Gateway Trilogy

E.E. HOLMES

Lily Faire Publishing
Townsend, MA

www.lilyfairepublishing.com

ISBN 978-0-9895080-0-1 (Paperback edition)
ISBN 978-0-9895080-2-5 (Digital edition)

Publisher's note: This is a work of fiction. Names, characters, places and incidents are either the product of the author's imagination or are used fictitiously.

Cover design by James T. Egan of Bookfly Design LLC
Author photography by Cydney Scott Photography

For Joseph, who believed in me, and for Dylan, our greatest creation.

What beck'ning ghost, along the moon-light shade
Invites my steps, and points to yonder glade?

—Alexander Pope
"Elegy to the Memory of an Unfortunate Lady"

CONTENTS

PROLOGUE

I COULDN'T MOVE. Terrifying faces leered at me, weirdly distorted, as in fun house mirrors. A hand reached out, finding my own hand and clinging to it. It felt familiar, like holding my own hand, and I grasped it for dear life. Cries and moans and pitiful shrieks echoed inside my head, forming no distinguishable words. Deathly white hands, their coldness emanating palpably toward me, were clawing at me, though they seemed unable to make full contact. I felt a scream building inside me, but it was as though my lungs had forgotten how to take air, my voice to produce sound. Suddenly a single voice that contained many whispered in my ear. "The Gateway is open..."

The hand holding mine slipped away from my scrabbling fingers, and I fell through space as the cry inside of me fought its way to my lips.

I woke shrieking; my body was being attacked not by groping arms and legs, but only by twisted bed sheets. I sat shivering uncontrollably in my drenched T-shirt; the oppressive July heat had turned icy in the midst of my terror. As the nightmarish images faded from my eyes, I forced myself to breathe slowly and deeply, and felt the breeze turn warm again. My tiny bedroom swam back into focus.

"It was only a dream, Jess. Get a hold of yourself."

I squinted at the clock. It was 3:00 AM. A glance toward the door showed the eerie flickering glow from the television in the living room. A slightly muffled voice was promising that the Gut Buster 2000 would transform my body or my money back. Guaranteed.

"Damn it, Mom," I muttered as I slid out of bed. I peeled the sweat-soaked T-shirt from my body and tossed it onto a pile of dirty clothes by my door. I grabbed a clean one from my laundry basket and pulled it over my head as I shuffled out to the living room.

She always did this. I hadn't even heard her come in, but it had to have been after 1:00 AM, because that was when I'd finally given up calling her cell and fallen asleep. Walking toward the front of the apartment, I knew exactly where I'd find her: passed out on the couch, her shoes still on, if they'd made it home. Sometimes the shoes didn't make it home.

My bleary eyes scanned the living room. On the television, the Gut Buster had been replaced by a helmet-haired man hawking diet shakes; apparently insomnia and obesity were regular bedfellows. A single red pump lay abandoned on the floor in front of the threadbare sofa alongside a pair of empty wine bottles. The only detail missing from the familiar scene was my mom, who was not sprawled on the sofa, where I'd assumed she'd be.

I noted that it was the shoe that should have been in a pair, not the wine bottles, and then laughed humorlessly at my own joke. I found the remote and turned the TV off, then bent to pick up the empty bottles. I nearly slipped in a puddle of chardonnay and caught myself on the arm of the sofa.

I looked down and gasped. "Shit!"

My sketchbook lay sodden on the floor, the pages curling and stinking from sitting in stagnant wine. The sketch on the top page, a landscape of Central Park I'd been working on, was completely ruined. I closed my eyes, took a deep breath, held it, and then blew it out slowly. Then I turned and flung the ruined sketchbook onto the kitchen table, where my mom would see it when she woke up. She hadn't done it on purpose, but I didn't care. Let her feel guilty about it.

I scooped up the wine bottles and deposited them into the sink. I'd wash them out in the morning; I didn't want to deal with it now.

I considered heading into my mom's bedroom to clean her up, but decided I was too pissed off to deal with that, either. I would check to make sure she was breathing, but that was all she was getting from me tonight. As I headed to the front door and thrust the deadbolt home, I became vaguely aware that something was wrong. There were sounds of sirens outside, and voices shouting... frightened voices. Sirens in New York City were a permanent part of the soundtrack, but this was not the warped sound of passing cruisers. This was close—just outside the building. I could hear them screeching to a halt, the sirens abruptly cutting out as car doors slammed. At the same time I could hear raised voices in the hallway. One of them sounded like our landlady, Mrs. Morelli.

A sudden pounding on the door sent my heart into

palpitations for the second time in ten minutes. Cautiously, I pressed my eye to the peephole.

"NYPD, is there anyone at home?" The voice was loud and businesslike, belonging to a weathered, middle-aged officer.

Oh, for God's sake. What did she do now? I took a steadying breath. Reluctantly, I pulled the chain and opened the door.

"What can I do for you, officer?" I kept my voice polite and neutral.

"Sorry to disturb you at this hour. Does Elizabeth Ballard live here?"

"Yes, sir, I'm her daughter."

"Is she here in the apartment now?"

"Yes, sir, she's asleep. Can I ask what this is about?"

The officer hesitated in answering, instead glancing down at a small spiral-bound notebook in his hands. I seized the opportunity to continue.

"Look, I know she doesn't have the cleanest record, but if she's done something, I'm sure it was only because..." My voice died in my throat. For the first time, I noticed that Mrs. Morelli was standing just off the man's shoulder. Something was wrong with her face; her eyes were red-ringed and glistening, her flyaway gray hair tousled into a frazzled halo around her head. Her mouth was opening and closing like a fish's out of water as she stared at me.

Something inside my head clunked heavily into place. I'll never understand how I knew, but the knowledge was almost instantaneous as my mind quickly synthesized the officer, the sirens outside, the vacant couch. Realization thundered down on top of me like some sort of mental avalanche. I forced my body into motion and ran for my mother's bedroom. I could hear the officer's footfalls behind me, his shouts for me to stop. I burst through the door and my eyes darted around, taking in the rumpled, empty bed, the open window, the curtains hanging askew from the dangling curtain rod. I heard the cries of the people outside and their cries became my cries. But as I rushed to the window, I realized that the woman who usually comforted me when I cried was not there to hold me. My mother was gone.

I

HOMECOMING

I PRESSED MY ACHING HEAD AGAINST THE COOL GLASS of the bus window, wishing the rain outside would stop hammering against it so I could sleep. After four hours of sitting, with only a ten-minute pause to stretch my legs at a rest stop in Connecticut, my entire body felt cramped, as though everything were bent at the wrong angle. The bus was nearly silent, except for the coughing of an elderly man somewhere toward the front and the faint, tinny sound of music seeping from the headphones of the man sitting beside me. His mouth hung open in a comical caricature of sleep, his head bobbing from side to side. I felt a stab of jealousy; I hadn't slept like that in nearly a month.

Since receiving my acceptance letter to St. Matthew's College in the mail, I had imagined over and over again how my grand escape would play out. I'd crossed the days off my bedroom calendar with a kind of desperation, flipping forward to the month of August where I'd scrawled the word "FREEDOM!" across August twenty-first. If I had known then the preciousness of the time slipping past, I would have grabbed hold and tugged ferociously in the other direction. Now here I was, finally on a bus to Boston, and wishing with every fiber of my being that I could go back—as far back as I could—and never reach this point again. It still felt like a nightmare, more horrible than the one I'd had the night it happened.

I shook myself away from the image to which my mind drifted whenever I wasn't consciously fighting it: the open window, the curtain fluttering in the breeze, the white sheeted figure on the pavement below. Almost desperately, I tried to distract myself. This was becoming increasingly more difficult to do since Frank had fallen asleep.

Frank was not a friend; in fact, he was barely an acquaintance. He was just the guy who happened to sit down next to me when we boarded the bus at the Port Authority. Normally, I didn't enjoy talking to strangers in social situations. I wasn't antisocial or anything; small talk just wasn't my strong suit. But my need for distraction overrode my isolationist tendencies, and so when Frank turned out to be a talker, I just went along for the ride. Contributing as little to the conversation as I could, I let Frank talk my ear off from 42nd Street all the way to the Massachusetts border.

Frank, it transpired, was a butcher from Newark, New Jersey, who was on his way to Boston to visit his sister. He had once won $10,000 on a scratch ticket, which he spent on a used Harley Davidson, and had been married and divorced three times to the same woman, whose name he had regrettably tattooed on his forearm. I watched the offending "Lisa baby" rise and fall as Frank's arm rested on top of his impressive beer gut. He also snored. Loudly. So loudly, in fact, that it might have accounted for a couple of those divorces.

I seriously considered waking him up to regale me with more stories about the unpredictable market price of veal or the time he was *that close* to being initiated into the Hells Angels. It would have kept me out of my own head for a little while. Inside my head was not a great place to be at the moment.

"Attention ladies and gentlemen, we will be arriving at South Station, Boston in approximately fifteen minutes," the driver's heavily-accented voice crackled over the tour microphone, interrupting Ryan Gosling and Rachel McAdams, who were feverishly sucking face on the bus' tiny, dusty television screens in the kind of fit of passion that made housewives desperate.

I turned my head to watch the Mass Pike flash past in a wash of rain and caught sight of my own reflection in the glass. I laughed out loud. I looked like absolute hell. A great first impression I was going to make, showing up on Karen's doorstep looking like a herald of the zombie apocalypse.

I pulled a mirror out of my bag. My own eyes stared back at me; dark brown, owlish, and much too large for my face. I'd worn my jet black hair down, the streaks of purple peeking out around my shoulders. I'd dyed them myself, at first just to piss my mother off, but then they kind of grew on me, and I'd kept them. But after hours of leaning against my seatback, it was a tangled mess. I never should have tried to wear it down anyway, not with that kind of humidity. I braided it loosely back and secured it with one of the elastic bands that permanently resided around my wrist. I snapped the mirror shut and tossed it back into my bag where it clanked ominously amongst the rest of the contents, an indication it may never resurface. I always had too much stuff in my bag.

It was bad enough to crash down into Karen's life like this, but doing it in the dead of night somehow made it worse. I felt like I was sneaking in, like I was some sort of criminal. I knew it was stupid but I couldn't help it. Who wants to be the burdensome orphaned kid in the house?

I did my best to stuff this feeling away somewhere in the back corners of my mind, but it was pretty crowded in there. Suppressing unpleasant emotions was quickly becoming a talent of mine. Karen hadn't done or said a single thing to make me feel this way; in fact she'd done everything a person could do to make me feel the complete opposite. I'd been prepared to dislike her, to understand within moments why my mother had left her, and the rest of her family, far behind her. But Karen was being so damn sweet. It was unnerving. I felt like one of those kids from a fairy tale, about to find out that the kindly old woman was only giving me candy to fatten me up so she could shove me into her oven and roast me for dinner.

I'd asked my mother many times about her family. It was a subject I brought up with great care, weighing her mood and expressions carefully before I ventured to mention it. More often than not, my mother would just sigh and shake her head a little sadly and say, "Oh Jess, honey, let's not dig up the past okay? There are some things that are better left buried."

But over the years I had managed to learn a few things about my estranged family. Karen and my mother were twins and they had grown up in the Back Bay area of Boston. They had once been very close, inseparable in fact, just as you would have expected twins to be. I was never able to discover the reason for their falling out, but I knew that the rift was irreparable, at least from my mother's point of view.

Karen and her husband Noah had no children of their own, instead devoting their lives to their careers as big-time corporate lawyers. They still lived in the Back Bay with my grandfather in a brownstone. Since my grandfather landed on the other side of the family divide, I'd never met him either—though he was apparently too senile to know who I was, even if I had been allowed to see him. I learned very quickly not to bring him up; the resulting drinking binge was always catastrophic, and my mother and I wouldn't speak for days.

My mother was right up there with Pinocchio as one of the world's worst liars. My mother could pretend she didn't miss her family, but it was bullshit, pure and simple. As a child growing up in a variety of too-small apartments across the country, I often lay awake beside her in the bed we shared, inhaling the booze she breathed on me as she talked in her sleep. Hearing Karen's name spoken in desperate tones was an almost nightly occurrence. But an outsider witnessing the chain of events immediately following my mother's death would never have suspected that Karen was a virtual stranger to me: There she stood on my doorstep only hours after hearing the news. She'd thrown her arms around me like a daughter.

"Oh, Jessica, you poor darling, I am so sorry!" She kissed the top of my head and cradled me like it was the most natural thing in the world. In the numbness of shock and denial, I let her. I let a lot of people do all kinds of things I probably should have been actively involved in. The funeral arrangements, the terminating of the lease on our apartment, the execution of the will, my college arrangements; these were all overseen by Karen as I watched dimly from inside some sort of semi-transparent cocoon. That was one thing I learned about grief; the world doesn't stop even though it feels like it should.

I only vaguely remembered agreeing to Aunt Karen's insistence that I come to live with her. Had I been in my normal state of mind, I would have been too horrified to agree to such an arrangement. After all, I was eighteen, technically a legal adult, and to be honest I'd been taking care of myself for a good long time. I should have said no. Thanks for the concern, but I'm not your problem. Trouble was, I couldn't get myself to say much of anything coherent for a while.

The one good thing about going to stay with Karen was that I wouldn't have to be there for long. I'd come out of my walking coma about three weeks after the funeral. As I packed up my things, aided by a sympathetic Mrs. Morelli, I came to my senses. My mother would never have wanted me unloaded onto Karen like this, not when they hadn't so much as talked to each other in almost twenty years. It was too late to go back on the arrangement, but I promised myself that I would be out of Karen's hair in one year. I would find myself a job near St. Matt's, save up as much money as I could, find myself an apartment near the campus by the next summer, and that would be that. I had no intention of permanently reestablishing connections my mom had wanted to sever.

The bus splashed and spattered its way into the brightly lit portico of Boston's South Station.

"Welcome to Boston, folks. Please remember to check under your seats and take all of your belongings with you. Have a great night and thank you for riding with Greyhound," the exhausted driver chanted. The fluorescent interior lights flickered to life with a hum and the passengers began to stir slowly.

Frank grunted himself awake, looking disoriented. He blinked sleepily at me.

"We're here already? That was quick, huh?" He yawned, scratched his stubble, and stood up. His joints popped like a handful of little white snappers on a summer sidewalk. "Guess I better put this Yankees hat away, or I might get my ass kicked, huh?"

I smiled weakly. It was at least the tenth Boston/New York rivalry reference he'd made.

The people began to trickle slowly toward the front of the bus. Frank helped muscle my duffle bag down from the overhead rack and I joined the shuffling queue. A nervous feeling was mounting in my stomach. It was depressing to feel anxious about arriving at a place that was now "home."

§

Out in the downpour, I pulled my sweatshirt hood over my head and started squinting around for Karen's car. I didn't have to look for long.

"Jessica! Over here!" She flagged me down from beneath an enormous plaid umbrella.

I waved back half-heartedly and heaved my duffle bag toward her. She met me halfway and sheltered me under the umbrella.

"Is this everything? You don't have anything to get from under the bus?" She grabbed the handles and helped pull.

"Nope, this is it. I shipped everything else to St. Matt's yesterday."

We jogged to the car. It was a gleaming black SUV, what my mother would call a "look-at-me car." Ironic, considering people always stared with their mouths hanging open at our ancient green Volkswagen—probably shocked that the thing could even function. Mom had called it "vintage." I'd called it a good reason to carry an organ donor card. My mom had dubbed her deathtrap "The Green Monster," after the infamous left field wall at Fenway Park. Sometimes moving around in that car felt like a tour of the nation's seediest auto body shops. But every time I opened my mouth to tell my mother to sell the damn thing, I just couldn't; it was the one piece of home she'd brought with her. Now that she was gone, I'd felt like a traitor selling it. But room and board wasn't cheap, and there was no parking for freshmen on campus anyway. Adios, Green Monster.

Karen and I slammed the car doors simultaneously. She tossed the dripping umbrella into the backseat and looked over at me, grinning. The knot in my stomach loosened just a little. She actually looked genuinely glad to see me.

"So, Jessica, how—"

"—Actually, it's just Jess, if you don't mind. Everyone calls me Jess."

"Oh. Right, sorry. So, Jess, how was your trip?"

"It was fine. No traffic or anything."

"Good, good. I know the Pike can be a nightmare sometimes," she said as she started the car and pulled onto the street. "We'll be home in just a few minutes. You must be starving. Did you eat at the rest stop?"

I shook my head. I was a junk food junkie, but fast food and long bus rides were a dangerous combination, so I'd skipped the McDonalds.

"I had Noah order some food so that we'd have something for you when you got here. I'm not much of a cook." She made an apologetic face.

"That's okay, neither was my mom." I smirked a little, my memory flooded with smells of charred, brick-like casseroles and other failed culinary experiments.

Karen laughed. "That's true; we did have that in common. Noah just picked up some Thai food. Is that okay? We could grab a pizza or something on the way home if you don't like Thai, there's a great little pizza place just around the—"

"—No, no, Thai food's fine."

"Oh, good. We eat Thai a lot, especially because our favorite place is open so late. And they'll deliver to my office!"

We drove by a stretch of designer stores I would never even attempt to go into; I liked to shop as much as the next girl but I didn't want to get depressed over the price tags. Most of it wasn't really my style anyway; I tended to haunt vintage stores. Karen, on the other hand, probably frequented them. Even at midnight in the pouring rain, her impeccably-styled pixie cut was flawless and her makeup looked airbrushed. Her clothes were simple and casual, and yet gave the distinct impression of very high quality. Her features had a familiarity that made my heart ache.

She caught my eye as I gazed at her and I swiftly looked away. I fished for a topic of conversation.

"Do you and Noah work near here?"

"Not far at all, just into the business district on the other side of the Prudential Center." She pointed up at the towering outline of the skyscraper. "We both work for the same law firm, but you wouldn't know it, considering how rarely we see each other during the day." She rolled her eyes. "Our case loads very rarely converge."

We pulled along Marlborough Street, which was lined with beautiful brownstones, packed shoulder to shoulder like stately soldiers permanently at attention. Karen swung the car into its narrow spot, palming the wheel with one hand with the effortless expertise of a true city dweller.

"Nice one."

"Thanks," she replied. "I have to say, parallel parking was one skill I had to learn as a city girl. You should have seen Noah try to do it when he first moved here. It was pretty pathetic. We lost several good bumpers and pissed off a lot of neighbors." She squinted out of the steaming windshield and sighed. "Well, this rain isn't letting up any time soon. We might as well get this over with."

We flung the doors open and darted around the back of the car to retrieve my bag. Noah had been silhouetted in the window as we'd pulled up, and now bolted down the steps to help us. Though only outside the car for about thirty seconds, we were drenched by the time we crossed the threshold into the entryway.

"Hi Jessica," Noah said. There was an awkward moment as he tried to decide whether to hug me or shake my hand. He compromised by patting me on the shoulder. "We're glad to have you."

"She prefers Jess, actually," Karen said.

Noah raised his eyebrows and turned back to me. "Right. Sorry, Jess." I'd only met Noah once, on the afternoon of my mother's funeral. I could definitely tell that he had once been really good-looking. His hair and moustache were still thick and shiny, though streaked liberally with gray. He was tall with what was once an athletic build, though he'd softened up with age. He wasn't as social as Karen, at least not around strangers; I could relate to that at least. After the funeral he didn't seem to know what to say to me, and so he'd said very little. He'd stared at me a good deal though, and I recognized the symptoms of someone freaked out by my appearance. He had eyed my fishnet tights, combat boots, and dyed hair with definite disapproval. From the sideways glances I was getting now, I could tell not much had changed.

"I'll show you around, Jess. Noah, honey, bring the bag up and then we'll all have a bite to eat," Karen said.

Noah and my bag disappeared up a polished oak staircase and Karen gave me what she called the "grand tour." I could tell that she meant it sarcastically, but I couldn't see what there was to be sarcastic about. Their apartment was... well, amazing. They had purchased the ground floor apartment first, and then bought the second floor as well when it became available. They then renovated both floors into a single apartment. It all had the look of a five-star hotel. Intricate oriental rugs dotted the hardwood floors and an eclectic collection of artwork adorned the walls like jewelry. I was pretty sure the one over the mantelpiece was a real Picasso; I almost choked on my gum when I saw it. The downstairs comprised a living room and dining room, both full of antique furniture; a gourmet kitchen, which Karen called "all for show," since she was rarely home to cook; a mahogany-lined study; and a magnificently appointed bathroom. As we went from room to room, I instinctively kept my hands in my pockets; I felt like a second-grader on a museum field trip, forbidden to touch anything. Upstairs Karen and Noah had a master suite with a four-poster bed and Jacuzzied bathroom. Karen's office was also on this floor, contained behind leaded glass doors. She turned a last corner and opened the door on the right.

"And here's your room," she said. "I hope everything is comfortable for you."

I stared around, gaping. Every inch of wall space was covered in bookshelves, from floor to ceiling, and each shelf was bursting with more books than I'd ever seen outside of a public library or bookstore. In the corner were a bed, an armchair, and a nightstand. A matching bureau stood against the opposite wall, and a mirror hung on the inside of the door.

"I know it's not completely ideal," Karen said. "I mean, there's no closet in here and no room for a desk, but you can use the closet right out in the hall for whatever won't fit in the bureau. And I remembered seeing all the books in your room at home, so I thought you might not mind being in here. Obviously we've been using it as a library."

I walked around, examining the shelves. "I can't believe how many books you have."

Karen looked pleased. "Well, I've always been a reader, so was your grandfather. And your mother, as I'm sure you know. I've taken out all the law books, so we won't have to come in here bothering you with work stuff. And I put your mother's books in here too."

"My mother's books?"

"Yes, she left a number of boxes of books behind when she left home. I'd been saving them in the attic for... well, I'm not really sure why, but they were here, and I thought you might like to have them in your room. I hope that's okay.

"Thank you," I managed. Familiar names leapt from the bindings: the Brontë sisters, Jane Austen, Shakespeare, Edgar Allan Poe. A few of them even looked like first editions. Being surrounded by so many familiar stories was like reuniting with old friends, and I fought fiercely against the tears that threatened to well up in my eyes. I really didn't want Karen to see me cry, and quite frankly I was tired of crying. It was starting to feel redundant.

"I'll just let you get settled and then why don't you come on downstairs and we'll have something to eat," Karen said, tactfully backing out and closing the door.

We ate sitting on the floor around the coffee table in the living room. Despite the initial impression that nothing in the house should be touched, Karen and Noah were pretty casual about their place, with Noah kicking his shoes off in the middle of the living room floor, eating his Pad Thai while leaning on the pristine cream sofa. Not quite so brave, I sat on the rug and leaned over the coffee table to eat. We watched the end of a baseball game.

"You know, this might be illegal around here, harboring a Yankees fan," Noah joked.

I didn't bother to correct him about my complete lack of association with the Evil Empire. Instead we talked about the plans for the following week. I only had ten days before I was scheduled to move into St. Matt's.

"So I thought we could drive out together in the morning and try to beat the rush onto campus. Noah and I both took the day off," Karen said. She poked around in her noodles and speared a hunk of tofu.

"I can just take the train out; it stops just outside campus. I've just got the one bag to bring. I can get myself unpacked okay."

Karen was shaking her head before I'd even finished speaking. "Don't be silly, Jess, it's no trouble. We want to help, right Noah?"

Noah nodded absently in agreement, his eyes fixed on the game. "Mm-hmm, absolutely."

Karen winked at me. "See? All settled. I've never been to St. Matthew's before anyway. I want to see where you'll be going to school."

I surrendered, though still feeling like a nuisance. We finished eating and I helped clean up. Foil-wrapped leftovers and take-out containers populated the fridge, teetering on each other like an edible game of Jenga.

"See how domestic my lovely wife is? Betty Crocker incarnate," Noah said, balancing the half-eaten container of Pad Thai on a pizza box.

"Oh shut up, would you?" Karen said. "Jess, let's get you to bed, you look absolutely wiped out."

Washing up in the marble bathroom felt odd; my toothbrush and toothpaste looked like squatters illegally occupying the pristine counter. As I climbed into bed less than ten minutes later, sporting sweatpants and one of my favorite old tees, a quiet knock sounded against the door.

"Come in."

Karen poked her head around the doorframe, a pair of stylish square-framed reading glasses perched on the end of her nose.

"Are you all settled in? Do you need anything?"

"I'm all set, thanks."

"Okay, good. I just wanted to say good night." She looked like she wanted to say more than that. She lingered in the doorway for a moment before she spoke again. "Jess, I just want you to know something."

I waited.

"The fact that I haven't been in your life—well, it wasn't by choice. I'm not blaming your mother or anything. Our falling out was both of our faults, but I just want you to know that I loved her very much. We loved each other."

"I know." I wasn't just humoring her; it was the truth. She'd been absolutely distraught about my mother. I'd seen it firsthand.

"And asking you to stay here—I don't want you to think of it as charity or something." She cringed a little at the word. "You're family. These were terrible circumstances to meet under, I know. I wish it could have been while your mother was still alive, but that wasn't meant to be. I'm not sure if we'll ever know why she jumped, but…"

My head snapped up. "She didn't jump."

Karen looked taken aback. "I thought the police ruled it a—"

"—Well, they were wrong. She didn't do that. She would never have done that." Without ever intending to, I was almost yelling.

"I… okay. I'm sorry." Karen didn't seem to know what else to say, and so she just mumbled a quick good night and shut the door.

I stared at the door for a long time, my blood pounding angrily in my ears. I knew I'd been rude, but I couldn't help it. It was the same reaction I had every time anyone even suggested that my mother's death was a suicide, and somehow hearing it from Karen made it even worse. She had no right to make assumptions about my mom, not anymore. She hadn't spoken a word to her in years. She hadn't followed her around the country, dealing with the collateral damage she left in her wake. I had, and I would have known if my mom was suicidal. Self-destructive, yes. Perpetually drunk, absolutely. Suicidal? No way.

I gazed around in the darkness, watching the odd angular shadows the bookcases made on the ceiling. As my anger ebbed away, I became aware of how exhausted I felt, though the fatigue refused to extend to my thoughts, which were still whirring. Sleep fought for several hours with my emotions before it finally won.

2

———

FAMILY TIES

I STUMBLED DOWN TO THE KITCHEN THE NEXT MORNING, having slept much later than I'd meant to. Vaguely disturbing nightmares had interrupted my sleep regularly until near daylight, at which point I had finally been able to drop into a few hours of good, deep sleep. When I opened my eyes again, it was nearly 10:30 AM. I halted at the bottom of the stairs at the sound of my name. I listened carefully.

"Jessica had no right to yell at you like that. I could hear her from downstairs," Noah was saying. "She had every right. I should have known better than to bring it up," Karen replied.

"Well, if you ask me, that's indicative of a nasty temper."

"I don't remember asking you, actually."

"Yeah, you didn't really consult me on much of this at all, did you? We don't know anything about this girl."

"She's Lizzy's daughter, Noah. That's all I need to know."

"I think a few more details would be nice! Does she really need to dress like that? The neighbors are going to see her hanging around and call the police!"

"Oh relax, will you? She's got a unique style, there's nothing wrong with that."

"Are you sure she isn't into witchcraft or devil worship or something like that?"

"Noah, don't be absurd, please! She is a nice kid who happens to dress a little differently from what you're used to. That doesn't make her a punk. In fact, she must be an exceptional student to get a full ride to a school like St. Matthew's. And anyway, she's been through a lot, moving all over the place, a different school every six months, and now she loses her mother. If she's acted out a bit, looks-wise, you can hardly blame her. The kid's just expressing herself. Honestly, Noah, you didn't used to be this much of a stiff when I met you. In fact, I happen to remember a certain pair of leather pants that you—"

"—Yeah, yeah, alright. But couldn't you at least bring her down to Newbury Street and buy her some—"

"—If you think I'm going to tell that girl how to dress, you are out of your—"

"—Fine, it was just a suggestion. I'm going to work on those depositions."

I heard a chair scrape the floor and footsteps stomping down the hallway as Noah headed to his office. When I heard his door close, I arranged my face into an impassive expression and walked down into the kitchen.

"Good morning, Karen."

"There you are! I was debating whether or not to go check for a pulse," Karen said as I shuffled over to the table.

"Sorry. I guess I was really tired."

"Don't apologize! I remember when I used to be able to sleep like that! I miss it. Nowadays I can't force myself to sleep past 8:00 AM, no matter how badly I want to. My guilty conscience always drags me out of bed." Karen walked over toward the cabinets and then stopped. She spun around and eyed me critically. "Are we okay? You and me?"

I returned her gaze for a moment. A part of me wanted to say, "No," but I bit it back. I wasn't angry with her anymore, not really. She'd only made the assumption that everyone else had made, including the police. Everyone except me.

"Yeah, we're okay."

"Good." Karen opened a cabinet and eyed the contents with a sheepish expression. "It would seem your choices for breakfast are Lucky Charms or All-Bran."

I had to laugh. "Who eats the Lucky Charms?"

"Well, I may not be able to sleep like a teenager, but I can eat junk food with the best of them," Karen admitted.

"And the All-Bran?"

"Noah is attempting to reform me. A futile effort, but I let him try anyway. Would you like to be reformed, too?" She waved the stern-looking box at me in mock temptation.

"Lucky Charms it is." I replied. "I'll eat anything as long as it comes with a side of coffee."

"Industrial strength," Karen promised.

As I sat down to eat, my mind wandered to a question I'd had the night before: Was I going to be introduced to my grandfather today? I hadn't really expected to see him last night; I'd arrived so late that I figured he would already be asleep. But now that the morning had come, my curiosity about him was piqued again. Come to think of it, I didn't remember Karen even pointing out his room.

"So, where's my grandfather?"

"What?" Karen looked up swiftly from her *Wall Street Journal*.

"I thought he lived with you. My mom always said that he was with you in Boston."

"Oh." Karen put her paper down and surveyed me over the top of her reading glasses. "I think you misunderstood. Your grandfather doesn't live in the house with us. He's in a permanent care facility outside of the city. How much did your mother tell you about your grandfather's... condition?"

"Not a lot, actually. When I was little I would ask questions about our family, before I understood that she didn't like to talk about it. She'd told me that he had dementia and couldn't remember things anymore, and that was why she wouldn't take me to see him when I asked."

Karen just nodded. I felt a little pang of guilt as I realized it must be hard for her to talk about it too. Still, it didn't stop me from pressing the subject.

"So, do you see him often then?" I asked as I brought my empty bowl to the sink.

"Certainly, I do, as often as I can—which isn't saying much, I guess, with work being what it is. I really should be a better daughter. But as your mom said, his mind is gone—he can't even remember who I am, so I try not to beat myself up over it."

"Is he close by?"

"Yes, relatively. He's in Winchester, about half an hour from here." She paused and then added, "He was a good man. He loved his girls, and I know that he would have loved you too. I'm sorry that you never got to know him."

The sudden shift to the past tense unnerved me a bit, but I continued anyway. "Would it... I mean, if it's okay with you, could you maybe take me to see him?"

"Jess, I really don't think that's a good idea."

"Look, if you're too busy, I can just call a cab or—"

"—No, it's not that!" Karen snapped. "It's not a question of how busy I am! It's just a very stressful and emotional experience to see someone in that condition." She gave a little involuntary shudder. "I wouldn't feel right taking you just after your mom... well, I just don't think this is a good time."

"Look, I'm sorry if I upset you, but don't you think that's my decision? He's my grandfather and I've never met him. I have every right to—"

"—You haven't upset me," Karen said. "I just wasn't prepared to... let's get you settled here and off to school and everything first, okay? We can talk about it again when you're back for Christmas break."

I shrugged, deciding to let it go for the time being. Karen was lying, though. She *was* upset, I could tell. Her formerly calm face was flushed with emotion and she couldn't seem to refocus on her newspaper. Frustrated, I made my way back to my room to start unpacking, and resolved to figure out how to see my grandfather on my own.

As it turned out, I didn't need to. Later that afternoon, Karen appeared at my bedroom door and informed me that she would take me to see my grandfather later that week, if I still wanted to go. I agreed immediately, though I was surprised by the offer. I think she felt guilty about her initial response to my request. When the morning of our visit dawned, however, there was no doubt about it; she was a ball of nerves.

I noticed it the moment I came down the stairs on Friday. Her usually cheerful greeting sounded subdued and muffled, as though she'd been crying. When she turned around to hand me my bowl of cereal, my suspicions were confirmed. Not even Karen's usually flawless makeup could entirely obscure the red puffiness around her eyes and at the tip of her nose. The sight gave rise to an immediate wave of guilt, and I felt like shit for bringing the whole thing up.

"We'll get going right after breakfast," Karen told me, in a brave attempt at her usual lighthearted tone.

"Karen? Are you okay?"

"Fine, Jess, totally fine. Just a little cold, that's all. Or maybe allergies, I'm not sure." She shrugged airily. "Do you want to stop for coffee on the way? I think I'm gonna need a little pick-me-up."

"Sure." I took the cue and quickly dropped it. If she wanted to tell me why she was upset, great. If not, it was her business. I thought I could understand, though. She hadn't physically lost her dad, as I had my mom, but he was gone just the same. In some ways, I could see how that could be worse than if he had actually died.

I waited in the car while Karen ran into Starbucks and emerged a few minutes later with a pair of frothy lattes. We drank them in silence, following the highway out of the city and into the quieter northern suburbs. Karen always listened to talk radio, a nod to her political vigilance. I couldn't really tolerate the rightwing sentiments, but I let the sanctimonious voice of the host drone on, harmonizing with the smooth hum of the car's engine. It was an oddly lulling sound. As we pulled off the interstate and onto a quiet tree-lined street, Karen spoke.

"So just remember, Jess, his mind is pretty much gone. He recognizes me occasionally, but not often. And naturally he won't know who you are because he's never met you. I told him about you, of course, but I don't think he remembers any of that. And sometimes..." she paused here, as though searching carefully for the right words. "Sometimes he says things that don't make any sense. So just try to remember that he's not mentally sound anymore."

I swallowed hard, as some of Karen's nervousness started to rub off on me. We rounded the bend and arrived in front of a white Victorian with gingerbread trim and a wooden sign on the gate that read "Winchester House for the Aged." A wide porch wrapped around the outside of the house, dotted with empty rocking chairs. One glance at those forlorn chairs and I found myself having to fight a sudden and alarming urge to cry.

§

The house had clearly once been a private residence converted for its new purpose. The shape of the house had a distinctly turn-of-the-century feel, but the renovations were clear. Telltale modernity reared its ugly head in sharp contrast to the original features; insulated windows stared blankly from fluted window frames, and window air-conditioning units protruded like so many blemishes. Reinforced metal handrails and handicapped ramps added the final touch of indignity.

Inside, the high-ceilinged entryway housed a sort of reception desk. A nurse was seated there.

"Good morning, Mrs. Hunt. You're here early this week." She slid a clipboard toward Karen, who clearly knew the protocol and signed in.

"Yes, I brought my niece up from New York to see her grandfather." Karen inclined her head toward me.

"Oh, how nice! Well he'll be very glad to see you both, I'm sure. Let me check the schedule to see if he's in his room." The nurse smiled brightly and turned her back on us to use the telephone.

I looked around while we waited. The entryway opened into a fireplaced sitting room. Sunlight streamed through the white lacy curtains. A number of small tables and armchairs were set up around the room in cozy, inviting arrangements. The room was so quiet and still that at first glance I thought it was empty. However, as I let my eyes wander more slowly over the room, I realized that wasn't the case.

There were five residents scattered about the room, all completely motionless. An ancient shriveled woman in a blue fleece nightgown was propped in a wheelchair by the window, presumably to admire the view, though she seemed wholly unaware of the existence of any outside world at all. Two old men were hunched over a chessboard; whose turn it was—anybody's guess—for they just kept staring at the board in a puzzled way, as though unsure of its purpose or relation to them. Two white flossy heads perched on bony shoulders were visible over the back of a pink sofa, facing a silent television set with the closed captioning flashing across the bottom. No, I was right the first time: The room was empty. God, someone please shoot me before I get that old.

"Jess? We can go upstairs now. The nurse says that Dad is in his room." Karen pointed toward the entryway staircase. I followed her upstairs.

The staircase looked like a portrait gallery for a family that had never known youth. We passed photo after photo of elderly people, all donors to the home and its programs. Every single frame bore a gold name plate bearing the donors' names and, grimly, their birth and death dates. I could barely repress a shiver but kept reading them. It was like walking through a wall-papered, gilt-framed graveyard.

At the top of the stairs we entered the very first room on the left. It was a surprisingly bright and cheerful room, with tall windows that faced the morning sunshine, which fell across the floor in an orderly geometric pattern. Frilly white curtains hung in the windows and the two beds were covered with bright patchwork quilts. There were suggestions of illness of course: a wheelchair, an industrial-looking shower, several hospital monitors and IV stands. But the overall feel was of one's own home, not of an institution. I had a sudden rush of affection toward Karen for finding a place like this for her father.

"That's him over there," Karen murmured in my ear, pointing to a plush green armchair facing the window. It was the kind of chair I'd always envisioned a jolly old grandfather would sit in, with slippered feet and a head ribboned by pipe smoke, an image no doubt conjured from literary sources. The man who occupied the chair bore little resemblance to the grandfather I had imagined for myself.

He was staring out the window, not blankly, as the woman downstairs had done, but with palpable expectation. He was startlingly gaunt, with hollow cheeks beneath severe cheekbones that seemed determined to break the surface. His posture was spring-loaded; he was leaning toward the window and clutching the arms of his chair with white-knuckled intensity. His hair was white and flyaway, and he was wrapped from the waist down in an afghan. Sitting so, he gave the impression of a seeded dandelion in a pot, stretching toward the sunlight. He seemed completely unaware that anyone had entered the room.

Karen led me across the room, a gentle pull at my elbow. We sat together on a matching green sofa facing the chair. Up close, I could see that my grandfather's lips, terribly chapped and dry, were moving very quickly in some sort of silent stream of words.

"He usually does that. I've never actually been able to figure out if he is really saying anything. He hardly ever speaks aloud anymore," Karen whispered to me. Then she turned toward her father and said in a loud clear voice, "Dad, I've brought someone to visit you."

I watched my grandfather closely. Something stirred in his eyes and he twitched his head a bit. I realized that on some level, he had acknowledged we were there.

"Dad? Dad, I want you to meet someone. This is Jessica." She paused and threw me an apologetic look. "I mean Jess. This is Jess. This is Elizabeth's daughter. This is your granddaughter."

"Um, hi, Grandpa. It's nice to meet you finally," I said. It felt so silly to even try to communicate with him.

I thought he might have adjusted the angle of his head ever so slightly, as though in response to the sound of my voice. I opened my mouth to speak again, but I didn't know what else to say, so I snapped it shut.

Karen stood up. "I'll leave you two to get acquainted." She tiptoed quickly out. Her voice had that muffled sound again, a betrayal of too much emotion.

I sat with my grandfather for a very long, very silent minute. I felt more comfortable just looking at him now that Karen had left the room. I watched the subtle, steady movement of his mouth. I leaned in closer, trying to see if I could understand what he was saying, but it was impossible; he was either speaking too quickly or the movements were not forming real words at all.

"I really wanted to meet you. Sorry it took so long," I said finally.

Again, the slight cock of the head.

"Mom didn't speak of you very often because it made her sad, but I know that she loved you very much."

I had the strangest impression that he was listening. His mouth was hardly moving anymore, and there was something cognizant in his eyes. Encouraged, I went on. "Mom told me that it wouldn't be any use to come and visit you. She said that you wouldn't even know we were here, and so she didn't want to put me through it. Karen told me the same thing. But you do know I'm here, don't you?"

It wasn't really a question. He knew I was there, I was sure of it now. His hands looked as though they had loosened their desperate clutch on the armrests, the knuckles not quite so white and taut.

"Mom died. I know Karen told you. I just want you to know that she loved you very much and she just had a hard time seeing you like this. She wouldn't want you to think that she had forgotten about you." It was more than I had ever intended to say to him, particularly seeing as he was in some sort of vegetative state. I couldn't even say for sure that my mom had felt that way; after all she never told me as much, not in so many words. But I found that, with him unable to respond, I could say what I wanted to without worrying about his reaction. I don't know. It was like praying, or confession, or something. At least I imagined it was, never having set foot inside a church. Feeling a sudden flood of pity for the poor old man, I reached out and covered his spidery old hand with mine.

What happened next happened so fast I couldn't react.

It was as though I had flicked some invisible switch. His hand flipped and jerked suddenly upward and clamped mine in an iron grip; I wouldn't have believed someone so old and frail could grasp so tightly. He pulled me with such force that I flew off the sofa and was suddenly on my knees before him. His face, so carefully trained on nothingness a moment before, was staring at me with a desperation I could not fathom. His eyes were still cloudy, but something was awake behind the veil, and that something terrified me.

"Send me back!" he cried, with a voice hoarse and cracked from disuse. His other hand clutched for mine, claw-like, and grasped it just as tightly.

I could say nothing; I couldn't move, such was my shock at the sudden awakening of the unwakeable. He pulled at me again, so that my face was inches from his.

"I've seen it, Elizabeth! I've seen it! Send me back! I want to go back!" His voice broke and shuddered as he shook me in his hands. He was staring at me with such intensity and desperation that I couldn't breathe.

"I'm... not... Elizabeth!" I managed to choke out.

"Send me back, do you hear me? I've seen it! I've seen it!" His voice rose to a tortured shriek and he shook me harder, his hands crushing mine. I tried to scramble to my feet but he held me down.

"I can't send... I don't know what you're talking about! I'm not Elizabeth! Let go of me!" I gasped.

At that moment the door burst open and Karen flew across the room. She threw herself between us and wrenched my grandfather's hands away. I cried out in pain as I was flung to the floor, sliding into the wall where the back of my head cracked into the windowsill. For a moment everything in front of my eyes disappeared in a bright flash of blindness, and I had to shake my head to regain my vision. When my eyes refocused, Karen shimmered into view, cradling my grandfather in a comforting embrace. The old man was crying inconsolably on her shoulder.

"It's okay, Dad. It's okay," Karen cooed, stroking his withered old cheek.

His eyes were turned again to the window, looking far beyond anything visible to the living eye, and his mouth was moving rapidly again between his sobs, in a silent mantra I could now recognize.

"I've seen it. Send me back."

When his sobs had quieted, Karen carefully extricated herself from him and knelt beside me on the floor.

"Jess, are you okay?"

"Um, yeah. I think so," I replied, unable to repress the quiver in my voice.

"I'm so sorry, honey. He hasn't done anything like that in years. I would have warned you if I'd thought he was capable of any sort of outburst."

"No, I... it's okay." I tried to rise. The room spun.

"Don't try to stand up, sweetie. I think you gave your head a pretty good whack on the windowsill. Just sit for a minute, I'll be right back."

I must have looked frightened because she added, "Don't worry about Dad, he's calmed down now. Just don't touch him."

I sat on the floor and closed my eyes, trying to relocate my center of balance. My grandfather gave no further acknowledgment of my presence. The only visible evidence of his outburst was his newly anxious expression and the tears that still glimmered damply on his cheeks, reflecting the sunlight.

Karen returned a moment later, followed by the nurse from the reception desk. The nurse's formerly jovial expression was twisted with motherly concern as she bent over my grandfather, a syringe flashing in her white-gloved hand. He vanished behind her for a moment and when he reappeared again, his face had lightened into the attitude it had worn when I'd first seen it: expectant, eager.

Karen brought me a cold compress, and I sat with it pressed to the back of my head until I began to feel steadier. Then she helped me to my feet and walked me downstairs without a backward glance toward the old man in the chair. She walked me out onto the porch, where she sat me firmly in a rocking chair.

"Just wait out here while I sign a few things and then we'll head home," Karen said, and headed back to the reception desk.

I stared out across the lawn of the Winchester House for the Aged, wondering what it was that my grandfather saw out of that upstairs window that I was missing. I was trying to shake from my thoughts how desperately he had begged me to send him back, though "back to where," of course, I had no idea.

A voice drifted out of the open window behind me.

"...wasn't due for another dose for at least two hours."

"Well, then I'd question whether what you're giving him is strong enough to do the job."

"But Mrs. Hunt, he hasn't had a single spell, not once in five years. Why, the last time was when your sister came to—"

"—Yes, I know when his last *spell* was, thank you," Karen said, sounding for the first time like the lawyer she actually was. "And I'm quite sure I'd asked you not to mention my sister's visit."

"Yes, of course."

"Just do what is necessary to ensure that this doesn't happen again. I won't have my father upsetting himself or anyone else. Do I make myself perfectly clear?"

"Certainly, Mrs. Hunt. We will continue to do everything we can," the nurse replied.

"Thank you." Karen's boots tapped out a sharp staccato as she marched out. She softened her stride as she stepped onto the porch and looked down at me.

"Ready to go home?"

"Sure." I shrugged in what I hoped was an offhanded way. I didn't want her to think I'd overheard her conversation. I stood up carefully and followed her to the car. She'd just gotten seat-belted with the key in the ignition when she stopped and looked at me.

"So are you sure you're okay?"

"I'm fine, really," I insisted, not sure if I was telling the truth or not.

"Oh my *God*, look at your hands!"

I did, and realized that both of them were beginning to bruise, bleeding in a few spots where my grandfather's unclipped fingernails had dug into my skin. I hadn't felt the pain, probably from the shock of the whole experience and then the bump to the head, but now that I had perceived their appearance I also noticed that both of them were aching dully.

"Ow!" I said in surprise.

Karen heaved a long sigh and turned the key. "What a family reunion, huh? I'm sorry. I guess you can see now why I was so reluctant to bring you to see him. He is very rarely like that, so I'm sorry you had to see him on such a bad day."

"Is that what he always says? When he... freaks out?"

"No. I have heard him say something similar before, but it's different every time. He's just so far gone now, that he rarely makes any sense."

"He thought I was my mom. He called me Elizabeth."

Karen's eyes flashed anxiously, first to my face, and then to my hands again. She opened her mouth to say something and instead bit her lip. We drove home in loaded silence.

I'd never been around anyone who was mentally unsound, and it wasn't an experience I wanted to repeat now that I'd had it.

27

I'd heard friends talk about grandparents or great-aunts with Alzheimer's disease and dementia, but this was different than what they'd described. There had been a real urgency, a real sense of purpose to my grandfather and his strange words, though they made as little sense as the ramblings of any senile person. Somehow I couldn't convince myself that he was simply losing his mind as a natural part of aging. I would never forget the way he had stared into my eyes, and I felt uncomfortably haunted by the fact that I couldn't help him when he'd begged it of me.

3

IN THE CARDS

THE MORNING OF MY MOVE-IN TO ST. MATT'S dawned muggy and hot. Noah looked like he'd run a marathon after loading the car and had to re-shower and change before we could go.

"Are you sure you don't want to change too, Jessica?" Noah asked, a little too casually.

I smiled as sweetly as I possibly could. "No thanks, Noah. I'm pretty comfortable just like this." I'd dressed as "goth" as my wardrobe would allow that morning. I liked to think of it as a combination farewell gesture and middle finger.

At least the SUV had air-conditioning, something neither our ancient car nor our apartment had back home in New York. The ride was only an hour long and passed quickly, but the closer we got, the more nervous I became. By the time we pulled off the highway and into view of the campus, I'd gnawed half of my fingernails off.

St. Matt's was a college recruitment brochure come to life. Large, ornate wrought-iron gates enclosed the entire campus. The buildings were imposing, with ivy that tangled rampantly across their stone and brick façades. Wiltshire Hall, the largest and most impressive of the buildings, overlooked the quad, an enormous clock tower crowning it like royalty. The lawns and plants were beautifully manicured, and monstrous oak trees stood as sentinels around the grounds, shading lounging students beneath their leafy canopies. The students already looked at home, reading on blankets, playing Frisbee, and talking on cell phones as they strolled down the cobblestoned sidewalks.

We pulled up in front of the row of freshman dorms. Dozens of students in identical bright orange T-shirts were assisting the new students in hauling their belongings into the dorms. They were filling up giant wheeled laundry bins and dollies, going in and out with everything from pillows and lamps to couches and computer desks, swarming around like a hive of co-ed bees.

We got out of the car and were immediately descended upon by three students all bearing the uniform of the move-in crew.

"Hey, welcome to St. Matt's! What's your name?" the girl in front bubbled, consulting a clipboard.

"Uh, hi. I'm Jess Ballard."

"I'm Katie," she said, pointing unnecessarily to her name tag, on which her name was clearly printed in bubble letters. "Let's see here..." she muttered, running a finger down her list. "Ah, here we are, Jessica Ballard. Okay, it says here you're in room 312, Donnelly Hall. Is that what your packet says?"

I checked it. "Yup."

"Excellent. And these must be your parents?"

"My aunt and uncle, actually."

"Great! Well nice to meet you all. Jess, here's your name tag." She handed me a tag with my name on it, printed in the same bubble letters. Unfortunately, it said "Jessica." Not wanting to seem rude, I peeled it off the paper backing and stuck it grudgingly onto my black tank top.

We began loading my stuff into an available laundry bin. A lot of my things had been shipped from New York, so we didn't have nearly as much as some of the perspiring students around us. A freckly redheaded kid with his sleeves rolled up heaved the bin into the elevator for us. We followed him down the hallway on the third floor, where a small whiteboard confirmed we were in the right place. "Jessica Ballard and Tia Vezga, Class of 2017" was printed in girly purple lettering. I smudged my thumb quickly through the "–ica," leaving my preferred moniker. The door to my room was already open.

The initial effect was a little dreary; after all, there were definite visual similarities between my new bedroom and your standard-issue prison cell. But I firmly told myself to snap out of it. This room was the symbolic opposite of a prison cell. It was a fresh start, a new beginning. I settled on a metaphor that suited my artist's temperament: It was a blank canvas.

Well, an almost blank canvas. There was a large pile of boxes and bags on one of the beds already; it looked like my roommate had gotten here first.

It took until lunchtime to unpack everything. Karen insisted on staying to help; Noah and the freckly kid dragged my stuff up from storage that had been previously shipped, and then Noah excused himself to have a look around the campus. Karen and I had just finished a sandwich break when my roommate came in.

"Oh good, you're here!" she squealed, tossing a plastic shopping bag on her bed and bounding forward to greet me.

Tia Vezga was a very pretty girl, with a heart-shaped face and long shiny black hair that hung in a thick curtain down her back. Her eyes were heavily lashed and deep brown, and they crinkled as she smiled.

"It's so nice to meet you! I hope you don't mind, you weren't here yet, so I picked the bed on the right."

"No, I don't mind at all. It's nice to meet you too." I noticed almost immediately her total lack of reaction to my wardrobe choices; she didn't appear wary or disappointed—a positive sign. "This is my aunt, Karen Hunt," I added, hoping to avoid another "Is this your mom?" moment.

"Nice to meet you, Ms. Hunt."

"You too Tia," Karen replied, looking very pleased that my roommate was so obviously friendly.

Tia turned back to me. "I would introduce you to my parents but they're still in the bookstore. I think they're trying to buy one of everything." She rolled her eyes. "So Jess, where are you from?"

"Um, all around really, but most recently New York City."

"Oh, cool! I've never even been to New York! My family's from St. Louis."

"Well, I've never been to St. Louis," I said. Not that I'd ever wanted to go there, but there was no need to mention that.

"Yeah, well, it's not exactly the excitement capital of the world, is it?" Tia said, almost reading my mind. "Hey, you're just about unpacked!"

"Yeah, I've been here for a few hours."

Tia looked at her pile of boxes and suitcases, a little crestfallen. "I haven't even started."

"I'll give you a hand," I offered. "Just let me walk Karen out."

Karen looked up from the empty boxes. She'd been looking for little things to keep her occupied for the last fifteen minutes or so, but everything was now put away. She seemed hesitant to go as she and I walked toward the door.

"I can stay and help Tia, too."

31

"No, Karen, you and Noah should head home. It's so hot. You've done enough manual labor for the day."

"What about your books? Do you want me to go with you to buy—"

"—No, really, I'm fine. You guys head back to the air conditioning."

Karen nodded resignedly. "Okay then. You're sure you have everything? You'll call if..." her voice trailed off, as though she couldn't think of anything to say.

"Sure."

"Okay, then. I'm going, I'm going. Have a good semester."

I waved her down the stairs, trying my best to look independent or grown up or something, anything to wipe that worried look off her face.

As I walked back into my room, I was accosted by a girl in a skimpy sundress.

"Oh my God, do you live here?" she asked, pointing to my room. She was very tall and willowy, with flat-ironed, bleach-blonde hair and a complexion that could only be attained by sleeping nightly in a tanning bed. Her sequined dress was so low-cut it was like her boobs were actually staring at me. Who the hell lugs boxes around in an outfit like that?

"Uh, yeah, I do."

"Oh fabulous! We're neighbors! I'm Gabby Taylor. I'm just across the hall in 311. It's nice to meet you!" she gushed. Her eyes raked over my hair, my face, and my clothes. For a fleeting moment, a look of triumph seemed to twist her features, but as suddenly as it had appeared, it was gone.

"Hi, I'm Jess Ballard," I said as Tia leaned out of our room, tossing an empty cardboard box against the wall. "This is my roommate Tia Vezga."

"Hi, Tia." Gabby performed the same quick little inventory. This time she looked put-out and shook Tia's hand with a little less enthusiasm.

Tia seemed to notice none of this. "Nice to meet you, Gabby. Where are you from?"

"Oh, I'm from Connecticut. I went to an all-girls high school, so I'm thrilled to be going co-ed finally. My boyfriend isn't though. We've broken up like five times since I got accepted here. He's so jealous." She rolled her eyes.

"Oh, um... that's too bad," Tia said.

"Oh, not really. We just keep making up. And anyway, if we do break up for good, it's not like I can't find someone else around here," Gabby whispered, eyeing an upperclassman who was hauling a futon down the hall with his T-shirt sleeves rolled up. "Can you believe some of the guys here?" She winked coquettishly.

Tia just gaped. She seemed lost for words.

"Well, I'll come visit when I'm all unpacked. See you girls later!" Gabby disappeared into her room.

Tia looked at me blankly, and I grinned at her.

"Wanna ditch this whole unpacking thing and go scope out some guys?" I asked her, batting my eyelashes. She laughed and we headed back into our room.

"Well she was... nice," Tia said. I had a feeling that Tia always gave people the benefit of the doubt, even when that person had removed the doubt so forcibly.

"Sure," I agreed. "Be careful, though."

"Careful?"

"She was sizing us up, didn't you notice?"

"Sizing... what?"

"I don't think Gabby likes competition." I unfolded a blue pinstripe comforter and tossed it onto her bed. "She thought you were pretty. She wasn't happy about it." Tia finally caught up. Her olive complexion immediately flushed pink. "I wouldn't worry about it, Tia. I think she'll get her fair share of attention, don't you?"

Truer words were never spoken. There was a line of guys forming, trying to bring boxes to Gabby's room. Her boyfriend, who looked like a linebacker or something, watched the testosterone parade with a darkening expression. He departed a half an hour later, after a highly audible lovers' spat. If Gabby had been momentarily worried about competition from me or Tia, her fears should have evaporated by now. She had already created quite a disturbance among the male population.

Unpacking Tia's stuff was very different than unpacking mine. To begin with, all of her boxes were carefully labeled with little index cards. When I examined one of the index cards closely, I saw that it listed every item in the box in tiny, precise handwriting. And when I opened the box, everything was either wrapped in tissue paper or fitted in so neatly that I probably could have hurled the box out the window and not disturbed the contents. Everything was coordinated, from her bedspread to her picture frames to her little cup for holding pens and pencils. When we had finally finished, her half of the room looked like it had been staged for a catalog shoot. She gazed over it with a nod of satisfaction.

"Now I think what I really need is some stuff for these walls," Tia said.

Her eyes wandered across to my side of the room, where I'd managed to get a bunch of stuff up on the walls around my bed and desk.

"Oh, wow, Jess, did you draw these?" Tia asked as she walked over to examine my hodgepodge of wall hangings more closely. I'd stuck some of my own drawings up there among the magazine pages and photos and stuff.

"Yeah, some of them."

"Wow! You're really good! Are you an art major?"

"I don't know yet."

"Well, I can't even draw stick figures," she declared. "I'm definitely not going to be providing my own artwork. And these walls are so depressing unless you get something to cover them!"

"Sounds like you ladies are in need of the poster sale," a voice answered from the doorway. We both turned to see two guys standing there. One had sandy hair that stood out in cowlicks above his lightly freckled face. A Polaroid camera hung around his neck. He was wearing one of the bright orange moving day T-shirts. The other was dark-haired and tan, dressed in jeans and a sleeveless T-shirt. I recognized him as one of the guys who'd been carting Gabby's stuff around.

"There's always a poster sale in the student center the first week of term," the sandy-haired boy continued, bending down and scooping up a neon pink flyer that had been lying half-hidden under one of our empty boxes. He reached out to hand it to me.

"Thanks," I replied, taking the flyer.

"I'm Sam Lang. I'm the guys' R.A. on this floor."

Tia and I both introduced ourselves. Sam shook both of our hands with a very firm grip.

"And I'm Anthony, Sam's much more attractive and likable friend," the dark-haired boy added. He held his own hand out, seeming to flex his muscles as he did so.

"Hey," I said, shaking his hand quickly.

"Have any heavy lifting left to do?" Anthony asked. "I'm offering my services."

"No, we're good, thanks," I said. My smile was slipping off my face.

"Ignore him, he's obsessed with himself," Sam cut in, rolling his eyes. "Seriously though, can I help you with anything? Have any questions or anything like that?"

"Yeah, can we find out why some of our sizable tuition can't go

34

to some air conditioning?" I asked, moving toward the window in hopes of catching a breeze. The air was stubbornly motionless.

Anthony laughed far longer than the comment warranted, but Sam just nodded with a grin. "Not the first person to ask me that today, you know. It's brutal now, but the heat's really good in the winter, and believe me, we're gonna need it." He seemed to get a shiver just thinking about it.

"Well, that's good at least," Tia said, though she sounded like she was having a hard time sounding excited about blasting heaters when our whole room felt like a sauna.

"You girls want a personal tour of the campus?" Anthony asked.

"No, I think we helpless females will find our way around eventually," I said.

"Are you sure? I'd be happy to..."

"Down boy!" Sam ordered, shoving Anthony away from the door. "Head back across the hall, that blonde girl seemed to be enjoying your company, although I can't imagine why."

Anthony threw Sam a dirty look, but complied. "Goodbye, ladies. Don't miss me too much, now."

"Yeah, we'll try not to die of broken hearts in your absence," I said with a sugary smile.

Anthony winked and swaggered toward Gabby's room.

Sam looked mortified. "Sorry about him. I can't take him anywhere. He can't be held responsible for his actions; he's from New Jersey. Now ladies, I have been delegated the thrilling task of Polaroid duty." He grimaced and lifted the camera from his shirtfront. "This task has endeared me to some, but unfortunately lots of other people run screaming in the other direction when they see me coming."

Tia and I both laughed.

"Now, would you do me a favor and just let me take one picture of each of you? The res-life staff wants to put them up on everyone's bulletin boards next to their names. Something about helping everyone with matching names to faces. It'll be quick and painless, I promise."

Picture taking was not my favorite thing in the world, but Sam seemed properly penitent about asking us to pose, so I pasted on a smile and let Sam take my picture.

"Wow, so it looks like the moving in is almost done!" Sam said as he shook out the pictures, waiting for them to develop.

"Yeah, it took a while, but I think we're about done," Tia agreed.

"I think I've still got boxes from last year that I never unpacked."

"So you're not a freshman then?" I asked.

"Nope, a junior. You have to be at least a junior to be an R.A. Well, if you're done with unpacking, you should head over to the carnival."

"There's a carnival? On campus?" I asked.

"Yeah, and it's great! Here." He scooped another flyer off the floor and handed it to me. "It's the big welcome event. They really pull out all the stops; you should definitely check it out."

"Okay, thanks."

Sam handed Tia her photo. "Here you go, Tia."

"Ugh, I'm making that weird squinty face again!" Tia groaned. "Why can't I smile like a normal person?"

"Oh, come on, it looks fine!" I said.

"And Jess... oh, wait." Sam started to extend his hand toward me and then stopped, a puzzled expression on his face as he glanced down at my photograph.

"What, did I blink?" I asked. I always did that in pictures. Or I'd rock the "Exorcist look" with glowing red eyes.

"No, it's just... It didn't develop right." Sam dropped the photo into my outstretched hand.

I looked down at it. There I was standing in the middle of the room, looking a little sheepish but otherwise the shot was unembarrassing. But there was something wrong with the photo. All around the right side of me was this weird amorphous white shape. It looked like a bright, oddly shaped cloud of smoke. There was another smaller blob in the upper left corner near the ceiling. I'd never seen anything like that in a photo before.

"See?" Sam said. "I must have gotten a glare coming in the window or something. Can I try one more?"

"Okay." I forced another smile.

"Oh, you know what? That's the end of the film," Sam said, opening the back of the camera.

"Aw, shucks! Does that mean I don't get an embarrassing picture of me stuck up in the hallway for everyone to see? I'm heartbroken!"

"Don't worry Jess, I wouldn't want you to feel left out of the fun! I'll get some more film. I'll be back later for your photo shoot," Sam said.

"Oh, goody," I said with a big thumbs up.

"See you around." And with a wave Sam left, fiddling with his camera, a bewildered expression on his face.

"So what do you want to do, Tia? Do you want to hit that poster sale?" I asked, tacking my peculiar photo up with the other stuff on my wall. Camera malfunction aside, it was kind of cool-looking.

"No, not right now. I think I need a break. Do you want to go walk around? Maybe check out the carnival?"

"Sure."

As we headed out the door, Gabby and her roommate were leaving their room too.

"Hey, girls! Have you met Paige yet?"

We introduced ourselves to Paige, a tiny, mousy girl with tightly-curled black hair and an unusually high voice. She looked about five years too young to be in college.

"Are you girls going to the carnival?" she asked.

"Yeah, we're headed there now," Tia said.

"Great, we'll join you!" Gabby said.

I wasn't thrilled about spending time with Gabby, but Tia was too polite to say no, so we followed them out. It was finally cooling down. The setting sun took just enough of the heat out of the air to make it warm and balmy. We could see the lights and hear the shrieks of people on the carnival rides. A Ferris wheel, blinking brightly, rose like a slow-motion firework above the commotion.

"Wow, they really went all out for this!" I said.

"My sister graduated four years ago and she still talks about the carnivals!" Paige said. "Come on, let's get some food!"

We wandered through the crowd to a row of booths selling traditional carnival fare. I stood munching my fried dough, Paige and Tia both devouring enormous caramel apples. Gabby stood agonizing over the number of calories in the various options before settling on a small bag of popcorn. I considered throwing the rest of my fried dough at her, but settled for wafting it under her nose and saying loudly, "Mmmmm, doesn't this smell good?"

We tried our hands at some carnival games, even though Tia insisted they were rigged. We tossed plastic rings around the tops of bottles and shot darts at balloons. We aimed water pistols at targets and even played a few rounds of Whack-a-Mole. We had no luck scoring any of the tacky prizes until we tried a game in which we had to toss ping-pong balls into fishbowls.

"Come on, Tia, let's try it! I think we should have a mascot for our room!" I urged as I pulled her toward the booth.

Tia made a face. "No one can win those things, it's such a scam!"

"Oh, don't be such a downer, Tia! We can do it, come on!"

I handed two bucks to the guy running the booth. He looked bored out of his mind; it must be depressing having to work at a carnival, watching everyone else having a blast. He handed us three ping-pong balls each.

"Sink a ball, win a fish," he droned.

Tia went first. She missed her first shot, sending her ball pinging off the rim of a bowl. She threw me a withering look that clearly said, "See? I told you!" I went next. I missed the bowls completely. On Tia's second shot, our luck finally kicked in. The little white ball spun around the inside of the rim before plopping into the water and bobbing cheerfully.

"Hey, I won! I don't believe it, I won!" Tia cried, as the somber game attendant scooped out the ball and handed us the bowl. Inside swam a flamboyantly-blue little beta fish whom we secretly dubbed "Sequins" after Gabby's ridiculous dress.

We were giving Gabby a hard time, but I had to admit her tactics were effective. No fewer than three different guys had offered to win prizes for her, and now she was tottering around carrying two neon teddy bears and a giant SpongeBob SquarePants. If her haul of carnival toys was any indication, Gabby was going to be very popular.

I couldn't convince Tia to come on the Ferris wheel with me; she had a thing with heights. So Paige and I rode together, taking in the stunning sight of the campus and the lights of the city beyond, while Tia stood below holding the fishbowl.

By the time we'd ridden all the rest of the rides we'd wanted to go on, it was nearly ten o'clock. Stifling a yawn, I suggested we head back to the dorms. Gabby looked disappointed.

"But it's still early! Let's just go see what's on the other side of the rock wall before we go," she whined.

We squeezed through the crowd past a whirling ride that looked positively nausea-inducing, and found that only two attractions remained that we had not seen. The first was a station at which a sketchy-looking guy was trying to persuade onlookers to step onto a scale so he could guess their weight. Needless to say, we slid by that one without making any eye contact. The other was a purple velvet tent with a sign on a stand that read: "Tarot Card Readings by Madame Rabinski."

"Oh cool, a psychic! Come on, let's get our fortunes read!" Gabby urged.

"I'm game," Paige said at once.

I groaned. "You guys, I don't want to waste my money on *this*."

"What do you mean, 'waste your money?' Tarot cards are cool! I had mine read before and it was spooky how accurate it was. Some of these psychic ladies are for real," Paige said.

"Yeah, and some of them are scam artists," I said.

"Tia, how about you?" Gabby asked.

"I don't know. That stuff kind of freaks me out. I think I'll stay out here with Jess."

Gabby and Paige disappeared into the tent while Tia and I waited, Tia practically bouncing up and down with anticipation. For someone who was "freaked out" by tarot cards, she certainly seemed anxious to find out what happened. Finally they ducked back out through the tent flaps, both looking awestruck.

"Well, how was it? Was it any good?" Tia asked.

"That was awesome!" Paige whispered.

"She knew so much stuff—so many details!" Gabby added.

"Like what?"

"She knew all about my relationship with my boyfriend from home. And she told Paige that she'd made a very last minute decision to be here."

"Which is completely true!" Paige said. "I only got off the waiting list two weeks ago! I was all set to go to another school!"

Tia was biting her lip. Then she turned sharply to face me. "Jess, I think I want to try."

"*You* want to do this? You thought the fishbowl game was a scam, and now you want to get your fortune told?"

Tia looked a little embarrassed, but she nodded. "Well, yeah, sort of. I mean, it might be fun, just to see if anything comes true. It sounds like she's pretty good."

"I doubt she said anything she couldn't have guessed." I grumbled.

"How do you explain her knowing that I had a boyfriend?" Gabby asked.

"Well, you're wearing a claddagh ring upside down, for starters. Everyone knows that means you have a boyfriend," I suggested, pointing at her hand. "*And look at your outfit*," I added silently.

Gabby crossed her arms, hiding her hand. "Okay. What about Paige's recent decision to come here?"

I snorted. "Gabby, we *all* made recent decisions to come here! That's how choosing a college works!"

"That's not how she—"

"—Relax, Gabby!" Tia said. "It's just a carnival attraction—for fun... that's what we're supposed to be having right now, remember?" She turned to me. "Just for fun. Who cares if it's real or not? You don't have to get yours done, just go in with me!"

I rolled my eyes. "Fine, fine. Just don't blame me if I start laughing uncontrollably in the middle of your reading."

We entered the tent together. Tia went first, dragging me behind her. Inside the dim interior, a woman sat alone at a candlelit table.

I could barely repress a roll of my eyes. Madame Rabinski looked exactly like my own stereotype would have painted her. She was wearing vaguely gypsy-ish attire: A long, ruffled, red skirt and a peasant-style blouse. Her dark hair tumbled loose and wild around her shoulders, framing a dark-eyed, sharp-featured face. She was probably about forty years old, though the low light in the tent made it hard to tell. She raised a hand in greeting; her silver bracelets jangled and her fingers were adorned with clunky old rings. It took all my strength not to turn right around and walk out.

"Hello, girls. You would like your tarot cards read?" she asked, gesturing to a chair.

"How did she know?" I whispered dramatically to Tia as we sat down.

She elbowed me hard in the ribs, and then turned a friendly smile on Madame Rabinski. "Yes, we would. Well, I would, she's just here to watch."

"So's the fish," I added, plunking the fishbowl down on the table.

Madame Rabinski turned a penetrating stare on me. "A non-believer?"

"No, Sequins the Fish is a firm believer in the occult," I answered, straight-faced. The gypsy's eyes narrowed at me.

"Five dollars, right?" Tia said hurriedly.

"Yes, my dear." Madame Rabinski held out her glittering hand. Tia dropped the money into it. Madame Rabinski still had her eyes on me, and they were narrowed in dislike. She reached into a little blue velvet bag and extracted a very old set of tarot cards. She set them carefully on the table.

"What is your name, my dear?"

"Tia Vezga."

Madame Rabinski shook her head as though to clear it and her eyes darted to me, before she asked again, "I'm sorry, what is it?"

Tia repeated her name, more slowly.

"And your birthday, Tia?" Madame Rabinski continued.

"June twenty-seventh."

"Very well then, Tia, if you would shuffle the deck three times and then cut it for me, please," Madame Rabinski said, pushing the stack of tattered cards across the tabletop toward Tia.

Madame Rabinski couldn't seem to concentrate on what Tia was doing because she kept looking at me. She continued to periodically shake her head, as though there were a sound that was bothering her. I started to squirm under her gaze. What the hell was she looking at me for? I'd behaved myself... mostly.

Tia cut the cards and looked up expectantly. Madame Rabinski tore her eyes from me and started to lay out the cards with shaking hands. She'd only laid four cards on the table when she stopped abruptly, staring at what she saw. She re-gathered the cards and shuffled them once quickly, before starting to lay them out again. It was too dark to see what was on them.

"Impossible," she muttered, scooping the cards up again.

"Sorry?" Tia asked, frowning.

Just then, Madame Rabinski's violently trembling hands dropped the rest of the deck of cards to the floor. Her hands flew up to her face in a gesture that looked like she was trying to shade her eyes from a bright light.

"I'm sorry, but your friend will have to leave now," she whispered, her eyes squinted nearly shut.

"Huh?" Tia and I said together.

"You! You!" the woman shouted, pointing at me. "You need to leave!"

"What? Why?"

"Yeah, she hasn't done anything!"

"Your energy... I just can't concentrate... so many voices at once!" She looked at me, and her expression was undoubtedly horrified. "Your energy is overwhelming me! I'm sorry, but you must leave this tent right now."

"Fine, we're out of here," Tia snapped, grabbing my elbow.

"No, Tia, you stay." I pushed her back toward her seat.

"No, I'll go with you, Jess. You're right, this was stupid."

"Tia, you paid your five bucks. Get your cards read, okay? I'll take my *energy* and wait for you outside."

Tia opened her mouth to argue, but I didn't stay long enough to let her. I turned on my heel and exited the tent. I threw one last glance at Madame Rabinski as I closed the tent flap; her face had gone pale and she was clutching the edge of her table so hard that her knuckles were white. She was still staring at me like she'd seen a ghost.

I was so distracted that I nearly walked into a guy standing just outside the entrance.

"Whoa! Easy there!" he said.

"Sorry. I didn't see you," I said. I stepped back and looked up into one of the most attractive faces I'd ever seen. He was tall and square-shouldered, with dark chestnut hair that lay carelessly across his pale forehead, and had a handsome profile with a straight nose and pronounced cheekbones. When I caught his eye, his face broke into a disarming smile that crinkled his warm brown eyes. I returned his smile before I'd even thought about it.

"I was thinking about getting my fortune told, but judging by your dramatic exit, I think I'll pass," he laughed.

"Yeah, save your money," I said.

"That bad, huh?"

"Total rip-off. You'd be better off trying the fish game." I held up Sequins for him to see.

"Maybe I'll try that," he said.

Just then, Gabby tapped me on the shoulder. "That was quick! What happened?"

"What a whack job! She kicked me out!"

"She did?" Gabby looked sort of pleased.

"Yeah, she said my *energy* was distracting her," I snorted.

"Ooh, what does that mean?" Paige asked.

"It means she's nuts!" I turned back to my handsome stranger. "Like I said, totally not worth..."

He had walked away. I looked for him through the crowd of milling students, but he was gone. Damn.

Tia appeared from between the tent flaps. Gabby and Paige descended on her.

"So? What was it like?" Gabby asked.

"Okay, I guess," Tia shrugged. I thought she threw a glance at me, but it was very quick. "She said some stuff that was pretty accurate. Like she said that I was interested in going into medicine or the sciences."

"Are you?" Paige asked.

"I'm declared in the pre-med program."

"See?" Gabby said, rounding on me. "There's no way she could have known that."

"Fine, whatever, she's omniscient," I muttered. "Should we head back to the dorm?"

Just then, much to my relief, Gabby got a jealous text from her boyfriend. The ensuing domestic dispute distracted everyone on the walk back to the dorm. But something else was distracting me. If Madame Rabinski had just been putting on a performance to make me a believer, she was a very talented actress. What actress could make herself turn pale or make her own hands shake? Was it possible that my "energy" really bothered her that much? And what was it she had said at the end? "So many voices?" What the hell was that supposed to mean? Whether she'd been joking or not, Madame Rabinski had seriously freaked me out.

Back in our room, Tia pulled a pair of striped pajamas out of her top drawer.

"So, that was pretty weird, huh?"

"Just a little. What happened after I left?"

Tia shrugged. "Just my reading."

"She must have said something about practically hurling me out of her tent! Didn't she apologize or anything?"

"Yeah, she did. She said that she was really sorry, but that your energy was very intense and she couldn't concentrate on my energy while you were there."

"Oh." Well, that was anticlimactic. I grabbed my shower caddy and slid my feet into my slippers. "Well, my energy and I are heading over to the bathroom to brush our teeth. Want to come with us?"

Tia made a sharp intake of breath through her teeth. "I dunno, Jess. I'm not sure that I can focus on my dental hygiene in the presence of your intensity."

And with that we both laughed and trekked across the hall to brave the terrifying and uncharted territory of common-hall bathrooms.

4

ENTER EVAN

TIA AND I WERE FAST FRIENDS, THOUGH IN MANY WAYS we were polar opposites. Her meticulously packed belongings and color-coordinated accessories I noticed on move-in day were merely symptomatic of full-scale neat freak syndrome. Her school books were arranged in order by subject on her desk in a maddeningly straight row, like a freshly stocked shelf of boxes at a grocery store. She ironed her underwear and organized her drawers by color. She made her bed with hospital corners and had been caught red-handed on several occasions lint-rolling her throw pillows.

My brilliant system of organization involved piles: the book pile, the binder pile, the miscellaneous-papers-I-have-yet-to-organize pile. I had no system for where or in what order I put away my clothes, but at least they were clean and usually not very wrinkled. Luckily, Tia didn't seem to mind being the Felix to my Oscar.

"I love those boots," Tia said on the first day of classes, as I laced myself into my favorite knee-high purple Docs—a fifteen minute process.

"You can borrow them if you want. They'd fit you."

"Oh, please, can you imagine me in those things? I'd look like a moron!"

"Um, thanks?"

"No, no, I don't mean that *you* look like a moron," she said, picking up one of my shirts from the laundry pile, a black lace tank decorated with silver studs. "I just mean that I can't pull off your look. On you it looks so great, but on me... well, I'd just look silly."

"Okay, if you say so," I said. I stood up and grabbed my bulging messenger bag. "Well, I'm ready. Let's go!"

I was taking Astronomy, Introduction to Art History, French III, and Sociology, but the class I was really looking forward to was my first one, Introduction to Shakespeare, which met at 10:00 AM in Turner Hall. And as luck would have it, it was Tia's first class too.

Our class was held in a huge lecture hall; there had to be about two hundred freshmen in it. Tia had confided in me that she was taking it to get her English requirement out of the way, but I was fully intending to enjoy every minute of that class. We found seats towards the front of the room, though not in the very front row, as Tia would have preferred. I coaxed her back to the third row, where we'd be slightly less prominent in the eyes of the professor. I was fishing my notebook and my Complete Works out of my messenger bag when a melodious voice echoed through the room.

"All the world's a stage, and all the men and women merely players; they have their exits and their entrances, and one man in his time plays many parts."

I looked up as our professor took center stage with a flourish. Dr. Trudy Marshall was a waifish little woman whose eyes were magnified to cartoonish proportions behind heavy-framed glasses. Her hair was long, wavy, and shamelessly gray, hoisted into a messy bun by what had probably been the nearest available writing utensil.

"Welcome, everyone. The Bard penned those well-known lines in his comedy *As You Like It*. They hold true in this class as in life. I hope that you will all choose the role of the inventive and active learner, rather than that of the reluctant idler. If you do, I promise that we will unlock many literary secrets together. Otherwise, you shall be horribly bored, I fear. The choice, as always, is your own."

She looked sharply around the room, her eyes sparkling. Tia sat up a little straighter beside me, and I could only grin. I loved this woman already.

The rest of Dr. Marshall's lecture was as stimulating as the opening. We were beginning with Hamlet, one of my favorite plays. The only downside to her class, as far as I could tell, would be the extra seminar block, which met at the freakishly early hour of eight o'clock on Friday mornings.

After English, Tia jetted off to her microbiology class and I made my way to the student center. I had an appointment at the campus employment office to get the details of my assigned on-campus job. My scholarship covered my tuition, but I had to supplement with a job if I was going to cover my living expenses. Much to my dismay, the only jobs open to freshmen were in the exciting world of campus food service.

46

Resignedly, I sat down on a bench in the main lobby to fill out my paperwork. I'd only written my name and room assignment when a sudden knocking caused me to look up.

The guy I'd nearly tackled in my rush to get away from Madame Psycho grinned at me from behind the plate glass window of the gift shop. I waved awkwardly and returned to my paperwork. I was probably the world's worst flirt. I don't think I'd ever flirted on purpose, and if I'd tried, I don't think it would have been interpretable as such by any male member of the species.

Knock, knock, knock.

He was still looking at me, and his face lit up when our eyes met again. He gave a casual wave. I couldn't help it. I looked behind me. There was no way this guy was waving at me. Had Gabby showed up behind me? I turned back around, my face red now. He nodded as if to say, "Yes, I'm waving at you."

He pointed down at the piles of T-shirts in the display, which he'd apparently been examining. He pointed at a gray one with the St. Matt's crest emblazoned on the pocket. He raised his eyebrows quizzically.

I must have looked confused, because he picked up the shirt and held it up in front of his chest, as though modeling it.

I smirked in spite of myself.

He tossed the shirt aside and picked up a second shirt, a blue one bearing "St. Matthew's College" across the front in silver lettering and modeled that one, too. Then he held one shirt in each hand and raised and lowered them like a scale. He raised his eyebrows again. His question was clear: "Which one?"

He raised the gray one. I shook my head and made a face. He raised the blue one. I gave him a thumbs-up and a nod of approval. He grinned and mouthed, "Thank you!"

"Here's your schedule," said a rather sharp voice.

I spun around, startled. The woman from campus employment was hovering over me, waving a yellow piece of paper in my face.

"Oh, um... thank you," I said.

"Are you finished with that form yet?"

"No, sorry. Just a sec." I scribbled in the rest of my information and handed over the clipboard. She thrust the schedule at me and disappeared into her office. I looked over the information. I would be washing dishes and serving breakfast in a hairnet three mornings a week. Hot.

I shoved the schedule in my bag and turned to go, glancing

again into the gift shop. The attractive window shopper had left, apparently having decided to give up on our silent conversation through the plate glass. Who was this guy and, more importantly, would I ever get to have an uninterrupted conversation with him?

The next couple of weeks passed with what I could only describe as clichéd quickness. On Tuesdays, Thursdays, and Saturdays I worked in the dining hall, which was about as miserable as I'd expected. Sam stopped by my room a few times over those first few weeks, occasionally with Anthony in tow. They provided an amusing insider's tour of the campus that included a secret entrance into the clock tower and the best hills for sledding on cafeteria trays when the weather got colder. Anthony didn't grow any more charming with time, although I had to be impressed with his persistence and his extensive collection of cheesy pick-up lines. I also noticed that Tia made extra passes with the lint roller when she knew Sam was stopping by.

We stayed friendly with Gabby and Paige, though I could only take the former in small doses. Gabby's soap-opera-style romance with her high school sweetheart lasted all of two weeks before she broke up with him for good. She then began the mysterious college ritual of "hooking up," something for which I could only ascertain the sketchiest definition; in Gabby's case it seemed to involve a lot of drinking, making-out, and awkward hung-over phone conversations. Watching the cycle repeat itself was all the encouragement I needed to stay well away from it. Not that I needed any other reasons to stay away from alcohol, having spent half my life cleaning up after my mom.

Tia only really took notice when Gabby bragged of "hooking up" with Sam in mid-October. This changed Tia's tone from mildly reproving to downright acidic, and we didn't hang out much across the hall after that, though Tia was much more inclined to be charitable when she heard that it hadn't worked out.

§

All in all, college was in many ways what I'd hoped it would be. The only times when I felt really sad were in the evenings when Tia called her parents. I never could catch much of the conversation, which was carried on in rapid, often exasperated Spanish, but I

48

could still sense the warmth and affection in her voice for her "Papi" and "Mami." It made my heart ache.

I knew it was only a matter of time before my own parental situation came up in conversation with Tia, and I braced myself for it. She finally asked me about it in our third week of rooming together.

"So, um, are your parents not around, or…?" Tia fumbled, not sure which version of her question would be the least offensive to ask.

"No, actually. I've never met my dad and I lost my mom this past summer."

"Oh my goodness, I am so sorry." Tia was always saying quaint things like "Oh my goodness" and even in the awkwardness of the moment it made me smile a little.

"Me too."

"So then, Karen is your mother's sister?"

"Yeah, her twin, actually. But she and my mom didn't talk anymore, so I'd never met her while my mom was alive."

"They weren't identical were they?" Tia whispered.

"No," I said quickly, stifling the image.

"Oh, good. Because that would have been a little too weird, don't you think?"

"Definitely."

"Are they alike in other ways?"

The bitterness in my laugh surprised even me. "Not even remotely. Karen is so put-together and my mom was… well, she was a mess, actually."

"Oh. We don't have to talk about this, Jess," Tia said.

"No, it's okay," I replied, suddenly feeling the need to unload it all. "My mom drank a lot. She was always screwing things up and then trying to make a fresh start, and that usually meant uprooting our entire existence every six months or so. I think I've lived in every major city in the U.S."

"That must have been tough, with school and everything."

"Well, it wasn't easy, but I got used to it. I always felt like she was running from something, you know? Not just with the moving, but with the drinking, too. There were things she just didn't want to deal with, but she never could get far enough away from them, whatever they were."

"How did she… I mean, was she sick, or…"

"It was an accident. She was drunk and she fell." Tia didn't need the details. I was sure she'd come to the same conclusion as Karen, and I didn't want her to, not when I knew it wasn't true.

"Is that why... well, your nightmares, is that why you have them?"

Damn. Apparently I hadn't done as effective a job as I'd thought in hiding that particular detail of my existence. She'd be bound to notice occasionally, sleeping six feet away from me, but I hadn't thought I'd been that obvious.

"Yes. They're getting better though," I lied. "I'm not keeping you up with my thrashing, am I?"

"No. I just noticed you were... restless," Tia said. Then she mercifully changed the subject.

I was hoping that the distraction of school would help get rid of the nightmares, but they'd only gotten worse. Though none could match that first one in their capacity to terrify me, all were vaguely disturbing. Sometimes, I could hear frantic voices calling my name out of the darkness. Other times, I would find myself lost in a strange cloudy landscape, struggling to navigate my way out. Still other dreams revealed me walking down a long, subterranean tunnel, drawn toward a light that both fascinated and frightened me. Without fail, I would wake up feeling jittery, sick, and unable to go back to sleep. If it kept up, I would have to start taking coffee intravenously just to get through my classes.

§

In the two weeks following Halloween, I saw my bookstore crush twice more. The first time was, naturally, in the last place on campus I would have wanted to see him.

I dragged myself out of bed the morning after Halloween, squashing an impulse not to hurl my alarm clock across the room, settling instead for smothering it with a pillow. A quick glance in the mirror confirmed I did not need to bother with makeup—I'd fallen asleep with it on, after a late night of horror movies and junk food with Tia and Sam, and it still looked surprisingly intact.

I smiled as I remembered Tia, wrapped in two blankets like a burrito, only her forehead and eyes visible, shrieking and cursing me for talking her into this movie night. I had chosen a couple of obscure Japanese films for the occasion, low in the blood-and-guts department, but chock-full of psychological scares. By the time we finished the second one, she hurled the entire bowl of popcorn at me, then spent the next half hour cleaning it up with a dustbuster.

I braided my hair quickly, the purple streaks playing peek-a-boo in the plaits, and brushed my teeth as I slipped on my black Converse sneakers. I was careful not to wake Tia, who despite the promise of permanent trauma, had slept pretty soundly. My footsteps crunched on some rogue popcorn kernels as I snuck out the door. I left a note on our whiteboard for her: "Forgive me, roomie?" with a sad face. I taped a bag of Skittles, her favorite candy, beneath it as a peace offering.

I arrived just on time for my shift, and checked the message board for my assignments. Left buffet line, cereals, and condiments. Could have been worse, I noted as I pulled on my gloves and greeted Paige, who also worked this shift. At least I wasn't scraping dishes this morning.

"What was with all the screaming from your room last night?" Paige asked. "I almost called res-life on you guys."

"Ah yes, the Japanese horror movie-fest. Tia was a little underprepared for the content."

Paige laughed as she poured a massive box of maple syrup into a stainless steel vat. "So I assume you won't be hosting another one?"

"You assume correctly. I don't think Tia will ever let me pick the movie again."

"Sounds like it'll be Disney movies and science documentaries for you from now on."

I grimaced and tucked my long braids into the obligatory hairnet. Then I donned my plastic gloves and started filling the plastic serving trays with Cheerios.

The dining hall stayed even emptier than usual for a Saturday morning, which made sense considering how many kids had been out partying incognito the night before. Gabby had invited us to a party she was attending, but we'd declined. Halloween had probably been fun at one point in history, but now it just seemed like an opportunity for girls to prance around in the trashiest outfits they could legally get away with in public. After several years in a row of being unable to purchase a costume that covered my ass, I'd gone on strike.

I was getting bored at the buffet line, and was amusing myself by separating the Froot Loops by color, when I looked up and saw him staring at me from across the room. It was the same boy from the carnival, sitting by himself at one of the tables under the window.

Catching my eye, he raised a hand in greeting. Automatically I waved back, and then realized I was waving a spoon covered in blueberry yogurt. Turning bright red, I dropped the spoon and retreated to the bowels of the kitchen, begging Paige to switch assignments with me. Stuck on dish duty, she happily agreed. I spent the rest of my shift volunteering for the least visible tasks.

The next time I saw him was almost a week later; he was heading up the crowded stairs of Wiltshire Hall while Tia and I were trotting down them. He grinned at me and winked. Momentarily dazed, I turned my head and followed his progress up the stairs until he disappeared around the banister.

Tia stopped a few steps down from me. "Did you forget something?"

"No," I said, ripping my eyes away from the empty hallway above me. "I just saw someone I knew."

"Was it T-shirt Boy?" Tia asked, smirking. She had taken to calling him that since I made the mistake of telling her about him.

I rolled my eyes. "Yes, but his real friends call him 'Campus Apparel Man.'"

"Oooh, can we go back up and find him? I want to see what he looks like!"

"No, I don't have time to be a psycho-stalker just now, thanks," I said as I passed her on the staircase. I ignored the little part of me that was willing to risk psycho-stalker status just to talk to him.

To tell the truth, I was a little annoyed with myself. It wasn't like me to obsess over some boy, especially one whose name I didn't even know. It was thoroughly Gabby-like behavior, and I hoped it wasn't becoming a pattern. I seemed to be able to interact with the rest of the male population without devolving into an idiot.

November brought gusty winds, the chill of oncoming winter, and the due date for my first major paper for Professor Marshall's class. Of the required twelve-page length, I had completed exactly zero. I had no excuse, really; I'd done it to myself just like always. Somehow, without a deadline looming directly over my head like some invisible guillotine, I was incapable of motivating myself to work. It was one of the few traits I'd inherited from my mom; I always knew that one day, as much as I hated to admit it, I would be recreating her frantic patterns around the kitchen in the morning, gathering up the bits of work that I'd scattered around the house, and swearing frantically under my breath as I tried to put on my shoes and eat a Pop-Tart at the same time. It seemed to be, alas, my fate. But I also knew that I worked best under pressure, and somehow, I never left things so late that I didn't miraculously finish on time. So it was with only a mild fluttering of panic that I set out for Culver Library at 8:00 PM on Thursday night. I had a whopping twelve hours before my paper was due. No problem.

At least I wasn't alone. As I walked through the main reading room with my laptop bag slung over my shoulder, heads were protruding from almost every cubicle, and the faint, rhythmic hum of typing pervaded the otherwise silent room. As I turned the corner to find a more private spot in the stacks, I spotted Anthony, his face inches from his laptop screen. I smirked to myself. He was hammering the delete button and muttering to himself, a pencil clamped between his teeth. I fought the urge to make some snide comment about his obvious writer's block and contented myself with the knowledge that he, too, was suffering.

I settled myself into a well-lit, forgotten little cubicle nestled among large dusty volumes of Russian history. I carefully unpacked and laid out my paper-writing survival kit, which consisted of my laptop, my binder full of notes, my copy of Hamlet, a two liter bottle of Diet Coke, and a family size bag of Peanut M&M's. And so, taking a deep breath and popping a red M&M into my mouth, I got to work.

It was slow going. My brain didn't seem to want to conform itself to the task at hand; it kept wandering to stupid things like a compulsion to line up all the blue M&M's, or counting how many times the word "to" appeared in the "To be or not to be" speech (fifteen, as it turns out). Eventually though, I was able to discipline myself, and after a few hours I had written seven pages. By midnight I only had the conclusion left to write.

It was around that time that I started experiencing the distinct feeling that someone was watching me. I kept looking over my shoulder as though someone had called my name, but I was completely alone. I didn't consider myself easily spooked, so I didn't think I could blame it on the solitude.

After about the twentieth glance over my shoulder, my eyes alighted on a biography of Rasputin, his eyes staring down at me from the cover with a mystical and piercing expression. I laughed out loud, and my laugh echoed softly back to me. I decided that it was the book causing my edginess and turned it backwards, allowing Rasputin's voodoo magic to work on someone else. I returned to my work but instead of refocusing, I started thinking that I would rather be stabbed, poisoned, shot, and drowned than finish this damn paper.

By one o'clock I had to run to the bathroom, having drained my entire supply of Diet Coke. The library was completely deserted, the table lamps casting a dull orange glow over the room. A work-study student had replaced the librarian at the main circulation desk. His head was drooping in a comical nod, his mouth hanging open, his ears deafened to my presence by enormous headphones. I wouldn't have minded a job like *that*, I thought, as a vision of the dining hall popped into my head. Hairnets to headphones would have been a definite upgrade.

Feeling much better, I returned to my lonely spot in the stacks. I turned the last corner that would reveal my cubicle and promptly shrieked.

There was a boy standing at my carrel, leaning over the partition and reading my computer screen. At the sound of my scream he jumped away from the desk; clearly I had frightened him as much as he had frightened me.

"I'm sorry! I didn't mean to scare you," he gasped.

I recovered myself. "No, please don't apologize. I'm sure I frightened you more, screaming like that. I just didn't realize anyone else was left in here."

"Neither did I. And here I thought I was the worst of the slackers tonight."

As I calmed down, I got a good look at him, and realized with a start that it was the boy from the carnival and the gift shop. I actually had to bite my tongue to keep from blurting, "T-shirt boy!" Note to self: kill Tia for coming up with that nickname. Even in the dim light of the stacks his looks made my breath stutter. My heart continued to pound, but no longer out of fear. I found that I couldn't help smiling back, and hoped that I wasn't grinning like an idiot.

"You're talking to a world-class slacker," I said.

"You're writing that paper for Marshall's class, huh?" He pointed over his shoulder toward the glow of my laptop.

"Yeah."

"Looks like you're nearly done. How's it going?"

"Okay, I guess. Just trying to finish up."

"Well, I wish I was as far along as you. I've still got at least three pages to go." He smiled again. Wow, was it infectious.

"You're in Marshall's class, too?" I couldn't believe I'd never noticed him there before. The more I looked at him the more difficult I found it to look away.

"Yeah. I think I've seen you there, haven't I? The section with the eight o'clock seminar block, right?" he asked, leaning casually against a shelf. My heart seemed to skip a beat. He'd noticed me.

"Yeah, that's the one. I don't remember seeing you," I admitted. My face felt hot. I was blushing. *Why* was I blushing?

"Well, what are there, about two hundred freshmen in that class? And my attendance hasn't exactly been exemplary—a side effect of an eight o'clock start time." He winked at me. It was the sort of thing I usually found obnoxious, but somehow I didn't mind. "My name's Evan, by the way. Evan Corbett."

He held his hand out. I reached over the partition to shake it, but before I could even grip it properly, I released it with a gasp.

"Your hand is freezing!" I cried.

"Oh, yeah, sorry about that," he laughed, shoving his hand into his pocket. "Poor circulation. Plus, I picked a really drafty carrel near the windows. Can't get too comfortable or I'll fall asleep and that'll be it for my paper!"

I just smiled, rubbing my fingers. The cold was lingering, and my blood was rushing oddly in the veins of my hand.

"So, do you only tell your name to warm-handed boys, or..."

"Oh, sorry! I'm Jess Ballard."

Evan's grin widened "Oh, excellent!"

That didn't seem like the appropriate response. "Sorry?"

"Oh, it's just that my sister's name is Jessica, so I know I'll be able to remember your name. I'm not always great with names. Somehow I think I would have remembered yours, though."

"So uh, how is your paper going?" I wanted to keep talking to him, but I felt awkward; conversations with boys who took my breath away were not an activity I engaged in frequently. Or ever.

"It's not original or earth-shattering, but I think I'll manage a decent enough grade, if I can just get it done." He sat on the desktop and crossed his arms. "Don't you ever feel like it's futile to try to write something original about a play that's been around for four hundred years?"

"I know what you mean. I'm definitely not breaking any new ground here. If generations of doctoral students haven't come up with it, I'm sure I won't."

"Exactly. So, are you an English major, Jess?"

"I haven't decided yet, actually."

"Good for you! I've never understood why people declare majors before they even get here," Evan said.

"Really? I feel like everyone I know has already declared." I said.

"Please! Half of them will change their majors three times before they graduate. There are so many classes to take here. Why would you want to limit yourself so early? Take a little of everything—explore a bit, you know?" Evan gestured around the library to make his point. There were more books there than anyone could ever hope to read in three lifetimes.

I felt a lump rise in my throat. I tried to fight it down, but it caught me off guard. It must have shown in my face because Evan suddenly looked concerned.

"Hey, are you okay?" he asked, standing up and taking a step toward me.

I took a step backward and nodded. "I'm fine. It's just that... my mother used to say stuff like that to me all the time."

As soon as I said it, I was shocked at myself. It was tough enough to talk about my mom at all, let alone with a complete stranger. But something about Evan put me at ease. His expression was so open and honest, I found myself confiding in him.

"She died over the summer. She kept telling me how jealous she was that I was going away to school, that I should take every kind of class I could so that I wouldn't miss anything."

"I'm sorry. Sounds like she was a smart lady," Evan said gently.

I found I could smile. "She had her moments."

"Well, then there's my mom. There's not a good idea on earth that she hasn't come up with herself; just ask her." He rolled his eyes. I knew he was lightening the tone for my benefit and I appreciated it. He went on, "She was really unhappy when I started playing lacrosse—wanted me to continue on the piano instead."

"That's a good skill to have, playing the piano. I wish I could," I said.

"Yeah, well, my mom used to make me practice two hours a day when I was younger." He grinned as my eyebrows floated up in spite of myself. "I know, huh? Some hobby. I think she's still in a bit of denial that I'm not going to be a hotshot concert pianist."

"Um, is there such a thing as a hotshot concert pianist?"

He chuckled. "No, actually, I guess there's not. Anyway she got over it pretty quickly when I got a lacrosse scholarship—turns out it was worth my time after all!" His forehead wrinkled thoughtfully. "We've met before, haven't we?" he asked.

"Yeah, we have, actually. A couple of times, I think."

"The carnival, right? Outside the fortune teller's tent? And the gift shop."

"I think so," I said.

"And somewhere else, I think."

"Oh, just around, I guess," I said. In reality I could have told him every single place on campus I'd ever seen him, every time he'd smiled at me. But at the risk of sounding like an obsessive stalker, I refrained.

"Here." He picked up my copy of Hamlet and one of my ballpoint pens (not, to my relief, one of the ones I had been gnawing on). He opened up the play and started writing in it.

"Hey! Stop defacing The Bard!"

"There," he said, closing the book and tossing it back down on the desk. "I wrote my number in there."

"Your number?" I asked blankly.

"Yeah. My phone number."

"Your phone number?" I repeated. My brain had officially stopped working.

"Um, yeah. You know... telephone?" He raised his hand to his ear in the universally recognized gesture for a telephone.

"You could have used my note paper instead of my book!" I said, pulling myself together and feigning annoyance, lest he think me mentally incapable of understanding the word "telephone."

"Yes, but this way, it's in your favorite book, so you won't lose it. And you have to look for it. It's on my favorite page. Think of it as a little scavenger hunt. When you find it, give me a call. Maybe we could hang out sometime. Good luck finishing your paper." He flashed that knee-weakening smile again. He started to walk away through the stacks.

He was just about to disappear around the corner when I called after him.

"Evan?"

"Yeah?"

"How did you know it was one of my favorite books?"

He just grinned again and slipped away between the stacks.

I stood in the semi-darkness, clutching my well-loved book, thinking how much more I liked it now that he'd written in it.

I forced myself not to open the book to look for his number. I told myself it would be a sort of reward when I had finished the paper. An hour later I stumbled exhausted through the main reading room, my final product in my hand. Yawning, I let my eyes scan the carrels. I was disappointed not to see Evan there; maybe he'd beaten me to the punch and finished his paper first. I ignored the impulse to look for him in the smaller reading rooms and headed back to my room for a few hours of sleep before class.

Tia was curled up in a ball under her comforter, snoring peacefully. She had finished her paper early, of course. It had been sitting neatly on top of her printer for three days, mocking me. I wanted to wake her up to tell her about Evan. She'd definitely think my meeting a dating prospect was well worth being woken out of a dead sleep. But my bed was calling to me. I decided my gossip could wait and I fell on top of my blankets fully clothed, sneakers still on my feet, and was asleep in minutes.

"Rise and shine, you overachiever."

Tia woke me fifteen minutes before class, a pitying look on her face and two cups of coffee in her hands. She was so obnoxiously perky in the morning.

"I didn't even hear you come in! What time did you finish?" she asked as I rolled out of bed and raced around the room to get ready.

"Around three. Hours to spare," I replied, grinning at her horrified expression.

She bit back whatever scolding comment she had for me and contented herself with shaking her head at me in disbelief as she handed me my coffee.

"Hey, if you don't like my study habits, you shouldn't be such an enabler."

"What do you mean, an enabler? I don't help you procrastinate!"

I waved my coffee cup at her. "Sure you do. You caffeinate me."

"Fine, I'll take it back then." She reached for my cup, but I danced out of her reach as I pulled on my sweatshirt.

"You wouldn't want to do such a thing, would you, Ti? I might fall asleep in class and miss something important. You wouldn't want that on your conscience, would you?"

Tia stuck her tongue out at me and slung her bag over her shoulder.

"Besides," I continued, keeping my voice purposely nonchalant as I grabbed my bag and paper off my desk, "if I were asleep, how could I tell you about the guy I met last night?"

Tia's mouth fell open as I bounced past her out the door.

"Excuse me! Hello? You met a guy in the library in the middle of the night?"

"Yup."

"I don't believe this! I could dance naked on the fifty yard line in the middle of a football game and not meet a guy! Who is he? How did you meet him?"

"Have you actually tried dancing naked on the—"

"—Jessica! Focus! What's his name?"

"His name is Evan Corbett. He's a freshman, and he's in Dr. Marshall's class with us."

Tia almost choked on her gulp of coffee. "He's in this class! You mean we're gonna see him right now?"

"I guess so, yeah."

"So how did you meet him?"

"He was there finishing his paper, too. I was in the bathroom, and I guess he walked by my computer and stopped to see if I was working on the same assignment. And I came back and he was still there and—well, we just started talking. Oh, and he's T-shirt Boy."

"You're *kidding*!?"

"Nope."

"Oh my goodness, Jess, you have to point him out to me! Does he sit near us? Would I have seen him before?"

"I don't know. Actually, I don't remember seeing him in that class. But there are so many people. Besides, he says he doesn't, um... always make it to class." I tried to say this last bit quickly. I didn't want Tia prejudiced against Evan before she even met him, and skipping class was a surefire way to incur Tia's disapproval.

Happily, if Tia did disapprove, she didn't mention it. As we entered the lecture hall and took our usual seats in the third row, Tia stayed standing, craning her neck eagerly toward the entrance as though someone had just announced the imminent arrival of a celebrity.

"Is that him? What about him? No, he's blonde; you said he had dark hair. What about him in the red sweater?"

"Ti, will you shut up? When he shows up, I'll tell you!"

The hall filled quickly. By two minutes of eight nearly every seat was taken, but there was still no sign of Evan. Professor Marshall arrived at eight o'clock on the dot, closing the door behind her.

"Where is he?" Tia whispered as she pulled her notebook out of her bag.

"I don't know. He's not here," I hissed back, scanning the room again, though I was sure I hadn't missed him.

"He wouldn't skip class today, would he? Not with a paper due!"

"Maybe he's just late."

But an hour into Professor Marshall's lecture, it looked like Evan wasn't just late. I hadn't listened to a single word as Professor Marshall explained the dramatic function of the character of Polonius. I was too busy worrying about why Evan wasn't there. He'd told me himself he was hoping to do well on this paper—why would he stay up half the night writing it if he wasn't going to bother to show up and turn it in? It didn't make any sense. I doodled aimlessly on my otherwise blank page, occasionally writing Evan's name without consciously meaning to do it.

"Jess, come on, let's go." Tia's voice suddenly sounded in my ear. I looked around. Everyone was getting up and packing their bags; Professor Marshall must have dismissed the class. I shoved my notebook back in my bag and joined the queue to turn in my paper.

"Ti, will you wait for me? I just need to talk to Professor Marshall for a minute," I said.

Tia nodded. She plopped her paper onto the pile and loitered in the doorway.

Professor Marshall smiled politely as I turned in my paper. "Thank you, Jessica. I look forward to reading it."

"Looks like you'll be doing a lot of reading," I said, waving a hand at the formidable stack.

"Occupational hazard. I'll survive."

"Um, Professor Marshall, I just wanted to tell you something."

"Sure, Jessica, what is it?" she asked as she started to pack up.

"Well, I just wanted to let you know that Evan wrote his paper."

"Hmm?"

"Evan. He wasn't in class today, but I know that he wrote his paper. We were both in the library last night and we were talking and he was almost done. I don't know why he isn't here, but maybe he fell asleep in the library or something."

Professor Marshall looked puzzled. "I'm sorry Jess, who did you say?"

"Evan."

"Evan who?"

"Evan Corbett. I only really met him last night and I know he misses class a lot, but I didn't want him to get in trouble. I..." My voice faltered and died in my throat.

Professor Marshall's usually friendly face was suddenly shocked. All the color had drained from it, leaving it drawn and pale. Her hand moved convulsively to her throat, shaking as she clutched at the collar of her blouse.

"Professor Marshall? I... are you okay?" I reached a hand out toward her instinctively; she looked like she was going to faint.

She leapt away from me as though I had extended a weapon instead of a helpful hand. Her voice escaped her lips in a breathless whisper. "I... Jessica, why would you... Is this supposed to be some sort of joke?"

"What do you mean? Is what a joke?"

"If this is your idea of a joke, I don't think it's funny. Not funny at all," Professor Marshall continued, her expression transforming from fear to anger.

"I'm sorry, Professor, but I don't understand—"

"—Neither do I, Jessica. I would never have expected this of you." Professor Marshall seemed to be pulling herself together, but she still appeared deeply disturbed. I was still scrambling to understand what she was talking about.

"Professor, if I said something—"

"—Jessica, please go to Dean Finndale's office."

"Huh?"

"Just go. Now!"

I turned automatically and walked out the door. Tia was standing by the doorway, her mouth hanging open in disbelief. I walked past her and headed toward the elevator.

"I'll see you back in the room," I told her.

I waited for the elevator in silence. I went over the conversation with Professor Marshall in my head and struggled to make sense of it, but I just couldn't. Was she angry that I was trying to make excuses for another student? Did it sound as though Evan and I had been cheating? Had something I'd said somehow reveal a breaking of a school regulation? The gears in my head were whirring, but no matter how I considered it, I just couldn't see how anyone could take offense to what I'd said.

I got out of the elevator and turned right along the third floor corridor. I knocked lightly on the open door to Dean Finndale's office and her secretary looked up expectantly.

"Can I help you, dear?"

"Professor Marshall just told me to come up and see the Dean." I tried to keep my voice casual, so I didn't look like the naughty kid who'd been sent to the principal's office. I'd never even had a detention in my life.

"Do you have an appointment?"

"No, she just told me to come straight up."

"And your name is?'

"Jessica Ballard."

"I see. Let me check if the Dean is available now. You can have a seat right there till she's ready for you," the woman said, bustling out of her desk and around the corner. I'd barely sat down when she reappeared. "You can go right in."

"Thanks," I muttered, feeling slightly ill as she ushered me through the door.

Dean Finndale was sitting behind her desk, scanning a pile of papers from over the top of pointy, red-framed reading glasses. I recognized her from an address she gave to the freshman class during the first week of classes. She looked up as I entered.

"Jessica, right?"

I tried to smile in greeting. "Hello, Dean Finndale."

She nodded toward a chair facing her. I dropped into it obediently.

She smiled at me. "We haven't met before. How is everything? Are you settling in okay?"

"Yes, I am, thank you."

"And what can I do for you, Jessica?"

"I'm not sure, actually. Professor Marshall sent me up here."

Dean Finndale's forehead betrayed the tiniest of frowns. "And why did she send you?"

"I have no idea."

With her forehead still frowning, she reached behind her and rifled through a filing cabinet until she found a manila filing folder with my name typed onto the colored tab. She laid it open on her desk and scanned it quickly.

"Is there something you want to talk to me about? Are you having trouble in her class?"

"No! I like her class very much. I really don't know what I'm d—"

"—Dean Finndale?" The secretary poked her round face around the corner.

"Yes, Linda?"

"Professor Marshall is here. She'd like to have a private word with you."

Dean Finndale nodded. "Thank you Linda. Please tell Professor Marshall I'll be right out."

She turned back to me. "It sounds like Professor Marshall is here to explain. Would you excuse me for a moment, Jessica? Perhaps she can clear this up for us."

"Sure." What else could I do?

Dean Finndale smiled at me again and left, leaving me sitting alone, stewing in my own frantic thoughts. She'd only been gone for five minutes, according to the clock above her window, when she walked back in. It may have been my imagination, but she seemed to approach me warily as she sat back down. When she spoke though, her tone was even and calm.

"So, I just spoke to Professor Marshall."

"And?"

"Would you like to explain yourself, Jessica?"

"I'd love to, if I knew what it was I was supposed to be explaining," I replied, starting to feel annoyed now.

"Professor Marshall says that you told her you saw Evan Corbett in the library last night?"

"Yes, I did. We were both working on our papers for her class. It's the first time I've ever really spoken to him."

"You spoke to him?" Dean Finndale's eyebrows disappeared into her hair.

"Yes. What, am I not supposed to talk to people now? Is that against some sort of college regulation, no talking in the library?"

"You are claiming that you saw Evan Corbett in the library last night and that you spoke to him?" she repeated blankly.

"*Yes!* Now will you please explain to me why I'm being treated like some sort of delinquent? I talked to a boy in the library. I don't think that's really such a big—"

"—Jessica, please listen to me. You could not have spoken to Evan Corbett in the library last night. Is it possible you got the name wrong?"

"No, I'm positive that was his name. He introduced himself, he... what do you mean I can't have spoken to him?" I stopped short, completely wrong-footed.

Dean Finndale didn't answer right away. She was watching me through narrowed eyes and seemed to be sizing me up, coming

63

to some sort of conclusion. Finally her expression softened into gentle, almost fearful disbelief.

"You really don't know who he is, do you?"

"What do you mean, 'who he is?'" My mind was racing. Was he some sort of criminal? Was he banned from the campus?

Dean Finndale reached across the desk and placed her hand on my clammy one.

"Jessica, listen to me. It's impossible that you spoke to Evan Corbett last night. He's dead."

5

WHISPERS AND MESSAGES

I T FELT LIKE I WAS TRYING TO THINK THROUGH A FOG that had suddenly arisen in my brain. I heard the words, but they seemed unrelated, a random grouping of sounds that had no direct correlation to me or to each other.

"Jessica? Did you hear what I said?" Dean Finndale's voice drifted toward me. I nodded, and then shook my head to clear it. "Evan Corbett was a freshman last year. He did take Professor Marshall's class, but he died before the end of the first semester."

I said nothing.

"So you can see why Professor Marshall was so disturbed when you said his name. Naturally she was upset."

I nodded absently.

"Where did you hear about Evan Corbett?"

I focused on her. "I'm sorry?"

"Where did you hear about Evan Corbett? Did one of the upperclassmen tell you about him?"

"I've never heard of him before last night. I don't really know many upperclassmen."

Dean Finndale leaned forward. "Think Jessica. You must have heard of him somewhere. How else could you mistake the name like that?"

"I didn't mistake the name. That was the name he told me. I've never heard of him before," I repeated.

Dean Finndale's tone turned stern, almost defensive. "Jessica, listen to me. Whoever you met in the library last night was not Evan Corbett, and this is not funny."

"I've told you the truth—I'd never joke about a student's death! Why would you assume I would do something like that?"

"Jessica, I don't—"

"Look, couldn't someone be playing a joke on me? Couldn't this be a twisted frat prank?" I asked, though my mind was already rejecting the idea. If this was a joke, what the hell was the punch line?

The Dean looked startled; it was clear this thought hadn't occurred to her. I opened my mouth to ask her why, but quickly shut it again. She'd just done that familiar flick of the eyes, the mental inventory of all the aspects of my appearance that many people, such as Noah, so often made. I wore black and dyed my hair; I must be a troublemaker.

I could actually hear the fight to justify herself buried in the sternness of Dean Finndale's next words. "It seems an unlikely joke, Jessica. Our students were badly shaken by the loss of Evan. I can't imagine one of them making a mockery of him, just for a laugh. That's just not our campus culture... No, I think it much more likely that you made a mistake."

I didn't bother arguing with her; I couldn't summon the strength. I was reeling too wildly from what she'd just told me.

"I'll speak to Professor Marshall. It's clear to me that you did not do this on purpose. I will explain that it was unintentional," she continued briskly.

I nodded again. Why couldn't I formulate a complete sentence to respond to this?

"I'm going to call Dr. Leahy down in Health Services. I think he should be able to give you the name of someone you can talk to."

"Someone I can...?"

"Yes, Jessica. A professional."

That did it.

"You're sending me to a shrink?"

"If by shrink you mean a licensed psychiatrist, then yes, Jessica. I think it's a good idea if you speak with him, in light of... recent events." Her eyes flicked almost imperceptibly to my file, still open on her desk. *Recent events.* My mom. She thought I was some sort of ticking mental time bomb because of my mom. Anger shot through me like a current. I couldn't stop it.

"I'm not crazy!"

"I never said you—"

"—You're sending me to a psychiatrist aren't you? Isn't that what you do with crazy people?" I asked, my voice rising.

"Jessica, please calm down."

I stood up involuntarily. "No! I'm not going to calm down! I'm not a liar! I'm telling you the truth!"

"I'm not calling you a liar. *Sit down*, Jessica." It wasn't a request.

I perched unwillingly on the end of the chair. "But you don't believe me."

"I believe that *you* believe what you're saying. I don't think that you're being deceitful. I think that you made an honest mistake because you're tired and confused. Now, I want you to go back to your room and have a rest. I'll email your professors to excuse you from the rest of your classes today. Get some sleep and call Dr. Leahy when you are feeling more rested." Her voice had an unmistakable note of finality. I was dismissed.

I stood up. I opened my mouth to speak and quickly closed it again. I was at a loss for words. I turned to leave.

"Jessica."

I stopped, but didn't look at her.

"I've asked Professor Marshall not to mention this to any of the students. I am asking you to do the same. We don't want to scare anyone with a simple misunderstanding."

I turned my back on her and walked out the door into the hall, ignoring the cheery goodbye from the secretary. Professor Marshall was nowhere to be seen, thankfully.

I let my feet carry me automatically back to Donnelly. I was trying to put together the pieces of everything that had happened in the past twelve hours.

I was sure of one thing. I *had* talked to Evan Corbett last night. I hadn't been asleep. I hadn't been dreaming or hallucinating. He had been standing there beside my desk, talking to me.

But if Evan Corbett really was... I could barely force myself to think the word *dead*... then how had I spoken to him? There was only one explanation. I hadn't seen Evan Corbett. I had seen Evan Corbett's ghost.

I rejected the word as soon as I'd thought it. It didn't fit what I'd seen. I ran through all the images I had of ghosts in my mind. Glowing white figures. Floating translucent beings. White sheets with eyeholes cut out of them. Casper the Friendly Ghost. All of them taken from movies and fiction because that was where ghosts belonged; I didn't believe in any of this stuff! None of them had any relation to what I had seen. Evan had been... well, solid. I hadn't been able to see through him. He'd been standing firmly on the ground. There was nothing ghostly about the way he'd sat in my chair or shook my hand.

But even as I thought it, I knew it wasn't true. I remembered the intense chill that filled my body when he touched my hand. At the time I had chalked it up to a poorly-heated library and my own giddy reaction to his touch—but now...

I had read somewhere that ghosts were cold, that touching them was like dousing yourself in icy water. Where had I read that? I couldn't place it. I tried to compare my own experience to this description. There was no doubt about it. The more I thought about it, the more I realized that what I had felt when Evan had touched me had been no normal chill; it had been much too cold for that. And what about the strange rushing in my veins? It certainly wasn't a normal physical response to a human touch, no matter how attractive the human.

My thoughts carried me in a fog all the way back to Donnelly. Tia had already gone to her next class, but our white board showed that her thoughts were still with me. "TEXT ME WHEN YOU GET BACK!" it insisted in bold red letters. I pulled out my phone and sent her a quick message: "In the room," and then sank onto my bed and tried to catch up on my sleep, but it was no use. My brain wouldn't shut off.

By the time Tia rushed breathlessly through the door, I had thought myself into a pounding headache. She threw down her bag and perched on the end of my bed, her face all crinkled with worry. "Are you okay? What happened?"

I hesitated. I had been considering what I would tell her since I had arrived back to the room. My initial reaction was to make something up, to tell her nothing of the bizarre reality I had landed myself in. But the fact was that she already knew too much. I'd told her every detail of my encounters with Evan and she'd seen Professor Marshall flip out at me. I could think of no explanation I could give her that she would actually swallow; she was one of the most observant people I knew. No, I would have to tell her the truth. The whole truth. Every ridiculous, unbelievable word of it. And then I would have to wait and hope that our new friendship was strong enough to stop her from running screaming from the room.

"Well, I went to see Dean Finndale."

"Yeah, I saw you get in the elevator. But why did Dr. Marshall send you up there in the first place?"

"She... thought that I was playing some kind of cruel joke on her." Even though it wasn't true, it was hurtful to imagine that Professor Marshall would think me capable of that.

"What kind of joke? I don't understand."

"Neither did I. So I went up to the Dean, and she, um... explained to me why Professor Marshall was so upset."

"And?"

I panicked. "Tia, I'm going to tell you everything, but I need you to promise me something before I do."

"Okay," she said at once.

"I want you to promise me that... that you won't look at me any differently." My voice cracked. Tears of fright were clouding my eyes, but I couldn't stop them. I rubbed them away with the back of my sleeve.

"What do you—"

"What I'm going to tell you is going to sound really crazy. It happened to me and I still don't think I believe it." My voice went up about an octave as I fought for control. Was this what a panic attack felt like? "I just—you're my best friend here and I really don't think I could handle it if you..."

"Jess, calm down! Take a deep breath! Now I promise you, whatever it is, we are still friends, okay? We will deal with it, and you will be fine. I'll help you. Just tell me what's going on."

I swallowed and caught my breath. "Dean Finndale told me that Evan Corbett isn't in Professor Marshall's class this term, but he was last fall. He was a freshman here last year. But he... died. He's dead."

I have to hand it to Tia; she took it well. Her face certainly betrayed shock, but she recovered quickly. She just closed her eyes and seemed to be thinking hard, her head nodding slowly. After a few seconds, she opened her eyes and said, "Well. That explains Professor Marshall's freak-out."

I burst into relieved laughter. "So you believe me? That I really saw him?"

"Of course I do! Jess, you're not a liar, I know that! And the look on your face when Professor Marshall started shouting—I knew something was seriously wrong and it was pretty obvious you had no idea what she was talking about." Tia slid off the bed and started pacing. "So what they're saying is that you... saw a ghost or something?"

"No, *they* are saying that I'm mistaken. That I heard the name somewhere and somehow got confused about who I talked to in the library last night. At least, that's the story that Dean Finndale is telling Professor Marshall."

"But you haven't heard of him before, have you?"

"No. Definitely not."

"And what about last night? I'm not trying to doubt you or anything, but I think we should at least consider all the possibilities. Do you think there's any chance you were asleep? Could you have been dreaming?"

I knew Tia was just trying to be thorough, so I considered it. I'd had some very vivid dreams lately, it was true. But I was quite sure I had never been asleep last night until after I'd returned to the room. And I'd been walking back to my desk from the bathroom when I'd seen him. "No, I really don't think I could have been. I remember the whole night clearly. And I was using all my usual tricks to keep myself awake."

"The candy and the Diet Coke?"

"Yeah."

"And anyway, even if you were asleep, that wouldn't explain how you dreamed about him," Tia pointed out, continuing her pacing.

"That's true."

"Did they tell you anything else about him? Like, how he died or anything like that?"

"No. Only that he was a freshman and that he was in Dr. Marshall's class last year."

Now that I thought about it, it seemed odd that Dean Finndale hadn't given me any other information. Wasn't some sort of explanation in order? I'd been in too much shock to ask for any details.

"Here," Tia said, grabbing my sketchbook, which she threw at me.

"What am I doing with this?"

"Draw him. Exactly how you remember him. And then jot down anything he told you about himself."

"What for? What good will that do?"

"We need a record of what you saw. It's the only way we can prove whether or not the boy you saw really was Evan Corbett." Tia looked resolved, like she had formulated some kind of plan. Thank goodness for her organized, sensible mind. I looked around for a pencil and something in my open bag caught my eye. My copy of Hamlet.

"My book!" I cried, diving for my bag.

"What? What?" Tia yelled.

"He wrote in my book! He picked it up and wrote his phone number in there! He told me to call him sometime!" I started to flip through the book from back to front, my eyes flying over the pages.

"JESS! Why didn't you tell me? That could prove everything!" Tia said, dropping to her knees next to me as I searched feverishly.

"I forgot," I said, wondering simultaneously how the hell I could have forgotten such a thing. My shaking fingers searched for the page. "Here it... no,"

Tia looked over my shoulder and then waved her hand dismissively. "No, that's not it. You said it's a phone number."

"Yeah, but I didn't write this," I whispered, my heart speeding up.

"Are you sure it wasn't already there? Is this a used book?" Tia asked, cocking her head to the side so she could look at the back cover.

"Yeah, by *me*. This is my copy of the book, Ti. I didn't get this in the bookstore; I've had it for years. I know every page of this book. I've read it about twenty times and *this wasn't here!"*

I let the book fall all the way open so that Tia could see it more clearly. In the top corner of the page, in the margin, there were visible words. They did not look as though they had been written with a pen, as I had seen Evan do. Instead, they looked as though they had been burned onto the page, the edges blurring from black to brown. It was not what I had been looking for, and though I didn't understand what they meant, the words sent a spasm of vague emotion through my body. I read them over again and again.

Help me. Find Hannah.

6

ELUSIVE

THIS WAS WHAT EVAN HAD WRITTEN TO ME. It wasn't a pick up line; it was a cry for help. But why did he need *me* to help him? And who in the world was Hannah? I turned my gaze wordlessly on Tia. She was mouthing the words over and over again, as though willing them to make sense.

"Do you know who—"

"—No idea. I don't even know anyone named Hannah."

"No one back in New York? Or any of the other cities you lived in?"

"Nope. Definitely not anyone who could be that important."

"Then it must be someone connected to Evan. That's the only thing that makes sense. Maybe we'll find something about her in the library." Tia stood up.

"Wait, the library? We're going *back* to the library?"

"Of course," she said, then saw the look on my face and quickly sat down again beside me. "Calm down, we're not going to bring a Ouija board or anything. But the library is the best place for research, and we've got to find out what we can about Evan. And now we've got someone else to search for, too," she added, tapping the cover of Hamlet.

"Thanks, Tia."

"What for?"

"For believing me. For helping me. Thank you," I said quietly.

She smiled gently at me. "Of course, Jess." Then she winked and added, "You are way more interesting than any of my other friends."

"Interesting. There's a euphemism if ever I've heard one."

As I bent to put my copy of Hamlet back in my bag, I noticed for the first time the text on the page that Evan had chosen. He said it was his favorite page. A shiver ran down my spine as I realized I was looking at a page of Act I, scene v, in which Hamlet speaks to the ghost of his father. And beside Evan's cryptic scrawl was one of the play's most memorable lines: "There are more things in heaven and earth, Horatio, /Than are dreamt of in your philosophy." I never understood the line better than I did in that moment.

I was still tired, confused, terrified, and a bit nauseous, but at least we had a plan. I was doing something; it beat sitting around and torturing myself with questions I couldn't answer. I flipped open my sketchbook and started drawing Evan, while Tia compiled a list of resources we could access in the library. I always drew best when I had the subject right in front of me, but Evan's face was burned very clearly in my mind. All I had to do was close my eyes and he was waiting for me behind my eyelids, holding perfectly still while I worked on his likeness.

"Wow, you weren't kidding. He really is good-looking," Tia said when I had finished.

Sketch and notes in hand, we set out for the library. It felt surreal to be back in the reading room under such different circumstances; but I found, to my surprise, that I wasn't afraid. Tia, on the other hand, looked oddly pale under her olive complexion. Her face was set and determined, though her eyes kept darting around the room at every little sound. Something inside me told me that Evan wasn't there. I didn't know how I knew it, but I was sure I would sense it when he was around. I realized that I wasn't dreading seeing him again at all. The feeling in my stomach that I had taken for dread was actually excited anticipation, which drained quickly when my instincts told me there would be no encounter. Not today, anyway.

Tia began an internet search while I dragged out the previous year's yearbook from a glass case near the circulation desk. Tia had already had luck by the time I returned to our table.

"I found his obituary." It sounded like an apology.

"Oh, right," I said, pulling my chair over to read it. Of course if he died, he would have had an obituary. Still, I felt very strange sitting down to read it. Tia had pulled up the *Boston Globe*. The listing of the obituary looked so impersonal, like a help-wanted ad.

CORBETT, Evan, 19, freshman at St. Matthew's College in Worcester, MA. A lacrosse player and award-winning musician, Evan graduated the top of his class from St. John's Preparatory School in Danvers, MA. Evan is survived by his loving parents, William and Rebecca Corbett; his grandparents, Verna Corbett and Thomas and Gladys Shaw; and his beloved younger sister

Jessica. Wake will be held at Kendall Family Funeral Home on Tuesday, November 15th from 3:00 PM–8:00 PM and funeral at Our Lady of Nazareth Church in Lexington, MA on Wednesday, November 16th at 10:00 AM. Private burial to follow. In lieu of flowers, the family has asked that donations be made to the Scholar Athlete Scholarship Fund at St. Matthew's College, which is designating a special scholarship in Evan's name.

"Are you okay, Jess?"

I turned to look at her. She was watching me with an anxious expression.

"His funeral was a year ago today."

"Oh, goodness. This is terrible."

"It doesn't say how he died."

"It usually doesn't," Tia scrolled back up through the other obituaries on the page. "None of these list cause of death at all. Sometimes they'll ask for donations to certain kinds of hospitals or disease research funds. You can usually get a clue that way, but otherwise they spare those kinds of details."

Well, that was understandable. We'd certainly spared the details in my mom's obituary, and not only because there were so many unanswered questions; the thought of anyone reading about her death, looking for tidbits to satisfy some kind of twisted, morbid curiosity was more than I could handle.

"But did you see this?" Tia continued, pointing at the name "'Jessica'. You were right about his sister's name."

"And the musician thing," I added. "See, it says he was an award-winning musician. He told me that he played the piano, that his mom made him practice all the time."

Tia looked at the paper I'd scribbled my notes on. "And lacrosse too. You said he was here on a lacrosse scholarship." She started shaking her head in disbelief. "Wow, Jess, there is a lot of confirmation here. Let's keep looking."

Tia went back to her internet search and I started scanning the freshman class photos. I'd only been at it a minute or so when I gasped out loud. Several people sitting near me looked around in annoyance.

There he was, staring up at me with that easy, friendly smile, the smile of someone who wasn't embarrassed to be photographed. His face was clean shaven and angular. His hair had the same messy elegance. I stared down at him with an odd feeling, like I was waiting for his image to come to life and start talking to me. Apparently that was the kind of thing that happened to me now.

"Here he is." I ran my finger gently over his face.

"Jess, he looks exactly like your sketch. You weren't exaggerating, he really is gorgeous."

"Was gorgeous."

I thought about Evan at the moment that picture was taken, not an inkling that his life was drawing so precariously near its end. Did he have any sense that his time was limited? Did the time slip fluidly by him as my time with my mother had flashed past me, with no warning about how precious it had become? His contented smile suddenly disturbed me. I slammed the book shut.

After another hour of digging, Tia tracked down an article from the *Boston Globe* and printed it out for me to read.

"This is how he died," she whispered.

WORCESTER, MA. Authorities were called to St. Matthew's College early Thursday morning around 5:00 AM responding to a 911 call. The caller, a groundskeeper at the college, reported that he had found an unconscious student on the grass outside MacCleary Hall on the south side of the campus. Paramedics and police arrived to find the body of nineteen-year-old freshman Evan Corbett at the base of a stone wall. It appears that the victim fell off of the wall and rendered himself unconscious. The apparent cause of death was hypothermia, and it is believed that the victim, who could not get back into his dorm, succumbed to the below-freezing temperatures. An investigation is currently underway and police are looking for any witnesses that can corroborate or dispute the apparent circumstances of this death, which is currently being ruled accidental.

So that was it. He had frozen to death. It didn't seem like it could be true; did people really freeze to death nowadays, on modern college campuses? How was that possible? My mind wouldn't absorb the information on any level but the hypothetical, and I was thankful for that.

We scoured the library and internet for any other information we could muster for the rest of that evening, and whenever we could find the time between classes. Our search of the yearbook and student directory had yielded three Hannahs. Two of them were currently freshmen and therefore had probably never even met Evan. Tia, bolder than I would have imagined, cornered the third after finding her room assignment in the campus phone book.

"She'd heard of him, but had never actually met him," she reported glumly the following Friday afternoon.

"How did you manage to bring that topic up?"

Tia shrugged. "I told her that I had been appointed as a liaison to the Student Athlete Scholarship Committee and that we were starting a scholarship in Evan's name. I told her we were looking for students who knew him, to take a quick questionnaire."

"And how the hell did you come up with that?" I asked, stunned.

"Well, I had to tell her something."

"And what if she'd said yes? What would you have done then?"

"I would have given her the questionnaire," she said, as though it were obvious.

"You actually made up a..." I shook my head. Of course she'd made the questionnaire. She was Tia. She'd probably established a real scholarship committee, just in case.

"Not that we would have gotten much further after that. How could we even start to explain what we really wanted even if we found the right Hannah?" she said.

"Seriously. I mean, does he have to be all cryptic about it just because he's a ghost? Couldn't he have told me why he wants me to find this Hannah person in the first place?"

Tia sighed and slung her bag over her shoulder. "Are you sure that you don't want to come to class? I'm sure it would be okay if you did."

I shook my head and tried to smile. "Not today. I don't think that would be a good idea."

"You don't think you could handle it?"

"I think I could handle it just fine, actually. It's Professor Marshall I'm worried about. I think Dean Finndale was thinking more of her than she was of me."

Dean Finndale had "suggested" that I take two weeks off from classes. She claimed concern for my nerves and well-being. I refused to miss my other classes, but in the case of Professor Marshall's class, I had agreed, though not because I thought I needed some sort of mental health sabbatical. I couldn't face Professor Marshall again quite so soon. It was too late in the semester to be switched out of her class so, since I couldn't spare her my presence entirely, I thought giving her a short break to recover herself was the least I could do. Tia, of course, thought that any solution that threatened my academic well-being was a poor one.

"You said that Dean Finndale had explained to her that it was just a mistake," she said.

"Getting an explanation and accepting it are two different things. I think I'd like to give her some time to accept the lie, since I can hardly tell her the truth."

"Oh, alright then. You can copy my notes again."

"Y'know this is a dangerous pattern we're getting into, Ti. Pretty soon I'm going to be too spoiled to attend any of my classes. It's just so much more convenient when you do all the work for me." I yawned and stretched out on my bed.

"Oh, shut up!" Tia huffed, rolling her eyes. She swung around and bounced out the door.

Trying to be good, I extracted my copy of Othello from my teetering stack of Shakespeare paperbacks and attempted to read Act I; there was no reason to be completely behind on class material. It was hard to concentrate, and I'd barely read three pages when there was a knock on the door.

I hopped up and opened it. "I told you Tia, I'm not going to—"

Karen stood in the hallway, her expression an odd combination of grim determination and fear.

"Karen! What are you doing here?"

"Your dean called me this morning," she said quietly.

I felt goose bumps rise on my forearms and my heart start to race. I should have known this was coming. I was absolutely not ready to have this conversation, but it looked like I was having it, so I stepped aside and gestured into the room.

"Come in."

Karen nodded and walked briskly into the room. She set a large cardboard box down on my desk. "I was going to mail this, but under the circumstances, I figured I'd just bring it with me. I thought you could use some snacks."

"Thanks," I replied as I shut the door. I'd never been less hungry in my entire life. "Sam will be thrilled."

Karen sat on the bed and stared at the wall for a moment. I sat down opposite her and tried to catch her eye, but she seemed determined not to look at me.

I finally broke the silence. "I suppose you'd like an explanation."

Karen continued looking at the wall as though it had spoken instead of me. "Jess, I don't even know what to say. Are you alright?"

"I'm okay, although I'm pretty sure several people are questioning my sanity."

"Are you… can you tell me what happened?"

She still wasn't looking at me. *Oh, God, she thinks I'm nuts. She thinks she's invited a lunatic into her house.* I could barely keep my voice from shaking. "I can only tell you what I told Dean Finndale. Did she tell you my side of the story?"

"Yes."

"I don't know what I can tell you, other than that. I can't explain it and I can't force it to make sense. Dean Finndale wants it all to be a misunderstanding, and quite frankly, so do I; but unfortunately I'm not lying and I'm not exaggerating. Nothing like this has ever happened to me before. I don't really know what else to say."

"I don't think you're lying. I'm just trying to think. I just don't know what to do," Karen told the wall.

I took a deep breath. I had to give her an out. She wasn't going to take it herself, so I had to give it to her. I spoke as quickly as I could, to get it over with. "Look, Karen, we're only just getting to know each other. You aren't obligated to deal with this. When the term is over, I'll come back to your place and get my stuff. I'm sure I can find a place to stay during the break until the spring term starts and then I'll work on finding an apartment for the summer. I'll just need a few days to…"

Karen finally recovered herself enough to look at me. "What?"

"I said I can find someplace else to live for—"

"—No, Jess! That's not what I want!" Karen's face crumpled into a horrified expression. "I don't want you out of my life because of this… this thing that happened to you."

"You don't?"

"Of course not! I'm just worried about you, that's all. And I need you to bear with me, because I have absolutely no idea how to deal with this," she said, running a shaking hand through her usually impeccable hair.

"That makes two of us."

Karen gave a trembling laugh that died out quickly. She lifted a hand to my face and stroked my cheek softly. I jerked my face away, startled by the emotion of the gesture. She dropped her hand.

"You must have been so scared."

"I still am."

"I'm so sorry you've had to deal with this, after everything you've been through." Her voice became bitter. "I should have done something to protect you."

I felt my brow furrow in confusion. "Karen, what could you possibly have done?"

"Oh, I don't know, I just... I'm just... I mean of course you're right," she said. "I just feel helpless that I can't do anything."

"You are doing something. You're still here. And you haven't written me off as a head case. That's everything."

Karen smiled sadly at me and reached as though to touch me again, but thought better of it. "We'll get you through this, all in one piece, I promise." She stood up. "I have to go talk to the dean again, and then I have some phone calls to make. Work stuff, it never ends. We can talk more over Thanksgiving weekend. We'll figure it out, okay?"

"Okay."

Karen gave me one long, appraising look and marched out. I let out a long sigh that I felt like I'd been holding in since I'd opened the door and seen her standing there. Karen knew everything and she wasn't going to disown me. I didn't realize until that moment how worried I'd been about it. Feeling lighter than I had in days, I decided to stop being such a chicken, and sat down at my computer. Within twenty minutes I had composed a carefully worded email of apology to Dr. Marshall. I decided to toe the official line, so to speak, and told her that I had mistaken the name, that I had no idea who Evan had been, and that I had never meant to scare or hurt her in any way. Then I settled back down with my copy of Othello.

Not five minutes later, Sam swung his head into the open doorway.

"Hey, Jess. Playing hooky again?" Sam let his mouth fall open in mock horror. "You know as an official member of the Residence Life staff, it is my solemn duty to report such detrimental behavior to the powers that be."

"Is it also your solemn duty to annoy me when I'm trying to read? Because you're doing a fantastic job."

"I've got skills," he said, flopping onto Tia's bed. She'd be so relieved that she'd just lint-rolled the comforter.

"Aren't you supposed to be in class, too? Don't you have trig right now?"

Sam just grinned sheepishly.

"Ah, now we see the corruption of the system!"

"Hey, you'd skip too if you were in my position!"

"Oh, yeah? And what position is that, may I ask? And please don't say a position of authority, because I will be forced to hit you with this book," I said, brandishing my weapon.

"The position of avoiding Gabby like the bubonic plague," he replied.

"What? Why?" I sat up and flung my copy of Othello to the side.

"She's stalking me!" he cried. "She actually swapped her entire schedule around just so she could get into my section of trig! No idea how she pulled that one off. The deadline to drop or switch classes was over a month ago!"

"I have a feeling Gabby usually gets what she wants," I said.

"Yeah, you're not kidding. I told her that I didn't want to date her, and she just stared at me. It was like I was speaking Mandarin-Chinese or something. She literally had no idea what I was saying. She totally ignored me, started talking about seeing a movie together next Friday." He sighed. "So what's your excuse? You're not usually this much of a slacker, are you?"

I kept my voice casual. "Just tired. I've read this play twice before anyway."

Sam's eyes fell on my desk and quickly lit up. "Hey is that...?"

I followed his gaze and burst out laughing.

"Yes, it's a care package from Karen. Hand-delivered, not ten minutes ago. Help yourself."

Sam looked surprised. "Your aunt was here? Why?"

"Just in the area. Lawyer stuff."

He jumped up and snatched the box, peeking inside. "Oh man, she went to Mike's Pastry again!"

"We do have a dining hall you know. It has food and everything. Surely in your two and a half years here you've managed to find it."

"I was just there an hour ago, in fact," Sam said as he poked through the box of baked goods. "But nothing the cafeteria ladies can rustle up can compare to Karen's designer desserts."

"My hairnet and I are offended."

He selected a chocolate cannoli and demolished it with a single bite. "Seriously, do you think your aunt will adopt me?"

"She might. She's all about taking in the strays."

"My mom always sends me trail mix. What college student of sound mind wants to eat trail mix?" he said. At least, that's what I think he said, his mouth stuffed indecently with chocolate crème.

"So, I did actually have a reason for coming here," he continued. "I mean, other than just to bug you and steal your food. I have come to extend a very prestigious invitation to a soirée this very evening."

"Soirée?"

"Oh, yes, a very classy event. There's even a dress code."

"Okay, I'm intrigued. Go on."

He swallowed the rest of the cannoli. "Okay, so I'm out of fancy lingo. Anthony is hosting a party in his room tonight. Do you and Tia want to come?"

"Anthony? Anthony who makes inappropriate remarks every time he sees me, Anthony?"

"Aw, come on, he's not that bad."

"He's a pig."

"Okay, he is of the swinish persuasion, but so what? There'll be a ton of people there. You won't even have to talk to him."

I had to admit I was tempted, despite the location of the festivities. I hadn't been much in the mood for socializing recently, but suddenly I felt like distraction was exactly what my overwrought brain needed.

"So, what's with the dress code?"

"Football gear. There's a football game on tonight, Patriots versus the Jets. Anthony is a die-hard Jets fan, and his roommate Nate follows the Pats religiously. Every time they play each other, they host a gathering in their room; loser foots the bill for the beer."

I wrestled my care package away from Sam and fished out a chocolate éclair. "Sorry, I don't watch football. And I definitely don't own anything with the name of a football team on it. I don't know if you guys can let me in."

"Oh, come on, you know you don't actually have to watch the game. There'll be lots of people hanging out doing other stuff, too. Just say you'll come."

I pretended to be torn; but honestly, it sounded fun, even if we did have to put up with testosterone overload. After everything that had happened, I was ready for a night of just being a regular college student. "Okay, I'm in."

"You're sure you can pull yourself away from the Shakespeare? You know, you might have missed something the first five times you read it."

"I'll risk ignorance in the name of a social life."

"Excellent!" he said. "Do you think you could convince Tia to come, too?"

"Consider her clubbed, sacked, and dragged."

Sam's smile doubled in size. Then he reached into the care package, grabbed a lobster tail, and swallowed it whole.

7

CHIVALRY IS DEAD

E VERY SINGLE TOP THAT TIA VEZGA OWNED was laid out around our room, arranged in a spectrum from red to purple. Unbelievable. Even when she was messy she was neat. "Well, that's it. I have nothing to wear," she announced.

I was lounging on my bed, wearing the same distressed skinny jeans and black sweater that I'd been wearing when Sam had stopped by that afternoon. Then again, she had a romantic investment in the evening.

"What are you talking about? It looks like The Gap exploded in here. Of course you have stuff to wear. I still vote for the red one."

"I don't know about that one. My sister gave it to me last year and I still haven't worn it. It's a little low-cut."

I threw my hands up. "Tia, just because it doesn't completely cover your clavicle doesn't make it low-cut! You look fabulous in it, and the color goes great with your skin. Now put it on and let's go!"

Tia scowled, but trusted me enough to pull off her conservative blue button-down and throw on the red top. "You seem a little eager to start watching football," she said.

"Nope. Just to get out of the room. Football will merely be the background noise."

Tia ran a brush through her hair and threw one last anxious look at the centimeter of cleavage she was showing. "Fine, let's just go before I lose my nerve."

We bundled up in our coats and hurried down the frozen pathway to Harrison Hall, where Anthony lived. Anthony was a junior, but through a stroke of luck had wound up with one of the few on-campus suites that wasn't snatched up by seniors in the housing lottery. The suites were supposed to be really big and comfortable, with their own bathrooms and kitchenettes. Tia and I were both excited to see the inside of one.

85

"You came!" Sam's face lit up like a Christmas tree as he opened the door. His eyes swept Tia approvingly. Color flooded her cheeks until they almost matched her top.

"I told you we would," I said, punching him in the arm.

"Come on in. Throw your coats in the bedroom, and then come hang out," Sam said, pointing vaguely behind him to the left.

Well, the suite might have been big for four people, but for forty? It was packed wall-to-wall with students, most in glaring team colors and clutching red Solo cups. The smell was a little overwhelming. Tia was already crinkling her nose.

"Does every boy's dorm room smell this way?"

"I'm gonna go with yes," I replied. I could distinguish stale beer, dirty laundry, and another sort of sour smell, not unlike foot odor. The whole olfactory nightmare was capped off with nauseating amounts of cheap cologne.

We wedged our way through the crowd, dropped our coats onto the outerwear mountain forming on the bed, and went to look for Sam. We knew right where he'd be; we just followed the sound of the television.

"Hey, over here! Come sit over here!" Sam was waving from an overstuffed gray sofa. He immediately shoved the guy sitting next to him onto the floor to make room for us. The kid, a Jets fan, was too engrossed in the game to notice he'd been displaced. Even with him gone though, there was only room for one of us to squeeze in. Sam was looking hopefully at Tia and had conjured a cup of beer for her, seemingly out of thin air.

"You sit there, Ti, I'm gonna grab a drink," I said.

"But where will you sit?" she asked with a slightly panicked look.

"Oh, I'll find a spot. Maybe Sam can assault someone else." I gave her a gentle nudge in the direction of the sofa and started worming my way towards the kitchen.

I saw a few people that I recognized from around campus, but most of the partygoers were seasoned upperclassmen, well-versed in the ways of beer pong and hangovers. Loud music with lots of thumping bass warred with the cheers of the diehard football fans crowded around the TV. It was a miracle the party hadn't been busted, though the rules were less strictly enforced in the upperclassmen's dorms.

The kitchen was as crowded as the rest of the apartment. A tarp had been laid across the floor, and the soles of my shoes stuck to the residue of beer that it was keeping off the linoleum. A group of about ten guys was crammed around a folding table, tossing ping-pong balls into geometric arrangements of plastic cups, ragging on each other when they missed, cheering and chanting when they sunk one. A few overly-dressed-up girls hovered nearby, hoping a stray shot might bring some attention their way.

"Hey, Jess!"

Anthony's voice had that unintentionally loud quality of someone who had already had a little too much to drink. He flung an arm around my shoulder, breathing beer in my face. The stick-thin girl to whom he'd been talking gave me a sour look and slunk away.

"Hey, Anthony," I said.

Anthony grinned stupidly and tightened his arm around my neck, giving me a noogie like I was his kid brother. "I told Sam I'd get you in my room eventually!" He tried, and failed, to wink. "'Course I always imagined there'd be fewer people."

"Charming."

He completely missed my sarcasm. "You look great." His eyes might as well have been groping hands. "I really dig the goth look you've got going on. Really hot."

"Great, because when I got up this morning, my first thought was 'What could I put on today that Anthony Messina would find hot?' Glad to see my mission in life has been fulfilled." And with the bitchiest smile I could muster, I turned away.

He grabbed my wrist. "Hey, don't be like that! I was just kidding! Just tell me why you give me such a hard time, huh? I'm a nice guy." He attempted an innocent look.

I looked pointedly down at my wrist, which he was grasping a little too tightly. He followed my gaze and quickly released his grip.

"Lemme get you a beer, okay?"

"I was actually looking for the soda. I'm not really a drinker."

Anthony seemed not to hear me and bent over the keg for a minute, trying to get me a drink, but there was something wrong with the tap.

"What the hell! I just untapped this one!" He whacked the nozzle on the rim of the keg.

"Anthony, seriously, it's fine. I just wanted a—"

"—No, no, I got this!" He held up the nozzle to see if it was clogged. A jet of foaming beer shot out of the end of it and blasted him in the face. "Shit!" he spluttered, dropping the tap and coughing.

A few bystanders started laughing, but I tried to stifle mine. Anthony mumbled something about changing his shirt and stalked off, his expression stormy. Another guy made his way to the tap and filled his cup without a problem. I had a definite smirk on my face. Sometimes karma was frustratingly absent, but sometimes its retribution was swift and satisfying. I grabbed a soda and went back to the living room.

I could see Sam and Tia sitting on the sofa together, looking very cozy. Sam was explaining the finer points of the game to Tia, who was leaning in to catch what he was saying. Sam's hands were drawing complicated diagrams in the air in front of him, and Tia was nodding seriously. Even when she was flirting she acted like she was in class. Just then, a Jets fan got up off the floor in front of the TV. I stole his spot, but instantly regretted it; the floor was grimy and smelled like feet.

"Hey, you're back!" Tia's face was flushed and voice slightly breathless.

"And you're still here." I looked pointedly at Sam's hand which was lying back to back against Tia's. Tia's expression was a little giddy, a giddiness that had nothing to do with the untouched beer in her hand.

"You find the drinks okay?" Sam asked.

"Yup," I answered and left it at that. No reason to kill the lovebird buzz with details of Anthony's ill-fated flirting. As it turned out, though, the buzz was about to be killed regardless.

Sam glanced up and then groaned, "Oh, *great*."

At that moment the door opened and Gabby stepped in. If she was hoping to attract some attention, mission accomplished.

"Oh, it's just something I threw together," she gushed to the guy who opened the door, mouth agape.

Gabby was wearing what looked like a man's Patriots jersey, but she had… well, altered it. It had been transformed into a skin-tight minidress with flared sleeves and a plunging neckline. A pair of bright red peep-toe stilettos completed the look.

"Sam, there you are!" Gabby squealed, the crowd parting for her like the Red Sea. "Anthony said we had to wear Pats gear. What do you think?" She executed a slow spin, hands on her hips.

"It's… something, alright," Sam replied. His eyes flicked uncomfortably over to Tia.

"I know, right? And to think I almost threw out all my ex's clothes that were hanging around my room!" she said. No one within a mile missed the inference.

Then Gabby noticed for the first time that Tia was sitting next to Sam. A shadow passed over her features but a second later she was beaming. She recovered herself quickly; I had to hand it to her.

"Oh, hey, girls. I didn't know you were coming. We all could have walked over together."

"We didn't know we were coming either till this afternoon, when Sam invited us," I said.

"Oh, *Sam* invited you? That was nice." Gabby said through her teeth.

"Wasn't it?" I agreed.

"We should all walk back together, though," Tia said, ever the peacemaker.

Gabby gave a noncommittal response that sounded like "huh," and then traipsed off towards the kitchen, her derriere working overtime.

When I looked back at Tia and Sam, the Gabby-frost had settled in. Neither of them looked in the mood to cuddle anymore. Sam stood up abruptly and put his hand out for Tia's cup.

"Ready for a refill?"

"Yeah, sure. Thanks," Tia replied.

Sam grabbed the cup and disappeared into the throng.

Tia looked over at me, looking somewhat distressed, and then saw me grinning.

"A refill? Did you even drink any of that?"

"It was warm. What are you smiling about?"

"The look on Gabby's face. It was priceless," I said.

Tia frowned. "I can't believe this. Did you see what she was wearing?"

"Was there anyone who *didn't* see what she was wearing?"

"Jess! This is not funny!"

"Yes, it is! It's hilarious, and I'll tell you why," I said, hopping up into Sam's spot on the sofa. "Gabby has shown up in what I would venture to say is the most desperate outfit I've ever seen, and Sam's still not interested! In fact, I think she's scared him off even more. I think you should be laughing your ass off."

"Ha, ha, ha," Tia said.

"Ti, you like him, don't you?"

Tia gave me a look that clearly said I was stating the obvious.

"Then don't let her get in the way. Show her that class and self-respect can still get the guy. I think she needs to learn it." I hopped up and went after Sam. It was time to play matchmaker.

I found him back at the keg trying to avoid Gabby, who was now cooing over the shot that Anthony had made in the current round of beer pong. Anthony was definitely enjoying her company.

Ignoring her, I walked up to Sam and whacked him in the arm. "Man up, Lang."

"Ouch! Hey, what was that for?" Sam said, rubbing his arm.

"Do you or do you not like my roommate Tia?"

"Of course I like—"

"—No, I mean seriously, Sam! Do you want to date the girl or not?"

Sam was dumbstruck for a moment and then the light bulb went on. "Yes."

"Okay, then," I grabbed the other empty cup from his hand and tossed it into the sink. "Then enough with the beer, she doesn't drink it." I handed him a soda from the stash in the fridge. "Bring her this, it's more her speed. And when you sit back down, tell her that there is absolutely nothing going on between you and Gabby. Then ask her what she's doing on Friday night."

"Are you sure—"

"—She's free. Take her to dinner at that little Italian place on the south corner of campus; she gushes over how cute it is every time we walk by it. She's allergic to roses, but she loves daisies and lilies. She doesn't like horror movies or anything with blood and guts, so suffer through a romantic comedy. Have her back by ten-thirty because she likes to get eight hours of sleep."

Sam stared at me like I'd just handed him a winning lottery ticket. "Anything else?"

"Yeah, hold her damn hand when you get back in there, will you? She's had it in prime hand-holding position for at least half an hour."

Sam's grin went from ear to ear. "Yes, ma'am!"

I watched him as he walked back into the living room. He definitely had a little more swagger in his step. He sat back down next to Tia and handed her the soda. Whatever he said next had her nodding and smiling, and five minutes later he was holding her hand.

Touchdown.

For the next couple of hours, there were three really interesting things happening in the room that had most everyone's attention occupied. The first, and in my opinion, least interesting, was the big game. There was some kind of outburst about a blown call and neither team could seem to make much progress, so the score kept creeping up by field goals. Also, some player, who was apparently important to the

Jets, got injured and was carried off the field. Under cover of all that excitement, interesting development number two was blossoming quietly on the sofa. Sam had moved successfully from hand holding to a full-out arm around the shoulder, and Tia looked like she was going to explode with happiness. They were whispering and laughing a lot, paying absolutely no attention to the television. The third and final spectacle was Gabby. Gabby always drew attention no matter what, but she seemed a woman on a mission tonight. The cozier Sam and Tia became, the louder and more obnoxiously drunk Gabby became. She had upped the ante at the beer pong table, making the players take a shot with her every time they scored a point. She was practically glued to Anthony and he wasn't complaining. No one was surprised when the two of them stumbled down the hall and disappeared into the bedroom. Let the hook-up cycle of regret continue.

Finally the game ended with huge cheers from the Patriots fans. Tia and Sam looked around, startled that it was over or perhaps that there had, in fact, been a game in progress at all.

"Is it over?" Tia asked.

"Yup," I said, climbing to my feet. My ankles were numb from sitting cross-legged too long.

"I'll walk you girls back," Sam offered.

"I'll get the coats," I said, hobbling down the hall towards the bedroom.

I opened the door and stopped dead. Gabby and Anthony were on the bed. It was dark, but I could sense quite a bit of movement happening.

"Whoa, sorry," I muttered. Mortified, I started backing out of the room. And then I heard something that utterly froze me in my tracks.

"Anthony, NO! I said get off of me! I want to go home!" Gabby sobbed.

I flung the door open and slammed my hand down on the light switch. The room flooded with light.

"What the hell!" Anthony growled. "Find your own damn room! Can't you see we're busy here?" He was on top of Gabby, one hand grasped around her waist, the other pushing her dress up around her hips. He'd removed his shirt and belt.

"Party's over, asshole," I said. "Rise and shine, time to go home."

Gabby, her face a map of mascara-stained tear tracks, struggled to sit up.

"No, stay there, babe. You're confused. You don't want to go anywhere. Jess was just leaving," Anthony said, his voice somehow managing to sound reassuring and threatening at the same time.

"You're right, Anthony. She is confused. And *we* are leaving. Right now." I marched toward the bed and tried to grab Gabby's hand, but Anthony jumped up and stood between us. He was surprisingly steady on his feet considering how much booze was on his breath. My heart started pounding but I stood my ground.

"She's not going anywhere. She's with me. I'll make sure she gets home," he snarled.

"Look at her. She's in no state; she needs to go home. NOW," I said.

"Exactly. Look at her... she walked into this party half-dressed. What do you think she wants?"

"—Not this. She clearly said NO. Her outfit has *nothing* to do with it."

I tried to reach around him, but he grabbed my wrist. "Let go of me," I said through gritted teeth.

"Listen, you bitch. You had your chance. Get your nosy ass out of this bedroom and keep your mouth shut or you'll be sorry." He tried to shove me aside, but lost his footing and stumbled. We fell into the wall and slid to the floor. I was pinned to the ground.

Anthony shook his head to clear it. Then he saw me under him and grinned lazily. "On second thought, I like you right where you are now. How 'bout we stay put?"

I opened my mouth to shout, but Anthony clamped a huge paw over my face. Panicking, I bit him as hard as I could. He let out a roar and pulled his hand back to strike me. I turned my face aside; my eyes clenched shut, waiting for the pain.

It never came. I heard a grunt and Anthony rolled off me, moaning. A huge hardcover book lay on the ground beside us. My eyes flew to Gabby, but she wasn't looking at us. She was crying and pointing into the corner of the room. I followed her terrified gaze.

Nothing. There was nothing there.

"Gabby, what..."

My question became a shriek as I felt hands grab the back of my sweater and drag me away from Anthony. My hands clawed around to free myself and closed around what I thought was a wrist, but it was shockingly cold. Gasping, I released it and spun around. There was no one there.

A second book lifted itself off the shelf under the window and hurled itself above my head across the room. This time it hit

Anthony on the shoulder causing him to roll even further away from me.

I skittered across the floor like a crab. Covering my head as another book flew through the air, I ran in a crouch over to the bed. I grabbed both of Gabby's hands and yanked. She slid off the bed and clung to me, crying into my neck.

"What the fuck? What the *fuck?*" she sobbed.

A fourth book soared across the room, whacking Anthony in the back. I stared frantically into the corner of the room, trying to force myself to see someone or something that would explain what was happening.

Anthony clambered to his feet, his expression livid. He was staring at Gabby, apparently convinced, as I had been, that she had thrown the books.

"I'm gonna kill you, you—"

Wham.

This time a lacrosse stick flew across the room and nailed Anthony right above the eye. He staggered back into the wall again and slumped to the floor, motionless. I just stared at him wordlessly. And then, just above his head, I saw it. In the small square mirror hanging on the wall, a reflection had appeared.

My head snapped back to the corner. Nothing. No one.

I stared back into the mirror. A dark figure, shoulders heaving, fists clenched, stared not back at me, but down at Anthony. I watched him reach for another book, and then stop, hand outstretched, as he caught my gaze. His eyes were blazing and his handsome features were twisted in anger, but I recognized him right away.

Evan.

Anthony was coming to. Blood began to seep between his fingers as he clutched his face. His angry yells finally sent people running into the room.

"What the hell is going on in here?" someone yelled.

"Anthony? What happened to you?"

"Jess? Gabby? Are you okay?" I could hear Tia's frightened voice from the doorway.

I glanced again in the mirror. Evan had vanished. Taking advantage of the sudden crowd, I dragged Gabby across the room and out the door, shoving past people. I felt as though my heart was going to beat its way out of my chest. Sam grabbed a blanket off the sofa and wrapped it around Gabby, who was on the brink of full-on hysteria.

I pulled her around to face me. Her teeth were chattering and her eyes were spherically wide. "Gabby, look at me. *Look at me.* Did he hurt you?"

With seeming difficulty, Gabby forced her erratic gaze to my face. Slowly she seemed to recognize me and then almost imperceptibly, she shook her head.

"Are you sure?"

A tiny nod.

Sam and Tia looked their questions silently at me.

"I'll explain later," I muttered. Let's get her back to the dorm."

"Can she walk?" Tia asked.

"Where are her shoes?" Sam added.

"Probably somewhere in there." I hitched my thumb back over my shoulder at the bedroom. "And we're not going back for them. She can barely stand up, let alone walk home in stilettos. Sam, can you carry her?"

"Yeah, of course," Sam said, and without hesitation scooped her up and hefted her into his arms. "Let's go. I'll talk to her about reporting this to campus security as soon as she sobers up."

We hurried back to Donnelly Hall in the crystal night, the air painful and sharp in our lungs. Tiny sparkling snowflakes sliced through the air on needling gusts of wind. The silence was oppressive, and the echoes of our footsteps sounded oddly dead against the pavement. The only other sound was Gabby's soft, fluttering sobs inside the blanket. Sam walked us to the door and promised he would meet us in our room after he had dropped Gabby off at the campus medical center to be checked out.

As soon as the door to our room was shut, I told Tia everything that had happened. Whatever Tia may have thought of Gabby, it didn't reduce her outrage at Anthony's actions. And when I reached the point of Evan's arrival, her mouth just dropped open.

"Jess, you're kidding me! Please tell me you're kidding me," she whispered.

"I wish I was," I said, flopping into my chair after ten minutes of pacing. "But he was there! I saw him in the mirror. It was like he was coming to my rescue! Somehow he sensed that I was in danger and he just showed up and started throwing things! And thank God he did, because I don't even want to think about what would have happened if he hadn't."

94

"Did Gabby see him? Did Anthony?"

"I don't *think* so. He only seemed to appear in the mirror and Gabby had hidden her face by then, she was so freaked out. Does it really matter though? I mean, they both saw inanimate objects being hurled through the air! What the hell are they going to think?" I ground a fist into my temple. My head was pounding.

"And no one else saw anything? What about the people who came into the room first?"

I thought hard, trying to extract my objective memory from the web of terror that had entangled the experience. "No, definitely not," I finally said. "The last thing to get thrown was the lacrosse stick and that was before the door opened. But it doesn't matter, does it? There were two witnesses! How am I going to explain this? What the hell am I going to do?"

"You're going to corroborate everything Gabby says... whatever her explanation is for things flying around the room, you back it up."

"Corroborate? Tia, Evan was there! You don't think I'm lying, do you?"

"Of course not!" she snapped. "Don't be ridiculous! I believe you, because you are my best friend and you don't lie. Not to mention the fact that you are completely sober and in total possession of your faculties. And that's just it, Jess. You're the only one in the room who was!"

"So what? Do you think they're just going to forget what they saw?"

"Actually, yes, I do. Think about it, Jess. Gabby probably won't have a very clear memory of any of this. You saw how drunk she was; she couldn't even walk, and Anthony wasn't much better. And even if either of them does remember something, do you really think they'll trust their own memories?" Tia said in her most reasonable, Tia-like voice.

"No, probably not."

"Exactly! You wouldn't believe it yourself if it weren't for everything that's happened this year with Evan. If you'd never experienced any of that, would you be telling me this right now?"

"No," I said, nodding my head in understanding, "I'd think I'd had some kind of freak out in my panic or that I'd been seeing things." I took a deep breath and blew it out. "And you think this will work?"

"Of course it will."

At that moment there was a quiet knock on the door, followed by a muffled voice. "It's Sam. Can I come in?"

Tia and I looked at each other in silent agreement.

"Here goes nothing," she said, and got up to open the door.

8

ENTER PIERCE

TIA, AS USUAL, WAS RIGHT. Sam believed our story at once, as did everyone else at the party who had discovered us in the aftermath. But they weren't really the ones I was concerned about. The real test came the next day when we saw Gabby, curled up in silky pink pajamas and fluffy slippers on the futon in her room, looking absolutely exhausted and slightly green from her hangover.

"It's like, a total blur," she said, nibbling on a saltine cracker. "I remember freaking out and I sort of remember you coming in and Anthony yelling, but the whole thing feels like it happened on one of those spinning rides at a carnival. How did we get back to the dorm?"

"We brought you back," Tia cut in, before I could answer. I fought the smirk that was trying to pull my lips up. She obviously didn't want Gabby to know she'd been whisked back to Donnelly in Sam's arms. Not that I blamed her.

Gabby accepted the story I told her without question.

"Good, I hope I got him in the junk with one of those books!" she hissed. "What an absolute creep! It's just so weird, because he seemed so nice at the party."

"Right." I'd known he was a creep from the first time I'd met him. In Gabby's lexicon, "nice" and "hot" were synonymous.

"So, are you pressing charges or something?" Tia asked.

"I don't know yet," Gabby said, chewing on her lip. "But I am definitely going to say something to the Dean. He shouldn't be allowed to live on campus, forget hosting parties."

Anthony wouldn't be hosting another party again for a long time. He was put on probation and lost housing. Gabby wouldn't get the police involved, but she did get up the courage to go to the administration and they took care of the rest. I refused to go within

97

ten feet of him, but Sam, who probably would have liked to kill him, agreed to talk to him for me.

"He's got a wicked shiner and three stitches above his eye," Sam reported. "You really clocked him good, Jess."

One of two things had happened. Either Anthony didn't remember what had happened and was taking our version of events as fact, or he did remember what happened and he was either too scared or too proud to admit what he'd actually seen. Either way was fine with me. I wasn't about to try to dig any deeper as long as he was cooperating.

And then there was me. I didn't know how to feel about what had transpired. Of course, I was glad that nothing worse had happened to me or to Gabby, and so I was grateful that Evan had shown up. But then again, *Evan had shown up!* The ghost I'd been trying to convince myself didn't exist, or that at least was not haunting me, had appeared again. He'd rescued me, like some paranormal knight in shining armor. My heart was calling for him to appear again so that I could thank him, but my head was telling my heart to shut up before I became known as the campus nut job, walking around chatting up a dead boy or getting carted off to the nearest available psychiatric facility.

I started spending time in the places I'd seen him, haunting them as I thought he ought to, both wishing and not wishing to see him. It was a strange combination of anticipation and dread. When I confessed as much to Tia, she looked thoughtful.

"Maybe you should try to contact him."

"Really?"

"Yes. He left you a message he thought was important, but he didn't explain it. How can you help him without more information?"

"Yeah, I get that, but still..."

"Look, I'm not saying we should break out the tarot cards or anything, but maybe you could try to... I don't know, call him, or something."

I laughed weakly. "This whole conversation sounds nuts."

Tia laughed too. "I know. But I've been thinking about it, and I think it might be worth a shot."

"But how do I do it? I never tried to see him any of the other times he showed up. I don't think it's something I can control."

"Maybe not, but I've been doing a little research..."

"Of course you have."

Tia went on as though I hadn't spoken, "I think maybe you should go to the spot where he died. People who study ghosts believe that spirits are tied to the places they died. I think you might have a better chance of seeing him there than anywhere else."

I scraped the purple polish from my thumbnail, considering. "What if it doesn't work?"

"Then we can add it to the list of all the other stuff we've tried," Tia said. "What's the worst that could happen?"

I glared at her.

"Okay, I withdraw the question. But just think about it."

I did think about it. For the next three days, every time I walked by the narrow alleyway between the quad and MacCleary Hall, my gaze lingered on the base of the rock wall where Evan had died. Finally I decided Tia was right. Evan had asked me for help. I had to find a way to give it to him, even if it scared the hell out of me.

The Thursday night following the party at 2:00 AM, I pulled on five layers of warm clothes and stuffed a blanket, a flashlight, and my copy of Hamlet into my bag. Tia, already in bed, offered one last time to go with me, but I shook my head.

"He reached out to me for a reason. I think I need to go alone."

"Well, take your phone. If you aren't back in an hour, I'm coming to get you. I know you want to see him, but it isn't worth freezing to..." she stopped abruptly, horrified with herself.

"Death," I finished quietly. I pocketed my phone and walked out the door.

The campus was icy and still under a steely mass of clouds that threatened snow at any moment. Here and there, a light glowed from a dorm window. A raucous laugh echoed faintly in the otherwise silent darkness. I kept my eyes on my feet as they crunched through the dirty snow.

The alley next to MacCleary Hall was darker than I'd hoped. The nearest lamppost's bulb was out, and I wondered if it had been like that since Evan's death—and if that was why no one had found him that night. For a moment I pictured him, a huddled mass at the base of the wall, and then closed my eyes and forced the image to recede.

I ducked into the alley and pulled the blanket from my bag, bunching it into a makeshift cushion to sit on with my back to the wall. I clutched the flashlight in one hand and the book in the other. Then I closed my eyes and took a deep unsteady breath.

"Evan?"

At first I called to him quietly even in my head. A slight breeze rustled by me, but there was no other answer. I thought his name again, louder.

"Evan?"

Nothing. I called for him silently over and over again as the minutes ticked by and I shivered in the cold. This was stupid, this was so stupid. The only thing I was going to find out here was a raging case of pneumonia.

I pulled my glove off with my chattering teeth and rifled with stiff clumsy fingers to the page Evan had written on. I placed my numb fingertips to his message and tried again, this time out loud.

"Evan?" I called, my voice a hoarse whisper.

"Jess? What are you doing out here?"

My shriek would have woken half the campus, but the cold froze it in my throat. The voice came from the darkest corner of the alleyway. As I watched, the shadows materialized into a form strolling casually toward me, clarifying and congealing until I recognized him.

Evan's face looked genuinely alarmed as he approached me. He was wearing the same sweatshirt and jeans he'd worn when I saw him in the library. He looked as real as anyone I'd ever seen, but no clouds of frozen breath wafted around him as he drew closer.

"You came!" I said.

"I was walking by and I saw you here! You shouldn't be out here by yourself in the middle of the night. It's freezing." He crouched down next to me.

"I know," I replied. His nearness drove the cold even deeper into my bones, but I didn't care. I couldn't believe I was looking into his face again.

"What are you doing out here?" he asked again.

"I was looking for you," I answered. I felt fear fluttering through me, but it was a wild, detached thing. I was afraid of something, but it wasn't him. It couldn't be him.

He looked puzzled. "For me? Out here? Why?"

"I... thought you'd be here. I didn't know where else to look."

He was too bright in the darkness, illuminated from some unseen source. A disturbed shadow flitted across his features.

"Why didn't you just try my room? I live right over..." He pointed toward MacCleary Hall, but dropped his hand quickly, looking momentarily confused.

My heart, already beating frantically, sped up to a panicked flutter. A terrible thought crossed my mind. "Evan... don't you know what's happened?"

He scowled and opened his mouth to answer me, and flickered out of focus, like an image in an old movie. He blinked out of sight and appeared instantly ten paces away, his hands shoved into his pockets. "You really shouldn't be out here. It's late and we've got class tomorrow," he said.

"No, Evan, we don't," I said slowly. "*I* have class tomorrow."

He gave me the strangest look, like I'd suddenly started speaking in tongues, and shimmered out of sight again. He reappeared on the other side of the alleyway, leaning against the wall.

"How did you do on your paper?" he asked, almost desperately. The outline of his form was wavering, like a fluttering candle losing its battle with the darkness.

"I..." I was completely unprepared for this possibility. He didn't know. He didn't know, and I didn't want to be the one to have to tell him.

I swallowed hard. "I got a B plus."

His expression relaxed into a smile. "Not bad for a procrastinator!"

"Um, yeah, I guess so." I tried to smile back, but my face wasn't cooperating. "How about you?"

"I got a B. Not my best work, but I'll take it. I'd better start earlier on the next one though. I'd hate to have to explain less than a B average to my mom."

"She's pretty strict, huh?"

"Let's just say it will not be a pretty winter break for me," he said.

His form seemed stronger now, brighter. It was almost as though, by pretending he was still alive, he was more likely to stick around and talk to me. But how was I ever going to find out about Hannah if we had to carry on this conversation as though he weren't a ghost? I decided to take a chance.

"Hey, I have a bone to pick with you."

His eyes widened. "Am I in trouble?"

"Yes, you are." I thrust a cold-stiffened hand into my bag and fished out my copy of Hamlet, which I flourished in his face. "You said you wrote your phone number in here, but I can't find it. Didn't you wonder why I never called?"

He started at the copy of Hamlet as though trying to remember where he'd seen it before. "I..."

"You said you wrote it on your favorite page, but I've searched it cover to cover, and all I've found is this." I clumsily thumbed to the message he'd left me and held it up so he could read it.

He just stared at it, dumbstruck.

"Who's Hannah?" I asked.

His outline began to shiver again, threatening to blink out of existence. I tried again.

"Who's Hannah, Evan? Who is she and how can she help you?"

He started fading dimmer and dimmer in the darkness as he shook his head frantically. "I... I can't... I don't want to..."

"Please Evan! How can I help you if I don't know who she is?"

His expression darkened. "Stop it! Just stop it, Jess!"

"Evan, please? Don't you know what's happened to you?" Tears brimmed up in my eyes and clouded my waning view of him. I brushed them fiercely away.

He shimmered out of view and reappeared so close to me that I gasped. The cold emanating from him washed over me like waves.

"Why are you crying? Why are you sad?" he asked, and reached out a hand toward my face.

"Because you're here," I said. "Because you're here and you shouldn't be. Because you're dead."

His hand hovered just an inch from my face. For the briefest of moments he stared into my eyes, his expression twisted with unimaginable pain. Then he was gone.

I sat in the absence of him for what felt like a very long time, letting the hot tears cool and freeze as they rolled down my face. Finally, I willed myself to stand and trudge stiffly back to Donnelly Hall and to Tia so that I could tell her the terrible truth: Evan didn't understand what had happened to him. He didn't even know he was dead, or at least, he didn't want to face it. Evan might have answers, but he wasn't going to give them up easily. In fact, he might never talk to me again.

§

The cold snap continued over the next couple of weeks. We had reached a total dead end in our search for more information about the elusive Hannah; but with the end of the term staring us in the face I tried to concentrate on the crushing onslaught of exams and final papers.

"Course catalog is out!" Tia called as she entered the room on the last full day of classes. It was miraculous that she could have opened the door at all; as usual, she looked like some sort of transient forced to carry all of her worldly possessions with her wherever she went. One would think that someone so organized would realize that she didn't *need* to bring six classes worth of books around with her when only two of those classes met that day.

"Ti, our room is the size of a closet. Why do you shout every time you come in?" I asked, half-exasperated, half-amused.

"Oh, I know, I'm sorry," Tia shrugged, efficiently filing away her mountain of books and tossing the catalog onto my bed before plopping down onto her own. "Force of habit, I guess. I always had to shout up the stairs when I got home—my mom's office was on the third floor."

"Why do we need a course catalog?" I asked.

"To pick next semester's courses, obviously. Did you think they were going to let you walk onto campus after break and just pull some out of a hat? They have to plan these things, you know."

I pulled the catalog towards me and was shocked by how heavy it was. "Whoa! How many courses are in here? I mean, how many classes can one person possibly take?"

Tia laughed as she pulled out her own catalog. "At St. Matt's? About a thousand." She wasn't exaggerating. "And see, they've got a detailed description of each one, so you know what you're getting yourself into." She had already pulled out a highlighter and was busily highlighting different course titles, adding little pink sticky notes beside possible options.

"So, do you have any idea what you're going to take? How the hell are we supposed to pick?" I was already feeling daunted just looking at the choices; decision-making was not my strong suit. The little packet of course options they'd sent to incoming freshmen over the summer had been bad enough.

"Well, there are restrictions. I mean, you can't just take whatever you want. Lots of the courses have pre-recs and things like that. They'll have an 'O' listed next to them if they're open enrollment. That means anyone can take them without any prior required courses. And they list them in ascending order from there by department. The earlier they are on the list, the fewer pre-recs needed."

I didn't respond. I didn't think this narrowed things down much.

"Haven't you thought any more about a major yet?" Tia asked, somewhat sternly, I thought.

"Well, I haven't definitely decided on anything. I was thinking maybe Art History, but I'm trying to leave my options open."

"Well, then just get your common requirements out of the way; everyone has to take those. And check these out, too," she suggested, plunking herself down next to me and flipping forward a few pages. "There are a whole bunch of art courses."

We sat quietly contemplating our choices for a half an hour or so. I took Tia's lead and borrowed a highlighter to mark my options. Tia didn't have much trouble selecting her courses, having already declared her major and met with her advisor. Sometimes she was so productive that she gave me a complex. She tried to be helpful, even going so far as to suggest that I enroll in microbiology with her. "To fulfill your science requirement!" she trilled.

But one withering look from me obliterated that idea. Finally, after much grumbling and biting of my fingernails, I had decided: I would take Intro to Journalism, Art History II, Intro to 3D Drawing, Sociological Theory, and Poetry 101. Feeling satisfied, I was about to close the course catalog when something caught my eye.

"Hey!"

Tia jumped and almost choked on her Skittles. "What is it?"

"There's a course in parapsychology!" I shouted, my eyes hungrily scanning the page.

Tia scooted closer so that she could read over my shoulder. "You're kidding! You mean they actually teach that stuff in schools?"

"Apparently. Listen to this! 'Introduction to Parapsychology gives the student an overview of the field of parapsychology, including exploration and discussion of the phenomena of psychokinesis, extrasensory perception, and theories of *survival of consciousness after death!*' I don't believe it! There's someone right here on campus who can help me!" The weight in my stomach was lifting already, I could feel it.

"Who teaches it?" Tia asked, snatching the catalog so she could read it for herself. "Professor David Pierce. I wonder if... wait, Jess! It's a senior seminar class, look." Tia pointed to the course number, her face falling. I grabbed the catalog back and felt my happiness extinguish as quickly as it had flared.

"But maybe you could still go talk to him! Even if you can't take the class, at least you could tell him what's going on," Tia suggested, keeping her voice low even though there was no one else in the room.

"No way. I have no idea who this guy is! What am I supposed to do, walk into his office and say, 'Hi, I'm Jess. I see dead people?'

That's the last thing I need—another professor thinking I'm crazy. One is enough for this semester, don't you think?"

"But Jess, he *teaches* paranormal psychology! He obviously believes in that sort of thing, why else would he..."

But I was already shaking my head. "*No,* Tia. I'm not telling anyone about this, not unless I know I can trust them! I'm not going to parade this around like I'm some sort of freak show!"

Tia's face blushed pink. "I didn't say you were a—"

"—I know!" I said, instantly ashamed that I'd snapped at her. "I know you were just trying to help, but I'm already unsure whether I believe myself; I just need some information—something that might help me figure this out. I need to get into that class."

Tia nodded in understanding and slid off the bed and over to her desk, where she got ready to tackle her biology exam review. "Well," she said, as she flipped open the enormous textbook, "the only thing to do is go visit Professor Pierce and see if he'll sign you in. Worst he can say is no."

I agreed, but I wasn't about to accept no for an answer, not after everything that I'd seen. I was determined about that, at least.

§

Despite my conviction to get into the parapsychology class, and as much as I talked about it for the next two weeks, it still took me until the very last day of finals to get up the nerve to go see the professor.

David Pierce's office was tucked away in a remote corner of the fourth floor of Wiltshire Hall, the oldest and most imposing of the brick buildings on the sprawling campus. The rumor was that Dr. Pierce had requested to work out of Wiltshire because it was the most likely building on the campus to be haunted, though what process of deduction he had used to reach that conclusion was a complete mystery. It seemed unlikely that a professor hoping to be taken seriously as an academic and a scientist would demand an office based solely on this criterion; after all, the entire science department was housed in that building. But the student body swore up and down that this was how Dr. Pierce came to be holed up in that particular spot.

In fact, there were many stories about ghosts that supposedly resided in Wiltshire, frightening the wits out of wayward students and unsuspecting custodial staff. I had even heard a story on my campus tour earlier that spring, when the overly-perky student tour guide had recounted, in what she obviously thought to be a spooky voice, the tale of a Jesuit monk who haunted the bell tower and performed Gregorian chants on stormy nights. I supposed it was as likely as not that many of these stories had only surfaced because Professor Pierce's presence there suggested them, but nevertheless, recent events had given them a faint ring of truth—or at least the taint of possibility.

The determination that had carried me out of my dorm and across the length of the campus had faded considerably by the time I reached Wiltshire Hall, and had all but disappeared as I climbed the final flight of stairs. I had convinced myself the night before that it would be very simple. I would just go up there, knock on the door, and ask to be signed in to the class, citing my fervent interest in all things paranormal, and a deeply-held ambition to become a ghost hunter. If that line of bullshit failed, I would simply have to beg and plead. But as I drew nearer and nearer his door, I began to feel that my plan was a feeble one. I didn't know the first thing about parapsychology; I hadn't even believed in ghosts until a few weeks ago!

I reached the office door and stood staring mutely at the name "Prof. David E. Pierce, PhD" as though hoping that the letters themselves would give me permission and save me the trouble of having to confront their namesake. Beside the door was a corkboard on which a number of newspaper and magazine clippings were pinned. There was a photocopy of a review of Professor Pierce's latest book, "Science or Science Fiction? The Paradox of Parapsychology." Beside that was an article torn from a magazine, entitled "Parapsychology and Christian Philosophy." And below that, someone had added a local paper's profile of a woman who claimed to be a medium. I'd just started reading it in spite of myself when a sudden clearing of a throat from inside the room confirmed that the professor was indeed there. With a deep breath that I couldn't quite get to fill my lungs, I knocked on the door.

"Come on in," said a man's voice. He sounded irritated. Great, just what I needed: to catch him in a bad mood.

I pushed on the door, which opened into a veritable disaster of an office. Every inch of wall space from floor to ceiling was covered in bookshelves, save one very tall, very narrow window that overlooked the courtyard—or at least, it would have if you could have seen out of it; a large dusty plastic ficus plant obscured most of the view. Precariously placed piles of books, papers, and file folders were teetering on every available surface. The place smelled like a cross between a library archive room and an airport smoking lounge. In the corner, nearly hidden by the oversized desk and its abundance of papers, was a very old, very cozy-looking brown leather armchair in which sat the mysterious Professor Pierce.

"Can I help you?" he asked, looking up from the book he was reading.

My immediate impression of David Pierce was that he would look more at home in the back of a VW van with a joint hanging out of his mouth than he did in this office. His hair was long and black, pulled into a ponytail even longer than mine. His face was overgrown with a poorly trimmed beard and mustache. He wore a threadbare purple Henley, ripped blue jeans, and an ancient pair of brown Doc Martens. The only aspect of his appearance that could be considered a nod to academia was a pair of horn-rimmed glasses perched tentatively on his nose, as if unsure whether they really belonged there. His eyes were blue and very inquisitive, and they bore into mine like drills as he waited for my response. I was instantly intimidated in spite of myself.

"Um, hi, Dr. Pierce. My name is Jess Ballard. I'm a freshman." I didn't know why I included this last bit of information—maybe I thought my timid manner needed some sort of excusing.

"Ah, shit. Am I your advisor? Do we have an appointment to pick your classes or something?" Dr. Pierce started to get up from his chair.

"No, my advisor is Professor Holden, Art History," I answered.

"Oh." Dr. Pierce plopped back down in the seat, but did not pick up his book. "So, what do you want?"

His bluntness did nothing to help my courage. "I was hoping you could help me, actually. I saw that you teach a class in parapsychology, and—"

"—And you thought I'd be kind enough to sign you in even though you aren't a senior and you haven't taken any of the pre-recs," Dr. Pierce finished.

I stopped short. It sounded pretty ludicrous when he put it that way. "Uh... yeah, actually, that's pretty much it."

Professor Pierce made a sound that was halfway between a laugh and a snort. "Ballard, is it?"

I nodded.

"Ballard, do you know what page I'm on in that book right there?"

"I... what?"

"I asked if you know what page I'm on in that book I was reading when you came in."

I felt thoroughly confused. Was he testing my psychic abilities or something? "I have no idea."

"It's the same page I've been on since eight o'clock this morning. That was three hours ago."

"Okay."

"And would you like to know why I've been on the same page for three hours?" Professor Pierce asked conversationally, crossing one leg over the other.

"Sure."

"Because you are about the hundredth lower classman who has made the trip all the way up here to try to get into my class. A class that *specifically* states it's only for seniors, and which has been full since last spring anyway." He stopped as though to gauge the effect of these words on me.

"I... I'm sorry," I faltered, back-pedaling. "I didn't realize the class was so hard to get into."

"Well, it is. This happens every year. It's the most popular class in the whole goddamn college. Lucky me."

I could feel my hope slipping away. I tried again. "Professor, are you sure there's no way to get into the class? I mean, can't you make an exception? I'm... um, I'm really interested in parapsychology." It sounded lame before it even came out of my mouth, and I knew it.

"Do you know why so many kids want to take this class, Ballard? They think it's a joke. A fucking blow-off course, you get me? They think it's gonna be a barrel of laughs, sitting around telling stories about haunted graveyards or their dead grandmothers leaving them messages on bathroom mirrors."

I was starting to get flustered now, and not just because a professor was swearing at me like a sailor. This wasn't going well. "I don't think it's a blow-off—"

"—Well, quite frankly, Ballard, you don't sound any different than any of the other kids who've come up here looking to get signed in. Why should I make an exception for you and not any of them?" He seemed to think it was a rhetorical question and, by extension, that the conversation was over. He returned to his book with a smug expression.

I could feel my temper boiling just below the surface. After months of confusion and terror, after my mother and Evan, the dreams and the voices, I was at my wits' end. But in spite of all of that, I just couldn't bring myself to tell this man the real reason I was there. If he wasn't going to believe that I wanted to be in the class for the usual reasons, he'd probably laugh right in my face at the real reason. I tried to keep my voice even so that I wouldn't betray how close I was to completely losing it. But I couldn't keep the bitterness out of my voice. "You know what, forget it. I'll find someone else to help me. Enjoy your book." I turned to leave.

My hand was on the doorknob when Professor Pierce suddenly spoke. "What do you mean, 'someone to help you?'"

I whirled around, all pretense gone. "What do you care? I'm just another presumptuous freshman, right?"

"Aren't you?" he asked, with the first flicker of real interest.

"No! I don't give a shit about an 'easy A' or whatever lame reason people usually take your class. If you knew the first thing about me, you'd know I don't need a pity grade to boost my GPA."

"So, then why do you want to be there? And don't feed me that line about being interested in parapsychology." Dr. Pierce had gotten up from his chair. He was eyeing me shrewdly, and seemed completely unfazed by my profanity.

"Of course I don't want to be a goddamn parapsychologist! I thought all this paranormal stuff was bullshit until..." I didn't know how to continue without telling him more than I wanted to. Luckily, there seemed to be no need.

"Until something happened to change your mind," he finished for me, giving me an appraising look. It was like being X-rayed.

"Yes."

Several seconds passed. Professor Pierce wasn't signing me in, but he also wasn't writing me off. I cooled off enough in the intervening moments to recognize that this was an opportunity. He was intrigued, I could tell. If I played this carefully, if I didn't blow it, this might just work out. I decided to press my luck and try again, but I didn't want to give him too much information; I wasn't sure that I wanted to trust him with that yet. When I spoke again, I kept my voice calm. "Dr. Pierce, I'm sure that there are lots of kids who take your class for the wrong reasons, and that sucks. But would you be willing to make an exception for someone who needed to take it for the right reasons? I think your class might be the only way for me to understand what happened to me." I hesitated and then added, "What's still happening to me."

She shoots, she scores. He was examining me now like I was some interesting new specimen. Perhaps it was the guarded manner in which I spoke, but he didn't press me for any more details; for this I was both surprised and grateful. There seemed to be an internal struggle going on between his desire to keep presumptuous freshmen from his ranks and his eagerness to gain what could potentially be a new case study.

After a moment that felt like an hour, he spoke. "I could let you audit the class. You wouldn't get any credit for it." He kept his eyes trained on my face.

Relief flooded me. "Thank you, Professor. I don't need the credit, just the information."

It was as though I passed some sort of test. Dr. Pierce continued to look at me inquisitively as he held his hand out for my registration form. I waited quietly while he fished a pen from behind his ear and scrawled his initials on the crumpled paper. Expressing my thanks again, I left the room at a jog, before he had a chance to ask me anything else.

Well, it hadn't gone exactly as I'd envisioned, but all things considered, I was relieved. I'd managed to get signed into the class without giving Professor Pierce too much of my story. I was happy that he'd been ready to accept my claim of having experienced something out of the ordinary. I suppose I shouldn't have been too surprised, once I thought about it; after all, his entire career was based upon his ability to believe that the impossible might be possible. Still, I felt like I was living on borrowed time. I didn't have to explain myself that day, but that wouldn't last very long. Sometime soon, I would have to tell David Pierce exactly why I was taking his class. I just hoped he turned out to be less of a jerk than he appeared.

9

UNEXPECTED GIFT

I HAVE ALWAYS HATED WAITING ROOMS. My whole life I've had this mortal dread of having to sit in a waiting room. I actually have a theory about this. Waiting rooms are basically torture chambers designed to heighten anticipation and breed fear in those of us unlucky enough to have to wait in them. Whatever lurks on the other side of the door is never as bad as what the waiting room has prepared you for; I knew this, yet I would always break into a cold sweat as I sat there, *waiting*.

Every waiting room is only a slight variation on a universal waiting room design concocted, I believe, by scientists well versed in color combinations that trigger irrational emotional responses in unsuspecting victims. Walls, if not a sterile white, are painted in some pastel color, perhaps a peach or pale blue. Hung upon these innocuously hued surfaces are framed pictures, most of them neutral in content—a watercolor bouquet of flowers, a wheelbarrow of gardening supplies. Scattered among these are pictures meant to calm us with their cute or humorous depictions: Children playing doctor grin preciously down at you; kittens clinging precariously to tree branches above silly captions like "Just hanging around!"

To escape the hypnotic stare of these photos, you can amuse yourself by counting the ficus trees sprouting from baskets, or by flipping through magazines that no one but waiting room personnel subscribe to. When these inane distractions fail to calm you down, you can look around at the other people sitting scattered around the room, but the barely contained panic on their faces will only amplify your own. When they took me to the hospital the night my mom died, I refused to go sit in that damn waiting room; I just sat outside on the sidewalk with a police officer. Hell must have a waiting room... or be one.

And so I found myself outside Dr. Thomas Hildebrand's office, which had a particularly horrible waiting room, though I had a feeling that my actual appointment was, for once, going to be worse than the waiting room itself. Karen had offered to stay with me, but I'd sent her out for coffee. There was no reason to subject both of us to the waiting room torture, and I really didn't want the added pressure of knowing she was there. I think I'd freaked her out enough, quite frankly. And I also hadn't quite forgiven her for making me go through with this in the first place.

Karen had pasted on a carefully lighthearted demeanor from the moment she'd picked me up for winter break, but I wasn't fooled. She hadn't yet recovered from Dean Finndale's phone call or my feeble explanations, and I could tell that there was something she wasn't telling me. Her eyes kept darting to me anxiously the whole way home and all throughout dinner. I finally faked a headache and went up to bed at eight o'clock just to get away from her. My escape was only momentary. She dropped the real bomb when she came up to say good night.

"You can't be serious."

"It's a condition of your return to St. Matthew's for second semester," Karen said.

"Can they even do that? How do they have a say in my personal life like this? It's none of their business."

"It becomes their business when they start investing scholarship money in you. You are an investment, Jess, and they want to see a return."

"And if I refuse to go?"

"It's this or you lose your scholarship."

"But a *shrink?*"

"There are worse things in the world, Jess. It might even be good for you, the whole Evan thing aside. You haven't even really dealt with your mom yet."

"I'm dealing."

"Well, now you can talk to a professional, someone who has experience with these things. You may be surprised at how much it helps."

"I'm pretty sure you couldn't be more wrong about that," I grumbled.

Apparently she decided it wasn't worth trying to convince me, because she left me alone after that—or so I thought. When I awoke sobbing from my familiar nightmares in the middle of the night, her slippered feet were there, casting a long shadow under the door in the light from the hallway. I'm sure she, like everyone else, thought I was completely nuts, or that I was going through some sort of post-traumatic stress thing. The difference was that she was the closest thing I had to a parent now, and she probably felt responsible for keeping me from falling apart.

But no amount of Karen's well-intentioned hovering could help me, because she only understood a tiny fraction of the chaos inside of me. Of course she knew that I missed my mom. However well I tried to hide it, the truth was that I felt like I'd lost the better part of my identity. As we'd bounced around the country, ruthlessly ripping up whatever shallow roots we'd managed to grow, my mother had been the only constant in my life. It was always just us—no father, no brothers or sisters, just us. My mother may have been a veritable disaster, but she was my disaster, and I felt utterly lost now that I didn't have her to take care of. Yet even as I struggled with the terrible weight of her absence, the finality of it all, I was suddenly being forced to question how final it really was. Evan was dead, but he had appeared to me, even protected me. Was it so outlandish, so impossible, to think my mother might do the same? How could I let go of her if a tiny part of me was clinging to the hope that the next ghostly face to appear would be hers?

§

The secretary's saccharine voice broke through my musings. "Jessica? Dr. Hildebrand will see you now." I stood up and followed her through the door and down a narrow hallway.

"Would you like to hang up your jacket?" she asked, gesturing to a coat rack in the corner.

"No, thanks," I said. It was probably childish, but having my coat with me made me feel like I was just passing through.

The secretary knocked quietly and then, without waiting for an answer, opened the glossy, paneled door.

Dr. Hildebrand's office was full of pretentious mahogany furniture. The doctor was sitting at his desk, his various diplomas and certificates floating above his head like halos. He was overweight and balding with a bulbous nose and a weak chin that he compensated for by jutting his jaw out thoughtfully.

"Jessica. So very nice to meet you." Dr. Hildebrand's voice was unctuous and fluid, like one of those narrators on self-help tapes. He probably was one, actually.

"You too," I lied.

"Won't you sit down?" He gestured to a chair that I was very glad wasn't a sofa. I sat.

"So Jessica, why don't we talk about why you're coming to see me and what we hope to get out of these sessions."

Unable to identify a question that required an answer in that, I just nodded.

"I spoke with your dean. She is very concerned about you and would feel better if you had someone to help you sort things out. I think you might feel better, too." He smiled smarmily. "I'd like to be that person. Is that alright with you?"

"Whatever." Like I had a choice.

"Splendid," he said as he pulled a leather-bound notebook out of his desk drawer and prepared himself for whatever it was he did. I could think of nothing that was less appropriately suited to my definition of "splendid."

"So, Jessica, I want to start out by getting to know you a bit better. Why don't you tell me about your childhood?"

"What do you want to know?"

"Oh, just anything at all that you would like to tell me about your life growing up."

I assumed that "nothing at all" was not an option, so I stuck to the basics. He started writing feverishly before I'd even opened my mouth.

"Well, I lived with my mom growing up. I've never met my dad. We moved around a lot; I was born in New York City. Then we moved all the way across the country to live in San Francisco, but I was too young to remember it. From there we moved to L.A., then to Seattle, then to Chicago, Milwaukee, Houston, Albuquerque, Richmond, Charleston, Cleveland, D.C., and finally back to New York again. My mom died this past summer, so I went to live with my aunt while I'm attending St. Matt's. I'm moving out soon, though." I felt compelled to tack on this last detail. I really didn't care what this guy thought of me, but I didn't want to give the impression of being a charity case.

"And why did you move around so much, Jessica?" Dr. Hildebrand asked, tapping his gold pen loudly against his blotter.

"My mom liked a change of scenery every once in a while."

"Mm-hmm." Dr. Hildebrand smiled, jotting a note on his paper.

I could feel the blood rushing to my face, splashing my carefully-concealed anger right across my features. "And what was it your mother was so eager to run from?"

"I never said she was running. She wanted to see the country, to have as many experiences as possible."

"Certainly, certainly," Dr. Hildebrand said, clearly humoring me. I was just a little disturbed though; I did always have a feeling that my mother was trying to keep something at bay, an indefinable something that she never wanted to catch up with her. Our moves were always sudden, spurred by no change of circumstances I could identify other than my mother's apparent restlessness. "Life's getting stale here, kiddo! Time to open a new door," she'd always tell me. I usually went without complaint because complaining had never turned the Green Monster around, but it was always odd to see the gleam of relief in her eyes as we drove on to our next destination, leaving whatever mess she'd made far behind us.

"How did the frequent moves affect you?" Dr. Hildebrand continued, with the maddening air that he already knew the answer and merely needed my confirmation.

"It wasn't so bad. I had to adjust to new schools, new kids, things like that," I said, downplaying it with a shrug. It had generally been miserable, but I'd always been a bit of a loner anyway. I'd never stayed in touch with any of my friends.

"And did you find that difficult... adjusting?"

"It was fine." I wasn't about to hand him psychological ammo.

Recognizing that he was not getting over this particular wall, he moved on. "Let's talk about your mother's death," he continued, almost cheerfully.

I shot him a look that should have fried him where he sat. Sadly, he remained uncharred. "I'd rather not, thank you."

"Now, now," he began in what I can only assume he meant to be a fatherly tone. "We can hardly get to the root of your behavioral issues if we can't even discuss the source."

I smoldered. So I had behavioral issues, did I?

"Why don't you tell me *why* you don't want to discuss it," he prodded again.

I barely repressed a roll of my eyes but couldn't keep the biting sarcasm out of my voice. "Well, Dr. Hildebrand, I don't actually know you at all, and you don't know me, so I'm sure you can understand why I don't exactly want to have a heart-to-heart with you about something so personal."

"But I'm trying to get to know you, Jessica. That's the whole idea of you being here," he explained in a tone dripping with condescension.

I narrowly avoided shouting expletives at him and channeled my excess frustration into my rapidly bouncing leg.

"Now, Jessica, I can't really get a handle on your current mental state if you refuse to discuss your mother's suicide, which I'm sure—"

"—My mother did not commit suicide!" I growled. My fingers clutched at the leather armrests of my chair, digging in against the emotion.

"Oh, I see." Dr. Hildebrand sighed as though he had just come to a brilliant conclusion. He walked out around his desk and perched on the end of the chair right across from me, leaning his elbows forward on his knees, surveying me thoughtfully.

"What do you *see*?" I hissed between my clenched teeth.

"Jessica, Jessica. I understand, my dear. Of course I understand."

I was unsure of many things at the moment, but I was pretty damn sure that he did *not* understand.

"I can see perfectly well why you would want to believe that your mother's death wasn't a suicide," he said.

"And I can see perfectly well why you would like it to be one," I shot back.

Dr. Hildebrand's oily eyebrows arched up in exaggerated confusion. "I'm afraid I don't follow. I certainly wouldn't want such a—"

"—Of course you do!" I flung the words at him like verbal grenades. "That would fit me very nicely into one of your predetermined little pigeonholes, wouldn't it? The perfect explanation for the set of behavioral issues you 'see' me 'exhibiting.'"

"I was merely pointing out that the circumstances of her death were—"

"—Undetermined. That's what the coroner ruled her death: Undetermined. It was an accident. My mother wouldn't..." My voice trailed off as I bit back the vulnerability that was fighting its way to the surface. This man would *not* see me cry.

"Very well, then. I can see we aren't going to make any headway with that particular issue. Perhaps next week."

"Don't hold your breath."

"Why don't we focus instead on the event that brought us together."

This was it—the part of this conversation I had been dreading the most, the part I couldn't dodge and couldn't justify in any sane way. If I told the truth, I was certifiable. But what lie could explain it away?

"Why don't you tell me about what happened between you and your English professor," he said, pen poised at the ready.

I was done with the polite pretenses. "What about it?"

"Do you have an explanation for your actions that you'd like to share with me?"

For the tiniest fraction of a second I considered telling him the truth. I imagined the look of wariness and fear that would flit across his chubby face; it was tempting, just to see his reaction. But my defenses quickly shot the impulse down.

He took my silence as reluctance instead of indecision and tried to prompt me further. "Well, did the two of you get into some kind of argument?"

"No."

"Did she perhaps give you a poor grade on a paper? Embarrass you in front of the class?"

"No," I repeated blankly. Why was he asking me these questions?

"Can you think of any reason why you chose to target this particular teacher? Why her and not another of your professors?"

Oh. "You think it was... some sort of practical joke," I realized out loud.

"Not a very funny one, to be certain, as I'm sure you can see in retrospect," Dr. Hildebrand said.

I stood up. "Okay, we're done here."

"No, my dear, your session lasts an hour. We still have half of your—"

"—No, I mean I have nothing more to say to you." I pulled on my coat.

"Now, Jessica, I disagree. Let's not be brash here. There is still much to be discussed, but if you won't be open about things, then..."

Something in my expression made him stop. Whatever he saw there told him that he would make no more headway with me today.

Damn right he wouldn't.

I stalked straight through the waiting room and out to the car in silence. Karen put the key in the ignition, but didn't turn it.

"I'm sorry you had to do that today."

Surprise registered dimly in my brain. That wasn't really what I'd been expecting her to say.

"Those shrinks think they know everything, but they don't. They don't know a thing about you, just remember that. You aren't some case study they can just pick apart." Her voice was unexpectedly bitter.

I didn't know what to say. It was like she'd stolen my line.

"So... does that mean I don't have to go back?"

Karen hesitated. For a moment, from the look on her face, I thought that she might actually let me off the hook. "I think it's important for you to go. Your school arranged it, and I know that your dean is rather insistent on the point. I think, in the interest of staying on the administration's good side, that you should continue to see Dr. Hildebrand. It's not worth risking your education."

§

My winter break taught me the truth behind the clichéd observation that the holidays are a difficult time of year. My mom had always made a huge deal of the Christmas season, even though she seemed to have little to no awareness of the fact that it was actually a religious holiday. We drove hours out of whatever city we were living in at the time to get a real Christmas tree, preferably one we could chop down ourselves. There was even one time she almost got herself arrested when she stopped on the side of the road to cut down a tree that turned out to be on someone's private property. She'd plied the man with Christmas cookies and a sob story to get us out of that mess. Karen laughed herself into tears when I told her about it.

"So does that mean you don't want to get a tree? I have a fake one in the basement we usually use," she said.

"Ugh! A fake tree? Are you trying to kill me, Karen? What is sadder than a man-made tree?"

She looked a little sheepish. "I guess you're right. I just hate cleaning up the needles."

"I'll clean up the needles. You won't even be able to tell we dragged foliage through the house, cross my heart," I promised. "My mom would probably come back to haunt us if I let you have a fake tree while I was living here."

I meant it as a joke, but neither of us laughed; Karen looked almost nauseous and I sat silently struggling again with that nagging possibility I could just never shake. Evan had convinced me ghosts existed; that much now I knew for sure. Did that mean I might roll over some restless night and find my mom sitting by my bed, humming one of her made-up tunes that she used to lull me to sleep? I couldn't decide if the thought comforted or terrified me. Maybe a little of both.

Despite the loss that Karen and I were feeling so acutely, we managed to have a very nice Christmas. We double-teamed Noah and convinced him that he would like nothing better than to drive out to a nearby tree farm and trudge around behind us through the snow while we selected the perfect balsam, and then chop it down for us. I was a little disappointed when I came home from some shopping the next day to find that it had been professionally decorated by Karen's usual interior designer. There was no denying that it was very beautiful, though I thought it lacked a certain charm due to the absence of homemade paper ornaments and stale popcorn threaded on a string.

I had to admit it was nice sleeping in on Christmas morning. My mother, a child at heart, had dragged me out of bed every year at the crack of dawn, too eager to wait to give me my presents, no matter how hungover she was or how scant the money was for gifts. Karen seemed pretty excited about giving gifts too, but apparently not excited enough to prevent me from sleeping until nearly ten o'clock.

After a big breakfast of cheese omelets and bacon (Karen was intensely apologetic, having attempted to cook the bacon on her own and turned it into what Noah euphemistically referred to as "Cajun style"), we sat down to open gifts. Karen glowed as I unwrapped a beautiful new leather portfolio for my artwork and several expensive-looking sweaters. I thanked her profusely and pulled one of the sweaters on over my pajamas to reassure her that I really did like it.

Karen complained that I'd surely spent too much on the boots I bought her, feeling guilty, no doubt, that she'd been eyeing a similar pair while we'd been out on Newbury Street. I told her that Tia, who never paid full price for anything, had helped me find them on eBay, so I hadn't paid the laughable sticker price from the boutique. Noah seemed genuinely pleased when he unwrapped a book I'd bought him about the history of Fenway Park. He wasn't treating me like a leper, so I could only assume that Karen hadn't told him about my disturbing new talent.

When the rustle of wrapping paper finally died away, we all settled into the trademark quiet contentment of Christmas afternoon. Noah engrossed himself in the history of his favorite sports team while Karen and I watched *Miracle on 34th Street* and tidied up under the tree. The rituals were at once familiar and strange, like a jarring note misplayed in a favorite song.

As I crammed the last of the crumpled gold paper into the trash bag, a small, unobtrusive object caught my eye, tucked partially under the tree skirt. I knelt down and slid it out. At first I thought it was an article of clothing, but as I picked it up, I felt a solid, flat shape beneath the material. A gift, then, wrapped in a scrap of faded blue fabric and tied with a frayed white ribbon.

I turned to ask Karen about it, but my voice only made it halfway to my lips. A small piece of paper tucked under the ribbon answered my unasked question. In a tiny, elegant hand was the following message:

Jessica,

This was your mother's, once upon a time. Now it rightfully belongs to you. I'm sure you will find it interesting.

There was no signature. My heart beating inexplicably fast, I tugged gently at the ribbon and followed its featherlike fall to my knees. I unfolded the fabric, an ancient watered silk, and revealed the object inside. A small, leather-bound book rested in my palm. It was by far the oldest book I'd ever handled. Its binding was frayed and tattered; its leather surface was a fawn color, looking more like raw animal hide than processed leather. The texture had been worn to an incredible softness. It took less than a moment to take all of this in before my attention was entirely occupied with the image burned into the leather. It was a line drawing, almost primitive in style. It depicted a woman's hand in profile, cupped with the palm up, as though waiting for someone to drop something into it. Above it was another hand, identical to the first, but palm down and facing the other direction. In the space protected between these two hands was a symbol composed of three spirals, reminiscent of a pinwheel. I stared at it as one hypnotized. I could barely tear my eyes away from it to open the book. When I finally did, my disappointment was instantaneous. The rough-cut pages were all blank.

Crash!

Startled, I turned to the doorway. Karen was kneeling there, gathering up dripping shards of porcelain with visibly trembling hands. She looked up and tried to smile, but only managed a grimace.

"Sorry," she murmured. "Slipped out of my hand." A puddle of eggnog was spreading across the floor.

I got up to help her, but Noah waved me back down. "I'll get some paper towels," he said, hopping up from the couch.

Karen just nodded and kept her eyes carefully on the remnants of her mug.

"Karen? Is this from you?" I asked, holding up the book.

When she raised her gaze to me, her casual tone didn't match her wary eyes. "Oh, yes, I'd forgotten all about that."

"Was this really my mother's? I don't ever remember seeing it before."

"Yes, it was. She left it here, actually. I didn't even remember I had it. I found it in the basement last week when I was digging out the Christmas wreaths."

"It's really... what is it?"

"Just an old blank book. I don't know where she got it—you know your mother and books. She probably found it in an antique shop or something. Anyway, I thought you might like to have it. Be careful with it, of course. Something that old should be handled with care."

She walked into the kitchen—*fled* may have been a better word for it. I realized as I watched her whip around the corner that I didn't believe a word she had just said to me, except maybe for the part about handling the book carefully.

I looked back down at the book. Why would she take the trouble to wrap it so distinctly from the other gifts, setting it apart as something special, but then claim to forget about it? Why the note, if it was just some old thing she found lying around? It didn't make sense that she'd forgotten to give me something of my mother's, especially when, as the note said, she thought it "rightfully belonged to me."

Then of course there was the mystery of the book itself. She'd obviously seen it before, because she knew that the pages were blank, although I supposed she could have just glimpsed at them when she came in the room. Why would my mother have such a thing and why, in all the time she had it, did she never write in it?

All through the rest of the evening, I kept the odd little book cradled in my hands, tracing and retracing its cover. Finally I trudged up to bed around ten-thirty, after nodding off during the middle of *It's a Wonderful Life*, which I was pretty sure I would never get to see in its entirety. Balancing my mother's book on top of my stack of other gifts, I was almost to my room when I heard Karen's voice, hushed but urgent, from her office.

"...had no right to send it to Jessica without talking to me first."

Silence. She was obviously on the phone.

"Oh." Her harsh tone was suddenly confused. "Well, if you didn't send it to her, then I'd like to know who did!"

Silence. Karen was tapping something sharply against her desk.

"I understand that, Finvarra, and that may very well be the case in the end, but it wasn't my decision. There wasn't anything I could do to persuade Elizabeth against it, as I explained to the Council."

The unusual name caught my attention. Who in the world was Karen talking to?

"We'll just have to agree to disagree on that and see what happens. But I will not actively go against my sister's wishes. You know as well as I do why I can't do what you ask."

A longer silence. I could hear Noah puttering in the kitchen below me.

"I understand, Finvarra. Oh, believe me, I intend to. And please speak to the others and find out who has done this. Whatever the disagreement on this situation, you and I both know this was not how it should've been handled." Another pause. "Very well. I'm sorry to have bothered you. Good night, then."

I didn't stay put long enough to hear her hang up the phone. I was already safely shut away in my room when I heard her slide her door carefully open and close it again.

IO

DROWNING

MY MOTHER'S BOOK WASN'T MENTIONED AGAIN by Karen for the remaining two weeks of break. She did, however, seem unusually quiet and a little jumpy. And of course, she said not a word about her mysterious late night phone call to this Finvarra person. I had stowed the book carefully in my sock drawer, taking it out only when I was alone to examine it.

Further inspection revealed little else. I thought about using it as a diary; the blankness of the pages seemed to suggest it. But when I sat down to write, a sudden, unexplainable fear gripped me. My fingers started to shake, and I couldn't bring myself to put pen to paper. Only when I had put the pen away and closed the book again did my breathing ease and my nerves calm themselves. After that, I wrapped the book in my favorite St. Matt's sweatshirt and tucked it gently into the front pocket of my duffel bag, ready to return with me to school.

I tried not to waste the free time at my disposal. I sketched a lot, and I realized how much I had missed it while I was so busy and distracted at school. I also exhausted every avenue I could think of to locate the elusive Hannah. Trying to take a page from Tia's book, I took to haunting the Boston Public Library, telling Karen I was trying to get ahead on next semester's reading material. I was enough of a bookworm to pull it off, thank goodness. I managed to locate two more potential Hannahs. One lived on the street where Evan grew up, and the other attended the sister school that sometimes held social functions with Evan's all-boys high school. I found them both on Facebook and stalked their photographs; there were none that included Evan. Emails to both girls yielded nothing; the neighbor had only known him casually and the second had never even met him. Frustration mounting, I took to locating every mention I could find of Evan, on the internet, local papers, everywhere, which I pasted together into a morbid scrapbook. I even found a memorial Facebook page set up in his honor, which I joined. On the wall I simply posted: "I'm trying. I promise."

I also suffered through three more fruitless sessions with Dr. Hildebrand, during which he talked a lot and I answered his questions in one-word sentences... and threw him filthy glares. Karen drove me back and forth to them in stony, silent solidarity.

I took the train back to St. Matt's on the fifteenth of January, two days before classes started up and the first day that campus opened for the new semester. Karen seemed upset that I was leaving early, but if she wasn't going to be honest with me, I could see no reason to stay.

The dorm was quiet when I arrived Saturday morning, but by that night it had repopulated, the gathering snow storm whirling students through the doors on gusts of blustery wind. I knew that Sam would be there early too, since R.A.s had to oversee student arrival, so I swung by to visit him. He had one of the worst sunburns I'd ever seen.

"Nice tan! What beach did you lay on all break?" I asked.

"I wish. My family went skiing. This is windburn," Sam said. "And it hurts like a bitch, I might add."

"That sucks. Still, at least you did something interesting, which is more than I can say for my break."

"That bad, huh?"

"Mind-numbing."

"Didn't you even get to..." Sam glanced past me out into the hall and shouted, "Really, O'Reilly? In a paper bag with the name of the liquor store on it?" He jumped up and leaned out the door. "I'm walking down to your room in thirty seconds, and I better find that bag full of junk food or something else that won't get you put on housing probation!" He turned back to me, incredulous. "Seriously, it's like they're getting dumber every year. I should go take care of that."

I laughed. "No problem. I'll catch you later."

Sam stopped me in the doorway. "Hey, when Tia gets back, have her stop by. You know, if she wants to."

"Sorry, lover boy, she's not back yet, but I'm sure she'll come running as soon as she gets here." I patted his cheek a little harder than necessary.

"You two are so cute. I could just eat you up."

Sam blushed even redder. "Yeah, yeah, alright," he

grumbled, and took off down the hall after O'Reilly and his poorly disguised contraband.

After unpacking my stuff I headed to the student center, where I found a nice surprise in my campus mailbox. The final paper I'd written for Professor Marshall's class was tucked into a big manila envelope along with a letter. The paper had earned me an A, I noted with a mixture of relief and pride. The letter was a relief too, containing an apology from Professor Marshall, who had read my email and was very sorry about her "overreaction" to my "honest mistake." The whole reconciliation was something of a lie, of course, but I felt better anyway. I emailed her when I got back to the room, thanking her for her note and accepting her invitation to have coffee and a chat when classes resumed.

Tia called to let me know that she would not be back until Sunday afternoon. "Mami" couldn't bear sending her little girl back to "that place" without ensuring that she had one last day of home-cooked sustenance. Leave it to a mom to mistrust institutional food. Tia actually ate the healthy stuff, for the most part. In fact, with the exception of the occasional bag of Skittles, Tia ate healthier than any normal college kid should.

I fully intended to use my alone time that night to do a last spot of non assigned reading, but by ten o'clock, I was whacking myself in the face with my book as I dozed off. Rather than risk permanent facial damage, I lay the book aside, clicked off my reading lamp, and drifted to sleep quickly.

I couldn't be sure what the sound was that woke me, but suddenly I was awake. It hadn't been another dream, as far as I could remember. I rolled over and looked at my alarm clock, glowing like a neon sign in the darkness. 2:37 AM. I heard loud music thumping next door, punctuated by raucous laughter. I briefly considered chucking one of my shoes at the wall, but I thought this may not be an obvious enough hint for them to quiet down, so I rolled over instead and pulled my pillow over my head.

The pillow dulled the sound enough that I should have been able to drift back off but I found that I couldn't. It wasn't the music that had wakened me at all. My feet were cold; they were bundled in fuzzy socks and my comforter, but they were as cold as if I'd stuck them out the window into the January air.

And there was another sound, indistinguishable at first from the racket bleeding through my wall. It was a steady dripping sound, as though I had left a faucet only partially shut off in the bathroom. I tried to ignore it, but once my ears had picked up on it, it was all I could hear—like the ticking of a clock in an otherwise silent room. I'd just made up my mind to crawl out of my bed and take care of it when I remembered that I didn't have a bathroom. No bathroom and therefore, no faucet.

My heart was suddenly beating rapidly. Somehow I knew there was something I didn't want to see on the other side of my pillow. I couldn't say how I knew it, but I was certain that if I pulled that pillow away, I would not be alone. For a moment I was completely unable to move; my muscles had actually forgotten how to respond to my brain, which was screaming at me to leap out of the bed and out of the room as fast as I possibly could. Instead, I did the one thing I had absolutely no intention of doing; I flung the pillow off my face and looked for the source of the sound.

What I saw was as mystifying as it was horrifying, and it was all I could do to stop from screaming aloud. At the foot of my bed, hovering just above my achingly cold feet, was a figure. In the darkness, I could not immediately make out the details, but as my terrified eyes quickly adjusted, each newly visible aspect multiplied my fright. The figure was that of a small boy, no more than seven or eight years old. He was dressed in a pair of jeans, a red jacket, and dirty white sneakers. Unwillingly, my eyes were drawn to his face. Black hair was billowing hypnotically around his eerie, green-tinged complexion. His eyes were so dark they looked almost black, and his expression was mirroring my own terror.

As he raised a tiny, pale hand out towards me, I noticed for the first time that there was a faint glow surrounding the boy. It didn't seem as if the light was emanating from him, but I could see no other source. The light was unsteady somehow, wavering across the fearful little face so that it rippled in and out of focus. The quality of the light was familiar, but it wasn't until the boy's mouth opened and emitted a stream of bubbles that I realized why. The boy was standing at the foot of my bed and yet he was very clearly submerged in water.

Before I could control it, a scream ripped from my throat, followed by another, and then another. I couldn't stop, even as the ghostly form before me shook his head in protest. I screamed and screamed until I heard commotion in the hallway and a pounding on my door. Finally the door flew open and my room was flooded with light.

"Jess! What the hell? Are you okay?" I recognized Sam's lithe form tearing across the room toward me, but I still couldn't silence my own voice. My eyes remained trained on the spot where, moments before, the drowning boy had reached out to me and where now there was nothing but empty space.

"Jess! JESSICA!" Sam was by my side then, grabbing me by the shoulders and shaking me harshly. He grasped my face and wrenched my head around until I was forced to look at him. The sight of his living, familiar features turned my screams immediately to sobs. I buried my face in his neck and his arms closed around my heaving shoulders.

"It's fine, everything's fine," Sam called to the small crowd of students crammed into my doorway. "She had a nightmare or something; go back to your rooms."

From the reactions it was clear that this was a rather anticlimactic conclusion to the uproar I had caused.

"A nightmare? Are you kidding me?"

"Did you hear her?"

"The whole campus heard her!"

"I thought we were going to find a serial killer in here."

"Hey! Did you hear me? Clear out and shut up, before I write you all up for the party you're throwing in there!" Sam shouted.

The muttering turned momentarily mutinous and then died out as the crowd dispersed.

"It's okay, Jess. Take a deep breath now, and try to calm down." Sam said as I struggled to master myself. "Where's Tia?"

"N-not back y-yet," I managed to stammer.

"Can you tell me what happened?"

I picked my head up from his saturated T-shirt. His eyes were burning with concern.

"I... I think I had a nightmare," I gasped.

"You *think* you had a nightmare? You're not sure?"

"I... well, it m-must have been, I guess. But it just seemed s-so real." The vision of the boy danced before my eyes and I fought to dislodge it.

"What was it about? Do you want to tell me?"

I was too rattled to think up anything but the truth, so I told Sam exactly what I'd seen, making a mental note to draw it all out later when my hands stopped shaking. In an effort to salvage a scrap of my dignity, I made it sound as though I hadn't known that I was wide awake.

Sam let out a low whistle when I'd finished. "Well, damn, I would have freaked too. What, did you watch another horror movie last night or something?"

"No."

"Well, good. I was afraid you were going soft on me."

I laughed weakly. "Sorry if I scared the crap out of you."

"Yeah, I'm not gonna lie, I think I was about as scared as you were for a minute there. But I'm glad you're okay. And you definitely subdued that party next door. I was going to have to bust them up soon, and I really wasn't looking forward to that. So thanks!"

"Um, you're welcome?"

Sam waited for me to stop crying, and after about the fiftieth time I told him he could go, he went. I didn't sleep the rest of the night, and instead turned all the lights and the TV on, made myself a mug of tea and some ramen noodles in the microwave, and then sat down with my sketchbook. I had no desire to relive the visitation that had just awoken me, but I had to be sure to record what I had seen before time distorted it. I knew that this was another ghost, as Evan had been, though who he was or why he had visited me I had no idea. Was he a ghost who was always on the campus? Had he died on the property as Evan had? And, most crucially of all, why, why on earth were ghosts seeking me out? Were ghosts going to start appearing to me everywhere, scaring the living daylights out of me or following me around like lost puppy dogs? Was this boy really only the second I'd seen, or had there been others that I hadn't even recognized as ghosts? I had no idea if I would ever be able to find out who the boy was. I had no information to go on other than what I'd seen.

Sighing, I tucked the sketch away and tried to distract myself with a stream of syndicated 90s TV sitcoms. My parapsychology class with David Pierce would begin in less than forty-eight hours. Now if only I could keep myself awake until then.

11

ENERGY

T HE MYSTERY OF THE BOY AT THE END OF MY BED pretty much solved itself. No super sleuth mission was required, as with the Evan situation. The next morning in the dining hall during my break I snagged a newspaper to scan while I ate my cereal. What I saw on the bottom of the first page demolished what little appetite I had. The boy from the previous night grinned up at me from what looked like a posed portrait taken for school. Beside the photo ran the following article:

CAR RUNS OFF QUANNAPOWITT RIVER BRIDGE, LOCAL BOY KILLED

Local police were called to the Quannapowitt River Bridge yesterday afternoon in response to a 911 call that a car had gone into the river. Officers responding to the scene spotted a red 2007 Toyota Corolla submerged beneath the surface, as well as a man clinging to one of the steel bridge supports. Emergency responders were able to lower an officer to the man to rescue him. The driver, Robert Mulligan, 42, of Worcester, revealed that his son was still trapped inside the car. All efforts were made by local rescue teams, but the boy, seven-year-old Peter Mulligan, did not survive. The car, with the boy inside it, was removed from the water several hours later by use of a crane. Mulligan is being held in police custody under suspicion of drunk driving, an offence for which he has been arrested twice before, his license having been suspended in 2003 for a similar...

I couldn't read anymore. Further words were obscured by the thought of poor little Peter Mulligan, deep in the Quannapowitt River and reaching out, for some reason, to me. I stared blankly into my cereal bowl, helpless. What in the world was I supposed to do? He'd looked so scared, and all I could do was scream at him, just as terrified.

I was staring at Peter's picture so intently that I didn't see Tia until I walked right into her.

"Tia! What are you doing back already? I thought your mom was keeping you until tonight?"

"I escaped early," Tia said, dropping her matched luggage to hug me. "I wanted to make sure I had everything organized for classes tomorrow. I didn't want to be rushing around with..." She paused, eyed me critically. "You look awful! What happened?"

I glanced pointedly at several students walking past us into Donnelly. "Nothing happened. Come on, I'll help you carry your stuff upstairs."

I knew Tia wouldn't drop it, but at least she got the hint and changed the subject. We lugged her suitcases down the hall and into our room, but had barely sat down when Gabby sidled in and shut the door behind her.

"Sorry, girls. I need to hide out for a bit."

"Uh, hi, Gabby. How was your break?" Tia asked, never too flustered to be polite.

Politeness be damned, that was my motto, at least when it came to Gabby. "Why can't you hide in your own room?" I asked.

"Because the person I'm hiding from is still in my room," she explained. She pressed her eye to our peephole and groaned. "Ugh, he was not up to my usual standards."

"I didn't realize you had usual standards," I mumbled. I tossed my newspaper on my desk, picked up my introduction to poetry anthology and tried to ignore her. She went on as though I hadn't spoken.

"Scott O'Reilly threw this killer party last night, Tia," Gabby said. She abandoned her post at the door and sat on Tia's desk chair instead. "I wish you could have been there. It was an absolute blast, and he has some of the most delicious friends on the basketball team."

"Oh, that's... good," Tia replied. She looked like a deer caught in headlights, poor thing.

"I thought I'd picked a winner. I mean, he was total eye-candy, but one drink too many, and what a disappointment. Let me tell you, he had the equipment, but he did not know how to use it," Gabby sighed, pulling her suggestively tousled hair into a messy bun on top of her head.

Tia had lost the ability to form words. I watched her in amusement for a moment or two before I leapt in to rescue her.

"Yes, well, as interested as we are in this random guy's equipment, could you spare us the details, please?"

Gabby glared at me. "Okay fine, Jess, why don't you tell us about your night instead? It was pretty exciting, after all, with you waking up half the dorm with your hysterical screaming."

Well, shit. So much for breaking the news to Tia gently. I could have picked Gabby up by the straps of her push-up bra and hurled her into the hallway.

"Hysterical screaming? Why? What happened?" Tia exclaimed.

Gabby answered for me. "Oh, it was very exciting, Tia. She had a bad dream, poor little thing."

Tia's look was far too knowing. I smiled grimly.

"Yup, just a bad dream. You know me and those pesky dreams."

Tia stood up and marched resolutely to the door. She put her eye to the peephole.

"Oh, look at that, Gabby, your overnight guest just left. Looks like you've got your room back."

"Oh, good," Gabby said as she stood to leave. "Well, I'll see you ladies later. Try not to scare us all to death again tonight, Jess."

"I'll see what I can do."

Tia closed the door. "Okay. Talk to me. What's happened now?"

I left out nothing, and even tossed her the morning paper, which I'd saved as proof of just how accurate—and terrifying—my unwanted new talent was becoming.

Tia, who had been completely silent through my entire explanation, just stared down at the paper, her head shaking very slowly.

"So, it's not only Evan then."

"No, I guess not."

"I wondered why he would be appearing to you, since you didn't know him or anything. But now it's not just him anymore."

"No."

When she raised her eyes and spoke, her voice was nearly a whisper.

"Thank goodness you start that class tomorrow, Jess."

I thought about the number of ghosts that could conceivably find their way to me and felt suddenly nauseous. "My thought exactly."

§

I trudged through the newly fallen snow to Professor Pierce's class with a kind of fierce satisfaction. I felt proactive, something

I hadn't felt since my first day in the library researching Evan. I'd stayed up half the night reading my textbook. It read like most science textbooks: clinical and full of unemotional jargon. The text felt like it had very little to with the very emotional experiences I'd been having. Still, I was confident that Dr. Pierce would be able to explain it all, and somehow I'd start to find the answers I needed.

"Jess! Hey!"

I looked up to see Sam trotting toward me.

"Hey, yourself," I answered, stopping so that he could catch up with me.

"Where are you off to?" he asked.

"Um, I've got class in Harrison."

"Yeah, I figured that much out, seeing as you're walking straight for the front door," Sam chuckled. "I meant what class have you got now?"

"Introduction to Parapsychology."

The response was predictable. "What? But you're a freshman! That's a senior seminar! How the hell did you manage that one?"

"My devilish good looks?"

Sam was shaking his head in disbelief. "Wow, I'm impressed. I can't believe that Pierce cracked and signed you in."

"It's not the coup you imagine, Sam," I lied, more smoothly than I would have thought myself capable. "One of my high school teachers in New York was a buddy of his. He emailed Pierce and that's how we got introduced. Anyway, I'm just auditing."

"Oh. Well, still. I had no idea you were interested in that stuff. I mean, after the whole nightmare thing, I kinda figured that would be outside of your comfort zone."

I just shrugged and tried to change the subject.

"What class are you off to?"

Sam flung his arm around me. "Introduction to Parapsychology."

I was too shocked to remain cool. "What? But you're only a junior! How did *you* get into that class?"

"One of the perks of campus employment. I'm Pierce's lab assistant." His voice contained a hint of pride.

"Will someone please explain to me how everyone else winds up with these interesting jobs and I'm stuck doling out mystery meat casseroles in a hairnet!" I shouted.

"Calm down, I did my time in lunch lady land freshman year. It's just about the only job you can get in your first year. I just started with Pierce this past fall. I'm a bio major, so I got assigned to someone in the science department."

"What's it like, working for him? What do you do?" I tried to sound casual, though I was burning with curiosity.

Sam gave a knowing laugh. "Yeah, he's pretty intimidating at first. Comes off as a bit of an asshole. But it's been pretty cool, actually. I mostly just set up equipment and organize papers. I've also become an expert in the art of using the copy machine. So after a semester of generally not screwing things up, he told me I could take the class, if I wanted to. Think of it as one of the perks of the job, I guess."

He held the door open for me. It would be nice to know someone in the class, and yet, I couldn't help thinking that this was going to complicate things. A lot.

When Sam and I arrived in the lecture hall, there was a chair in the center of the floor in front of the lectern. It was draped in a long black swath of fabric that fell in folds to the floor. Everyone was pointing at it and murmuring with curiosity. Professor Pierce entered with a little smirk and deposited his bag by the desk before seating himself on the front table. He looked satisfied, so I guessed the chair was attracting the sort of attention he expected. He also looked ridiculously out of place. If anyone who didn't know him had walked in, they would have thought that some commune hippie had wandered in off the street, looking to score some weed.

He began talking, projecting a powerful voice out over the pre-lecture buzz. "Good morning everyone. I would like to sincerely welcome you to the first day of class. It is my hope that this will be a very informative semester for all of us, as we are stepping into a field about which little can be proven and even less can be rationally believed to be true. So let me say that if you are the kind of person who needs cold hard facts and formulas to underlie everything you deem worthy of study, you are in the wrong fucking class. I don't want you in my lecture hall. Get the hell out and do it now."

The room was oppressively silent. No one moved. The kid next to me wasn't even breathing. We were all Dr. Pierce's captive audience and he knew it.

"No one leaving? Brilliant!" He clapped his hands together. "Now, I could start throwing all kinds of scientific terminology at you today, but I think we'd best start with the kind of demonstration that you are likely to see with some frequency in here. It offers a fair example of the general content, as well as an accurate depiction of the kind of creative thinking required to get anything out of this class. It is the contention of many in the field of parapsychology that everything in the world has its own unique energy."

Pens and pencils started scratching wildly.

"I think many of us would admit that we can sense this among people. Our own individual makeups emit a certain frequency, so to speak, so that the feeling we get hanging around one person is very different than the feeling we get hanging around someone else. Would you all agree?"

There was a dull murmur of assent accompanied by some nodding heads.

All eyes were trained on the chair.

"Everything on earth has energy. We are all made up of energy; places have energy, inanimate objects have energy. Not every energy field is equally strong, nor is everyone equally sensitive to those energy fields. But they do exist, and it is a heightened sensitivity to these energies that we commonly refer to as a sixth sense. How many of you would say that you have a sixth sense?"

Not a single person raised his hand.

"Oh, come on, don't be modest, people! Someone must have had an experience in life where they sensed something based purely on a feeling. Anyone?"

A red-headed girl in the front corner raised her hand tentatively.

Professor Pierce swung around. "Yes, Miss …?"

"Taylor. Sarah Taylor."

"Okay, Miss Taylor. You've had an experience like this?"

Sarah looked like she already regretted putting up her hand, but she went on. "Well, I don't know if this is what you're talking about, but there was this one time, when I got home from school, and the house was supposed to be empty. But when I walked in the door, I… sort of felt that there was someone there who wasn't supposed to be."

"You didn't hear or see anything?" Dr. Pierce probed.

"No, everything looked normal. And I didn't hear anything either; it was all quiet."

"Unusual smells maybe?"

"No, nothing like that. But it was like I could feel someone in the other room. I just knew he was there."

"And was there someone there?"

"Yeah, my brother's friend had snuck in the window to borrow a

PlayStation game. Scared the crap out of me," she finished. A few people laughed, including Dr. Pierce.

"Well, not the dramatic conclusion we were all expecting, but effective nonetheless. So can you describe how you knew someone was in your house?"

"No, I can't really explain it. I just sensed it."

Professor Pierce clapped again. The sound echoed around the hall and several people jumped in surprise. "Ah, the classic response! She 'sensed' it. She cannot identify one of her other five senses as having a part in it, and yet she sensed it. People can have very strong energies that we can pick up on. But did you know that objects can have strong energies as well?"

A few people looked surprised by this revelation. Another student raised his hand, a boy this time.

"Yes, and your name is?" Dr. Pierce called, glancing at his roster.

"Ben Stanton," the boy replied in a carrying, confident voice. I recognized him as one of a crowd of basketball team members who were often in the dining hall at the same time I worked the breakfast shift. "So, I've got this pocket watch that used to be my grandfather's, right? And whenever I take it out of the case, I sort of get this feeling that my grandfather is in the room. Is that what you're talking about?"

"Sort of, yes. But part of your experience could be that you know that the watch belonged to your grandfather, so it is not necessarily the energy of the watch, but the sight of the familiar object that evokes the feeling of your grandfather's presence. On the other hand, it could well be that that object has a very powerful energy of its own. Did your grandfather like that watch?"

"Yeah, he wore it all the time."

"So would you say he was attached to it?"

"Definitely. My mom thought he should be buried with it, but my grandmother gave it to me instead."

"Okay, then. So your grandfather's pocket watch would be a good object for this particular exercise. There is a theory that objects to which people were particularly attached have an aura memory." Professor Pierce turned and wrote the term on the whiteboard behind him. A hundred heads bent in unison over a hundred notebooks and scribbled the same term with a hundred pens.

"That is, they retain the energy of the person who owned it," Professor Pierce explained. "The aura memory of a favorite or special object is especially strong. Those with a sixth sense can often feel and interpret that energy.

Which brings us to today's demonstration." Dr. Pierce waved with a flourish to the chair under the cloth. "We will test this theory," he continued, "through a group activity. Sarah!" He pointed at her suddenly. "Can you tell me what I have under that cloth?"

Sarah shook her head.

"Ben? Any idea?"

"A chair?" Ben suggested. We all laughed.

"Very observant, jackass," Dr. Pierce said. "And on the chair?"

Ben shrugged. "No idea."

"Ben, would you come on up here?" Dr. Pierce asked.

Ben stood up a bit reluctantly and joined Professor Pierce on the platform. One of his buddies chanted his name and Ben looked over at him, grinning.

"Okay, Ben. You have just told us that your grandfather's pocket watch makes you 'feel' the presence of your grandfather. What does this object under here make you feel?"

"Nothing."

"And why's that?"

"I don't even know what it is."

Professor Pierce smiled as though Ben had said the very thing he hoped he would say. "Ah. We have no familiarity with this object. It is a mystery to us. We don't know anything about it, and therefore, any information we can gather about it will come purely from our own abilities to tap into our sixth sense."

Professor Pierce was gazing around the room now at each of us in turn as though wondering which of us would be able to do it. I thought that his eyes lingered on me for a particularly long moment, but that might just have been my own paranoia. I didn't worry much about it. I was too curious about what was under that sheet, just like everyone else.

"As in any good scientific experiment, we are testing a hypothesis. But in order to do that, we need to have a control. Any science buffs want to explain for the humanities kids what a control is?" Dr. Pierce asked, clearly baiting us.

Just to spite him, a girl I recognized as a regular from the art building raised her hand.

"Yes, Miss ...?"

"Gonzales. Art major."

Dr. Pierce smiled appreciatively. "Yes, Miss Gonzales?"

"A control is a test sample that isn't exposed to any outside variables."

"That is correct, thank you. Notice we're using science-y words, for those of you who think we are somehow dealing outside the realm of legitimate science here. By removing all variables, we can be sure that none of those factors are affecting our outcome. The variables, in this case, are our other five senses and previous knowledge of the circumstances surrounding the object in question. Do you all follow me?"

"So," Ben said, "if I can tell you anything about what's under the sheet, it's because I used my sixth sense."

"Exactly. So, any guesses? Do you feel anything?"

Ben stood there staring at the sheet for about ten seconds. "Nope!" he announced finally.

We all laughed again.

Professor Pierce stepped around to stand beside Ben. "Okay, try this. Stand right in front of the chair and place your hands close to the outside of the sheet. Now concentrate for a minute or so and see if you can pick up on the energy of that object."

Ben stepped forward and did as he was told. He was so tall that he had to bend almost in half to put his hands at the level of the concealed object. He started moving his hands slowly through the air around the sheet. The look on his face advertised that he felt pretty stupid. I didn't blame him. He looked pretty stupid, to be honest.

After a couple of initial sniggers, though, the class seemed to be holding its collective breath. Finally after what seemed like forever, Ben straightened up.

"How about now, Ben? Any impressions?" Dr. Pierce asked.

"Well, I..."

"Shut up!" Dr. Pierce shouted. "Don't tell me a thing! Go back to your seat and write it down. I'm now going to open the floor. Anyone who is interested in trying may come down and attempt to sense the object. Don't share your thoughts with anyone. Write all of it down confidentially. It's very important not to censor yourselves. Any random thought you have while concentrating could be connected."

At first, no one moved. All the students were craning their necks around to see if anyone else was getting up.

"Come on people, now is not the time for bashfulness. Take the leap or you won't learn much in this class!" Dr. Pierce yelled.

Gradually, people began to rise from their seats and form a clump in the center aisle. Several people crowded around the chair at a time, their hands groping at the nothingness around the outside of the sheet. Even those who'd chosen not to wait in line were staring intently at the sheet, as though they had X-ray vision.

"What do you think? Do you want to give it a try?" Sam asked.

"No, thanks. I think I'm gonna sit this one out," I said.

"Not one for getting up in front of people, are you?"

"You could say that."

I watched Sam head down the aisle to join the queue of whispering students. I had no intention of drawing attention to myself in this class. It was bad enough that word had circulated that a freshman had somehow weaseled her way into the most popular senior seminar on campus, and that most people would eventually figure out that freshman was me. I wasn't about to get up in front of everyone and risk something weird happening. But that didn't mean I couldn't try from my seat.

From where I was sitting in the corner of the room, I had a clear view of the chair. Twiddling a pencil in my hand, I started concentrating on the sheet. I wasn't really sure how to go about it. I tried visualizing the object through the sheet, but nothing came to me; the sheet remained stubbornly opaque. Then I tried running through a list of small objects in my head, to see if anything stood out. Book, plate, picture, mirror, toy, dress, candlestick, hairbrush, hat. Nothing.

"Come on, what are you?" I thought.

No, that was the wrong question. The question wasn't "What are you?" it was "Who are you?"

I stared at the sheet and started to focus not on the object itself, but who had touched the object. I let my pencil doodle thoughtlessly across my notes. Who had held it? Used it? How did they feel about that object?

"It's mine."

A little voice had woken up in my head, claiming the object for its own. It was barely more than a whisper, but I could hear it clearly.

"It's yours?"

"Yes. It's my favorite."

"Your favorite what?"

"My favorite doll."

A doll. It was a doll. I knew it. The voice had just told me.

"Who gave you your doll?"

"Uncle Timothy. He buys me lots of toys."

"That's very nice of him."

"Yes, he's very nice to me."

"What's your name?"

"Lydia."

"Well, I think we can cross world famous psychic off my list of future career options." I jumped about a foot out of my seat. My pencil skittered across my desk and onto the floor. I hadn't even seen Sam coming back.

"Whoa, sorry! Are you okay?" Sam bent down to retrieve my pencil.

I tried to quiet my frantic heart with a steadying breath. "Yeah, I'm fine. I was just... spacing out. I didn't see you. Any luck?"

"I don't think so. I'm gonna write down what I thought of, but I'm pretty sure it's just bullshit. How about you, are you going to go up?"

"I was looking at it from here."

"Okay, everyone," Professor Pierce's voice cut across the low buzz of conversation. I looked around for the first time in a few minutes. Dr. Pierce was staring right at me, a curious expression on his face. Everyone had filtered back to their seats and were busily writing or whispering to a neighbor. "Let's record our thoughts precisely. I'll be coming around to see how we're doing."

I started to panic. I could still hear that tiny, faint voice echoing in the recesses of my ears. Should I write down what I'd heard? What if it was right? What did that mean? Maybe I should just make something up, just in case it really was true. I didn't want anyone knowing what I could do, if I really could do it. Of course, I didn't even know what "it" was. And why the hell was Professor Pierce staring at me like that? Did he know what had happened? Had I given myself away?

"Hey, what's that?" Sam asked. He was staring down at my notebook.

I followed his eyes to the page. There, beneath my notes about aura memory, was a face. It was the face of a little girl, about six years old, with very long, dark hair, and a gap-toothed smile. Under her face, I had written the words "Lydia" and "doll." As I stared at the words, I grew aware of a dull aching sensation in my right hand. It was a familiar feeling, the exact feeling I got when I'd taken a particularly long test that required lots of writing.

I tried to keep my voice casual. "Oh nothing, I was just doodling. I always do that when I'm bored."

"Who is that?" he pushed, pointing to the girl's face.

"Nobody. Just a face." I quickly flipped to a clean page. "So what did you come up with?"

Sam looked like he was going to ask me something and then decided against it. Instead, he tilted his notebook toward me. He had written the word "blue" and then a series of question marks.

"So, Mr. Lang? Any glimpses of a psychic nature?" Professor Pierce abruptly appeared over Sam's shoulder. Looking a little embarrassed, Sam showed his paper to Dr. Pierce.

"What made you write the word 'blue?'" Dr. Pierce asked. I noticed his eyes roving to my own page, which I had thankfully covered up. I tried to look mildly interested in Sam's findings.

"Well, I was staring at the sheet for a while and just when I was about to give up, I thought that the black of the sheet looked blue for a second. So, I just wrote down 'blue.' I thought maybe the object or something on it might be blue," Sam said.

Professor Pierce squinted at him. "I see. Interesting. And you, Miss Ballard?"

I shook my head. "I didn't go up." My voice cracked like a prepubescent boy's. Very smooth.

Dr. Pierce's features were marred for just a moment by something... disappointment? Then he walked away. He approached the chair and placed his hand on the black fabric. "Have we all solidified our thoughts?"

Everyone nodded eagerly, eyes glued to the sheet.

"Very well, then. I will reveal what is really under the sheet and we can discuss if your findings were in any way accurate."

He paused for another moment, clearly enjoying the building anticipation. Finally, he drew the sheet away, revealing first the feet, then the ruffled dress, then the chipped features of a porcelain doll.

The whole room erupted into conversation. Some people were eagerly comparing their notes to what they saw in front of them. Others were consulting neighbors. I was trying my damnedest not to vomit.

I'd known what would be under that cloth, but somehow that didn't lessen the shock of actually seeing it there; if anything, it intensified it. The doll was clearly very old, like something you would find on a dusty shelf in an antique shop. The braided blonde hair was matted on top, the plaits sticking out stiffly above the shoulders. The face had faded pink lips and rosy cheeks painted on. The nose had a chip on the end of it and the glass eyes stared vacantly out over the eager audience. Her wrinkled satin frock was lacy and…

"Blue!" Sam whispered, pointing unnecessarily at the doll. "Hey, the dress is blue! That's pretty cool, huh?"

"What? Oh, yeah! Good job!" I tried to sound excited rather than how I really felt: Seriously disturbed.

Sam's eyes widened as he remembered what I was hoping he would somehow miraculously forget. "Hey, you wrote the word 'doll!' You guessed what it was! Whoa, Jess, that is so weird." He didn't sound freaked out, thank God. Just impressed.

I played it off as best I could. "Lucky guess. More than just luck, actually. It was the angle I had from over here. I could sort of make out the shape of the feet under the sheet."

He bought it. "Oh. But still, it could have been lots of things with a shape like that. You can read my fortune any day."

"I see pain in your future," I replied in a mystical voice. Then I stomped on his foot.

I tried to distract myself by listening as other people shared their findings with the class. A surprising number of people had sensed something correct about the doll. One other person in the class had guessed what the object actually was, though she admitted she had pictured a rag doll, not a porcelain one. Five others had sensed it was a kind of toy. No less than ten different people had written down something about seeing a face or a pair of eyes, though most of them had thought it might be a photograph or a painting. Another handful had sensed that whatever it was, it belonged to a child. The overall level of accuracy was impressive, even to Dr. Pierce, who addressed us again when we'd all finished sharing.

"Excellent, everyone, thank you. I hope this exercise has gone a little way to help prove our theory about the existence of a sixth sense. It is imprecise, no doubt, and though we have done what we can to remove the variables, there are the ever-present factors of coincidence and pure dumb luck to contend with as well—assuming of course that you believe in luck or coincidence."

Sarah raised her hand. "Professor Pierce, where did you get the doll?"

"My wife and I found her in the eaves of our house when we renovated it. She dates back to the late 1800s."

After a twenty minute lecture on the properties of energy fields,

Dr. Pierce dismissed the class. As Sam and I worked our way toward the door, I came to a decision. I couldn't quiet the curiosity burning inside me. I had to know if my encounter with Lydia had any basis in truth.

I waited until we made it into the hallway, and then doubled back, telling Sam I'd forgotten my sketchbook. Sam had to get to his next class, so he went ahead without me.

§

Dr. Pierce was still in the lecture hall, wrapping the doll in bubble wrap and packing it away carefully in a shoebox.

"Professor? Could I talk to you for a minute?"

Professor Pierce looked up. He didn't look surprised to see me. "Sure, Ballard. What can I do for you?"

I took a deep breath. "I think you already know this, but I didn't tell you the truth before about not writing anything down during the exercise."

"Yes, I did know that. I was watching you during the exercise. I knew something had happened."

"Why were you watching me?"

Professor Pierce put down the shoebox and folded his arms across his chest. "Ballard, you told me you needed to take this class to help you understand things. That makes me assume that something of a paranormal or psychic nature has happened to you. It was under this assumption that I agreed to sign you into this class. Was my assumption correct?"

There was no point in denying it. "Yes."

"You can understand, then, why I might be more interested in your responses to these kinds of experiments than in those from the rest of the class."

"Yeah, I guess I can."

"Okay, then. You came here for help. I want to help you. But I can't if you don't trust me enough to tell me what's going on."

The man had a point. Why the hell was I even here if I wasn't going to take advantage of the potential help staring me in the face? This wasn't like telling Dr. Hildebrand. Here was someone who would believe me—maybe the *only* person who would believe me. Decision made, I nodded my head.

"Good, that's a start. Maybe you can begin by showing me what you came up with in class today?" I pulled out my notebook, flipped it open to the day's notes, and handed it to him. He scanned the page calmly, and then let out a low whistle. "Do you mind if I ask you a few questions about how you came up with this?" he asked.

"Sure. Only if you don't mind me asking you a few questions when you're done." I replied as I chewed on a fingernail.

"Yeah, I'll bet you have questions, Ballard. Damn! I'd have some if I were you," he muttered, more to himself than to me. Then he straightened up and tucked my sketchbook carefully under his arm. "Let's go up to my office. There's another class meeting in here shortly."

I followed him in silence up to the fourth floor of Wiltshire. It wasn't an awkward silence; we were both too lost in our own thoughts to bother with each other. When we got to his office, Dr. Pierce threw his bag into the corner and started rummaging through a filing cabinet.

"Have a seat, Ballard. And some coffee." He gestured over to a coffee maker perched on a stack of files in the corner. The pot was full; he'd obviously left it on while he was gone. Trying not to think of the imminent fire that would someday engulf this entire office and its contents, I poured myself a cup and tossed a sugar into it. I took a sip and immediately started sputtering.

"Sorry, I like my coffee strong."

"No kidding," I choked, reaching for several more sugar packets. It was by far the strongest coffee I'd ever had, and I was a coffee girl. "Why do you even bother brewing it? Just eat the grounds, it'd be quicker."

Professor Pierce looked for a moment like he was seriously considering the idea before throwing himself into his chair and laying open a file. "Okay, Ballard. Tell me what happened."

"Today?"

"Let's start with today. We'll move backward from there. Into the past is an appropriate direction when dealing with this kind of thing."

"What was that, ghost humor?" I asked with a smirk.

Dr. Pierce just grinned and waited for me to start. I described to him in as much detail as I could exactly what had happened during class. I told him about the voice, and about my hand seeming to draw without my realizing it. I tried to describe the quality of the voice, the way it sounded like it was coming through a badly tuned radio or a poor-quality microphone. Dr. Pierce just listened intently and scribbled on his notepad.

"And then Sam sat down next to me, and I sort of... snapped out of it," I finished.

"And you never saw anything? There was no visual of Lydia or the doll?" he asked. It seemed to be an important point.

I shook my head. "No, I never saw the doll. The only reason I knew it was a doll was because she told me. I couldn't have told you what it looked like before you pulled the sheet off."

Professor Pierce jotted that down. He read it all over in quiet.

"Professor?"

"Mm-hmm?"

"Am I ... right? About Lydia?"

Professor Pierce looked up. "You sure as hell are."

He extracted the file out from under his notepad and tossed it across the desk to me. It was full of papers, some recent, others very old and protected in plastic sleeves.

"That first one," said Dr. Pierce, pointing, "is the deed to my house. As you can see, the family name is Tenningsbrook."

I looked down. I found the surname of the original owners of the house along with their first names, William and Jane. The house was built in 1883. I flipped the document over. The second document was full of legal jargon that seemed to be about construction. It was dated ten years later.

"What's this, a building permit?"

"The next page will explain," Dr. Pierce said grimly.

I turned to the next page. It was the oldest newspaper article I'd ever seen. A quick scan of the emboldened headline made me gasp.

"It burned down!"

"Not completely, but yes, a large section of the house was destroyed. They had to obtain a permit from the town to reconstruct the damaged wing."

I felt my throat going dry. I continued reading the article, and only a few sentences further my fears were confirmed.

"Lydia Tenningsbrook," I whispered.

"She died in the fire. From what I can gather from the floor plans, her bedroom was in the wing that caught fire. By the time anyone was alerted to the blaze, it was already too late to reach her room. Her body was recovered the next morning."

"There's not a photograph of that in here, is there?" I practically squeaked.

"No, no, not of the body," Dr. Pierce reassured me. "But there is a photograph in there that might interest you to take a look at. Just a few pages further."

I flipped past an insurance claim notice and a death certificate that left me feeling nauseated before I reached it. It was a sepia-toned photograph that had faded with age. A dark-haired, mustached man in a black suit stood with his hand on the shoulder of a very serious but very pretty woman in a high-necked gown. Standing on the woman's right, her pale little hands clasped demurely, was Lydia.

There was no name, of course, but I knew who it was. She was the very same little girl whose face had smiled back at me from my notebook page, though the face in this photo bore no smile. Just like every old photograph of children that I had ever seen, she looked abnormally still and serious for someone so young. The sight of her living face, and knowing she was dead, made me light-headed.

"As you can see, the resemblance between your drawing and the photo is uncanny," Dr. Pierce said.

I couldn't respond.

"Can I ask you a few more questions now?" Dr. Pierce inquired.

"Okay." I closed the file more forcefully than I meant to and handed it back to him—I didn't want to stare at that poor little dead girl anymore.

"Do you remember if you saw Lydia at all? I mean, in your mind's eye, did you picture her while she was talking to you?"

"No. The first time I ever saw her face was when Sam pointed it out on my paper."

"I see, I see…" Dr. Pierce mumbled, scribbling some more. "And now, the crucial point: Has anything like this ever happened before?"

I hesitated. "Well, not exactly like this."

"Well, then tell me what *did* happen."

"I, uh, met someone in the library who turned out to be dead."

The statement hung in the air for a solid minute before Professor Pierce could respond.

"How do you know this person is dead?"

"Dean Finndale told me."

"And how does Finndale know this person is dead?" Dr. Pierce asked.

"Because it was a student who died here last year. His name was Evan Corbett."

Professor Pierce's eyes went wide. "You saw Evan Corbett here?"

I sat up straighter. "Did you know Evan?"

"No, I didn't know him personally, but of course the news of his death was all over the campus. Lots of bad press for the school, as I recall, and if there's one thing the administration hates, it's bad press." Dr. Pierce sounded a little bitter. I started to like him even more.

"Yeah. Well, anyway, I told my professor I'd talked to him, not realizing what he was. She flipped out and sent me to the dean and the dean sent me to a shrink. They both seemed to think I should keep my mouth shut and go on some behavioral meds." It was my turn to sound bitter.

Professor Pierce slammed his pen down on the table. A small pile of manila folders slid onto the floor, but he didn't seem to notice. "Well, they should have sent you to me, damn it! Narrow-minded people, that's the problem around here. Hush it all up, don't rock the boat, label 'em crazy and lock 'em away.

It's people like that who keep parapsychology on the outskirts of acceptable science. Doesn't even occur to them that you might be telling the truth!" Dr. Pierce was raging now, but I was smiling. He looked over at me and stopped in his tracks. "Something funny?"

"No, nothing, it's just—I wish I'd been able to say a little of that to the dean without getting expelled."

Professor Pierce's smile looked a bit more like a grimace. "Yeah, I wish I could say it without getting fired. Same boat, I'm afraid." He took a breath and sank into his seat again. "But, what's done is done. They should have sent you to me, but they didn't. No matter. You're here now and we'll do what we can."

"Can I ask you a question now?" I asked.

"Of course. I can't guarantee that I can answer it, but let's give it a try." He plunked his pencil down and drained his cup of steaming coffee without flinching.

"So... what's wrong with me?"

"What would make you think that there's anything wrong with you?" he asked.

I snorted. "Are you kidding me right now?"

"Ballard, there is nothing wrong with you. On the contrary, you have an ability that most people do not possess. It would appear that you are some sort of medium."

"A medium? What exactly does that mean?" I had heard the word before, of course, but it only conjured up images of gypsy women in turbans waving their claws over crystal balls, like that ridiculous fortune teller at the carnival.

"It means that you seem to be a channel of sorts for

communication between the living world and the spirit world," Dr. Pierce explained.

"A channel?" I didn't like the sound of it at all. "So I'm like some sort of... what, spirit telephone or something like that?"

Professor Pierce cracked a smile. "Not exactly. Let's make an analogy here. Think of yourself as having an extra antenna that most other people don't have. Spirits are each on their own frequencies, ones that living people either can't or won't acknowledge. You have the ability, by focusing your antenna in the right way, to pick up on those frequencies and even understand them."

That sounded a little more plausible, not to mention less frightening. "So where did I get this antenna? How come I have one and most other people don't? And why did I only just start tuning in?"

"Now those are questions for which I have no answer at all."

"And do all mediums experience what I do?"

"No. In fact, every medium experiences these things differently. Just as our personalities and points of view change the way we experience everyday situations, the same is true of medium experiences."

"So, the drawing thing?"

"Unusual, but not entirely unheard of. It's called psychic drawing, and there are other psychic artists out there, although," he stared again at my drawing of Lydia, "I've never seen anything from a psychic artist that was this detailed or accurate. Do you draw regularly?"

"Yeah," I said, "I've drawn since I was little. I do it all the time."

"And are your drawings usually this good?" Dr. Pierce asked.

"Um, I dunno. I guess so," I admitted, a little embarrassed, but pleased. I pulled out my sketchbook and handed it to him. He flipped through it page by page, nodding as he did so.

"Yes, it looks like your usual style. Very detailed, very life-like, strong attention to shadow and light." He saw my slightly surprised look, and explained, "I took an art class or two in my day. Believe me, it was a passion the world was better off without; I was terrible."

We smiled at each other as he handed it back, and he waited until I put it safely away in my bag before he spoke again. "So, Ballard. The time that you saw Evan in the library, was that the first time you ever saw him?"

"No, and he hasn't been the only one to seek me out."

For the next hour I gave Pierce all the details of every encounter I'd ever had with Evan, as well as my visit from Peter Mulligan. I flipped through my sketchbook to show him the drawings I'd done, and also the documentation I had collected: Evan's yearbook photo, the newspaper articles on Evan's and Peter's deaths. He bombarded me with questions and took furious notes. My initial hesitation to share with him had melted away, and now I was answering his questions with as much enthusiasm as he showed in asking them. There was something cathartic about getting all of these details out to someone, but it was more than that. When I was sitting there telling half-truths to Dr. Hildebrand, I'd only felt more nervous and self-conscious. In fact I'd been blatantly lying just so they wouldn't haul out the straitjacket. Even confiding in Tia, I hadn't had this same sense of freedom I felt now. Now with each word that I let escape my lips, with every question and answer, I was getting closer to the truth. This was a revelation that could lead to something, something concrete.

I had no idea what that something would be, but finally I was talking to someone who could really help me to understand, to find answers. And, perhaps best of all, he was someone who didn't treat my story with disbelief or fright.

"Okay, I think I've interrogated you for long enough," Pierce said at last. He was looking at me with concern; did I look that much like hell? "Are you sleeping?" he asked.

"No, not that well. I'm having a lot of nightmares."

"And do these nightmares have anything to do with Evan?"

"Yes," I admitted. "And… others, I think."

"Others?"

"Mm-hm. Other spirits, I think. Nothing as intense or clear as Evan or Peter, just voices and weird shapes, stuff like that."

"I see. Interesting." That was definitely one of his favorite words. "When did these dreams start?"

I squirmed uncomfortably. "Over the summer. The night my mom died."

We sat in silence for a while. I kept my eyes on my hands, watching myself pick away my nail polish, avoiding Pierce's gaze. Finally, Pierce stood up and went over to a shelf behind his desk. He pulled a book off almost immediately; he obviously knew his book collection well—I could respect that. He handed me the book. It had no title and when I flipped it open it was...

"Blank," I murmured, as a little wave of disappointment and déjà vu rolled over me at the thought of my mother's blank little mystery book.

"Not for long, I hope. I think you should record everything you can in it. Every dream, any encounter, with as much detail as you can recall. And keep sketching, of course. It will help me to track your patterns as a medium and maybe give us a little insight into who may be contacting you and why."

"Is there usually a specific reason for spirits to contact the living?" I asked.

"Oh, yes. Not a universal reason, mind you. Remember, spirits used to be people, as unique and varied as people are. Their reasons for contacting the living are just as varied, but we can generalize enough to say that spirits who are still here on earth are discontented for one reason or another. Either they don't know they are dead, or they do and they want to do something about it. Some just seem to crave human interaction. Others are looking for help.

The word "help" exploded in my brain. I flew over to my bag so quickly that Pierce leapt out of his chair.

"What? What is it?" he cried.

"You just made me remember something! When I saw Evan, I didn't just talk to him. He left me a message!" I dumped my bag out onto the floor in my haste to find what I was looking for. Finally I dug it out and ran over to Pierce, flipping pages frantically.

"Hamlet?" he asked.

"This is what I was writing my paper on. It was sitting on my desk that night. He picked it up and wrote in it."

Pierce's eyes went wide. "He wrote in it? You mean you had actual physical manipulation of objects when you..."

"Yeah, whatever, he picked it up off the desk, along with my pen and wrote in it. He told me it was his phone number, but when I looked at it later, I found this." I found the page and pointed it out to Pierce.

Pierce looked like I'd handed him the holy grail of paranormal evidence.

"But this isn't ink," he practically whispered, running his fingers just above the surface of the page, as though afraid to touch it. "I can't tell what it is." He was holding it comically close to his face.

"I know, I thought that too. It sort of looks like it was just burned into the texture of the paper, no indentations or anything."

"Jess, could I borrow this? I have a couple of chemistry buds I would like to have run some tests on it."

I hesitated. "Um, I don't know. Would it destroy the book?"

"Destroy this book? Are you insane? Do you seriously think I would let anything happen to this book?" Pierce looked thoroughly offended.

I cracked a smile. "No, I guess not. Okay, go ahead. As long as I can get it back."

"You have my word, Ballard. Undamaged and intact," Pierce promised with a gesture like the scout's honor. The thought of him as a boy scout made me smile even wider.

"What?" he asked with narrowing eyes as I grinned at him.

"Oh, nothing. I'm just... really glad that you're helping me," I said. "Thank you, professor."

"Thank you for coming to me, Ballard. I don't know how much help I'll be, but damn it, I'm going to try." He held out a hand.

I took it and gave it a good shake. "One last question."

"Shoot."

"This spirit antenna thing. Any chance it will just... go away?"

Pierce's smile faded away. "I don't think so, kid."

12

SWEETER DREAMS

I WAITED ANXIOUSLY AT THE BACK OF THE LECTURE HALL until class cleared out. It had been almost a month since I'd given Pierce my copy of Hamlet, and I was starting to get anxious. Finally at the start of class that day he'd caught my eye, pulled the book discreetly from his brief case, and nodded. In my anticipation I heard and comprehended exactly nothing that he taught us in class that day.

It wasn't just that I wanted to know what his "chemistry buds" had found; I also wanted the book back in my possession. I hadn't seen Evan at all since our encounter in the alleyway, and I was starting to go through this odd bout of withdrawal. I kept torturing myself with questions that there was no way to get answers for. Why hadn't he shown himself again? Was he scared, or angry with me because of what I'd told him?

I looked for him everywhere, my breath catching at every possible sighting. The appearance of a tall dark-haired figure from across the room would send my heart pounding into my throat.

A turn.

A closer look.

No Evan.

My excitement would quickly dissolve into irrational disappointment. And then I'd immediately start chastising myself. "*No, Jessica. We don't want to see ghosts everywhere we go. We don't want to be a freak, remember?*"

It should have been a convincing argument, but I remained stubbornly unconvinced.

In the meantime, the book wasn't the only thing that had been experimented on. I had spent a lot of my free time with Pierce in his office or in empty lecture halls, testing my abilities in a variety of ways. We had tried two more aura memory tests. About one object, an old hairbrush, I was able to pick up nothing at all. Pierce nodded, though, as if he had expected nothing less. Then we tried a gold locket. The response was almost immediate: A woman's voice popped into my head, claiming the trinket as her own. After only a few silent questions, I quickly opened my eyes and tried to mentally disconnect with a violent shiver.

"What happened that time?" Pierce asked.

"I just got screamed at."

"By whom?"

"Her name was Mary, and she was really angry that you took her things out of her house." I sounded more accusatory than I ever meant to sound, as though Mary's feelings had intermingled with my own.

"Did she tell you anything else?"

"She said that 'he' gave it to her, and that she had promised him that she would hold on to it forever. She sounded really upset... like I was trying to steal it or something. It's a locket, it's got his hair in it," I finished with a limp gesture toward the cloth, which did indeed reveal the locket beneath it.

Pierce looked grimly satisfied.

"So what's with the face? Did I pass or what?" I asked.

"You've just confirmed what I've thought would be the case. "Of these two objects, only one is associated with paranormal activity." Mary Dryden is a well-known inhabitant of the Dryden Inn in northern Vermont; the locket is on loan from a local historical museum there." He picked up the locket and held it out to me.

I cringed away from it. "Ugh, no! Didn't you hear me? There's a dead guy's hair in that locket!"

Pierce chuckled, but put it away. He went on, "The hairbrush was found under the floorboards during renovations in my brother-in-law's house. He's never had a speck of paranormal activity.

"So, I'm only picking up on objects owned by spirits who are still around?"

"Yes, that would appear to be the case."

"Well," I replied, shivering again, "if they want the activity at the Dryden Inn to calm down, I'd take that locket back."

Pierce had also suggested that I try again to make contact with a ghost other than Evan, but coward that I was, I hadn't quite gotten around to trying that one yet.

The cacophony of scraping chairs announced the end of class and promptly snapped me back into the present. I worked my way down the aisle as the last lingering students filtered out the door. Pierce pulled out the book and handed it to me with a kind of reluctance that only heightened my anticipation. I felt an odd sense of relief to feel its solid shape between my fingers again. I flipped automatically to the page with Evan's message. It appeared entirely untampered with, exactly how I'd remembered it.

"That," Pierce stated simply, "is quite a remarkable book, Ballard."

"I know. But, why, exactly? Did they find anything?"

"Yep. The boys ran the regular battery of tests. No fingerprints on the book other than yours and mine. No visible impressions made by any sort of writing utensil, even on the microscopic level. The chemical makeup of the message itself is in no way different from the chemical makeup of the paper it's written on. And remember how we thought the message looked as though it had been burned in? No chemical remnants or evidence of any kind of burning. According to the chemical and physical analysis, that message does not exist." Pierce finished cheerfully.

Speechless, I ran my fingers over the pages of my "remarkable book."

"And that's not all. Temperature measurements on the book itself turned up some pretty crazy shit, too. That book doesn't absorb transferred heat!" he announced.

"And what exactly does that mean? Heat transferred from what?" I asked.

"Anything! You know how when you hold an object, it warms to your body temperature? Well, you could toss that book onto a blasting radiator, come back an hour later, and find it as cool as if you'd just pulled it off your bookshelf."

I tried to focus on the way the book felt in my hand and I realized almost immediately that he was right. It remained cool to the touch, even where I'd been grasping it so tightly.

"Is any of that what you expected?" I asked.

"That's just it, Ballard, I had no idea what to expect. In all my years of paranormal investigation I've never seen anything quite like this book. I've witnessed plenty of poltergeist activity involving inanimate objects, but testing on the objects afterwards found them to be totally unremarkable, indistinguishable from other objects of their kind. The poltergeist activity had no lasting, measurable effects on the objects, as far as we could tell. But this..." Pierce just shook his head, apparently lacking the right words for what "this" was.

The book rested coolly in my hand.

"There's one more thing, actually," Pierce added excitedly, as though he'd only just remembered. He rifled through his briefcase and extracted a small stack of papers enclosed in a Ziploc bag. "The pièce-de-résistance!" he announced with a flourish, handing the bag to me. "These are some photocopies of the forms I was able to get my hands on. They're all from campus records, filled out and signed by Evan before he died. I had a handwriting analysis done."

I looked down at Evan's living signature and listened to the blood pounding in my ears.

"There wasn't a whole lot to go on, of course. Your message isn't very long, and usually, to get anything conclusive, they need a longer sample for comparison. But they did the best they could, and from what they had to work with they were able to determine that the handwriting in your book is consistent with Evan's known handwriting. See how he joins certain letters together? And they particularly noticed the 'Hs,'" Pierce pointed from the school forms to the message in Hamlet. In both instances, the "Hs" had been crossed in a single fluid motion that looked like a sideways "v."

"Yeah, you're right! It does look like the same person could have written it," I said, tracing my fingers over the telltale "Hs" and then handing the student forms back to Pierce.

"It's all promising evidence, Ballard. The best we could have hoped for, under the circumstances," Pierce told me.

"Well, thanks for getting it checked out. And for getting it back to me in one piece. Is there anything special I should... um... do with it?" Now that the book had been proven so important, it seemed silly to just bring it home and toss it on my desk.

"Well, don't lose it, whatever the hell you do," Pierce grumbled, shooting a covetous look at the book. "Just... hold onto it. Carefully!"

Taking his words to heart, I wrapped the book gingerly in my scarf and nestled it into my messenger bag. Pierce appeared slightly mollified, as though he was now sure that I wasn't going to start using it as a coaster or something.

"So any luck on tracking down the elusive Hannah?" Pierce asked as he packed up his own belongings.

I shook my head in chagrin. "Nothing. I've checked into every possible lead I could think of and they've all been dead ends. No family members, no classmates who knew him, nothing. And I can't find out anything else about his childhood without stalking his family, and I'm sure the last thing they need is awkward questions that I don't have any believable reason for asking. I'm starting to wonder if I'm looking in the right places."

Pierce looked stumped. "Hmm. Where else is there to look?"

"Short of the yellow pages?"

"Well, you could try asking him yourself," Pierce suggested. "Do you remember last week, the lecture on EVPs?"

"Of course," I replied. I wasn't likely to forget. Electronic Voice Phenomena, EVP for short, were voices that were captured on recording equipment, voices that were not heard by the human ear at the time they were recorded. Pierce had played several EVP sessions for us in class. The investigator conducting it, often Pierce himself, would ask questions hoping to elicit a response from spirits. Some of the "voices" captured had been pretty garbled and hard to make out, making the evidence pretty unconvincing. But others had very clearly spoken words that the entire class had been able to recognize. The most frightening one of all had been a harsh, male voice which, when Pierce asked, "Would you like us to leave you alone?" had responded unmistakably with, "Leave or I'll kill you!" It was pretty impossible to explain away.

Pierce opened his briefcase and extracted a little black voice recorder, identical to the ones he'd shown us in class. It was no bigger than a cell phone.

"Why don't you start fooling around with this, see if anything comes up?"

"What do you mean, fool around?"

"You know, let it run, ask questions, see if you get any responses."

"I'm not sure if—"

"—I know you think he's avoiding you. Maybe he is. But he's drawn to you, Ballard, there's no denying it. Even if he won't show himself, he could still be hanging around, and this might be a way to find out."

I stared at the little device doubtfully.

"Look, I'll even analyze it for you. You don't even have to listen to it, unless I find something relevant, okay?"

I took the recorder. "Okay."

Pierce tossed his briefcase down and hopped up onto the desk, looking me square in the eye. "We may have another opportunity to make contact, too. Ballard, I don't know what you're going to think of this, but I've been thinking about it for a while, and I think I could get permission from the school if we keep it hush-hush."

"Permission to...?"

"Conduct a paranormal investigation of the library," Pierce finished.

"Oh!" I don't know what I was expecting him to say, but it definitely wasn't that.

"What do you think? We could get my entire team together and run the whole gamut of equipment. Then we'll bring you in and see if we can make any sort of contact."

"What would I have to do?"

"In all likelihood, not a whole hell of a lot. Like I said, Evan is drawn to you, so it only makes sense to have you present for the investigation when the goal is to make contact with him. The right stimuli can work wonders when you are trying to instigate paranormal activity."

"And I appear to be the right stimuli."

"In this case, anyway. We haven't had any other reports of him walking abroad, have we? We have to assume he's only appeared to you. So, what do you think?"

"Will it work?"

"There are no guarantees, of course. A majority of paranormal investigations yields nothing. And when we do get something, most of it can be dismissed or explained away. Even some of our most compelling evidence is controversial at best. But wouldn't it be worth a shot, especially if there's a chance we can corroborate your story?"

I considered for a moment what it would feel like to have indisputable evidence of what I had experienced, to have others see what I had seen. There was no denying that the vindication would be sweet.

"Yeah, okay. Let's do it."

"Atta girl!" Pierce gave me a hearty slap to the shoulder blade that almost knocked me over. "I'll start the ball rolling and let you know as soon as I have anything definite. I'll have to do some serious ass-kissing, but it'll be worth it."

I had to agree. It would be.

I decided to wait to tell Tia about the investigation until I had more details. No sense in worrying a compulsive worrier when it may not even happen. When I finally received an email from Pierce at the end of March, explaining that the investigation would be the following week, Tia took it better than I'd expected. She was nervous, of course, but she thought it was a perfect opportunity to find out what we'd both been obsessing over.

Tia was almost as frustrated at our lack of progress on the Hannah-front as I was, and Tia didn't deal well with frustration. She was of the firm belief that, if you worked hard and persisted through trusted means of research, you could always find what you were looking for. When her tried and true methods failed, she only attacked them harder. Tia didn't do failure; I think it was a genetic thing.

But I had a renewed sense of hope in the entire situation. There was a plan, and the more I thought about it, the more I let myself hope that it would work. I was going to see Evan again. I just didn't realize how soon.

§

He was sitting at the foot of my bed. I had the distinct impression that he had been there for quite some time, just waiting for me to wake up. I wasn't startled, as I had been when I'd awakened to find little Peter Mulligan floating in very nearly the same place. No, something had alerted me gently to this presence before I'd even opened my eyes, and when my gaze fell upon him, it was with clear expectation of seeing him there. He nodded his head to me in greeting.

He looked exactly how I had remembered him, my sketch come to life. I would have thought him alive, except for the fact that I could see him so well in the dark. It wasn't that he was glowing; he simply seemed to exist on a different plane, a plane whose brightness illuminated him, almost like a spotlight. I imagined a photo of him being taken on a bright sunny day, and then cutting out his form and pasting him onto a photograph taken at night. That's what it was like.

"Hi, Jess," he said.

"Hi, Evan." I sat up in my bed.

We sat in silence for a moment, looking at each other. He looked a little sad.

"Are you really here?" I asked finally.

"Yes."

"Am I awake?"

"No."

I digested this information. "So I'm dreaming right now."

"Yes. But I really am here. This conversation is really happening."

"Okay." I'd accepted many more far-fetched things than that.

Another moment of silence.

"I thought you were avoiding me, because of what I said in the alleyway."

"I was. But I don't want to do that anymore. I don't want to be a coward. I didn't want to deal with the fact that..."

"You're dead," I finished for him. I hated saying it out loud, but it had to be easier for me than it was for him.

"Yes," he answered, as his calm face drooped into melancholy resignation.

"You're a ghost."

"Not right now. Right now I'm just my own consciousness, talking to your consciousness. I'm not taking any physical form. You're just picturing me this way because you know this is what I look like. This is how I exist, most of the time."

"And the rest of the time?"

"Sometimes I get lonely for people. When you've only got your own thoughts for company it can get pretty maddening."

"I'll bet."

"That's when I become visible. It's not easy. It took me months to figure out how to do it. I gather enough energy to materialize and that's when I can talk to people."

"Why didn't you just tell me what you were?" I asked, a little desperately. "It would have been so much easier if I'd known what you were. I told people about you, Evan. I've been trying to repair the damage for months."

Evan hung his head. "I'm sorry. I never wanted to cause you trouble, Jess, honestly. It's hard to explain, but all those times I talked to you, I wasn't... completely aware of what was happening."

"What do you mean?"

"When I'm like that—visible to people—I'm using all my energy to stay in a physical form. I don't have any capacity left to remember that I'm only pretending to be alive. It's like I'm concentrating so hard on imitating who I was, I forget what I am."

"So when you were talking to me, you... forgot you were dead?"

I couldn't imagine being able to forget something like that. Then again, I couldn't imagine being dead either.

"Yeah, I did. I couldn't help going to the carnival one last time. I wanted to be a normal student again, hanging out in the gift shop and eating in the dining hall. And that night in the library, I saw your paper there and it... brought me back to that moment in my own life. I couldn't resist the urge to go back to it, so I did."

"Because you were lonely?"

"Yeah," he answered. He leaned forward across the bed, his tone a little frantic. "I'm sorry, Jess. I didn't mean to confuse you or... scare you. I know I shouldn't try to relive things like that. But I just know—if I was still alive—that we would be... friends. I could recognize that as soon as I saw you. And I wanted to know what that would feel like. I'm just drawn to you, and I can't explain why. You draw me in. Don't be angry with me, okay?"

"I'm not angry, I promise," I said.

He leaned back again and smiled, relieved.

"How could I be angry, really? That night, at the party..."

Evan's face darkened but he said nothing.

"I know what would have happened if you hadn't been there. Thank you."

"You don't need to thank me."

"Well, maybe you didn't need to hear it, but I needed to say it."

We were both silent for a moment. Then another one of my myriad questions burst from me. "So, have other people seen you before?"

"Yes," he admitted sheepishly.

"A lot of people?"

"Maybe about twenty. None of them ever figured out what I was. I'd never talked to anyone before you, though."

"Why not?" I asked in surprise.

"I don't know. I guess it wasn't enough... just to watch you."

I shivered. I thought of all the times I'd seen him, and realized that he must have been near me much more than that. How many times had he been there, watching me like some kind of invisible companion? And yet, I couldn't help thinking about who I would want to talk to if I were a ghost, and it wasn't some random person I'd never met in life.

"What about your family?"

He shook his head desolately. "I can't."

"Why not?"

"I can't leave the campus."

"You mean you're trapped here?" I had a vision of spectral shackles around his ankles.

"I don't know how it works, but I can't see anything outside the gates of the school. It's like everything goes blurry after that and I don't know where I am. I've tried to go home before, but I can't find my way. I never get very far." His voice was shrouded in nonchalance. I wasn't remotely fooled.

"That's awful, Evan. I'm sorry."

He shrugged. "It's probably better. If I saw them, I don't know if I could stop myself from trying to talk to them. They're having a tough enough time. I can't go haunting them everywhere they go. They'll never get over it."

I slid slowly across the bed and sat next to him. I wanted to comfort him somehow. "I'm glad you spoke to me, Evan. Really. You're right, about what you said before."

"What did I say before?" he asked.

"I think in life we would have... connected." I reached out tentatively and laid my hand on his. It didn't feel cold anymore; it didn't feel like anything. I couldn't register any sensation of his touch. After all, this was only a dream.

He looked down at my hand in surprise and then raised his eyes to my face. An incredibly sorrowful shadow passed over his face and he closed his eyes for a moment. I started to pull my hand away.

"I'm sorry, Evan. I didn't mean to upset—"

"—No," he replied, opening his eyes. His fingers laced through mine and grasped them tightly. The shadow had passed. "Don't apologize. It's okay. It's just hard to think about."

"What is?"

"What it could have been like. With us. If I were still alive."

We sat again in silence, both looking down at our interlocked fingers.

"Evan?"

"Hmm?"

"Are there many of you here? Spirits, I mean? I've seen a few others, but..."

His voice was unexpectedly harsh as he responded. "Yeah. Yeah, there are lots of *us*. It seems to have gotten much more crowded lately."

"Lately?"

"Ever since you got here."

"Why? Why is that?"

"I have no idea."

"Do you think... do you think you're only drawn to me for the same reason they are?" I asked. I couldn't hide the sadness in my voice.

"No," he said immediately. "It's not just the pull you have on us. I feel that too, just like they do, but there's something else. I meant what I said, Jess. We would have connected in life."

We smiled at each other. I could feel my color rising and changed the subject.

"So, it's crowded. But it can't be everyone who's ever died here. I mean, not everybody becomes a ghost, do they?"

"No. From what they tell me, most people don't stay behind."

"Why are you still here?" I didn't know if it was a rude question to ask, but I wanted to know the answer so badly.

The response burst from him, his tone pleading, "I don't know! I'm not supposed to be. Somehow I missed the moment I was supposed to—I don't know what it was! I just remember I could feel a pulling, and part of me wanted to go, but part of me didn't." His voice was rising now. He raked a frantic hand through his hair. "Everything was telling me to just let go and follow whatever it was that was taking me away, but that little part of me just kept clinging on; and then, just as I decided I was going to let go... it had passed. I missed it."

He looked at me with such desperation that I couldn't help myself. I flung my arms around him. He went stiff with surprise, but then he responded, wrapping his arms around my back, winding one of his shaking hands into my hair. I could almost feel him. *"Let this be real, please let this be real!"* It was all I'd wanted from the first time he'd locked me with those eyes. I grasped tighter, willing myself to feel the solidness of his body, the wetness of his tears as they slid from his cheek to my neck. I grabbed his face between my hands and lifted it so that it was an inch from mine. Our eyes met. He understood my intention.

"We won't be able to feel it," he croaked.

"Yes, we will," I whispered fiercely.

He crushed his lips to mine. As he kissed me, my heart thumped wildly. My veins seemed to lift beneath my skin, fighting their way toward the surface. My breath was gone and my ears were ringing. The ringing got louder and louder. The sound was drowning me and I couldn't breathe as I struggled to hold onto him. He was slipping away and the noise was unbearable.

"JESSICA! WAKE UP!"

My eyes flew open and I gasped as my lungs inflated. I actually felt myself land on the bed with a forcible thump. As though I had just resurfaced from deep under water, I gulped the warm air in the room, my lips tingling and cold. The ringing noise continued, deafening me as I fought for breath.

"JESSICA!" Two hands grabbed the front of my sweatshirt and shook me roughly. I focused my eyes in the dark. It was Tia, and she looked positively terrified.

"You were floating!" she yelled over the ringing.

"I... what?" I could barely hear her. I felt feverish. What the *hell* was that ringing?

"You were floating in the air two feet above your bed, for goodness sake!" she repeated as she hoisted me out of the bed onto shaking legs. I still felt unsteady from lack of breath. "Get your shoes on, we have to go!"

"What? Why? What the hell is that noise?"

"It's the fire alarm! Someone pulled it, probably some drunk idiot—Can you walk?" She was practically holding me up.

I steadied myself on my own feet and slipped into my sneakers. "I'm fine. Let's go."

We stumbled down the staircase and out the front door, jostled amidst the crowd of grumbling, sleepy students. The clock tower on Wiltshire Hall read 2:15 AM. We were herded out onto the grass where we waited, shivering, to be let back in. Several guys next to us were shoving each other around and laughing loudly. They smelled like a brewery floor.

Tia was staring at me, still shaken. "What happened?" she murmured in my ear.

I led her away from the crowd to a vacant patch of grass under a massive pine tree. I sank into a sitting position beneath it and she knelt down next to me. I explained about the dream. When I told her about the kiss, she gave a sharp intake of breath, but didn't interrupt me. I felt a pang of guilt and hoped that Evan wouldn't mind that I'd told someone. It suddenly felt very private.

"When he kissed you... was that right at the end of the dream?" she asked.

"Yeah, just before I woke up. We were still kissing when..." Realization hit me. "Did you say I was *floating*?"

"Yes!" Tia hissed. She glanced around to make sure no one could hear her. "The alarm started sounding and I woke up. It scared the life out of me. I looked over and I couldn't believe you were still asleep. I started shouting your name to wake you, but I couldn't. You seemed to be talking in your sleep. And then suddenly you just... stopped breathing."

I gaped at her. I thought back to the breathless drowning feeling I'd experienced.

"Your lips were turning blue and your back was arching right off the bed and then... you just lifted up, blanket and everything. I freaked out, I ran over and grabbed you and shook you. That's when you woke up." Tia's voice broke and shuddered with a barely repressed sob.

"It's okay, Tia. It's okay, I'm fine," I put a comforting arm around her.

"I thought you were dying," she choked.

I just sat with her, rubbing her back until she calmed down. Sirens were sounding and colored lights flashed carnival-bright across the lawn. People were starting to get impatient, jeering at the firefighters and cops for keeping us out of our beds.

"Hey! So who is Hannah?" Tia turned on me, panic obliterated by epiphany.

"What?"

"You were talking to him! You must have asked him who Hannah was! What did he say?"

I felt my heart drop to the vicinity of my knees. I couldn't believe it. He'd been right there, answering all of my questions and I hadn't asked him the one thing I'd been dying to know for months. My face flushed in shame and I couldn't bring myself to meet Tia's eye.

"I didn't ask him," I answered in a small voice.

"You can't be serious! What do you mean you didn't ask him?" she demanded.

"Well, I... just didn't think of it. It all happened so fast, and all of a sudden we were kissing..."

Tia dropped her head into her hands. Her voice came muffled from between her fingers, like she was talking to a toddler. "Jessica. You haven't seen him in months. We've spent countless hours with virtually nothing to go on but a first name, trying to find out what this ghost could possibly want from you. And you 'just didn't think of it?'"

"It was a dream!" my voice grew louder and more defensive, as the weight of my mistake sank in. "I don't think I had any control over what I was saying or what he was saying. It all just... happened."

Tia took a deep breath but seemed to accept my explanation.

"Yeah, I guess you're right. Sorry I snapped at you. I was just hoping you would have found out more, that's all. I guess you'll have another chance soon enough, at the investigation."

I nodded and we fell into silence. I knew that I had lied to Tia, just a little. It *was* only a dream; Evan had told me as much. But it wasn't like a typical dream where I was just along for the ride, drifting wherever my subconscious wanted to take me. I'd been able to think clearly, to make choices. I had to admit that I'd really blown an important opportunity. I resolved that it wouldn't happen again. I knew what the first question was that I needed to ask Evan, if I ever got to see him again. My lips still tingled where they had met his. And there was *that* to discuss, too.

As I gazed over the crowd, something drew my eye to our window. Tia's striped curtain was swaying slightly. Beside it, barely distinguishable at first from the shadows around it, a figure loomed, a solitary hand pressed to the glass.

Evan looked down on me, his face a mask of sorrow. I gazed back until his form melted away again into the darkness.

13

MIXING MEDIUMS

THE NIGHT OF THE PARANORMAL INVESTIGATION had finally arrived. I'd been watching the clock for what I was fairly sure was five or six years as the hand crawled toward 10:30 PM with agonizing sluggishness. Finally I decided to abandon my unread book, and started to get ready.

As soon as I stood up, Tia threw her homework aside. "Jess, are you sure you want to do this?" She was positively dancing with anxiety, her feet flitting about beneath her as though independent of her control.

"No, I wouldn't say I want to. But I do want some answers, and I don't see how else we're going to get them," I said. But I wasn't exactly telling the truth. A part of me, the part that wasn't awash with skepticism or fear, did want to go—to see Evan again, no matter how strange the circumstances.

"At least let me come with you?" Tia asked.

"Ti, I have no idea what I'm supposed to do when I get there. I really don't know how this works. What I do know is that Pierce takes it very seriously and I don't think he'd appreciate my friends tagging along. Besides," I looked up at her as I finished tying my sneaker, "you'd be scared out of your mind."

"Oh, I know, you're right. I'd probably pass out or throw up or something," Tia said, flapping her hands helplessly. "I just hate the thought of you going by yourself."

"I'm not going to be by myself," I pointed out. "There's going to be an entire professional investigative team there with me."

"Oh, you know what I mean!"

"Just try to get some sleep, okay? I'll wake you up in the morning when we're all done."

"Oh, yes, I'll be sleeping like a baby, Jess!" Tia snapped. "Here, wait. Take this with you."

She dropped Pierce's tiny voice recorder into my outstretched hand.

"What do I need this for?" I asked.

"You said he wanted to review whatever you'd recorded on it, to look for evidence."

"Yeah, but I haven't even used it," I said. I'd dropped it onto my desk and forgotten all about it.

Tia grinned a little guiltily.

"Wait a minute. Did *you* use it?" I asked.

"I couldn't resist! It was sitting there, and it was so... scientific. I just ran it for a few hours on a few nights while you were sleeping."

I pocketed the recorder, shaking my head. "I can't believe you did my parapsychology homework."

Tia smiled. "You know me and homework."

I walked quickly across the campus, my head bent against the chill in the early April breeze. Even on the cusp of spring, the wind on the hill stayed stubbornly bitter. I kept the steps of the library in my sights and forced myself to march forward, though everything, even the wind, seemed to be encouraging me in the other direction.

I'd made up my mind not to tell Pierce about my dream encounter with Evan. I felt guilty about it, because I knew that Evan had given me information about ghosts that Pierce would kill to know. After all that Pierce had done for me, I really did owe it to him to keep him in the loop. But I couldn't make myself care about that when I thought about the privacy of the conversation, the intimacy of it. Didn't I owe it to Evan to keep my mouth shut? After all, I'd told Tia and immediately regretted it. No, I wouldn't tell Pierce, not yet anyway, and certainly not all of it.

The doors of the library were locked tightly. A boldly worded sign proclaimed that the floors were being waxed. The campus looked deserted, except for a pair of underdressed girls jogging hurriedly across the sidewalk. I could hear one complaining loudly about the library being closed.

"You'd think they'd wait until the summer to do that kind of stuff," she said, clutching her books to her as though they might warm her. I wondered what kind of strings Pierce had to pull to get the library to close its venerable doors against even a single night of academic enlightenment—it wasn't St. Matt's style.

I pulled out my cell phone and called Pierce.

He answered after a single ring. "You here, Ballard?"

"Yeah, I'm outside."

"I'll send Iggy to let you in. Anyone around?"

I glanced behind me. The two scorned studiers had vanished. "Nope."

"Alright, hang tight, he'll be right out." He hung up immediately. His tone was brusque, but excited at the same time. I had a feeling I was about to see Pierce in his true element.

I bounced on the spot for a few seconds, trying to keep warm, until the shadowy form of Iggy appeared in the frosted glass surface of the doors, amorphous at first, then solidifying into the very defined shape of a very large man. There was the clinking of a key in a lock and the right-hand door opened.

"Jess?" Iggy poked a heavily bearded face around the door frame. Did all of Pierce's friends look like displaced hippies?

"Uh, yeah," I said, trying to smile.

"Welcome to the party!" Iggy smiled back, revealing a large space between his front teeth. He pulled the door open and stepped back to let me in. He was every bit as big as his shadow had implied, at least six foot four, with broad shoulders and a very round stomach that was testing the elasticity limit of his Grateful Dead T-shirt. A worn purple bandana was tied around his head and several faded, greenish tattoos peeked out from under his sleeves. He wouldn't have looked out of place at a biker joint, except that he was so obviously friendly.

"Thanks," I said, as he held out a massive, callused paw for me to shake.

"So, you're the ghost girl, huh?" Iggy asked as we walked past the circulation desk to the main reading room.

"Is that what they're calling me now?"

"Naw, don't worry, I'm just teasin' ya. Pierce filled us in on the background of the investigation and all, and he told us you were gonna join us. Should be fun, huh?"

I just shrugged in response. The idea that this little adventure could be anything but terrifying or disappointing hadn't really occurred to me—fun was about the furthest thing from my mind.

"So you've actually seen a full-bodied apparition, huh?" Iggy asked.

"Unfortunately, yes. Several times."

"That's wild, man! I hope that means we'll get one tonight! I've only ever seen free-form stuff, and a few shadow forms, too." Iggy was looking at me with totally undeserved admiration.

The library reading room looked like a high tech stake-out. Two of the large tables had been pushed together in the middle of the room and were buried in wires, laptops and a number of closed-circuit television monitors. They must have been using every outlet in the place; there were orange extension cords snaking out in every direction like the roots of some crazy technological tree. Lined up on a third table were a number of gadgets I couldn't even identify. Pierce was leaning over the table, deep in conversation with a lanky younger guy. There were two other men setting up video cameras.

"Glad you could make it, Ballard!" Pierce said as he looked up. His eyes were aglow like a kid's at Christmas.

"Well, there was a kegger at the dorm, but I decided to skip it," I said.

"Good call. This is going to be way more fun than some drunken dorm party, I can guarantee you that!"

What was it with these guys and *fun*? It was like they didn't even appreciate the fact that we were about to spend the night in the company of dead people—by choice.

"Let me introduce you to everyone, and then I can give you the lowdown on the plan for tonight." Pierce took me by the shoulder and started steering me around the room, introducing me to his group one by one. The youngest team member, the one Pierce had been talking to when I walked in, was Dan, a recent MIT grad who was only a few years older than I was. He sat stationed at the tech table, barely looking up when Pierce spoke. Instead, he gave a half-hearted flicking gesture over his shoulder that seemed simultaneously to say "hello" and "don't bother me." He wore dark-framed glasses and his hair had the disheveled appearance of one who had just rolled out of bed.

"Dan is our tech specialist. He coordinates our technological components and makes sure that everything is running smoothly from one central location. He has live feeds to all of our video cameras and audio hook-ups to all our team members while the investigation is going on. And this is Neil Caddigan."

A slight man fumbling with the video camera looked up quickly and gave me an appraising glance which quickly jerked into a nervous smile. He extended a pale, blue-veined hand out to shake mine.

"Hi, Neil, nice to meet you."

"Charmed, Ms. Ballard. Very interested to work with you tonight. Very interested, indeed." Neil's voice undulated forth on the wake of a very refined-sounding British accent. His protuberant eyes were a strange, milky-blue color reminiscent of blindness. His stare made me uneasy; it had a vaguely hungry quality that was unsettling.

"Neil has just joined the team, while researching here in the U.S. He's a theologian and professor in London. He's been working on a book about hauntings of former religious sites, and St. Matt's used to be the site of a monastery. He's also a demonologist," Pierce said.

"You study...?"

"Demons. Yes, indeed," Neil said with a little bow, his eyes never leaving mine. He didn't seem to need to blink.

I must have been staring, because Pierce felt the need to clarify as he led me away. "Obviously, there are many religious beliefs that can be called into question in a field like this. Theologians are sometimes drawn to paranormal investigation as a means of further researching what we can gather about the theory of life after death. Surely you can see the appeal."

There was a sudden and insurmountable closing of my throat and I temporarily lost the ability to swallow, so I just nodded in response and tried to look calm. I didn't fool Pierce in the least.

"Ballard, we don't think there are any demons here. Seriously. Demon-free zone."

I tried to breathe.

Lastly, Pierce introduced Oscar, who shook my hand so hard he nearly dislocated my arm. Oscar looked like he'd just leapt from the deck of a barnacled fishing vessel. His face was covered in white stubble, and his skin looked several sizes too big for him, hanging loose under his chin and at his elbows. I wouldn't have been surprised to see a wooden peg leg sticking out from his battered jeans: Captain of the S. S. Paranormal.

"Jesus, Piercey, she looks like she's gonna yack. You sure she's up for this?" Oscar asked, eyeing me beadily.

"She'll be fine." Pierce said.

"I'm fine," I repeated, parrot-like.

"Oscar took me on my first paranormal investigation when I was a high school student. Bought me my first camcorder, helped me capture my first paranormal footage. We've been investigating together ever since." Pierce slapped Oscar fondly on the shoulder blade. Oscar grinned, revealing a gold tooth. "He also happens to be a New England historian, so that comes in rather handy on the research end of things."

"All kinds of sordid tidbits to dig up on this place. Had a field day with this one." Oscar winked. I was intrigued in spite of myself. Sordid tidbits at St. Matt's? It didn't seem possible.

"Okay, okay, we'll get to all of that. Let's not taint the sensitive, alright?" Pierce said. Oscar merely shrugged and went back to his camera.

Pierce led me back to the tech table where we waited for everyone to finish with their set-up work and then, when all the team members had gathered, Pierce laid out the game plan.

"Okay, Ballard, here's how this will work. This team has conducted quite a few paranormal investigations together and over time we've developed a system that we feel works fairly well to meet the challenges we're most likely to face. First of all, besides our live investigators tonight, we've got quite a bit of surveillance going on."

Pierce gestured to the television screens that were stacked like Tetris blocks on Dan's tech table. "It's important to back our personal experiences with visual and auditory evidence. That's where all this technological shit comes in."

"Technological shit? Is that an industry term?" I asked with a smirk.

Pierce chose to ignore me and went on, "So, the entire library has been rigged with HD video equipment, which has already begun recording. There are three cameras on each of the three floors of the library, positioned to cover as much area as possible."

I studied the dim gray displays on the monitors. I could make out the main circulation desk in the bottommost corner, the central staircase, and the corridor outside the bathrooms on the basement level. I also recognized, with a start, the carrels in the back of the Russian literature section, where I'd spoken to Evan. The view sent a shiver down my spine. The rest of the video screens were practically interchangeable, revealing cramped aisles of books bordered by nearly-identical groupings of desks.

"The cameras will be running all night. Dan will be stationed here, running communication with the team and monitoring the surveillance equipment. If an unmanned area starts showing some activity, Dan can alert us and we can get a team over there. Anything that shows up on the monitors will be documented in our log book, to be examined later. Hopefully, if there's anything to be seen, the cameras will catch it."

At this point Dan sat up straighter in his chair, as though to emphasize the importance of his role in this whole process.

"The other members of the team will be breaking into pairs to investigate the library. Each pair will have their own equipment to work with. First, every pair will carry an infrared camera, which will be used to visually document the experience. Since the audio on those cameras leaves much to be desired in the way of quality, each pair will also carry a wireless audio recorder to pick up any sounds, voices, or other auditory phenomena they might encounter. Finally, each group will also carry an EMF detector. This will alert you to any electromagnetic anomalies in the atmosphere."

"Sorry, you lost me at EMF. What exactly does that thing do?" I asked. Dan sighed dramatically. I shot him a nasty look, but otherwise ignored him. I couldn't afford to feign understanding; what if someone handed me one of those things and expected me to know what to do with it?

"Remember how we talked about energy in class?"

"Not likely to forget it, actually."

"Right. Well, everything has energy, and many objects have electromagnetic energy that is measurable. That's what the EMF detector does. Usually the kinds of things that have EMF readings are wiring, electronic devices, things like that. But there is a theory that ghosts use electromagnetic energy from the atmosphere around them in order to manifest themselves. The EMF detector can tell if there is a concentration of electromagnetic energy in an area. If we can't trace it to any material source, then it could be a sign of paranormal activity."

"And am I going to have to work one of these things?" I asked. "Because I inexplicably render most gadgets useless just by coming into contact with them. Kiss of death, I'm not kidding."

Dan shifted his chair protectively toward his toys.

Pierce laughed and shook his head. "We'll handle the equipment, don't worry."

"And what exactly am I supposed to handle?" I asked.

"You reel in the ghosts, girlie," Oscar replied as he limped by.

This was what I was afraid of. Was I expected to deliver on some sort of macabre party trick? Pierce read my mind and cut in before I could respond.

"We haven't really tested Ballard's abilities as a medium yet. She hasn't been aware of them long enough to thoroughly gauge them, or to understand how to get in tune with them. So she's just going to be here as bait, so to speak. The ghosts—or this one at least—seem to be attracted to her without any real effort on her part. Her presence alone should be an advantage here."

"We set the bait and see what bites. I like it!" Oscar cackled. Seriously, the fishing metaphors were *not* helping me separate him from Captain Ahab in my brain.

"So, then it's just going to be luck, whether I walk into the right part of the library at the right time?" I asked. It sounded like we were leaving an awful lot up to chance.

"Well, by splitting up we'll be able to cover more ground, have a better chance of tracking signs of activity. And the equipment will be our eyes and ears in even more locations. But still, I thought of that, so I asked Annabelle to join the group tonight. She's coming from her shop, so she should be here any minute."

A satisfied murmur went through the group of men, who obviously approved of this unexpected addition.

"Who's Annabelle?" I asked.

"She's a good friend of mine, a medium who lives locally. She's got a pretty powerful sense, great for locating concentrations of energy," Pierce said.

"When she hones in on a spot, there's a damn good chance that we'll get some action," Iggy added. Oscar grunted his approval.

"She should be here any—" Pierce was interrupted by a sharp rap on the door. "And that's probably her."

Iggy got up and trotted out to let her in. He appeared moments later not with the expected Annabelle, but with...

"Sam!" I cried.

"Jess?" Sam looked even more shocked to see me than I felt to see him. For a moment we just stared at one another.

"Hey, Sam, what's up?" Pierce asked sharply, rising from his seat.

Sam's startled face snapped to Pierce's and he seemed to recover. "Oh, Professor, you left these audio recorders in your office. These are the new ones that just came in. I figured you'd want to use them for the investigation," Sam said as he handed Pierce a small cardboard box. His eyes kept flitting over to me in confusion.

"Thanks, Sam, you're right. I'd forgotten these had come in. I appreciate your running them over," Pierce said.

"No problem. I'll um... see you tomorrow, I guess," Sam replied, still looking at me. I could feel my face reddening as I turned deliberately from his perplexed stare and feigned interest in a television monitor.

"Be up to my lab around 7:30 tomorrow morning at the latest. There's going to be a lot of material to review, and I need everything set up and ready for analysis by noon," Pierce said.

"Sure, no problem," Sam agreed, and without another word to me, he turned on his heel and left.

Great. Yet another thing I was going to have to explain to Sam that had no logical explanation. Except the truth, of course, which was just about the least logical thing I could think of.

Just as Sam's lanky figure disappeared around the corner, another figure took his place. It was a woman with familiar wild hair and a gypsy profile. The sight of her ejected me from my chair like an electric shock. "Oh, you have *got* to be kidding me!"

Only Dan seemed to have heard me. The rest of the team was up out of their seats to greet her. I just stood there, gaping. Annabelle was Madame Rabinski, the fortune teller from the carnival.

If my reaction was negative, it was nothing compared to hers. After flashing a wide toothy smile around the group of men, shaking hands and exchanging greetings, her eyes found me. As though I were a rabid pit bull instead of an aggravated teenager, she stepped backwards at the sight of me and tried to shield herself with Iggy's massive body. "What is this, David? What the hell is she doing here?" Annabelle shouted. Her expression was wild, and I momentarily forgot my annoyance as I realized that she was looking at me with unadulterated fear in her eyes.

It took Pierce's startled response for me to realize that she was addressing him; I'd only ever heard him called by his last name.

"Annabelle, what... do you two know each other?" he asked.

Annabelle ignored the question and continued glaring at me. "Why didn't you tell me about this?" she demanded.

"I told you there was going to be another possible medium! That was the whole reason I wanted you here, remember? What the hell is wrong with you?"

"What's wrong with me? Why would you bring her into this?" Annabelle shot back, defensive enough to step out from behind Iggy, who looked just as lost as Pierce.

Pierce turned to me, eyebrows raised.

I found my voice, not to mention my own anger. "Yeah, we've met, actually. She was scamming people with tarot cards at the fall carnival."

"*Scamming* people? How dare you—"

"—And she decided to try out some of her more theatrical

tendencies on me while my roommate was getting her fortune told." I made little quotation marks in the air, infusing my last two words with as much sarcasm as I could manage.

Annabelle opened her mouth to argue and then snapped it shut again. With her nose in the air, as though she was above addressing me again, she turned herself around to face Pierce.

"I did meet this girl at the carnival. And yes, I was giving tarot card readings, David, as you know I do. She entered my tent with her friend and completely disrupted the fields. I could hardly hear myself think."

I snorted and rolled my eyes. She looked daggers at me.

"What do you mean?" Pierce asked. He had that familiar note of scholarly interest in his voice, the traitor.

"I *mean*, I couldn't even pick up on the other girl. I was getting so many conflicting energies, so many life forces at once, that I couldn't focus on a single life to read the cards for. I was getting readings that completely contradicted themselves."

I noticed Neil perking up in interest, his pale eyes gleaming queerly.

Pierce frowned. "And you're sure it was Jess that was causing—"

"—Yes, of course I'm sure!" Annabelle snapped. "She was all but pulsating with it! As soon as she'd left, the atmosphere was instantly cleared. I can still sense a very strong spiritual presence around her now! And it's not pretty, David."

Everyone was suddenly staring at me like I was something fascinating stuck to the bottom of a petri dish.

"Professor, you're not actually buying this, are you?" I asked, but couldn't quite manage the proper tone of incredulity. My recent experiences were starting to give Annabelle's words an eerie ring of truth.

"Well, I trust Annabelle, if that's what you mean." Pierce turned back to Annabelle, whose untamed hair was practically crackling with anger. "Annabelle, I know that strange things are happening with Jess. She does, too. That's why she came to see me. That's why we've been working together. There's no point in running this investigation without her because she's the reason we're here."

Annabelle's eyes darted back and forth between me and Pierce, but she did not interrupt him.

"Now, if you don't want to stay, that's just fine. You can go, and I'm sorry if I've upset you. But it would be a big help to me if you stayed. Jess doesn't understand her abilities yet, and I think you might be able to help; that you might even *want* to help, given what you've sensed about her."

"Are you sure she'd accept the help of a *fraud* like me?" Annabelle sneered at me.

"I would think," Pierce answered for me, "that she would accept the help of anyone who might be able to help her understand what's happening to her."

I opened my mouth to reply, but my supply of sarcasm and bitter retorts had dried up. A lot had changed since I'd first set eyes on Madame Rabinski and her battered tarot cards. Hell, my whole damn world had been turned upside down. And as much as I hated to admit it, my own personal experiences had become even less believable than any carnival trick. Did my old prejudices even make sense anymore? Could I really doubt Annabelle's abilities after discovering my own? I felt myself deflate.

"You're right, Professor," I said quietly. I turned to Annabelle. "I'm sorry."

Annabelle said nothing, but after a moment of tapping her foot and glaring, she took off her coat and threw it on a chair. "Well, who's going to fill me in, then? Let's get this show on the road."

Oscar took this task on enthusiastically, launching into a description of everything they knew about Evan using Pierce's familiar battered notebook. Iggy distracted me by requesting some data. He held up a couple of complex-looking gadgets.

"Will it hurt?" I asked.

"Not unless you wrestle it away from him and beat yourself with it," Dan said, not taking his eyes off his computer screens.

"Charming," I muttered.

"Naw, they won't even touch you. They only record the atmosphere around you," Iggy promised.

He started running one of those EMF thingies up and down me like a security guard at an airport. His eyes widened as he stared at it and, with a low whistle, he then recorded whatever it told him into a spreadsheet, noting the time and exact area of the building in which we were standing.

"What?" I asked nervously. "Is it bad?"

"You are a walking EMF magnet, kiddo. Off the charts," Iggy said, looking at me like a long-anticipated Christmas gift. Then he picked up another item and held it up to show me.

"This is a thermal imaging camera. This part," Iggy explained, holding out a device that looked like a little security camera with a handle, "is used to scan the room to measure temperatures of different objects. Then we can watch for temperature fluctuations here." This time he showed me a little portable screen, black at the moment. "Watch this."

He pushed a red button with his massive thumb and the screen flickered to life. It was one of the oddest images I'd ever seen. As Iggy panned the room with the little camera, the screen reflected it back, but in a crazy, psychedelic spectrum of colors.

"Trippy," I said, watching the colors pulse and move.

"The colors represent the range of temperatures in the room," Iggy said. "The blue end of the spectrum is cooler, and the temperature increases as the spectrum approaches red, which shows the hottest temperatures. People and other living things appear in red, because of the body heat, see? When we get an unexpected heat signature, we call that a hot spot."

"And what does heat have to do with ghosts?" I asked.

"You're in Pierce's class, aren't you?"

"Yeah, but he never mentioned anything about heat."

"Sure, but I'll bet he was yammerin' on about energy," Iggy said with another gap-toothed grin.

"Just a little," I said.

"I don't yammer, asshole!" Pierce shouted from across the room.

"Supersonic hearing, that one," Neil muttered, rolling his oddly luminous eyes. I jumped at his voice; I hadn't heard him approach us.

"Anyway," Iggy plowed on, ignoring everyone else, "that means you've already heard the theory about spirits borrowing energy from their surroundings to manifest?"

"Yes." Evan had taught me that much.

"Well, that energy can take many forms. Sometimes, it can be electrical energy, such as from wiring or batteries. Other times it can be thermal energy, or energy in the form of heat." He tapped the glass of the screen again as he scanned the room and stopped on the strange, colorful image of Dan sitting at command central. He appeared in red, which feathered to orange and yellow, as did many of the machines around him. "See? Living people have lots of thermal energy. So do electronics and lots of other things, besides. A spirit can sap that energy in order to show itself."

I nodded my understanding, but suppressed a shiver. When I thought of the icy coldness of Evan's touch, I couldn't imagine heat having anything to do with it. I didn't mention this to Iggy, however, and let him carry on with his thermal doohickey.

Finally, our initial data was gathered and it was time to begin.

§

I could feel my nerves starting to jangle, like an out-of-tune piano some toddler was banging the hell out of. I gathered with the rest of the group, silhouetted in the slightly greenish glow of the night vision monitors. Pierce was reviewing everyone's instructions.

"Okay, kids, here's the deal. First of all, we need to remember that Jess has never done this before, so we need to explain everything, be explicit in our instructions, so she feels comfortable."

Pierce nodded at me in a reassuring way. I smiled weakly.

"We're splitting up into pairs so that no one is ever investigating alone. All pairs will keep in touch with one another using walkie-talkies. Don't put it down anywhere, or you'll be stuck without com and it will be harder to find you if you need... something," Pierce edited. I was pretty sure he was going to say "help."

Dan started tossing walkie-talkies around the circle. He did not throw one to me. Maybe he figured I wouldn't be able to catch it.

Pierce deftly caught his radio and continued, "We'll be covering as many floors of the library simultaneously as we can. Oscar and Neil, you take the basement. Iggy, you and Annabelle take the ground level starting in the main reading room. Jess and I will take the upper floor, including the stacks where the first sighting occurred. Dan will take the first shift at central command and watch the monitors. All suspicious hits, or anything Annabelle picks up on, should be radioed directly to me so we can get Jess over there as quickly as possible."

For some reason, Annabelle glowered at me. Bristling, I glared right back at her. What the hell was that, some kind of medium jealousy? I bet she was usually the one they radioed for in these situations. Well, she was welcome to it. I opened my mouth to tell her so, but just as quickly as the expression had appeared, she neutralized it. She was now looking over at Pierce, who was addressing her.

"Annabelle, did Oscar go over the entire file on Evan Corbett?"

Annabelle nodded her mane regally.

"So, you know what you're looking for?"

"Yes."

"Great. And please remember everyone, we can't rule out other spirit activity. This library is old and this is not the first reported sighting this campus has had, not by a long shot. Keep eyes and ears peeled and stay safe. Every pair make sure to take along an audio recorder, thermal, and camcorder. Every team member should have a flashlight."

Pierce handed a flashlight and the audio recorder to me. It was identical to the one he'd given me to test out EVPs in my dorm room, which reminded me that I still had the thing in my pocket.

"Oh, here, Professor. There's some stuff for you to go through on this," I told him, handing it over.

"Great! Do you think you got anything?" he asked, depositing it onto the tech table.

"I don't know. I was asleep. My roommate took some initiative and played detective," I admitted.

"Oh. I haven't met this girl, but I think I like her!" he said. Then he turned back to the waiting team. "Okay, everyone, fan out. Dan, let's go lights-out."

14

SHADOWS COME OUT TO PLAY

THE LIBRARY WAS PLUNGED INTO DARKNESS. I stayed where I was until my eyes began to adjust and the black receded to shades of gray, helped along by the dim light of the monitors. Flashlight beams cut swathes of visibility and bounced along as pairs headed toward their assigned locations.

"Ready, Ballard?" Pierce asked. His voice was calm on the surface, but there was an undercurrent of excitement bubbling beneath it.

"Ready as I'm gonna be," I said as stoutly as I could. I was very glad to be paired up with him instead of someone I barely knew.

We walked slowly and carefully in the direction of the main staircase. The circulation desk looked particularly creepy as the flashlight beams rippled across it. I had an unexpected flash of a childhood memory of the phantom librarian from an old VHS tape of the movie *Ghostbusters* that I'd watched until it wouldn't rewind anymore; I had to suppress a slightly hysterical giggle. Luckily, Pierce didn't notice. He had begun a thermal sweep, panning the camera back and forth across the path in front of us.

We ascended the staircase, the ancient wooden banister creaking ominously as we leaned on it. It was easy to see how people could get freaked out even in buildings devoid of ghosts. Shadows played tricks on our eyes, shape-shifting and darting in the wavering beams from our flashlights. Every little sound was enough to make me jump. I stayed just behind Pierce, letting him lead the way.

When we finally arrived in the wide, tiled hallway at the top of the stairs, Pierce stopped so abruptly that I almost walked right into him. He swept the entire area slowly from right to left with the thermal camera, and then holstered it onto his belt. He pulled out an EMF detector identical to the one Iggy had used on me. He turned and pointed it at me like I was some TV program he wanted to mute. A slow grin spread over his face.

"Iggy's right, you are an EMF factory!"

"You sure know how to flatter a girl."

"Sorry, couldn't resist," Pierce said, and turned away from me. "Do me a favor and stay at the top of the stairs, would you? You'll contaminate my field."

"Right," I said, trying not to be offended.

"And if you, y'know, sense anything or see anything, just let me know," Pierce added.

"Yeah, about that. Is there something special I should be doing?"

Pierce turned back around. "Just do what you did in class with the doll and the other objects we tested. Just try to clear your mind and be receptive. If there's anything here, it's likely to come to you."

I stood in my assigned location and tried to clear my mind, but it wasn't easy to do with Pierce creeping around like a cat burglar. It was much more interesting to watch him at work, so that's what I did. When he had walked the entire perimeter of the space and returned to where I was standing, he pocketed the EMF detector and sighed.

"It's reading pretty flat right now. Why don't we try an EVP session?"

I pulled the recorder from its spot, safely wedged in my back pocket. I held it out for Pierce to take, but he shook his head.

"Why don't you take lead on this, Ballard? Just remember to state the day, time, location, and team members present before you start."

"Okay," I replied uneasily. I'd heard the stating done on the other recordings we'd heard in class. I knew it was done to help organize and pinpoint activity. I was pretty sure I could handle that much.

I walked to the middle of the room and plopped down on the area rug. Setting the recorder on the ground in front of me, I pressed the record button and watched the little red light flash to life.

I took a deep breath. "Investigation of the Culver Library, March twenty-ninth. Location is the second floor, foyer. Dr. David Pierce and Jessica Ballard investigating. It is 11:07 PM. EVP session starting now." I looked over at Pierce and he smiled approvingly.

After a brief pause I asked, "What is your name?"

My voice echoed a little against the austere wainscoting and vaulted ceiling. I waited a few seconds to allow for a response, just like Pierce had taught us.

"How long have you been here?"

180

Silence.

I reminded myself that it was to be expected; the very nature of an EVP meant that we wouldn't hear it until we played back the tape. Still, I felt a little silly as I continued.

"How did you die?"

I listened intently. And then, a small cold breeze brushed the back of my neck. Gasping, I whipped my head around and stared into the blackness. I couldn't see anything.

"Ballard, what happened? Did you hear something?" Pierce hissed.

"No, I... it was just a draft, I think," I said. But no draft had ever made my heart leap into my throat like that. I clutched the back of my neck protectively with my hand: The hairs were raised and the skin was covered with goose bumps.

"Do you need me to come over there?"

"No, I'm okay," I said, and I was. My fear, surprisingly, had given way to curiosity. Had that been a draft, or something else?

Collecting myself, I asked my next question. "Did you just breathe on the back of my neck?"

Nothing happened.

"Why are you still here?"

My question was followed by what was unmistakably a derisive laugh, silvery and clear, from just behind me. This time, I tried not to move, though my instincts were screaming at me to run. Pierce, who had not responded, obviously heard nothing. I couldn't tell if I recognized the voice. Could it possibly be Evan? I didn't think so. I took a deep steadying breath and said quietly to Pierce, "Have you got the camera?"

"Yeah. You want it?"

"No. Just do me a favor and take some pictures right now. Concentrate on the area behind me."

I kept my eyes trained on the opposite wall, and sat very still. Trying to keep my voice from trembling, I asked, "Evan? Is that you?"

Another laugh, louder this time.

I frowned with concentration. This didn't feel right, it didn't sound like him. I kept my tone light. "Did I say something funny?"

Only the frantic clicking of the camera broke the silence. I could feel the air behind me growing colder by the second, as though I were standing with my back to an open freezer. My whole body grew chilled.

"Pierce, use the thermal!" I said. I heard Pierce fumbling to unholster the thermal camera, heard the beeping that meant it was turning on.

"Holy shit," Pierce whispered. "Ballard, don't move. It's right behind you."

"I *know*," I hissed back. My breath formed a little puff of steam in front of me.

"I asked you why you're still here!" I repeated.

"I've been waiting for you."

The voice shivered right beside my ear, and I knew this wasn't the voice I'd been longing to hear. This was someone else, someone I didn't know.

§

"PIERCEY! PIERCEY! We got a hit on the basement level!" Oscar's gravelly voice shouted over the two-way radio. I scrambled in a panic up off the rug. The sound had scared the life out of both of us and, I realized a moment later, severed the communication with whatever had been behind me. I could sense right away that it was gone; the heat that had been sucked from the atmosphere came gushing back over me as though an invisible dam had been holding it at bay.

"Okay, Oscar, we'll be right down," Pierce said into his radio. Then he turned to look at me, his face aglow with excitement. "What happened just now?"

"Someone was answering my questions from right behind me."

"Well, hell, I could tell *where* it was. Have a look at this." Pierce waved me over and began fiddling with the camera.

"What, did you catch something?"

I peered over Pierce's arm at the little digital camera screen. The image it displayed was of me just moments ago, cross-legged on the floor, mouth open in mid-sentence. Behind me was a strange white shape that looked eerily familiar. It was just like the shapes that had appeared in the Polaroid photo Sam took of me on my first day at St. Matt's. But, unlike that photo, when the misty cloud had taken no identifiable shape, this time the cloudy form of a human figure crouched just behind me, the profile and limbs clearly defined, down to the fingers outstretched as though to caress the back of my head.

"Shit."

"You said it," Pierce whispered under his breath. He scanned through the images he had taken in rapid succession. It was like watching a flip book. The figure's hand reached closer and closer toward me until the moment that the radio had gone off. At that moment the head of the figure had actually turned and looked directly at the spot where Pierce had been standing, as though the sound of the radio had only just alerted it to his presence. It was already fading away, the doorway behind it clearly visible.

"I've never seen anything like it, not in over three hundred investigations." Pierce's face was mirroring my own feelings. We had been very close to something and it had slipped through our fingers. He was clearly disappointed. I was somewhat relieved, and yet now that the fear had passed I was exhilarated. The investigation had only just started. What would happen next?

The truth was, not much for a good long time. As Pierce had warned, real paranormal investigation was about one percent action and ninety-nine percent mind-numbing boredom.

Oscar's "hit" on the basement level turned out to be nothing more than a well-concealed circuitry box that was making his EMF detector go haywire. When Pierce showed him what we'd captured upstairs, his jaw dropped.

"Why the hell didn't you just ignore me?" Oscar asked. "Nothing we were getting could possibly have compared to that!"

"No point, old man. Your call scared it away, whatever it was," Pierce replied. It was a testament to his affection for his mentor that he kept the bitterness in his voice to a bare minimum. Oscar looked appropriately ashamed at this news, and offered to head up with his equipment and blanket the area. Pierce let him, but I knew whatever was up there was gone. If it was going to show up again, I realized, it was going to be wherever I was.

Eager to review the footage further, Pierce suggested we head down to central command. The picture quality on the monitors was far superior to the tiny little camera screen, but the creepy-factor rose in proportion to the clarity of the image; by the time Dan had blown up the photos and fiddled with the contrast, I could barely look at it. Pierce, however, was eagerly analyzing and picking out details.

"The form seems male to me," Pierce said, his finger tracing it on the screen. "The face seems almost to have a shadow here, like a beard or something."

"The voice sounded male, too," I said. "But if it's male, what's with the dress?"

"Yeah, I noticed that too. The bottom of the garment has a flowing shape to it, like a gown or a cape or something."

"Or a robe," Neil suggested, making me jump out of my skin again. He was right behind me, leaning over toward the screen.

"Seriously, stop doing that!" I cried, throwing my hands up. "Can't you clear your throat or drag your feet or something? You're like a goddamn ninja!"

"Pardon?" Neil asked, brow furrowed. Apparently he didn't get my reference. Dan was snorting amusedly, but Pierce seemed not to have noticed the exchange. He was studying the picture further.

"A robe, huh? Yeah, I can see that," he said.

"The shape of the sleeve supports it, too," Neil continued, sliding into the seat beside Dan, and pointing with the tip of a pen. "It hangs down here, too wide for a typical shirt or coat. And see the slight bulge at the back? It looks like it could be a hood."

"A robed figure in the library. Hmm. I guess that would make sense," Pierce said.

"Um, how does that make sense? Why would anyone wear a robe in a library?" I asked.

Neil pulled a pile of files toward him and beckoned me over to him. "It makes sense because of the history of the library building itself. It is built on the site of an old monastery, so there is always the possibility that what you saw was the spirit of a monk, tied to the area from hundreds of years ago."

Somehow, an ancient monk didn't fit my vague perception of the presence that had spoken to me, but I listened. Anything was possible at this point.

"Or there was the Swords Brotherhood, which would be much more recent," Pierce suggested, and then turned to explain before I could even frame the obvious question. "They were this secret society on campus, back at the beginning of the 1900s, when the school was still an all-male institution. It was kind of like the Skull and Bones at Yale, a privileged fraternity of sorts. Not many records of its activities exist, but we know that it met in this building."

"A secret society? Wow, I didn't think this could get much weirder," I murmured, but something about it fit. I was finally starting to understand what Pierce had meant all those weeks ago when he'd first spoken of the vague certainty of the sixth sense. I hadn't seen the ghost with my own eyes, nor had he said anything to confirm or deny the idea of the Swords Brotherhood, but something in me was whispering that this was right. Instead of trying to ignore this whispering, I decided to start listening to it.

"Neil, you start going through those files and see if the photos can offer anything concrete on either possibility," Pierce said.

"Focus on that brotherhood. That's the right track," I added.

Pierce turned to look at me. His expression was surprised, but pleased. "You feel confident about that, Ballard?"

I nodded solemnly.

"Good. Good for you." Pierce unholstered his radio and called all of the teams back to central command to regroup. From the depths of the library, bouncing flashlight beams led the investigators back to us. Batteries were changed, equipment was swapped out, and memory cards were emptied with impressive efficiency onto Dan's computers. Pierce decided to reorganize as we entered into the second phase of the investigation. We all chugged some of Pierce's atomic-blend coffee, but I didn't feel particularly tired, despite the fact that it was now approaching three o'clock, a time Neil eagerly referred to as "the witching hour."

"I think we should refocus our energies on some new areas of the building we haven't covered yet, especially the stacks where Ballard had her encounter with Evan's spirit. That okay with you?" he asked me.

"Sure," I agreed. "I'm gonna run to the ladies' room first, though."

"Okay, everyone. We'll head back out in five," Pierce said.

My flashlight lit the way to the nearest bathroom, which was in the entry hall just beyond the circulation desk. I instinctively flipped the light switch when I entered the room, but then remembered that Dan had killed the power from the circuit breakers. So instead, I stood my flashlight up in the center of the tiled floor, casting a dim circle of light onto the ceiling and creating just enough illumination to see by.

Every sound echoed hollowly off the tile and unusually high ceiling, and I finished quickly, eager to get out of there. I was just refastening the walkie-talkie to my belt when I felt it: A creeping sensation beginning at my toes and crawling like insects up my legs and spine.

Swallowing back the fear, I slid the catch on the door of the stall and poked my head out into the bathroom. Nothing. No shapes, no shadows that couldn't be explained by the inanimate objects in the room. Calming my breath, which had begun to speed up, I walked to the sink and began to wash my hands.

An icy breath caressed the back of my neck. My face snapped up towards the mirror, where two faces stared back at me. The first was my own terrified reflection. The second was just over my right shoulder, shrouded by a hooded robe. I screamed as loudly as I could.

The scream pounded against my ear drums and multiplied itself as it shattered into echoes. The figure behind me did not react to it, except to raise a luminous finger to its shadowy lips. At his gesture, the echoes muffled and died, as though the walls that were creating them had suddenly decided to absorb them. I clapped a hand over my mouth and spun around to face him. Part of me expected him to disappear, but there he was, no more than a few feet from where I stood pressed against the cool porcelain of the sink. He had a slight glow that illuminated nothing but his own form, the darkness seeming to double around him. His face was gaunt and bearded, his chin pronounced, and I could see his dark hair in the recesses of his hood. I registered all of this in a fraction of a second before I was drawn to his eyes, deep pools of darkness set into his face.

Somewhere from outside the room, I could hear voices shouting and footsteps clattering toward the bathroom, but they were not nearly as loud as they should have been. The ghost's presence seemed to muffle everything except the sound of my own blood pounding in my ears.

"W-who are you?" I whispered.

"I've been waiting for you. It's been agonizing." The figure's mouth moved, but I didn't hear his voice in the room. It was in my head, echoing against the insides of my skull. I shook my head, trying to dislodge it. It felt unnatural for it to be there, an intrusion.

I took a deep breath. "That's not what I asked you."

"My apologies, witch. My name is William. I was a student here, just like you."

"Why did you call me 'witch?'"

William just stared at me. I tried another question.

"You were in that group, right? The Swords Brotherhood? Isn't that why you're wearing that robe?"

"I had the distinct misfortune of entering their ranks, yes." He had a slow, drawling voice.

"Why misfortune? What happened to you?"

"I was killed during one of our ceremonies. I was meant to be sacrificed—symbolically sacrificed, of course. But the brother playing the part of the executioner never intended the sacrifice to be symbolic. He slaughtered me." At this William parted the robe and revealed a dark stain splattered gruesomely on his white shirt. "They covered it all up, it was very hush-hush. The school paid millions... bribed the press... judges... lawyers... even the police. Expelled the brother immediately, doctored the records of the others. Even today, the only record of the case remains in sealed court documents. But I would not be silenced. I stayed so that others would know what happened to me. I haunted them all, until their precious little society disbanded altogether. But by then, I was stuck here."

"Ballard? JESSICA? Are you in there?" Pierce's voice bled faintly into the oddly deadened atmosphere of the bathroom. There was also a dull tapping sound, which I realized was his pounding on the door.

I turned to William. "Did you lock that door?"

"I did. I wanted to speak with you and I did not want to be disturbed, as we were so rudely interrupted earlier."

I ran for the door, expecting him to try to stop me, but he did not move. I pulled on the handle and tried to turn the deadbolt. It wouldn't budge.

"Jessica! Are you alright?" Pierce sounded frantic but very far away.

"I'm here! I'm here with the ghost from upstairs and he won't let me out!" I shouted back.

Again, the pounding on the door was reduced to a pathetic tapping by whatever William was doing to the room. Frustrated, I turned back to him. He was just staring at me, the slightest of smirks on his face.

"I'm not finished speaking with you," he said softly in my head. "When we've concluded our business here, I will gladly allow them access."

"What business could you have with me? I don't even know you," I replied, trying to keep the growing hysteria out of my voice.

"Don't play stupid with me, witch. I've been waiting a long time. We all have."

"We?"

"We've many spent years trapped between where we are now and where we are meant to go. We've been waiting for you." With that he

187

took a small but decisive step toward me. As he did, the room filled with a buzz of whispering, many voices at once, a quiet cacophony.

I turned and pounded on the door. "Pierce! Get me out of here!"

I could hear him saying something to someone else, and other voices behind the door, which had started to rattle. They were trying to get me out.

"So eager to go? But you've only just arrived." Another step toward me. I slipped away from the door and past the stalls, which gave me more room to maneuver away from him. It might have been pointless, trying to evade a ghost, who could conceivably appear wherever he wanted to be, but my flight response seemed unwilling to acknowledge this.

"You know, if you just stand still, this ought to be easier," William suggested.

I froze. "What will be easier?"

"This."

Without another word, William flew at me like smoke on the wind. His face, as it approached mine, was full of a manic kind of anticipation, and then I felt only an intense cold as he passed through me. It was the last thing I registered before the pain started.

It exploded inside me, expanding through every vein and tissue. Gasping and screaming, I fell to my knees. It felt like every cell in my body was freezing and crystallizing to ice.

"JESSICA!" The voices outside the bathroom grew instantly louder; whatever William had done to the room had lost effect the moment he'd attacked me. The door flew off its hinges with a resounding crash as Iggy barreled into it. The team flooded in.

Pierce crouched beside me, shaking my shoulders and shouting for me to look at him.

My vision was clouded and oddly fuzzy, as though I was looking through a fogged-up windshield. I tried to speak, but could only continue to scream as the sensation morphed from intense cold to a new feeling, as though I was becoming too expansive to be contained in my own body. Emotions that weren't mine skittered across the surface of my mind. Anger. Confusion. Desperation. They were William's emotions. William was inside my body.

"Help... me! He's in... here!" I gasped.

Pierce stared into my eyes with horror and I realized that he was seeing someone else entirely staring back at him.

"Move, David! Move! Jessica, look at me!" Annabelle's face

replaced Pierce's above me, swimming in and out of focus. Neil's face hovered over her shoulder as well, his eyes like saucers. I tried to speak to them, to explain what was happening, when the pain shifted again.

I was being torn apart inside, the very fibers that held me together were being severed, the connections between my body and whatever of me existed that wasn't my body. I began to shake uncontrollably, my screams reaching a new pitch, and I found myself wishing, for the first time in my life, that I was dead. William's anger and frustration fought for domination in my brain.

A tiny part of my consciousness was somehow able to focus on Annabelle, who had begun to chant something over me, though I could not hear the words over my own irrepressible shrieking. I could barely register the sound of her voice. The last conscious, desperate thought that rose through the waves of agony was not mine, but William's.

"I can't get through! Why can't I get through?"

And then the pain engulfed me and I knew no more.

15

DECEPTION

I WAS FLOATING. It felt like water, like warm, untroubled water. If I could have remembered being inside the womb, I imagined that this was what it would have felt like. My body felt wonderful, weightless, but my head felt strange, like someone had taken out the gray matter and replaced it with packing peanuts. My thoughts rustled around in there, trying to surface. It wasn't easy, though, and for a while nothing discernible or understandable came of it.

Presently though, disturbing images began to untangle themselves from the comfortable haze. I was vaguely aware that they bothered me, and I tried to push them back down. At first it was as easy as batting away soap bubbles, but soon they grew stronger and clearer, cutting through my cozy cocoon, turning the water cold and troubled. It rocked in my head like a stormy sea, bringing on waves of nausea.

I became dimly aware of my body, and as soon as I could feel it, I wished again for the numbness. There wasn't an inch of me that didn't ache horribly. The ache was being propelled through my body by my veins, my pulse pushing sluggishly as though the pain made my blood viscous.

Sounds began to reach me, muffled and warped at first, then with sharpening clarity. An intermittent beeping sound. An occasional click. A steady dripping. Two voices, one male and one female, were conversing nearby. I forced a reluctant eyelid open. A sterile white hospital room swam into focus. I turned my head slowly towards the door. It seemed to take the room a few seconds to catch up with me. When it did, I was able to focus in on Annabelle and Pierce standing just outside the doorway.

Annabelle tossed her head, looking every bit the fiery gypsy. "I have been doing this all of my life. Since I was a child, I've been sensitive. And I can tell you now that I have never seen anything like it before."

"So what are you saying, Annabelle? What is she?"

"My grandmother called them portals. She'd met only two in her lifetime, and what she described is exactly what that girl is doing."

"Yes, but you still haven't explained what the hell she's doing! What happened to her in there?" Pierce began at a shout, but dropped his voice at the end when he suddenly remembered he was standing in a hospital corridor.

"She attracts them, David!" Annabelle cried. "I don't know how she does it, but they are drawn to her! Their energy is everywhere, crowding each other out, trying to get closer to her. The ones she's seen are only the beginning of it!"

My skin began to crawl and my headache throbbed more strongly as I tried to absorb this information.

"They need her for some reason; maybe she can help them. I've only ever heard of one instance in which that could be true. And so have you, David. Something you've been trying to find for a long time." Annabelle began nodding her head slowly, in time to some silent beat.

As though it were contagious, as though he'd just registered the tune as well, Pierce's head started bobbing along with Annabelle's. "Durupinen," he whispered.

Annabelle shivered at the word and her eyes danced nervously over to me. I shut my eyes a little tighter, completely losing my visuals, but hopefully appearing to be asleep. *Durupinen.* I rolled the word around in my head, committing its strange sound to memory. *What the hell were they talking about? And why did they have to be so damn cryptic?*

"You can't be fucking serious, Anna." Pierce sounded excited now. "I mean, I spend half of my professional life trying to track down any verifiable proof of their existence and you're telling me that one of them just walked into my office and signed up for my class? Do you know how absurd that sounds?"

"Yes, I do! I know how ridiculous it is to even be *talking* about Durupinen like they're—I don't know—some kind of established thing. Stories of them are as unsubstantiated as vampires, but almost as pervasive, especially in the medium subculture."

"Unsubstantiated? It's like they don't even exist! Every lead has dried up, every original document vanished, every witness unable to recall his experience! For all intents and purposes, they don't exist! It's an academic's nightmare! It's freaking Atlantis!" Pierce was shouting in a whisper.

Annabelle dismissed his words with a wave of her hand. "David, *everything* we deal with is unsubstantiated! And you have to admit, it's the only explanation that makes sense."

I risked opening my eyes a fraction of an inch. Pierce was pacing like a caged animal now, his hand pulling absently at his beard as though he were plucking the hairs out one by one.

"If this is true, Annabelle, if she's really..." he trailed off, crushing the rest of the thought beneath his pacing feet.

"I know. She needs to talk to someone, and fast by the looks of it. Who does she have? Her mother? A grandmother? From what little I know it's always the women." Annabelle sounded truly frightened, which made my heart start to thump unevenly. My mother? What would my mother possibly have to do with this?

"Only an aunt, I think," Pierce said.

"Maternal side?"

"I believe so, yes."

"Has anyone called her yet? Does she know what happened?"

"The hospital called her," Pierce replied. "She's on her way from Boston. Should be here any minute, I'd think. Obviously, we left out the ghoulish details, at least for now."

It was Annabelle's turn to pace. "I don't think we should let on that we know about the Durupinen. The secrecy is... well, let's just say I have no idea what would happen."

"Well then, what do we do? We have to do something! My God, if they tried to use her again like that, Annabelle—"

"—I know."

"From what little myth and lore exist, it's not supposed to be like that. Something's wrong. Seriously wrong."

"I'm going to talk to her," Annabelle said.

"Do you think we should wake her?"

"Do you seriously think this can wait, David? Don't be an idiot!"

Apparently Pierce didn't think it could wait, because a moment later I heard Annabelle's hurried footsteps clicking toward my bed. I tried to feign sleep.

A moment of silence and then, "You're awake, aren't you?"

There seemed to be no point in faking it. I opened my eyes

and stared Annabelle in the face; she swam nauseatingly in and out of focus.

"Yes."

Annabelle sighed, a deep release that sent ripples through her hair. "How much of that did you hear?"

"Enough to be completely confused. Do you know what happened to me? Because if you do, you have to tell me."

"Jessica, I want you to listen to me. I know that we haven't gotten along well, and that you thought I was some kind of fraud. After last night, can you believe me now when I tell you that's not true?" Annabelle asked.

"Yes."

"Do you trust that I understand a lot about this kind of thing?"

"Yes."

"Then I want you to trust me when I tell you what I'm about to say." She shifted forward in her chair. "Your aunt is going to be here very soon, and I'm sure you've been wondering what exactly you should say to her. It is very important that you tell her the truth."

I tried to sit up and failed. "But I can't! She'll think I'm—"

Annabelle placed a gentle but firm hand on my shoulder, keeping me still. "You don't know what she'll think. You can't know until you tell her. But you must tell her."

"But—"

"—Jessica, listen! I can't say for sure what happened to you, but I think I understand enough to know that you must tell your aunt! Now! Tonight!"

"Do you think my aunt will actually be able to tell me what's happening?"

Annabelle was silent for a moment. "Yes. And if she doesn't, she should be able to take you to someone who can."

I closed my eyes and tried to breathe evenly again. I felt like I was going to vomit at any moment. Nothing made sense, nothing she was saying made any sense. "But she knows about Evan. She knows what happened first semester, because the dean told her. If she knew something about what's been going on, why wouldn't she have told me then?"

"I don't know. I'm sure she'll have her reasons," Annabelle said.

"Why can't you just—"

Annabelle stood up abruptly. "It's not my place. I—David and I—shouldn't be involved. Not in this. I know you're confused, but you have to trust us now. Can you do that? Promise me you'll tell your aunt what's happening. We'd do it for you, but..."

"You can't," I finished.

"It's the only way. Promise me."

"I will, but you need to promise me something, too."

She looked wary but let me continue.

"If Karen won't or can't explain what is going on, will you help me? Will you tell me what you know, or what you think you know?"

Annabelle hesitated, but something in my expression must have affected her. "I don't think it will come to that. But, yes, I will."

Reassured that I would soon have some answers, I gave in to whatever sedative was currently coursing through my veins and drifted into blissful unconsciousness.

§

When I woke again, several hours later, it was a different face I saw looking down at me.

"Jess, sweetie? How are you?" Karen whispered.

"I don't know." I stretched tentatively, but everything still ached like hell.

Karen's nose and eyes were red, and she was absent-mindedly shredding a Kleenex between her fingers. "What happened to you, sweetie? Can you remember anything about it? Your professor was here when I arrived, but he just said that you collapsed in the library. The doctors couldn't tell me a thing. They're still running all of your tests."

I glanced toward the corridor, where Pierce and Annabelle had been waiting. It was now deserted. I was on my own and it was time for the truth.

"Karen, I'll tell you what happened last night. I'll tell you everything, but please, just... don't interrupt me, okay? I want to get it all out before I lose my nerve."

Karen nodded and continued to pulverize her tissue.

Taking a deep breath that felt like fire in my lungs, I let loose the floodgates. I told Karen everything, from my many encounters with Evan to my run-ins with other spirits. I told her about my relationship with Pierce, and how he'd been helping me understand my abilities. Her face was absolutely inscrutable, but I didn't let myself stop talking long enough to attempt to decode it.

The only time I thought she would stop me was when I told her about William and what had happened when I was trapped in the bathroom.

Her hand grasped mine convulsively and her head started shaking back and forth, her mouth open in an "O" of perfect horror.

And, I realized suddenly, perfect understanding.

She started looking at me with a new intensity, her eyes taking a frantic inventory of every inch of me, looking for something she hadn't noticed before. She took me by the shoulders and shook me slightly, staring deep into my eyes. She ignored my faint groan of protest, searching, trying to see through me, to see *into* me. She saw only me looking back at her, shocked, and so she released me with a moan of relief and listened to the rest of my story with a shaking hand pressed over her eyes.

When I had finished, I thought the silence was going to stretch beyond my ability to wait it out. Was she waiting for me to speak? Was she ever going to speak to me again? I had just opened my mouth, with little real idea of what would come out of it, when she finally spoke.

"This is my fault. All my fault," she whispered.

"What? How can this be your fault?"

"I should have... maybe I could've done something to..." She didn't really seem to be talking to me at all. Abruptly, she was on her feet, digging through her bag and muttering unintelligibly.

"Karen, if you know something, you have to tell me."

I watched as a dozen emotions flitted across her face in quick succession, and I tried to make sense of the battle going on behind her eyes. Finally, something clicked into place and her face smoothed out.

"I can't."

My jaw dropped open. I didn't realize until that moment that I'd been expecting her to deny it. "You can't or you won't?"

"I can't. Not yet."

"Not yet?"

I struggled into a sitting position, ignoring the tug of the tubes in my wrists. Karen's careful expression faltered as she reached out a hand to push me back onto the pillow. I slapped it away impatiently. "So, let me get this straight, just so we're clear here. You know something about what's happening to me. In fact, I'm pretty sure you know everything about it." I took her silence as confirmation. "And in spite of the fact that whatever just happened almost killed me, even though I've been convinced for months that, on some level, I've gone insane, you aren't going to tell me what's happening. Is that what you're saying to me right now?"

Still Karen said nothing, though her face was twisted with something akin to agony.

"So what's it going to take, Karen? What kind of red flag or secret sign are you waiting for? Because I can't take much more of this."

"Jessica," she begged, her voice a hoarse whisper. "I just can't..."

"What are the Durupinen?"

As though an electric current had shocked her, Karen jolted out of her seat and skittered away from me until her back was pressed to the wall. "What... Who told... I never..." she spluttered.

Her reaction was all the confirmation I needed. Annabelle and Pierce had been right in their suspicions, whatever they meant. "If you won't tell me, I'll find someone who will."

"Who? Who have you been talking to?"

I had her spooked, and I had no idea why, but I kept my mouth shut and just waited.

"Jess, just listen to me, alright? You trust me, don't you?"

"Actually, Karen, I'm not sure that I do."

"Okay. Okay, you're right. I guess I deserve that," Karen said, and began pacing the room. I could practically hear her mind working. "Assumptions aside, then. If I asked you to trust me, just this one last time, would you do it?"

"That depends."

"On what?"

"On whether or not trusting you is going to get me answers."

"Jessica, I promise that if you trust me just this once, you will get some answers."

"When?"

"Soon. As soon as I'm possibly able."

"I'm listening."

Karen heaved a sigh of relief. "Good. Thank you. I need to get you checked out of here and home to Boston. Nothing they are doing for you here is actually going to help you. Once we get home, I will need a little bit of time to speak to some people. After I've done that, I'll know exactly what I can tell you, and also what we are going to do from here."

I considered for a moment. It sounded like she was hedging to a certain extent, but I could wait it out and see what came of it. I would take what I could get from the "people" she was going to contact, and then, if I wasn't satisfied, I would go to Pierce and Annabelle. I would force them to talk, if necessary.

"Fine. Let's get out of here."

16

―――――

NIGHTTIME VISITORS

I AM NOT SURE HOW KAREN MANAGED IT—maybe she threatened a lawsuit—but I was out of that hospital bed and into her SUV within twenty minutes. The nurse who helped me into the passenger seat looked like she was doing it against every fiber of good sense she possessed. Karen ignored her sniffs and general grunts of disapproval, and we were speeding east toward Boston just as the rising sun peeked, blushing diffidently, over the horizon. Noah stared at us as we walked in the door, his hair a too-dark haystack, his toothbrush suspended motionless, halfway to his mouth. I wondered, as I took in his bewildered expression, if Karen had even told him she was bringing me home. She insisted that I go straight to bed, and I was too exhausted to argue. I didn't need to be present for that discussion.

I lay in bed fighting the fatigue. Just the walk up the stairs to my room had my legs trembling. I caught sight of myself in the full-length mirror on the back of my door and nearly frightened myself to death. I was so pale, I could have been one of my own unwelcome visitors. Karen's grim but resigned expression as she helped me into bed was proof positive that she knew exactly what had happened to me, and that my symptoms were nothing less than expected. I bit back my torrent of questions and concentrated instead on trying to stay awake long enough to eavesdrop on her phone conversations. Unfortunately, she seemed to be anticipating this maneuver. Instead of going across the hall, she descended the stairs and shut herself into Noah's office. I barely had the energy to register my own disappointment. Whatever information I was going to get, it was going to have to wait until tomorrow. Or at least, that was what I thought as I let sleep carry me away again.

Damn it. Not again. Not here.

There it was, the increasingly familiar feeling that I was not alone in my darkened bedroom. My heart pounded a frantic tattoo against my ribcage and my breathing quickened, both ignoring the silent calming words my brain was trying to send my body, which still felt like it had been tossed off a cliff. I opened my eyes slowly, careful not to move any other part of my body. I was facing the wall of books against which my bed was wedged. There was, thank goodness, no face hovering between me and the rows of gilded spines.

I could sense movement, though, and eyes boring into my motionless back. Deciding I may as well get it over with, I struggled into a sitting position and turned around.

Two figures were silhouetted in the silver moonlight streaming through the open window. The curtains fluttered around them like silken wings. One figure, clearly female, was standing just in front of the window ledge, hands raised slightly from her sides, palms out. The other figure, crouched on the window seat, was diminutive enough to be that of a child.

I opened my mouth, but the upright figure spoke first.

"You see, Catriona? She's awake, and she's not even screaming," her velvety-smooth voice cooed.

"Well, that's one for you, I suppose," a bored voice answered. "Shall I pay up now, or...?"

"You can owe me, love. I won't forget," the tall figure replied. Then she turned toward me and added, "Hello, Jessica." She had a very strong English accent.

I found my voice at last. "Excuse me, but who are you?" I was proud that it didn't crack; I was doing a decent impression of composure.

The tall figure stepped into the middle of the room towards me, where the moonlight lit her features. She was slender and graceful, moving with an almost feline fluidity. Her skin was flawless and luminous, a beautiful shade of mocha. Her face was almost unnaturally beautiful, as though she had been airbrushed, with high cheekbones, almond-shaped eyes, and full lips which were curved into a curious little half-smile. Her hair stood out in a kinky halo all around her head. She had every appearance of an Egyptian goddess, except for the anachronistic outfit; she was dressed in skintight designer jeans, fur-topped stiletto boots and a low-cut suede vest.

I gasped out loud at the sight of her. Her smile widened, as though she expected my awe. Not surprising; a woman so beautiful must get that all the time.

"My name is Lucida. This is Catriona," the goddess said, gesturing offhandedly to the second figure behind her. "We've come to pay you a little visit."

Catriona slunk off the window seat and stood beside Lucida. She was just as beautiful as her companion, but the polar opposite. Her skin, also with an unearthly glow, was purest ivory. Her hair flowed in shining golden waves down her back. She was nearly a foot shorter than Lucida, which gave her even more of the appearance of a porcelain doll, and her features were heartbreakingly perfect, from her rosebud mouth to her wide, extravagantly lashed blue eyes. She looked like she'd walked off the cover of *Vogue* magazine, dressed in a devastating pair of black leather pants and a gold cashmere top that hung carelessly off one of her shoulders.

But the biggest difference between them was the expressions on their faces. Catriona looked apathetic and slightly annoyed, while Lucida's face was aglow with interest and excitement.

I swallowed convulsively. "Why are you here? What do you want from me?"

"Calm down, love, take a breath. Like I said, we're just here to have a little chat," Lucida said, smiling in what she evidently thought was a friendly way.

But I was too scared to calm down. "Look, I don't want to talk to you. I don't know why you all keep finding me, but I can't help you. I don't know what to do, and I'm sorry about that, but please just go away."

"What do you mean, 'you all?' Who else has..." Lucida began, but then Catriona put a hand on her arm.

"She thinks we're a Visitation," Catriona said, her tone indicating that it should have been obvious.

Lucida's expression cleared immediately as she shook her head and laughed a short, harsh note. "Of course she does. Not surprised, all things considered."

"Aren't... aren't you both dead?" I asked.

"No, Jessica. We are very much alive," Catriona said.

I considered this possibility. They both looked totally solid. Then again, so had Evan. He hadn't known he was dead, and so it was conceivable these visitors were in the same frame of mind, though I doubted it. It was obvious from their comments that they were aware, on some level, of what had been happening to me. I decided to take them at their word and accept that two unknown, living women were standing in my bedroom in the dark. If they thought this was going to calm me down, they were quite wrong.

"How did you get in here?" I demanded.

Lucida gestured lazily behind her. "Through your window. I suppose these weren't the smartest shoes for scaling the side of a building, I'll admit it. Pleasant surprise to find it unlocked, though. Thanks for that."

The night breeze lifted Lucida's cloud of hair around her, and I realized that indeed, the window hadn't been open when I'd gone to sleep.

"Okay, give me one good reason why I shouldn't scream at the top of my lungs and call the police," I said, put off by Lucida's strange composure. It was as though entering strangers' windows by moonlight was a regular occupation for her.

"Well, for one thing, I'd lose my bet, and that'd be a shame, wouldn't it?" Lucida said, shooting Catriona a gloating smile. "And secondly, how do you expect to understand everything that's been happening to you recently if you boot out the women with all the answers?"

"How do you know what's been happening to me?" The words tumbled out over each other in my surprise.

"Because once upon a time, it happened to me. To both of us," Lucida said.

"Why should I believe you?"

"Oh, stop being so bloody vague and just tell her already," Catriona said, running a hand through her magnificent hair. She turned to me. "Don't mind Lucida, she's always been one for the theatrics. I for one wanted to knock on the front door, but *no...*"

I felt one corner of my mouth twitch upward in spite of my fear. Lucida, however, looked aggravated.

"Yes, well we're here now, and I'm sure Jessica has lots of questions for us," she said.

"I've got a few of my own, Lucida." All three of us whirled around to face the door. Karen stood framed in the light from the hallway, her expression absolutely livid. Her arms were folded tightly across her chest.

Catriona looked instantly uncomfortable. Lucida's face fell, but only for a moment. She quickly recovered herself and hitched a smile back into place. She continued in the same unconcerned tone as before.

"Hello, Karen. So nice to see you again."

"I wish I could say the same, but let's not start with the pretenses so early, shall we? It sets a bad precedent," Karen said.

"Who's pretending?" Lucida looked around, as though she may find as yet undiscovered people hiding behind her. "It's been ages. You're looking... well." Her voice shook with a barely contained laugh, as though she were enjoying some private joke.

Karen seemed to get the punch line. "So are you. Remarkably so. I'm sure the Council finds that rather interesting."

"We take care of ourselves, don't we, Cat?" Lucida said, glancing back at Catriona, who was avoiding Karen's gaze.

"Karen!" I finally managed to say. "What is going on? Who are they and why do you know them?"

"Don't worry about it, Jess," Karen said, still not looking at me. "Lucida and Catriona are old friends. I'm sure they just wanted to meet you, but now they have and they'll be running along." Her voice rang with finality.

"But we just got here! And we've come such a long way, too! Surely you're not going to pack us off without a nice little visit, are you?" Lucida pouted, flopping into my chair and crossing her legs. "We've got so much to talk about."

"We have absolutely nothing to talk about," Karen hissed.

"Oh, I think Jess would disagree, isn't that right Jess?" Lucida said, turning to me.

"It's not Jess's decision, Lucida, and it's certainly not yours," Karen said. "It's up to the Council and they've assured me that—"

"—Oh, I think you'll find that the Council has had a change of heart, so to speak," Lucida said politely. "That's why we're here."

That stopped Karen dead. The color drained from her face. "No, Finvarra would have told me. I received no word of any new decision."

"Yeah, well, Finvarra's a busy woman, isn't she? Like I said, that's why we're here."

Karen turned to Catriona wordlessly for confirmation.

"It's true, Karen. The circumstances have changed," Catriona said.

"And just how have the circumstances changed, I'd like to know!"

"That's exactly what we've come here to explain. Isn't that lovely?" Lucida said. She was obviously enjoying herself. "But before we do, I think you've got a bit of explaining to do for Jessica here. Unless you'd rather I—"

"—No!" Karen shouted and then immediately deflated, her face crumpling and falling into her hands. "I'll tell her."

"Brilliant!" Lucida clapped her hands and folded her feet beneath her like a child at story time. "We'll just stay and listen, then."

Catriona sat carefully on the end of the window seat, throwing me a sympathetic glance before settling her gaze on the carpet.

Karen shuffled to the foot of my bed and sat heavily. When she looked up, her eyes contained a sadness I couldn't begin to comprehend.

"I owe you an apology, Jess. I've kept a lot from you, and I've left you searching for answers I could have readily supplied you with. I'm prepared for your anger, and the possibility that you might not forgive me, but I beg you to remember that it was your mother who made me promise I would never reveal to you what I'm about to say, and I do not break that promise lightly. If I thought it would have done any good at all, I would have told you right away. However, it seems that this has been taken out of my hands. It won't make much sense to you unless I start at the beginning. Please, hear me out."

§

As Karen began the story that would reshape the path of my life, her voice was quiet and gentle.

"When your mother and I were growing up, we were inseparable. We did everything together from the moment we were born. We connected on a level that even other twins couldn't understand. In all things, we were as one, until the day we turned four years old.

"The morning of our fourth birthday I awoke to find Lizzie talking animatedly to herself. As I took in what was happening, I realized that she was talking not to herself, but to someone else, someone I couldn't see. When she saw that I was awake, she smiled, and tried to introduce me to her friend, a boy named Michael. At first I thought she was playing a game with me, teasing me with a made-up story, but she became upset when I didn't believe her, and scared when I said that I couldn't see who she was talking to.

Crying and confused, she asked Michael to go away, and he did. But others soon took his place.

"Lizzie was scared of the people she was seeing at first, and I was scared for her, but soon she grew used to seeing her 'secret friends.' I tried to understand that she could not help it, that she was not excluding me from this part of her world on purpose, but I grew more and more resentful of these friends who were stealing my sister away from me. And so one day, when we were seven years old, I waited for one of Lizzie's visitors to arrive and then I went and got our mother.

"I was sure that when mother heard what Lizzie was doing, she would forbid her from having these secret friends. But when mother listened at the door, she merely closed her eyes and smiled softly to herself. 'Ah, my Lizzie is the Key, then,' she whispered, and entered the room.

"That was when my mother sat down with us and first tried to explain what we were, what had been passed down to us. For it was not just Lizzie, she assured me. We were both very special. Someday soon, I, too, would see the people that Lizzie saw, and we would grow up to fulfill the destiny that our mother had passed on to us."

Here Karen paused, scanning my face carefully as though something she said might have damaged me.

"I'm fine. Go on," I said.

"When I turned sixteen, I had my first encounter. Lizzie was in the habit of warning me when a visitor was present, and one day in the yard she warned me that a young man had arrived by the fence. I could hardly believe my eyes, for I'd been staring at the very same young man for the last several minutes, wondering who he was and if he needed directions. He was wandering rather aimlessly. In this moment, we realized that I had awakened to our gift, and that very soon we would be making use of our unusual abilities.

"On the night we turned eighteen, my mother sat us down and gave us a very old book. She explained that we were the next in a very ancient, very powerful line of women known as the Durupinen."

Catriona and Lucida both expelled a breath of reverence at the word. Catriona's eyes were gently closed, Lucida's uplifted and unfocused.

"Durupinen is an old Celtic word meaning 'gatekeeper.' The Durupinen are known by many names in as many languages as humans have created. The Durupinen were and are the keepers of the doors that separate the worlds of the living and the dead."

This was not happening. What she was saying was just not a part of the world in which I lived, the world that made sense.

"My mother explained that our abilities had been passed through the female bloodline for as many hundreds of years as human records could account for, and she was sure for many hundreds of years before that. The people we could see were souls, trapped on earth for a multitude of reasons. It was the calling of the Durupinen to open the doors they controlled and to help these trapped souls to whatever lay on the other side."

I choked on a lump that was rising slowly in my throat. "That's why the spirits found my mother? Because she was a... one of these gatekeepers?"

"Spirits, when they are ready to depart, can sense the presence of a Gateway."

My breath caught on the last word, my mind spiraling back to the night my mother died, the night of the very first dream, and a single whispering voice.

"The Gateway is open."

"What is it?" Karen asked. My face must have betrayed my shock.

"Nothing. A dream I had the night my mom died. It... a voice mentioned a gateway. Please go on. How does the Gateway work?"

"Each spirit Gateway, or 'Geatgrima' in the old tongue, is controlled by a pair of women linked by the same bloodline. By the joining of hands and the use of certain incantations, the Durupinen can open their Gateway, briefly, and allow the trapped souls to cross, using their own bodies to facilitate the passage."

"Their own bodies? What does that mean?"

"One acts as the Key, the entry point, so to speak, and the second acts as a sort of pathway, called the Passage. The soul enters the first body, crosses through the second, and arrives safely intact on the other side."

Here Karen shot a sharp look at Lucida, who inclined her head and returned her gaze steadily. I fought the panic that was trying to rise in me and held it at bay with another question.

"Which were you? The first or the second?"

"I was the second, the Passage. Your mother, as the first, was the Key. That was why she was sensitive to Visitations so early on. Often the spirits can sense when a Key is present, even if it is not yet active. This was how our mother knew that we had inherited the gift."

I could see a glaring hole in this explanation and how it could possibly pertain to me, but I did not give it voice. There was still so much I wanted to know.

Karen continued, "Mother trained us in the ways of the Durupinen. She traveled with us to meet the Council, which you have heard me mention tonight. The Durupinen have a hierarchy, just like any clan or group. She saw us through our training and soon we were able to begin fulfilling our birthright. The intention is that each generational Gateway remains open until the next is ready to take its place. There are exceptions, of course, such as when a Durupinen dies without the appropriate heiresses waiting. But the bloodlines are strong, and though it may take years, usually the gift can continue. Our mother's Gateway closed on our eighteenth birthday, as had her mother's before her. Unfortunately, our family's path would not remain so clear.

"Your mother and I were initiated into our roles as Durupinen and went through the appropriate training. Then, when we were at Harvard together—"

"—Wait. My mother went to Harvard? With you?"

"She never told you?"

"No. She told me she never went to college."

"She never graduated. But while she was there we roomed together, of course, as inseparable as ever we were. It only made sense; our newfound responsibilities to the Durupinen required that we be in close proximity to each other."

"But then she left."

"Yes, I'm getting to that. We were never quite sure when a Visitation would occur, or when a crossing would be required. But the need arose, rather urgently, one night in our senior year while we were home for winter break.

"A great part of the responsibility we bear is the secrecy, Jess. No one outside of the Durupinen can know what we are or what we do."

"Why?"

"Too dangerous," Catriona chimed in. I jumped, having all but forgotten she was there. "If people knew that we had the ability to communicate with the dead, there would be no peace for us."

"I don't understand. Why would it be so terrible if people knew?"

Lucida answered this time. "Can't you imagine what would

happen? Every husband who'd lost a wife would want a chat. Every mother who'd lost a child would want to see or hear from her little one. And what of the churches? The scientists? We'd be studied and exploited like bloody extraterrestrials, wouldn't we?"

Of course, she was right. What if I'd known such people existed, that I might be one of them? Wouldn't I, who had just lost my mother, have gone through any means to speak to her one last time?

"As I said, there was an urgent need for a crossing. This particular spirit was... rather insistent," Karen said, her eyes faraway. I did not need to ask what she meant. My own mind returned to the library bathroom and the hooded figure; I knew exactly what an insistent spirit was.

"It was late at night, and we had just invoked the opening of the Gateway. The spirits had just begun to cross when our bedroom door crashed open." Karen closed her eyes and gulped. "It was our father. He took one look at us and jumped to some sort of conclusion, though what exactly he thought was happening, we'll never know for sure. He was a devoutly religious man. The candles, the Summoning Circle—maybe he thought it was witchcraft or something. In any case, he panicked, ran over to us, and tried to pull our grasped hands apart."

Here, Karen seemed unable to go on. She was inhaling sharply through her nose. Lucida was perched on the edge of her seat, her eyes blazing with an unsettling combination of horror and fascination. Catriona was still staring at the floor, shaking her head minutely.

"Blimey, Karen, I never knew that," Catriona whispered.

"No one ever knew what really happened except for the Council. It was our request, and Finvarra honored it."

The three of them were silent with grim understanding, while I sat stewing in growing anticipation. Finally, I blurted out, "So, what happened to him? What happened when he pulled your hands apart?"

"He interfered with the Gateway. The spirit that was crossing was mid-journey when your grandfather made his own body a part of the path."

"It almost never happens, because the Durupinen operate in such secrecy. But it's not unheard of," Catriona said.

"When your grandfather's body became part of the path his own spirit was pulled partially from his body. That's the best way I can describe it," Karen said.

I could feel what little color I had draining from my face. I closed my eyes against a sudden wave of nausea. "Pulled... partially?"

"If it had been pulled fully, of course, he would have died. But we were able to close the Gateway and end the crossing before his entire soul could go through."

"But something happened to him. I mean, he's not okay," I said.

"No," Karen agreed, "he's not." She stood up and paced a moment, seeming to weigh her words carefully before she continued. "Our souls want to cross over. Even when they exist inside our bodies, they can feel the pull of the other side. That's why most people don't stay behind as ghosts. Most of our souls give over to the powerful pull and cross over immediately upon death. When your grandfather entered the Gateway, the pull was strong enough to tempt his soul to leave its house and seek its final home. We believe a small part of it actually did, leaving the rest of it both damaged and longing."

I couldn't even begin to deal with the concept of a final home, and so instead I asked a more immediate question. "But that doesn't make sense, Karen. If his soul was pulled from his body, why didn't yours or Mom's ever try to cross? You exposed yourselves to the Gateway all the time."

"It's in our blood," Lucida said. Her voice had a pride in it. "Those who inherit the gift of the Durupinen can't be pulled across while we are performing a crossing. Our birthright protects us."

I did not respond. My mind had just made a mental leap to the previous summer. My grandfather's tortured voice was echoing through my head. "I've seen it! Send me back!"

Karen went on, "Your mother was devastated. We both were, of course, but for the first time in our lives, Lizzie and I found ourselves in an irreconcilable situation. I felt it was our duty to continue with our roles as Durupinen. Your mother wanted to give it up."

Lucida made a sound like the quiet hissing of a cat. Catriona gave her a stern look which she completely ignored.

"Why would you want to keep doing this, after what it did to your father?" I asked. I didn't want to be rude, but my mother's point of view made a hell of a lot more sense to me than Karen's did. "When something you do nearly kills your family members, you stop. Right?"

"I can see why you would question my judgment on this, Jess, but this wasn't a matter of giving up some kind of hobby or something like that. This was an obligation we were born to fulfill. That was how Finvarra had explained it to us, and I still believed that. But your mother couldn't handle it anymore. She left."

"But she would still see the ghosts, wouldn't she? What could she do about that?" I asked. "I can't remember Mom ever doing or saying anything that would make me think she was seeing ghosts. I mean, I've only been seeing ghosts for a few months and half the people I know are ready to have me committed. How could she possibly hide that from me?"

"She performed a Binding," Lucida snarled, offering no further illumination.

I turned on her, aggravated. "Oh, that explains it completely! Thanks so much. I don't suppose it's occurred to you that I have no idea what you're talking about? If you're going to butt into this conversation, maybe you could at least explain your freaking spirit code words!"

Lucida opened her mouth to respond, but Karen cut her off. "She's right, Lucida, let me explain this to her, please. A Binding is a ceremony that a Durupinen can place upon herself or another in order to block the contact of outside spirits. It is only meant to be used very briefly and only in a dire emergency. It has been used in the past to protect a Durupinen from hostile spirits or other beings that may take the form of a spirit."

I gasped. "*Other* beings that—"

"—We'll get to that another night, Jess. Just stay with me right now, please," Karen said wearily. "Your mother performed the Binding on herself, but because she was the Key of our Gateway, all spiritual contact ceased for me, too. Without her connection to the spirit world, mine was severed."

Something in her voice made me hold my breath. It sounded like grief. The concept of missing the frightening Visitations was unfathomable to me.

Karen went on, "Your mother meant to protect us and our family, but she was not using the Binding as it was intended to be used. There are only a set number of Gateways in the world at any given time, and they all serve a very important purpose in handling the spirit activity. When one is closed for too long, the consequences can be catastrophic."

"The earthbound spirits need us," Catriona said. "Without us, they could be trapped here indefinitely. Spirits are drawn to a particular Gateway, and when they find it, they will try to cross through it until they succeed."

"Spirits were drawn to your mother for years but were unable to make contact. Over time, their need grew stronger and your mother's Binding spell grew weaker. The night that she died was the night that the spirits finally broke through," Karen said.

My blood felt like ice coursing through my veins. I was finally going to understand what happened to my mother. And after months of wanting just that, I suddenly realized that the truth may not be something I was ready for. But ready or not, here it was.

"When the spirits finally broke through the spell, all their many years of anguish took over. They tried to use your mother as a Gateway despite my absence. You should have a pretty good idea of what that was like, Jess. The very same thing happened to you on a smaller scale in the library last night."

And with those words, the terror of that night shifted into focus. William's words, his desperation, his insistence that he had been waiting for me, it all made sense now. I shuddered as I remembered the blinding pain, the feeling that my body was too full, that I would tear apart at the seams. That was what my mother's final moments had been like, only a hundred times worse. Her life had ended in a whirlwind of pain, confusion, and terror. It was worse than I ever could have imagined.

"I thought that she only left to protect us, and so that she wouldn't have to face what happened to Dad." Karen looked up at me, her eyes well-deep. "But it was more than that. She was pregnant, Jess. With you. She was terrified of what would happen to you if you ever inherited the gift. She was able to accept the risks for herself at first, especially when she was young and was wrapped up in the glamour and excitement of it all. But when she found out she was going to become a mother, all of that changed. She saw what happened to Dad and she panicked. You remember your mother, Jess. You know how fiercely she loved, in spite of all of her vices and failures. She wouldn't risk your life for anything, even your destiny. So she went into hiding and brought you with her."

I found my voice at last. "She was always running from something. That must have been the reason for all of the drinking. It was like she always expected someone to appear just over her shoulder if she let down her guard for even a minute. We moved all the time, and always without warning. I hated her for it."

"The Durupinen were searching for her," Catriona explained. "Her Binding spell wreaked more havoc than she wanted to admit. The spirit world was growing steadily more unstable without the proper number of Gateways to control it. It was crucial to track her down before... well, we weren't in time."

We all sat in silence for what felt like a long time. The only sound I could hear was my own breathing, and an occasional sniff from Karen.

Finally, I voiced what seemed to me to be the obvious flaw in this whole explanation. "But I can't be a Gateway. There needs to be two parts and there's only me."

This re-lit Karen's earlier fire. "That's what I've been trying to tell Finvarra and the entire Council for months. There's no reason for you to have known any of this. Noah and I were never able to have children, and there are no other females in your generation. The Visitations shouldn't be happening to you at all. The Gateway closed with your mother's death. There's something else going on here."

"Ah, Karen, but that's where you're wrong," Lucida said, seeming to savor the words. She was smiling, as though we'd finally reached the point in the conversation she'd been waiting for. "The Gateway is still very much open."

"Don't be absurd, Lucida," Karen snapped. "That's not possible and you know it!"

"I'll tell you what I do know, love. The Gateway is open and Jessica is a part of it."

"Oh, really?" Karen retorted. "Why don't you explain how that's possible, *love*."

"Because, like you, she's one of a pair."

"What do you mean, one of a pair?"

"I mean," Lucida leaned forward, her voice a velvety caress, "that she was not the only baby born to your sister eighteen years ago. Our darling Jessica has a twin."

17

HANNAH

T HOSE WORDS WERE FOLLOWED by the loudest silence I'd ever heard. I watched the fallout from the soundless explosion settle over all of us, drifting almost gently, like snow. And, like snow, it disappeared on contact as we absorbed its impact. Karen was the first to recover.

"That's not possible," she whispered.

"Of course it's possible. Genetics, darling! Twins do run in your family, now don't they? And not only is it possible, but, if you take a moment to consider, it's the only explanation that makes a modicum of sense," Lucida said.

Karen threw up her hands in frustration. "No, it's not—"

"—Why? Explain it to me," I demanded.

Lucida turned to me and flashed that feline smile again. "Glad to, darling. Your mother discovered she was pregnant and performed the Binding, just as Karen has told you. But things quickly went from bad to worse. She soon learned she was carrying not one child, but two, and both females, at that. A potentially intact Gateway contained in a single womb—an enormously powerful thing. You should understand that, Karen, having been part of one yourself."

Karen's mouth opened and closed uselessly.

"We can only assume she thought that by separating the babies and maintaining the Binding, she could protect them from ever coming into their birthright. And so, she did. She kept you with her, Jessica, and she gave your sister up."

I shook my head sharply, hoping to expel the image from my brain. "My mother would never do that. There must be another explanation. My mother made a lot of mistakes, but I just can't believe that—"

"—She may not have wanted to, but she was certainly able, because that is exactly what she did. She was, unfortunately,

213

misguided. No spell, however powerful, or distance however far, can stop the Durupinen from fulfilling their destiny; a fact I would have thought she understood quite well, being one of us herself."

"That's enough, Lucida. You can fault Elizabeth for many things, but don't ever blame her for trying to protect her child," Karen shouted.

"Children," Lucida said.

"How do you know this? Why should we believe you?" I pressed on as though Karen hadn't spoken.

Catriona leapt in, apparently hoping to mediate. "When your mother died, the Gateway should have closed for good. The Durupinen have ways of knowing when a Gateway has disappeared from the world and therefore when they must take steps to create another. But it didn't disappear. In fact, when her Binding finally shattered, the Gateway was completely open for the first time in eighteen years. That was only possible if the proper descendants were there to take her place. Finvarra began an investigation to find out more."

"I can't believe she did this without telling me," Karen said.

"And who are you that Finvarra, High Priestess of the Durupinen, needs to inform you of her decisions?" Lucida snorted.

"I'm the remaining representative from this family, damn it, and she should have told me! And don't you get all high and mighty with me, Lucida. Don't pretend you've got some sort of healthy respect for authority all of a sudden."

"Don't know what you mean, love," Lucida laughed, and turned her back on Karen. "We managed to track you down, but that was only half of the battle, of course. We needed all of the pieces to rebuild the Geatgrima. That's the real reason for our visit tonight. We've found your sister." With this announcement, Lucida pulled a folded up piece of paper from her cleavage, and began waving it around like she was trying to hypnotize me with it.

Two forces battled inside me at the sight of that paper. The first was a burning curiosity, flames of it leaping and licking at the corners of my mind. The second was like a shield, a self-preservation instinct that was begging me not to look. *"Too much, too much!"* it screamed. Whatever that paper contained might very well shatter whatever tenuous grasp I still had on my self-control. In the light from my lamp, backward words, like hieroglyphics, taunted me with their inscrutability.

Curiosity won.

I reached up and snatched the paper out of Lucida's hand. I half expected her to play keep-away, but she released it readily. I unfolded the well-worn document.

At first glance, I thought it might be a birth certificate. It had the same sort of medical document look, the same kinds of information. But the date didn't make sense. It was dated only five years ago.

"What is it, Jess?" Karen asked.

"I don't really know. It looks like some kind of medical record."

"A patient entry form, from the New Beginnings Group Home in New York," Lucida said, almost cheerfully. She was definitely enjoying herself.

I scanned the document. My mother's name caught my attention first, my eye drawn to it as though magnetically. It was typed in a sterile-looking font over the heading "Birth Mother." I then let my eyes travel up the page to the upper left-hand corner, knowing that was where I'd find the name I was really looking for.

Patient Name: Ballard, Hannah

The shock that should have registered was a dim and slightly discordant harmony compared to the warmth that filled me at the sight of that name. My sister. My twin. Hannah.

Of course, she was my Hannah, not Evan's. I'd been looking in the absolute wrong direction. He was trying to lead me to her, not just for himself, but for me, too. He knew that she would complete the Gateway, but in the process, she would complete me. It was the only thing he could really do for me.

Hungry to know what I could now, I read more carefully, swiping away at the blurring tears that were obscuring my view. I saw my own familiar birth date, the same screaming blank where "Birth Father" should have been listed. I also saw other familiar details; born in Brooklyn at New York Methodist Hospital. But then other words started to jump out, and my temporary elation morphed into panic.

There was a list of foster families; I counted seven. Other words leapt out as well. Antisocial behavior. History of hallucinations. Suspected paranoid schizophrenia. A list of medications I couldn't pronounce.

"What's wrong with her?" I demanded. I was surprised at how completely the panic gripped me.

Lucida's eyes widened innocently. "Nothing. She's a Durupinen. She sees ghosts, just as you do."

Karen had read over my shoulder and understood more than I had. "Enough of your games, Lucida. Tell her what's going on."

Lucida threw her a saccharine smile. "Well, put two and two together, love. Your darling mum thought the Binding would prevent you both from ever even seeing spirits, but that was not the case. What do you think would have happened to you if you'd been seeing ghosts and had no one to explain it to you? You've only dealt with it for a few months, and you nearly lost your bloody mind. Your sister is the Key, see? She's been chattin' away to the ghoulies since she knew how to talk. Problem was, there was no one around to explain things and make sure she didn't give herself away. So naturally, everyone thought she was crazy. Still do, come to that."

"We need to find her. Now." I said.

"I know. I'll help you," Karen promised.

"And so will we," Lucida added.

"Over my dead body! You've caused enough chaos here tonight, Lucida. Just get out of here and go back to London. I'm sure you have a report to deliver to Finvarra, and I wouldn't want you to miss an opportunity to play lapdog when you so excel at it."

Lucida seemed to be gearing up for a nasty response, but Catriona placed a restraining hand on her shoulder. "Look, we didn't want to come here—"

Karen laughed incredulously.

"Well, okay, I didn't. But Finvarra ordered us to, so here we are. But you're right. You need to deal with the fallout and we need to leave. But Finvarra did want you to contact her after we spoke."

"Oh, don't worry, I intend to," Karen said.

"Good. Well then, we'll be going. Out the door this time." Catriona slunk out, dragging Lucida behind her.

"Pleasure to meet you, Jess," Lucida called from the hallway.

Unable to return the compliment, I simply watched her go.

18

JAILBREAK

THE NEXT FEW HOURS WERE AGONIZING. As soon as Lucida and Catriona had made their escape, I was struggling out of bed and into my jeans. I was halfway to the stairs before Karen realized I was heading for the car. The shouting match that ensued was not pretty, but I was feeling the closest to crazy I'd ever felt in my life. I had a sister. A twin sister. And they had her locked away like some maniac.

Every fear I'd ever had about my own future had been her entire life. I felt so sick I was swallowing back bile every time I let myself imagine it. It was all Karen could do to get me to sit on the sofa in the office while she began a frantic string of phone calls. My entire body still ached with every beat of my pulse, but I barely noticed it. A new pain was taking over, the debilitating emotional pain of the unknown.

Karen talked to social workers, judges, and other lawyers. She'd woken them all in the middle of the night, but apparently she was respected enough that they were all willing to overlook that fact in light of her story. Unfortunately, their respect didn't seem to be enough, and her tone grew more frustrated with each subsequent conversation. I sat curled like a cat in a big leather armchair, fighting to keep my eyes open as I watched the bright oranges and pinks of dawn creep through the blinds and across the floor. Finally, Karen slammed the phone into the cradle with a resounding curse.

"What? What is it?"

"We can't get her released. Not legally, anyway."

"What do you mean we can't get her released? There's nothing wrong with her! She's not crazy!"

"I know that and you know that, but no doctor in the world is going to release her, not with her history."

"Call Finvarra, or whatever the hell her name is! She's in charge of all this Durupinen stuff, isn't she? There's got to be something she can do! I mean, Hannah can't be the first one of us to be locked up because people misunderstood."

"No, she's not, not by a long shot," Karen said. "But Finvarra is in London, and even her contacts would take time and money to work their magic. Money we've got, but we're out of time. We've got to formally open this Gateway and perform a crossing before one or both of you meets a fate like your mother did."

"So, now what? What do we do? Who do we call?"

"There's no one else to call. I told you they aren't going to release Hannah."

"But we *have* to—"

"—Jess, calm down! We're getting Hannah out of there, and we're doing it today. It'll just take a little more... creativity," Karen said, looking me square in the eye.

My exhausted brain was slow to catch up. "What do you mean?"

"I mean we're breaking her out."

In that moment my anger toward Karen twisted into something resembling respect and, although I didn't realize it at the time, I began to forgive her for lying to me. "I knew this was the most likely outcome," she said, "so I've been trying to weigh our other options, and I think I've come up with a plan B. How are your acting skills?"

I snorted. "Nonexistent, but just tell me what I need to do and I'll do it."

"I think the only way to get Hannah out is to send you in for her. We're going to pretend that I'm your mother, there to have you, my unruly daughter, evaluated and committed. While I'm meeting with the doctors, you need to find a way to get in, find Hannah, and get both of you out."

"Besides the fact that I have no idea how we're going to do any of that, I think it's a great plan," I said.

"Agreed. Go put on whatever you have in your wardrobe that would frighten Noah the most and let's go." She didn't need to tell me twice. I sprinted upstairs to the bathroom. I brushed my teeth and ran a comb through my hair, then thought better of it and teased it into a hopelessly tangled mess. I also traded out my St. Matt's sweatshirt for a shredded pair of gray jeans, a shirt made almost entirely of fishnet, and a little leather cropped jacket I'd bought in a consignment shop. A pair of knee-high black combat boots completed the outfit. Karen was waiting for me at the foot of the stairs, a file folder and my bag in her hands.

I spun to show off my outfit. "Scary enough?"

"Terrifying. Let's go."

§

The facility was a good four hours away, according to the frustratingly calm voice on Karen's GPS, and I worked hard to convince myself that no amount of grumbling on my part was going to make the drive any shorter. I stared out the window for a while, but my vision still had an odd, cloudy quality around the periphery, and the blurred scenery began to give me a headache. Instead, I closed my eyes and listened as Karen tried to formulate a plan.

"I'm sure there's some kind of waiting room. Just act lethargic and hopefully they'll let you sit unattended. I'll tell them you're on something. They'll buy it; no offense, but you look like hell."

"Yeah, well, I feel like hell, so I guess that's appropriate."

"Once you're in, try to stay out of the sight of the staff. This place isn't exactly a fortress, but it still probably won't be easy to find her. When you do, just find a way out and meet me at the car. I'll stall with the doctors to buy you as much time as I can. I'm sorry we don't have more to go on, but we'll just have to improvise."

"Whatever we have to do."

"I read up on the staff physicians while I was waiting for you to change. A couple of them have given medical evidence at some trials I've worked. They really are good people over there, not like some of the quacks I've seen on the stand."

"Not that it's done Hannah any good, since no doctor would ever believe what she's experiencing."

"Hannah could have done a lot worse than end up there," Karen said. "Durupinen have suffered far greater punishments for their gifts."

"Gift is a relative term I'm not ready to use yet," I retorted. Karen had the good grace to look contrite.

Finally, we pulled up to the New Beginnings Group Home. The sign might have said "Home," but the place looked like a miniature prison. Bars were affixed to the windows on both floors of the sterile white concrete structure. The cheerful tulips planted along the walkways looked as out of place as if they had been planted in the middle of the arctic tundra. A chain-link fence ran around the perimeter of the yard, but it appeared low and easy to climb. Despite my best efforts, I was practically hyperventilating by the time we found our way inside.

Karen grasped my shoulders tightly, and I let her steer me into the lobby. She sat me in an orange plastic chair and then marched to the front desk. I was repressing a horrible flashback of visiting my grandfather at the Winchester House for the Aged. As depressing as that place had been, there was something even worse about knowing that the patients here were just kids, spending what should have been the best years of their lives locked away in this prison of barred windows, cinder block walls, and ironic tulips.

I could see Karen gesturing rather frantically to the nurse at the front desk. She was clearly a better actress than I was. I wondered how many times she'd had to lie to keep the Durupinen's secrets. She'd done it plenty of times to me. The nurse, who was built like a linebacker, leaned around Karen to get a better look at me. Before I could even try to look drugged-out, she nodded, as though one glance at me had confirmed all that Karen had said. The nurse stood up and stomped her way across the tiles towards me. Karen followed, her expression the picture of motherly concern. "I'm sorry, I'm not sure what the delay is with her paperwork, but I can assure you, she is supposed to be admitted here. This is an emergency, court-mandated placement. Isn't there anywhere you can put her while we sort this out?"

"I guess I can put her in one of the detox rooms until the doctor clears it up," the nurse said.

"That's wonderful, thank you," Karen sighed. She turned to me and shook my shoulder. "Jessica? You need to go with Nurse Jameson. She is going to take you somewhere where you can lie down."

I glanced from the nurse's sour face to Karen's. Should I go quietly, or make a scene? Karen sensed my hesitation and tossed me a clue.

"Now don't give her any trouble, okay? Not like last time."

"I want to go home!"

"I know you do. We just need to get you cleaned up and then we'll go home, okay?" She smiled.

I looked back at the nurse now towering over me. Seriously, the woman was downright Amazonian. She was attempting to smile too, though it looked more like she was going to swallow me whole.

"You're lying! You're not gonna let me go home. You're just

gonna lock me up here, aren't you? Do you think I'm fucking stupid? I hate you, you bitch!" This last bit might have been overkill, but I figured it was better to overplay it than underplay it.

Karen went along with it, though. "Jessica! Do not use that kind of disrespectful language with me! I have had it! I said we would go home, and I promise that we will, but you are not going home in this condition. If your father sees you like this, he'll kick you out of the house. Is that what you want?"

"Yes!"

"Enough! Now, please let Nurse Jameson take you somewhere to rest."

"I hate you, mom! I hate you!" I shouted as the nurse hefted me out of the chair and across the hall. I chanced one glance over my shoulder. Karen was watching me anxiously. She gave me a quick thumbs-up, then pointed to her cell phone just as I lost sight of her around the corner. We'd agreed to text each other to keep in touch.

"Jessica, your mother told me she thinks you took some ecstasy at that party. Is that true?" Nurse Jameson's voice was low and gravelly.

"Yeah."

"Is that all you took?"

"Yeah. I mean, I think so. I don't really remember."

"Mm-hmm." Nurse Jameson released the death-grip on my shoulder long enough to extract a laminated I.D. on a lanyard from the neckline of her scrubs. She waved it in front of a small black sensor on the wall and the door in front of us swung open. It looked like I was going to have to steal one of those in order to get Hannah and me out of here. I wasn't up on my legal jargon, but I really hoped that wasn't a felony.

Nurse Jameson steered me into an identical corridor and then took an immediate right into a small, nondescript room that held nothing but a cot, a bedside table, and a black plastic trash can. In one swift motion she muscled me onto the bed and swept the trash can alongside it.

"You may start to feel sick when you come down, Jessica. Just aim for the trash can, okay? I'll have to clean it up if you miss."

"I'll do that," I mumbled letting my head fall limply back onto the pillow.

"Put those on," she told me, pointing to a greenish-blue pile of cotton fabric on the end of the bed. She walked to a small intercom unit on the wall. She pushed the button and said, "New intake in detox three. Urine kit and scrubs requested." Then she turned back to me. "Well? Put them on!"

I gaped at her. "Can't you give me some privacy?"

"Don't think so, sunshine," she barked. "I can't leave you until I'm sure you aren't hiding anything on your person. You'll get your clothes back when I'm sure they're clean. So, let's go, I've got a lot of other patients to see to."

Luckily, I'd already stuck my cell phone in my bra. I didn't know if that counted as contraband, but I wasn't going to draw attention to it if I didn't have to. I scrambled into the loose cotton pajamas as quickly as I could and deposited my clothes and boots into a small plastic bag before handing them over.

"Now lie down and try to get some rest. I'll be back in a few minutes to check on you, and if everything is sorted out with your paperwork, we'll move you to one of the resident rooms," she said. The door clicked shut behind her.

I held still for a minute or so, to make sure she was gone, and then crept up from the bed. As I neared the closed door I could hear voices nearby.

"...need to lock her in?"

"No, she's technically not committed yet, so we can't. But she'll be out cold in a few minutes anyway. Mother got home from a business trip and found her nearly passed out in the backyard."

"The backyard?"

"Trying to sneak in a window after being out all night. You should see her eyes. I'm not sure what she's on but it's not just ecstasy."

"Did you start your rounds yet?"

"No. Damn it, I'll never clock out on time now."

"I'll check the girls in South for you, if you want. They'll be back from the first lunch seating soon."

"Thanks. I'll see you tonight, Helen."

"Not me. I'm off tonight. Bye."

The squeak of two pairs of orthopedic shoes faded away.

I pressed my palms against the door and inched it open. The hallway was completely deserted. I slipped out and started in the opposite direction from the lobby. I'd only made it a few yards when a door began to open to my right. A nurse was backing out of it, wheeling some kind of cart. I ducked into the room directly across the hall and pulled the door shut behind me.

The room was large and bright, with buttery yellow walls and curtains striped in primary colors, like something you'd find in a preschool. Several groups of couches and comfortable chairs were situated around low, 70s style linoleum coffee tables, each of which was stacked with board games. I realized too late that there was someone sitting in the room, a boy about my age playing solitaire in the corner by the window. He made no sign that he had noticed me as I dropped into a chair, breathing hard. I needed to plan out my next move, but I had almost nothing to go on.

"So what are you in for?" he asked. His voice was unusually high and feminine.

"I'm not in. I'm just visiting."

"Really? You mean those are *your* wardrobe choices? Oh, honey."

Something about him made me feel edgy, but then again, they weren't going to let dangerous lunatics wander the place unaccompanied.

The boy sighed dramatically. "Well?"

"Well, what?"

"Aren't you going to ask me what I'm in for?"

"No, actually I wasn't. Should I?"

He pouted. "Well, yeah. I mean, I provided you with an ideal set-up. I must have piqued your curiosity, just a little." He gazed at me through a curtain of shaggy dark hair, and his eyes were amused.

"I guess I didn't want to be rude," I said.

"I asked you first. Are you calling me rude?"

"Yeah, I guess I am."

He arched one eyebrow. "Fair enough."

We sat in silence that was neither loaded nor awkward. It was broken only by the squeak of the nurse's cart on the linoleum and the crisp slap of the boy's playing cards onto the table.

"Depression, acute anxiety, attempted suicide, and an addiction to prescription pain killers. That's the short list," he said candidly.

"Thanks for sharing," I said. I was suddenly struck by inspiration. "Hey, do you know Hannah? Hannah Ballard?"

He narrowed his eyes at me. "What do you want with Hannah?"

I took that as a yes. "Do you know where her room is?"

"Why do you want to know where her room is?"

"Why is that your business?"

"Hannah is my business. We're friends."

I thought about cursing at him, but figured that wouldn't help me get the information I needed. Instead I said, "I'm here to see her. Trust me, she'll be glad you told me where she is."

"And how do I know I can trust you?" he asked.

"You don't."

He was silent for a moment, then smirked devilishly. "Touché. They generally keep the girls and boys separate, but those rules don't really apply to me. She's in room 218 South, one floor up and to the left, as far as you can go."

I thanked him and hopped back up, peeking through the little window in the door to make sure the coast was clear.

"I'm Milo, by the way."

"Jess." I glanced over at him, but he was still just flipping the cards. Flip. Flip. Flip.

"And you're sure you're not in?"

"Yeah, I'm sure." There was a doctor talking to the nurse with the cart, still only a few feet down the hallway.

"Did they just say you were coming for a visit? An evaluation? Because that probably means you're in," he continued.

"No. I think I would know if I were being checked in. I'm not."

"Fine, fine, if you say so. It just seemed likely, that's all." Flip. Flip. Flip.

He'd hit a nerve there, that was for damn sure. I twisted around from the door to confront him, but he still wasn't looking at me. "Likely? Based on what? Am I so obviously a head case, just from looking at me?"

"No, no. You look normal enough. The hair's a bit rebellious, but not a total giveaway."

I snorted. "What's that, an asylum fashion tip? Your haircut is looking pretty 'Emo' too, okay?"

"The lady doth protest too much, methinks," he quoted.

"Methinks the lady hath read Hamlet, too, smartass," I shot back.

"Sorry, I just call them like I see them."

"Okay then, what are you basing your brilliant deduction on, here? A whopping two minutes of conversation?" My voice had risen, which was not the smartest choice on my part, but Milo was supremely unconcerned.

"I guess you could say that I'm basing it on our conversation, yes."

Exasperated, I turned away from him and concentrated on making my escape. "Yeah, well, thanks for the diagnosis. I'll try to keep my mouth shut around the staff so they don't tackle me into a straitjacket."

"Good idea. The ones who talk to me usually wind up heavily medicated."

Flip. Flip. Silence.

I spun back around to face him. No Milo. No cards. Nothing. I scanned the entire room. There was no other door, no corner he could be hiding in.

Well, damn. Was I just going to see ghosts everywhere I went now? Utterly unnerved, I pushed my realization away until I had the time to deal with it, and snuck out into the now-deserted hallway.

Within moments, though, I was glad I'd met Milo, because I don't know how I would have found Hannah otherwise. As I headed straight for the staircase, I passed at least five other hallways I could have taken wrong turns down. Halfway up the stairs to the second floor, my phone began to vibrate. It was a text from Karen.

Doctor searching for paperwork. Where r u?

I texted back. *Almost to her room. How much time?*

15 min. Maybe 10. Enough?

Don't know. I'll try.

I stowed the phone back in my bra and took the rest of the stairs two at a time. I was fairly lucky as I stepped out into the south hallway; there was only one person in sight, and she was clearly a patient. Trying to look like I both belonged there and knew where I was going, I followed the room numbers to the left, past maybe fifteen rooms, until I stood directly in front of room 218. On my tiptoes, I peeked into the little window set into the door. The room was empty.

I tried the handle and found the door unlocked, a stroke of luck I had not expected. With a final glance down the hallway, I slipped inside and pulled the door shut behind me.

"Who are you?" a voice demanded.

I stifled a scream. The room had been empty, I was sure of it, but now a girl with stringy blonde hair was crouching in the corner, cowering.

"Hannah?"

"No! I'm not Hannah! I'm Carley! Why are you here? What do you want with me?! I already told them I wasn't going!" she screeched.

I opened my mouth and then shut it. There was something about the way the light didn't quite hit her, something about the way she seemed untouched by the shadows.

Holy shit! Two ghosts in five minutes!

I tried to keep my voice soothing. "Okay, Carley. Don't worry, I'm not going to take you anywhere. I'm just a patient here, like you. Can you tell me where Hannah is?"

"No! I won't tell you anything! You go away! They can't make me tell you anything!" she shrieked.

Without warning the light bulb in the lamp beside her flared to life and exploded in the same instant. With a miserable wail, Carley turned and crawled away straight through the wall.

I heaved a sigh of relief that she was gone and took stock of the rest of my surroundings. The room was small and devoid of personality, like a hotel room. Two twin beds and two small desks with matching chairs suggested that the room was meant for two occupants, though only one side appeared to be lived in. I chose the bed further from the window, the one stripped of bedding, and perched on the end. I'd made it here, and now there was nothing to do but wait.

I looked for a clue that might tell me something, anything, about my sister. Her side of the room reminded me of Tia's in its cleanliness. The bed was made with obsessive precision, the pillows lined up perfectly with the turned-down comforter. A number of books were arranged on a shelf behind the headboard. A quick glance confirmed that they were alphabetized, their bindings perfectly aligned.

The desk was covered in piles of matching books, the kind of black and white composition books I used to get in grade school. I walked over and picked one up. On the front cover, in tiny, precise handwriting was the name "Hannah Ballard." As I flipped through the pages, it appeared to be some kind of log.

April 18th

7:30 AM—Girl with blonde hair and freckles, art room. Gunshot wound to side of head. Self-inflicted? Standing by window with paintbrush. Tried to speak to me twice. Eye contact avoided—Jameson present. First sighting, 12 minutes.

8:47 AM—Assigned meds—two Valium and two Seroquel. Tongued and flushed.

12:30 PM—Old woman on back lawn during rec. time. Same one as April 6th, same location. (See log entry for April 6th at 11AM.) Not screaming this time. Sighting 45 minutes.

Tears welling in my eyes, I picked up another and flipped through it. Then another. And another. They were all the same. Encounter after encounter, ghost after ghost, for years on end. This had been my sister's existence.

"What are you doing in my room?"

I whirled around, dropping the book I'd been holding. There was a girl standing in the doorway, her hand resting on the handle. There was nothing ghostly about her. I would have known her anywhere.

Hannah was absolutely tiny. Her face was long and pale as porcelain, and the round, dark eyes that blinked confusedly seemed much too large, and old, to belong there. The resemblance to our mother in her fine, pointed features was so pronounced as to be startling. Her hair was chestnut brown and seemed unruly like mine; it sprung defiantly from the elastic band that struggled to hold it in a ponytail at the nape of her neck. Her entire frame seemed brittle and, despite how small it was, it seemed to take her considerable effort to hold it up.

It would be impossible to understand the emotions that ran through me at the sight of my sister. It began with a warmth that spread through me that concentrated behind my eyes, where it burned with repressed tears. The warmth drained almost as quickly as it had appeared as an icy fear chased it away. She looked so fragile, so breakable. The fear morphed into a fierce feeling, half-love, half-anger, and I knew at that very moment that I would destroy anyone who ever tried to hurt her again.

While this new world expanded and collapsed inside me, Hannah was staring at me, as though trying to decide something. Her expression seemed impassive, but her hands shook.

"You shouldn't be here. I took my meds. I haven't missed any in over a month. Why are you here?" Her voice fluttered when she spoke.

"I... came to see you," I replied, finally finding my voice.

"But you shouldn't be here. I shouldn't be able to see you." She squeezed her eyes shut and screwed up her face in concentration. After a few seconds she opened them again and refocused on me. Her expression morphed from surprise to frustration, and then fear.

"No! You aren't supposed to be here! They promised!" Hannah started to back away, her hand reaching for an intercom unit on the wall.

"Wait! Stop! Please don't press that button! Just hear me out! Hannah, I'm real, okay? I'm a real person."

Her hand hovered over the intercom switch but she did not press it. "What do you mean, real?"

"I mean I'm not a ghost. I'm not like the others you've been seeing."

Hannah shook her head ferociously from side to side, her voice rising shrilly. "Not ghosts. Hallucinations. Dr. Ferber promised that—"

"—Fine! I'm not a hallucination either."

"Are you my new roommate? They didn't tell me I was getting a roommate." Her voice hitched strangely.

"No, I'm not your roommate. I'm not a patient here."

"What are you doing in my room? Why are you touching my things?"

God, I was not ready for this! I didn't know which of her questions I should answer, if I would set her off into a panic, or if she would even believe me. I decided to answer as little as I could get away with. "My name is Jessica. I came to get you out of here. Don't you want to get out of here?"

"I don't want to *stay* here," Hannah said, "but I have nowhere else to go."

"What if there was somewhere else you could go? What if there was a home waiting for you, a real one, not another place like this? Would you want to leave then?"

Hannah sank slowly onto the end of the bed and began obsessively straightening the bedspread that had wrinkled around her. I noticed a number of thin scars that covered her wrists. "Yes, I would want to leave. But they would never let me. And even if they did, why would I go with you? Who are you, anyway?"

"I'm someone who understands what's been happening to you. Those people you've seen since you were little? I can see them too."

Hannah's eyebrows drew together and made her look surprisingly fierce. "I don't believe you."

"It's true." I took a step toward her, and sat across from her on the other bed. I moved cautiously, behaving as I would around a skittish animal. It was imperative that she believe me, that I say what I needed to get her to trust me. "I know everyone told you that they were hallucinations, but they aren't. They're ghosts, people whose spirits are trapped here. I can see them too, I promise you."

"No, ghosts aren't real. In therapy, they told me that my illness—"

"—You aren't sick, Hannah. They just don't understand what you can do. Listen, I can prove it. I just met your old roommate, Carley.

"You couldn't have. She's—"

228

"—Dead. I know. But I just saw her."

"I don't believe you," Hannah repeated.

"What about Milo?"

Hannah's frantic hands froze. She looked like cornered prey. "I... I don't know anyone named Milo."

"Yes, you do! He told me you were friends."

Hannah's eyes narrowed. "What does he look like?"

"Really thin with shaggy dark hair and blue eyes, likes to play solitaire in that common room downstairs."

"What did he say to you? Did he tell you anything?"

"He seemed pretty interested in sharing his personal information, actually. He told me he was committed here for depression, anxiety, attempted suicide, and an addiction to prescription pain killers. He's the one who told me how to find your room. He also told me I needed a new hairstyle and that he could tell I was crazy just by talking to me."

The corner of Hannah's mouth twitched up ever so slightly. "That sounds like something he would say." Her eyes bore into me. "You really did see him, didn't you?"

"Yes. I'm telling you the truth, I promise."

"That doesn't explain how you knew I was here or why I should go anywhere with you," she said, returning to her compulsive straightening of the bed.

I took a deep breath. I could only hope she was stronger than she looked. "About ten months ago I started having these Visitations—the same kind that you've been having for your entire life. Ever since it started, I've been in search of the reason why. And just last night, I got the answers I was looking for."

Hannah's eyes filled with tears. "Why? Why can we see them when no one else can?"

"It has to do with our heritage, our bloodline. You and I were both born into a line of women who have this... ability. We're related, Hannah."

"Related?" she whispered.

"Yes. We're sisters."

Hannah stared at me as though I had spoken a word in a foreign language.

"But I don't have anyone. I've never had anyone," she said blankly.

"I know. I didn't know about you, Hannah. I didn't know you were here, or I would have been here sooner. I'm so sorry."

"I don't have anyone," she repeated. "Only the dead people. I only have the dead people."

"But you do now, Hannah, that's what I'm trying to tell—" My phone buzzed to life again.

"Jess, have you found her yet?" Karen sounded out of breath.

"Yes, I'm with her now."

"The doctor started calling for your medical records, so I had to get out of there. They'll know by now that we made it all up. I pulled the car onto Preston Street, around the back side of the property. I'll wait here for you."

"Okay, we'll find a way out."

"Hurry, Jess, and whatever you do, don't get caught!"

I hung up. "Hannah, I'm really sorry, but we don't have a lot of time for explanations right now. I promise you that I will answer every question that you have, every one that I have an answer to. But right now we need to get out of here. Will you come with me?"

Hannah seemed frozen. She stared at me, her face disturbingly blank. Then she nodded almost imperceptibly and tried to rise shakily from the bed. Instinctively, I reached out a hand to help her up. She hesitated and then took it.

We both gasped.

A powerful current, almost like electricity, pulsed between us. Yet rather than wanting to break apart, the current only bound us more closely together. A gust of wind blew our hair around our faces, and the quiet of the room was suddenly alive with voices, bleeding through the walls, echoing from the floors, emanating from everywhere.

I wrenched my hand away from Hannah's and broke the connection. Hannah stumbled back from me and fell against her desk. We stared into each other's eyes, breathless.

"What was that?" she cried.

"I don't know, but I don't think we should let it happen again," I said. "Are you okay?"

She stood up gingerly. "I think so."

At that moment the intercom system crackled to life. "All residents please proceed to their rooms for afternoon rounds. All staff please take note, this is a code pink round. Please call the front desk for instructions."

"What's a code pink round?" I asked.

"It means someone is missing from wherever they're supposed to be. The nurses will be searching the rooms."

I groaned. "Damn it. I'm the code pink. They must have gone back to the detox room and found me missing."

"You were in detox?"

"Yeah. Well, I pretended to need detox so that I could sneak in and find you."

Hannah almost smiled. "You did that for me?"

"Of course I did." I tried to untangle my thoughts and focus. "We need to work together if we're going to pull this off. I'm going to need your help. What's our best chance to hide me until this code pink is over?"

Hannah thought for a moment. "I don't know. The kitchen maybe? If we can get down there, it opens out to the back parking lot. They leave the door open because it gets so hot with the ovens; I've seen it through the tray pass-through."

"Sounds like it's worth a try."

"We'll need to be quick, before they..."

A loud metallic click resounded through the room.

"...lock us in," she finished.

I flew to the door and pulled on the handle but I knew it was no good before I'd even tried. Hannah sank into her chair.

"It's too late. We can't get out that way."

"Come on, Hannah, think! Isn't there anywhere I can hide in here?" I cried. I chanced a look out of the little window in the door. A team of nurses was already at the end of the hall, opening the first door by swiping an I.D. through a sensor.

"No. I don't know how to keep them from finding you, unless..." her voice trailed away and her stare became glassy as it landed on the piles of notebooks.

"Hannah?"

She didn't move.

"HANNAH!"

She came out of her haze and rose unsteadily. "Get in the closet," she said.

"In the...? Hannah, no offense, but that's the first place they're going to look!"

"Just do it! Trust me."

What other choice did I have? I ran across the room, wrenched the closet door open and backed myself into the corner until I was pressed against the back wall.

"What are you going to do?" I asked.

"I'm going to call for help."

"Call who? Who could possibly..."

Voices just outside the door interrupted my question. I heard the beeping of the sensor and the snap of the lock as it released and the door swung open. My heart thudded against my ribcage.

I recognized the first voice to speak.

"Hello, Hannah," Nurse Jameson said. "Did you hear the announcement? This round will include a room check."

"Yes, I heard."

"Nurse Roberts has your meds. Please show your hands and swallow these."

"No."

"I'm sorry?"

"I said no. I'm not going to take those pills."

"It's not an option, Hannah, you know that," a kinder male voice said. "Either you take them voluntarily or we have to restrain you and administer them ourselves. It's your choice, but it would be a lot easier on all of us if you just took them."

"No," Hannah repeated softly.

"Hannah, we don't have time for this," Nurse Jameson sighed. "You've been voluntary for over a month now. What's the problem all of a sudden?"

Hannah stayed silent. I closed my eyes and tried, unsuccessfully, not to panic. What was she doing? How could causing a huge scene by refusing her medication possibly help our situation?

"Fine, have it your way," Nurse Jameson said. "We're coming in. Is there anyone or anything in your room that we should know about?"

"Not yet," Hannah said. Her voice was barely louder than a murmur. As she spoke, a cold draft swept the room and the temperature started to drop.

"What did you say?" Nurse Jameson asked.

"I said there's no one here that you should know about," Hannah repeated, a little more loudly. "But there will be."

My teeth started to chatter. I clenched them together to silence the sound. What the hell was going on? I chanced a peek though the slats of the door.

Nurse Jameson towered in the doorway, flanked by a short but burly male nurse. Hannah stood in the middle of the room, her head bowed as though in prayer. Her mouth was moving silently and her hands were clenching and unclenching at her sides. As I watched, her hair started blowing gently around her face.

"Hannah? Are you alright?" Nurse Jameson asked warily.

"What is she doing?" Nurse Roberts whispered.

Hannah's muttering grew faster and faster. It was impossible to tell what she was saying, but the effect was undeniable. The room was now so cold that I could see my breath. A familiar feeling began to creep through my veins, a sensation I'd felt only a few times before, but which I would never forget.

"Why is it so cold in here?" Nurse Jameson asked. She edged a step into the room and examined the thermostat on the wall.

But I knew why it was so cold. I'd felt it, and now I could see it. Ghosts. Everywhere. Materializing right and left, floating through walls, rising up from the floors. They were men and women, adults and children. A few looked like they'd stepped out of the pages of a history book, in antiquated clothing; others looked like they'd just walked in off the street. I recognized Milo and Carley among them. There were probably fifty of them in all, fading in and out of focus, flickering like eight-millimeter film images, hovering, floating and crouching everywhere. Whatever Hannah was doing was calling them to her, and they clustered around her like moths around a candle flame, forming a wall of the dead between her and the nurses.

Although Nurse Jameson could see none of this, she knew something was very wrong. She was backing away from Hannah like she was about to explode.

"Call Doctor Ferber," she told Nurse Roberts.

He unclipped a radio from his belt and raised it to his mouth, but before he could say anything, a small boy with a gaping head wound shot forward, thrusting his hands out for the radio. It flew out of Nurse Roberts' hand, arced through the air and smashed into the wall.

"What the hell was that?" he shouted.

"Hannah, I need you to calm down. Just take a deep breath and calm down," Nurse Jameson said, raising both of her hands in a gesture of surrender.

Hannah said nothing aloud, but inclined her head toward Milo, who disappeared then reappeared in the same instant beside Nurse Jameson. With a casual flick of his wrist, he sent her clipboard, papers, and I.D. soaring out of her hands and skidding across the floor.

Shock and terror had incapacitated me, and the worst part was that I didn't know who I was more terrified of, this army of the dead or my own sister.

Nurse Jameson turned to Nurse Roberts. "I need five milligrams of Haldol," she muttered. He reached back into the medical cart behind him, filled a syringe, and handed it to her.

Nurse Jameson took a cautious step toward Hannah, the syringe concealed behind her back. "Hannah, let's calm down and talk, okay? Can you tell me what's wrong?"

"Stay away from me," Hannah commanded. The spirits crowded around her rippled as each word passed through them.

Nurse Jameson took another measured step forward.

Nurse Roberts shadowed her.

"I told you to stay away from me," Hannah said, her voice quavering.

Around her, every ghostly eye turned on the advancing nurses.

Nurse Jameson and Nurse Roberts froze.

The room pulsated with a strange, cold power.

I held my breath. I could see Nurse Jameson's mind working furiously. She was trying to decide what to do. If she could see what was really advancing toward her, she would have run screaming.

But she couldn't. So, she stepped forward instead.

Hannah pointed a single finger at her.

The room exploded, glass shattering from the windows, the furniture upending, clothes and books scattering everywhere. I flung my hands up to protect my face as the closet door flew off its hinges. The ghosts surged forward as a single entity, blasting the nurses off their feet. Nurse Roberts crashed headlong into the medical cart and lay in a heap on the floor. Nurse Jameson collided with the wall behind her and crumpled onto the rug, the syringe thrust deep into her own thigh.

Only Hannah remained untouched amidst the wreckage. She stood as calmly and quietly as if she'd been meditating. As she raised her head and opened her eyes, the ghosts around her shimmered away into nothingness.

I crawled out of the closet on trembling legs. "Hannah? Are you alright?" I lay a gentle hand on her shoulder. She jumped a little, and looked at me with empty eyes, like she'd forgotten who I was. Then, something barely perceptible shifted in her gaze.

"Yes. I'm alright."

I wanted to ask her what the hell had just happened, but there was no time for that.

"We've got to get out of here, now!" I snatched Nurse Jameson's I.D. off the floor, grabbed Hannah's arm, and dragged her out into the hallway.

It was deserted; all of the patients were still locked into their rooms, their confused faces pressed to every window. We sprinted to the ward entrance. I mashed the I.D. against the sensor and the door swung open. Somewhere behind us, a distant door opened and voices began shouting. The door pulled shut behind us, quickly muffling them. I knew it wouldn't take long for the rest of the staff to be alerted to the absolute insanity that had occurred in Hannah's room, but I'd hoped for a few more minutes, at least.

"Which way to the kitchen?" I panted.

"Down those stairs and to the right," Hannah said.

I took the steps two at a time, but Hannah was falling behind. Whatever she'd done to summon the ghosts had left her weak and exhausted. By the time we reached the bottom of the flight, I was practically dragging her, and the voices on our tail were growing louder.

We used the I.D. again at the bottom of the steps, and I yanked the door shut behind us.

"They're catching up," Hannah gasped, clutching at a stitch in her side. "We've got to find a way to slow them down, or we'll never make it out!"

I glanced around frantically and my eyes found a fire extinguisher encased in glass on the wall.

"Give me your sweatshirt!" I cried.

Hannah yanked off her sweatshirt and handed it to me. I wrapped it around my arm and threw my elbow into the glass as hard as I could. It shattered on the first try. I grabbed the fire extinguisher and ran with it back to the door at the bottom of the stairs.

"Open the door again and hold it open this time!"

Hannah did as I asked. I ducked quickly through and found the sensor on the other side. The staircase above me was alive with shouts and echoing footsteps. I raised the fire extinguisher above my head and brought it down repeatedly on the sensor until it dangled uselessly from the wall. I flung the extinguisher aside and pulled the door shut behind us.

"Keep running!" I urged. "I have no idea if that will hold them, or for how long!"

We tore towards the kitchen. Behind us, fists pounded on the door, but it held.

A right, a left, another left.

"There!" Hannah said finally, pointing to a set of white double doors directly ahead of us.

I slammed the I.D. into one last sensor and we stumbled into an industrial-looking kitchen. We didn't stop to see who was yelling at us, or to check if they were on our heels. We darted around several large prep tables and a giant mixing unit towards the exit in the far corner of the room. We burst right through the exit and into the bright spring afternoon.

We skidded to a halt just long enough to spot Karen's car beyond the chain link fence, the engine snarling as she revved it impatiently.

"There she is!"

I grabbed Hannah's sleeve and tugged her across the lawn. We scrambled awkwardly over the fence and stumbled the last few yards to the car. I flung open the door, pulled us in, and we crumpled into a breathless heap in the back seat.

"Oh thank God, thank God!" Karen cried. "Are you okay?"

"We're fine, just drive. Drive!" I yelled.

With a squeal of the tires, Karen took off down the street and turned the corner like a NASCAR champ. For the next few minutes the car was silent except for our ragged breathing. I strained my ears for the sounds of sirens, but heard nothing.

"Aren't you worried the police will be after us? How many laws did we just break?" I said.

"It doesn't matter. I've already alerted the Durupinen to what we were planning. They have a long and illustrious history of laying false trails and bribing law enforcement. We're covered, I promise," Karen said.

When we finally merged onto the highway, Karen allowed herself a glance over her shoulder at us.

"You must be Hannah," she said.

But Hannah's eyes had fluttered closed and she did not answer.

19

TÉIGH ANONN

"IS SHE OKAY?" KAREN ASKED.

"I think so. They've got her on all kinds of meds, Karen. They seem to make her really weak," I said. "How did you do it? When I saw the sensor system on the doors, I never thought we'd be able to pull it off."

"It was Hannah. Karen, you won't believe how she got us out of there. It was insane. They figured out I was missing and they locked all the rooms down. Then these two nurses showed up, and Hannah just closed her eyes and suddenly it was like every ghost she'd ever met was there to help us."

The small part of Karen's face I could see in the rear view mirror looked alarmed. "What do you mean? They just showed up?"

"It was like she summoned them, Karen! It was like she could control them. She just concentrated for a minute and they all appeared out of nowhere. She used them to attack the nurses so we could get out."

"Tell me exactly what happened," Karen said.

I gave every detail I could pull from my frazzled memory. Karen was silent for so long when I'd finished that I got worried.

"Karen?"

"Yes."

"Was that... normal? I mean, for Durupinen? Can we all do what she did in there?" I thought of the number of times I'd tried to contact Evan without even a whisper of a response.

"No, Jess. That was something very... unusual," Karen said. Her eyes found mine in the mirror. "Jess, I don't want you to tell anyone about what Hannah did in there."

"Who would I—"

"—I mean the other Durupinen, especially. I don't know why Hannah was able to do what she did. Maybe it was a result of being

Bound for so long, I can't be sure. But I want to look into it for myself before we let anyone know about that particular... talent."

"Okay."

"Promise me, Jess. Not a word about it until I figure out more."

"I promise."

Hannah slept the entire car ride home to Boston, and it took both of us to get her up the stairs and into my room to sleep. I wanted to stay in the chair by the bed until she woke up, but Karen refused to let me.

"You need the rest as much as she does. Don't forget what you went through less than twenty-four hours ago. It was against my better judgment to let you do what you've done already today, but we had no choice. Now we do have a choice and you are going to sleep. No buts."

I but-ed anyway. "But I want to be there when she—"

"—I won't take my eyes off of her, I promise. And I will wake you when she's up."

Having pulled the rug completely out from under my argument, Karen gently pushed me onto the pillows of the sofa and tugged a blanket up to my chin.

"Sleep!" she ordered.

Like some kind of incantation, I suddenly couldn't resist the word; I'd sunk into unconsciousness before I could complete another thought.

§

By the time a voice roused me again, early morning sunlight had crept across the living room floor in wide golden stripes, falling across my body like warm embracing arms.

"She's up. I thought you'd like to know," said a voice much too close to me.

I shrieked in surprise and twisted around to discover Milo sitting on the windowsill, smirking at me.

Karen poked her head around the corner. "Jess? Are you alright?"

"Just a ghost," I grumbled. "Absolutely nothing out of the ordinary."

"An aggressive one? Do you need help?"

"Nope. Just an annoying one."

Milo positively beamed. "Stop, I'm blushing," he sang.

"Okay, well, Hannah just woke up. She was going to shower and get changed. She'll be down in a few minutes," Karen said.

"I know. The ghost told me."

"Oh. Okay. Well, I'll come get you when she's ready. Are you sure you're okay?" she asked doubtfully.

"Yeah, yeah, I'm fine. What time is it?"

"A little after seven. You've been asleep for fifteen hours. I told you you needed it."

"Wow. I'll be up in a minute." I turned back to my visitor. "Damn it, Milo, you scared the hell out of me!"

"Sorry!" he said gleefully, not looking sorry at all.

"What are you doing here? Why aren't you at New Beginnings?"

"What, and miss all the fun? Not on your life, girl! Besides, where she goes, I go."

"I thought ghosts were attached to the places they died. Don't you have to stay put?"

"Evidently not."

The phone rang in the kitchen. I heard the distant mumble of Karen's voice as she answered it.

"Anyway, I have a message for you," he continued.

"A message? From who?"

"From *them*," he replied cryptically, then added a mocking "Wooooooooo!" for effect.

I rolled my eyes. "Okay, Casper. What do 'they' have to say?"

"I've been instructed to tell you to hurry. They're impatient. They say they've waited long enough," he recited like a kid who'd memorized something for class.

"Am I supposed to know what that means?"

Milo shrugged. "Don't ask me. I'm just your roguishly handsome messenger boy."

"Fine. Well, I can't do anything until Hannah gets down here, so..."

"I can hurry her along," he offered, hopping up.

"Don't you dare! She's in the shower, you creep! Stay out of there!"

"Relax, honey. She's not exactly my type."

"Oh. Right. Well, stay out of there anyway."

He heaved a long-suffering sigh. "Fine, fine. I'll wait for her upstairs. I want to get a look around the place anyway." He faded from my view like a mirage.

"Stay out of my room!" I yelled. I could have sworn I heard a distant chuckle.

"Jess?" Karen had returned. "Are you, um... alone?"

"Yup."

"That was Tia on the phone. She sounded pretty worried. I think maybe you should call her."

"Oh, no! Poor Tia! She must be going crazy. I'll do that now, I... wait, what do I tell her?"

"As little as you can. We'll work on a cover story together later. Do you want me to bring you the phone?"

"No, I've got my cell."

"Would you like some tea with breakfast? I'm already brewing some for your sister."

"No, thanks. I'll stick to coffee," I said. Marveling at how strange the words "your sister" still sounded, I fished my phone out of my sweatshirt pocket.

Twenty-three missed calls. Seventeen voicemails. I scrolled through the missed calls; they were all from Tia's cell phone. Cringing internally, I pressed number three on my speed dial. It took less than half a ring for her to pick up.

"JESS! Oh, my *goodness*, I was so worried! What happened? Are you alright?"

"Hi, Tia. Yeah. I'm okay."

"Sam came by the room and said that he'd seen you at the library, but that you weren't there when they were packing up in the morning, and neither was Professor Pierce! The others wouldn't tell him where you'd gone. I didn't know what to tell him, since he wasn't even supposed to know you were there, so I just played dumb." Tia was babbling at warp speed now, and I could barely keep up.

I jumped in before she could start hyperventilating. "I just saw Sam for a second, so I don't think he really has any clue why I was there. I'll come up with an explanation."

"I've been calling and calling! Why didn't you pick up?"

"I've been... sleeping, actually," I admitted, feeling increasing twinges of guilt that I hadn't gotten in touch with her sooner. Knowing Tia, she'd probably paced a hole clean through our dorm room floor. "It was a rough night."

"But what happened? Are you okay? Are you hurt?"

"No, I'm okay, really. It was all just a little traumatic and Karen thought I should come home."

It was Tia's turn to sound guilty. "Look, I'm sorry I called you at your aunt's house. I know you haven't been telling her everything that's been going on, but I just had to know if—"

"—No, no, don't apologize. She knows everything now. I already talked to her. She sort of made me come home, actually. In fact, now that I'm up, I think she and I have a lot more talking to do. I'll call you later and explain everything, I promise."

"Okay, but please call soon, the suspense is killing me!" Tia moaned.

I laughed. "I will, I will."

"Good. Oh, and by the way I left you like ten voicemails. So, um, I guess you can just delete them."

"You left me seventeen voicemails, actually. And yes, I'll get right on that."

I said goodbye to Tia and tossed the phone aside. Moving gingerly, I got to my feet and padded into the dining room.

§

Hannah was sitting at the table, a steaming mug of tea clasped in her white-knuckled hands. She was staring into it as though it were speaking to her. I slipped into the seat across from her.

"Hi."

"Hi."

Hannah and I sat in silence while I waited for my coffee. I had so much to say to her and I had absolutely no idea where to begin.

Karen plunked a mug down in front of me and sat down at the table.

"Where's Noah?" I asked.

"Working, thank God. I still haven't had a moment to figure out what the hell I'm going to tell him."

"He doesn't know about any of this?"

"Not a clue. Oh well, I'll think of something. We always do." She took a large gulp of tea and savored it as though it were something a lot stronger. "Well, here we all are. And Hannah, you must have a lot of questions. I'll try to start at the beginning, and tell you everything I know. I'll ask Jess to fill in when I can't. Then we'll go from there."

Hannah still didn't look up from what was evidently a fascinating cup of tea. She did, however, nod that she was listening.

And so Hannah learned the truth. Karen told her everything she'd told me the previous night and, despite the absence of Lucida's snarky interruptions, I had an overwhelming sense of déjà vu. Hannah continued to stare at her mug, and I would have thought she wasn't even listening, except for a tiny crease of concentration that would appear in her forehead every now and then. I then told Hannah everything that had happened to me since August, starting with the death of our mother, the dreams, and my own ghostly encounters.

Finally, Karen and I had talked ourselves out, and there was a ringing silence pressing in on us from all sides.

"It didn't work," Hannah finally said.

"What didn't work?" Karen asked.

"The Binding. It didn't work. I still saw all those ghosts ever since I was little."

Karen's expression was miserable as she tried to answer. "I'm not sure exactly why that is, Hannah. That's a question for Finvarra, I think. I know that Bindings are only meant to be a temporary protective measure, so it's possible that it wasn't strong enough or lasting enough to keep you from Visitations. Your mother would have been devastated if she'd known."

Hannah scowled, but said nothing.

"So, what's next?" I asked Karen.

"Now that we have the two of you reunited, we must initiate your Gateway. Then it will be time for you to be trained in the ways of the Durupinen. If, that is, you are willing."

"We have a choice?" I asked.

"You do. There have been women over the years who have chosen not to embrace their birthright. But you should know that there are usually consequences to that kind of choice. If you choose never to become Durupinen, they cannot protect you from the spirits that will continue to seek you out. The ghosts themselves do not care about your choices, they sense only what you were meant to be; and they will find you, no matter where you go."

"That doesn't sound like much of a choice," Hannah said.

"No, I suppose it doesn't," Karen admitted.

"What does it mean, to be trained?" I asked.

"You would attend a school of sorts, set up by the Durupinen for the education of their Apprentices. Our training school is Fairhaven Hall, just outside of London, England, since that is the source of our family's bloodline. We are descendants of the Clan Sassanaigh, which originated in the British Isles."

"Wait, we'd have to move out of the country?" I cried. "What about college? What about St. Matt's and my friends? I thought you and mom went to Harvard?"

"We did, for a time, but only after our training. The training takes two years. The Durupinen have been able to establish an internationally recognized study abroad program as a cover for our clan school. You will be able to transfer back to the U.S. when your training is complete and your transcript will reflect that of a typical college."

"When would we go?" Hannah asked.

"As soon as possible."

I opened my mouth to argue but Karen silenced me with a weary hand.

"We'll worry about the transatlantic relocation later, okay? We have something more pressing to discuss. Because our Gateway has been closed for so long, we simply can't wait for the traditional initiation. We'll have to unlock the Gateway here and perform your first crossing before we go. Now that the two of you are back together again, the pull for spirits meant to cross through you will be stronger than ever. There's a real danger to both of you if we wait."

"That must be what Milo was talking about," I said.

"Milo?"

"The ghost I was talking to earlier. He's a friend of Hannah's from the group home."

"*Best* friend," Milo corrected. He had just appeared sitting on the kitchen counter.

"He's here," I told Karen. "In the kitchen."

Karen instinctively turned her head toward the kitchen, but then turned back to us. Her expression was almost sad. I realized that she actually *missed* seeing the ghosts that were all around us. Either she was insane or there was a lot about this entire Durupinen thing that I couldn't yet appreciate.

I continued, "He told me that they were getting impatient, and that we needed to hurry."

"I can hear them now," Hannah said. "They've been louder since I woke up."

I gaped at her, horrified. "You mean you can hear them all the time?"

She shrugged. "If I'm not medicated."

"What do you think, Hannah? Are you ready to do this?" Karen asked. "If we can cross them over, you may finally have a little peace."

It took Hannah a moment to answer.

"I don't like to think much about when I was little, but the earliest memory I can recall is sitting on my bed and talking to the ghost of a little girl in one of my foster homes. So many times I haven't even known if the people I've met have been alive or dead, and I may never know." Suddenly her voice grew stronger and she pushed her mug away from her. "But I'm tired of never being able to give them what they want. Some of them are so sad, so desperate, and they never understand why I can't help them. Now that I can, I feel like I have to do it, even if I'm afraid."

That settled it. I turned to Karen. "So, what do we have to do?"

"Well, I can help you with your first crossing. I've already spoken to Finvarra and she agrees that, under the circumstances, we should proceed immediately. I know you haven't learned the incantations or anything yet, but I can set everything up and handle the ceremonial aspects, if you girls can just follow my directions."

"Tonight?" I asked.

"Better not to wait any longer. What do you say?"

I looked at Hannah. "Up to you," I told her.

Her face betrayed the slightest suggestion of a smile. "It's not really up to either of us, is it?"

"Not really," Milo called.

Karen stood up. "Is that a yes, then?"

"Yes," we said together.

"I'm proud of you girls." Karen's eyes glimmered in the morning sunlight. "I'll get started."

§

We ascended the stairs to the roof, filled with anxiety and trepidation. As we emerged onto the rooftop where Karen had instructed us to meet her, the city of Boston was fading into purple twilight. All around us was a sea of buildings and their sharpening shadows, looking for all the world like a man-made garden reaching towards the dying sun. The breeze whipped between the buildings, carrying the echoes of the city up around us and raising gooseflesh on our arms.

Karen was standing in the middle of the roof, beckoning us forward. Candlelight lit her from below like a campfire. Her expression was uplifted and even a little excited.

"Welcome to your first Summoning Circle, girls. Come stand with me here in the middle, and I'll explain all of the aspects to you."

I glanced down. Drawn onto the roof with chalk were two perfect, concentric circles, about six feet wide. Four candles stood between the inner and outer circles, marking out a square. A strange swirling symbol was drawn in the center. I recognized it as the same symbol that was stamped into the front of my mother's old book.

For a moment I was frozen where I stood. A small voice in my head was shouting at me that this was not actually happening. It was a dream, it had to be. Things like Summoning Circles and rituals were not a part of my life, there was no way. But here I was, stepping carefully over that chalk line and feeling, as I did so, the decisiveness of that step. There was no going back.

Milo had materialized again, hovering uncomfortably around the outside of the Circle as though afraid to get near it. I wished I was out there with him, a happily uninvolved observer.

"All of this," Karen said, "will be explained in much greater detail to you in your studies, but here's the abbreviated version. I've drawn the Summoning Circle with chalk, but bear in mind the Circle can be created in a variety of ways. The four candles represent the classical elements. Have you ever heard of them before?"

I'd seen enough movies and read enough books to figure out what she was talking about. "Earth, fire, air and water, right?"

Karen nodded. "Exactly. All four of these elements must be represented in the Circle before the fifth element can be summoned here."

"What fifth element? What else is there?" I asked.

"The ancient Greeks called it 'Aether.' It translates roughly to 'essence.'"

"Spirit," Hannah said softly.

"Spirit, yes. The part of us that is not of this world, but the next. And now, it's time to call that element to join us. Are you ready?"

A shiver ran up my back and I took a shuddering breath. "Not at all. Let's get it over with."

Karen pointed to a green candle to her right. "Hannah, as the Key, you must come and stand by the candle representing earth. The earth is where the spirits are trapped, so that is where we must start."

Hannah nodded solemnly and took her place.

"Jess, you must come and stand here, by the candle representing air. This is the only element through which spirit can be conducted. As the Passage, that is your place."

As soon as I planted my feet beside that fluttering yellow candle, a steady whispering began in my ears. My heart began to race as I tried to decipher the voices, but there were too many of them tangled together. I could only comprehend the general tone: Anticipation. Excitement.

"Hannah, join your right hand with Jess's right hand," Karen instructed. Hannah reached her trembling hand for mine, and as I took it, I felt the same rushing electricity I'd felt the first time I'd touched her. The whispering voices magnified, now ringing inside my head. Hannah's widening eyes told me that she could hear them, too.

Karen's face was aglow. I realized that she had experienced all of this many times. She pulled a small book from her back pocket. I recognized it immediately as nearly identical to my mother's book, the one Lucida had left for me at Christmas.

"This is the Book of Téigh Anonn." The strange words rolled off her tongue with surprising ease. "It was presented to me when I was eighteen, and soon it will be passed formally on to you. It will be the focus of much of your training. For tonight, just listen to the incantation and try to repeat it as closely as you can."

Karen peeled the ancient cover back from the delicate pages. A sudden gust of wind blew the pages forward in a flurry, and then stopped quite abruptly on the very page Karen needed to begin the ceremony. She began to read, the words practiced and fluid:

> *"We call upon the powers endowed to us of old.*
> *We call upon the connection that binds us together.*
> *With the joining of hands and the joining of blood,*
> *The Gateway we open, the spirits we summon."*

At first all I could do was stand there with my mouth hanging open like an idiot. But then Hannah started speaking, and I automatically joined in. We repeated the first two lines, and then, with some prompting from Karen, the second two.

"Now, close your eyes and concentrate on a single phrase: 'téigh anonn.' It means 'crossing over' in the old language, and you must repeat it until the crossing has ended," Karen instructed.

"How will we know when it's over?" Hannah asked.

"Oh, you'll know, believe me. You'll feel it begin. You'll experience a flood of memories that aren't your own. They will belong to the spirits that are passing through you. And you'll feel a... tugging, I guess you'd call it. The pull of the other side is very strong, and although this Circle protects you from it, you are not immune to feeling its power."

"We're not forcing them, are we? To cross?" Hannah asked in a cracked voice.

"No. No one can force a spirit beyond the Gateway. It is a conscious choice of the spirit to step across the threshold and meet what's on the other side, whatever that may be," Karen assured her.

"What does that even mean, 'the other side?' Where are we sending them?" I asked.

"We don't know any more about it than they do. It is our job to open the doors, not to glimpse at what's behind them. We won't know until it's our own time to cross."

"That doesn't seem right," I said. "We could be sending these ghosts anywhere, couldn't we?"

"Or nowhere," Hannah added.

Karen shook her head fiercely. "No, I don't believe that. Does it make any sense to you that these doors would exist, or that we would exist to open them, if they just led to nowhere?"

"Well, no, I guess not, but..."

"Jess, do you remember what your grandfather repeated, over and over again, when you met him?"

"He said, 'I've seen it. Send me back,'" I said.

"Exactly," Karen said. "He saw it. And he wants nothing more in this world than to see it again. I may have shared your doubts once, but not anymore. We are sending these spirits where they are meant to be, and we have to have faith in that."

Hannah and I were both quiet. It was a lot to take in. Karen took our silence as assent and went on.

"There's another thing. I should warn you that you may feel spirits cross over that you recognize. That is, they may have appeared to you before in a Visitation or a dream. Don't be alarmed if that happens. Remember that this is their choice."

Hannah threw a panicked look out of the Circle at Milo, but he smiled and winked at her.

"No worries, sweetness," he said. "I'm with you."

Reassured, Hannah turned to me. "Are you ready?"

"As ready as I'll ever be."

Karen lit a final candle, a white one. She placed it on the ground between us.

"The Spirit Candle is lit. Let us begin."

20

SAYING GOODBYE

"**T**ÉIGH ANONN. TÉIGH ANONN. TÉIGH ANONN."

Flash.
A red paper lantern floating away over my head. A stolen kiss that tasted like cigarettes. A line of cocaine—like fire in my nose, my makeup-ringed eyes reflected blearily in a mirror.

Flash.
Being laced into a corset, feeling like my ribs would break. A man's handsome, mustached face, first smiling up at me from a rowboat, then choked with emotion at the end of a long church aisle, then pale and drawn in a coffin.

Flash.
Playing double Dutch, gangly legs flying beneath me. Chasing an ice cream truck up a city street, laughing. Hiding on a rusty fire escape, heart pounding. Staring into an empty refrigerator.

Life after unfamiliar life flashed before my eyes. It was all I could do to keep on my feet; the barrage of sensations was so overwhelming.

Flash.
A hospital room, clutching at my distended stomach beneath a white and blue hospital gown.

Flash.
A half-naked woman wiping lipstick from the collar of my dress shirt.

Flash.
Waiting for the subway, a kid strumming a guitar in the echoing tunnel.

"Téigh Anonn. Téigh Anonn. Téigh Anonn."

A hundred more lives flew by. I had no sense of time or space. I tried to focus on our incantation, holding on to myself for fear my own life would slip past me with the others.

A sudden spasming of Hannah's hand in mine grounded me in our own reality. I focused in on the life we were both experiencing at that moment.

Flash.
A balding man shouting angrily, his face crimson with rage. A boy stroking my cheek, telling me not to be scared as he roughly tugged at my shirt. A razor slicing cleanly across my wrist, drawing bright scarlet blood. Hannah perched on a windowsill in the moonlight, comforting me as I cried. A prescription pill bottle clattering on a tile floor.

Hannah's roommate Carley was making her exit.
And then...

Flash.
Blinded by a spotlight, climbing awkwardly onto the bench of a grand piano. A golden retriever puppy sitting beneath an enormous Christmas tree. A lacrosse stick tripping up my feet as I run, my arm snapping painfully. Watching snow through frosty eyelashes. Cold. So cold.

No. Please, no. I wasn't ready for this.

A dark-haired girl emerging from a striped tent. The same girl smiling shyly through a plate-glass window. And again, ducking quickly behind the doors of the dining hall, her face flushed beneath a hairnet.

Seeing myself through his eyes, feeling his rush of emotion at the sight of me, made it even more unbearable. My knees began to tremble and I fought to keep on my feet.

A friendly conversation in a darkened library. Uncontrollable anger, hurling books through the air at a crouching figure in a messy dorm room. A kiss. A wonderful, impossible kiss.

250

With a cry that was somehow both his and mine, my knees gave way and struck the ground. Hannah's hand gripped mine convulsively, maintaining our connection. Tears slid down my cheeks as we lingered, for just a moment more, on the only chance we'd ever had, reliving a kiss that could only ever be a kiss goodbye.

"No!" I moaned. "Wait!"

And suddenly, and I don't know how or with what part of myself, I was fighting the pull of the current, willing him to stay with me. I knew it was selfish and I knew I shouldn't be doing it, but none of that was stopping me.

"Jessica, let him go!" Karen's sharp voice penetrated my consciousness. "Focus on your task and let him go!"

"I can't!"

"Yes, you can! Now is not the time to mourn him!"

"It's okay, Jess. I'm ready to go," Evan's voice rose in a whisper a hundred times louder than the other whispers whirling around in my head.

"Aren't you scared?" I asked.

"No. I can feel it. It's good, whatever's waiting there. And you'll be closer to where I am than anyone, just on the other side of the Gateway."

"Let him go, Jess."

"Let him go."

What else could I do?

"Goodbye," I sobbed brokenly.

I let him go. I felt him slip away on a tide of strangers' lives, and, with a hollow thud, the door inside me closed.

§

I began to come back to myself. I could feel my knees protesting against the gritty tarpaper of the roof, feel the evening breeze on my face, which had broken out into a sweat. The strange worlds being played out behind my eyes had melted into blackness. I opened my eyes and found Hannah, on her knees beside me, still clutching my hand. She gave me a small, sad smile and then rested her head on my shoulder. We did not move for a very long time.

EPILOGUE

THE SUITCASE WAS NOT GOING TO CLOSE. I'd tugged and pulled and rearranged, and even sat on the damn thing. Mission impossible.

"I give up," I declared, flopping onto the bed.

Hannah looked up from her own suitcase and smiled. "Aren't there a few things you can leave here? I think the real problem is the shoes." Her bag had zipped shut with a single effortless flourish.

"I know, I know. Knee-high combat boots aren't space-savers," I sighed. "I guess I can leave the red ones."

I must have sounded pretty depressed because Hannah took pity on me. "Here, give them to me. I still have room."

"Thanks!" I tossed them to her one at a time. She caught them awkwardly and within moments they were zipped away, ready for the journey.

Hannah sank onto the bed next to me. She looked exhausted. Physical tasks still drained a lot of her strength. The aftereffects of years of therapies and drugs couldn't be erased overnight.

"Where's Milo?" I asked.

"Sulking. He really does mean well, you know."

"Yeah, right. If he had his way, my entire wardrobe would be in a trash bag instead of my suitcase," I laughed.

"No, he did like that one pair of jeans," Hannah said.

Much to my chagrin and Hannah's delight, Milo was still here. Despite his proximity to the Summoning Circle, when the candles had been blown out and the crossing completed, there he was, waiting for Hannah. I asked Karen about it, and she shook her head a little sadly.

"Some spirits just don't know what's good for them," she'd said.

And so here we were, preparing for a transatlantic trip with a ghost—and self-appointed stylist—in tow. It was a little more baggage than I'd anticipated, but he made Hannah happy, and so I grudgingly put up with him.

It had been four weeks since the crossing, and though I was

still heartbroken about Evan, the time had been fulfilling, too. Hannah and I were getting to know each other, and each day brought us a step closer to the bond that had been denied to us for so many years.

We sat up for hours past dark every night, and talked across the narrow gap between my bed and the matching one that had been crammed into our room during the intervening days. We asked each other endless questions, and our answers only triggered more questions to follow. It would be a long time, I thought, before we felt like we knew enough about what had passed to move forward.

She was shy, but incredibly smart. We both had a love for books, and she had many of the same favorites that I did. She was easy to smile but slow to laugh out loud—the sound of it seemed to startle her. She was exceptionally observant, reading people even more voraciously than she read books. In many ways, it was like the years of torment hadn't broken her. In other ways, it had.

She struggled with what could only be described as a sort of obsessive compulsive disorder. As ghosts and doctors wreaked havoc over the big things in her life, she fought for control over as many of the little things as possible. She was often unaware that she was doing it, but it seemed to help her keep her grip on things. She wouldn't talk much about the scars on her wrists when I finally mustered up the courage to ask her about them. She would only say, "It made me feel better."

Hannah opened up little by little each night, like one of those flowers that only bloomed when the sun went down. The only topic that seemed to close those shy petals tightly again was our mother. It seemed, as yet, a conversation she wasn't prepared to have. I tried not to push her. There would be time for that.

"Are we all packed up, ladies?" Karen asked. She stood in our doorway looking like a kid on the way to Disney World. Hannah and I both knew why she was so excited. This nerve-racking new chapter for us was a trip down memory lane for her. She was thrilled to be going back to Fairhaven Hall, even if it was only to get us settled.

"All set," Hannah confirmed.

"Well, then, let's get going! Bon Voyage!" she grinned, and grabbed the handle of Hannah's suitcase.

We made our cumbersome procession down the stairs and out to the car. Noah was there to help as well, still a little shell-shocked from the recent obliteration of his comfortable little world.

You couldn't blame the poor guy. He came home from work one day to the extraordinary announcement that he had inherited not one orphaned niece, but two (surprise!), and that both of them, accompanied by his devoted wife, would be disappearing in a matter of days to attend a school halfway around the world. Other than acquiring a permanently dazed look, he was handling it fairly well.

With Noah waving after us, we pulled away from the brownstones and into the heart of the city. We would not be heading straight to the airport yet. Our first stop would be a couple of days at St. Matt's, where I had a paper to turn in, two exams to take, and a lot of explaining and good-byes to take care of. It wouldn't be easy, but saying goodbye was apparently going to become a specialty of mine. I'd better start practicing.

As we left the city behind us, Hannah, with that uncanny perceptiveness I was just starting to get used to, seemed to sense my thoughts. She reached over and squeezed my hand. We didn't look at each other; we didn't have to. We looked instead at the life, at the world, ahead of us. A world beyond the only one we'd ever known had existed. A new home a world away from where we'd been. We had a lot of exploring to do, but from now on, we would do it together.

About the Author

E.E. Holmes is a writer, teacher, and actor living in central Massachusetts with her husband, two children, and a small, but surprisingly loud, dog. When not writing, she enjoys performing, watching unhealthy amounts of British television, and reading with her children.

To learn more about E.E. Holmes and *The World of the Gateway*, please visit www.eeholmes.com